A FURNACE FOR YOUR FOE

AN ANN KINNEAR SUSPENSE NOVEL

MATTY DALRYMPLE

WILLIAM KINGSFIELD PUBLISHERS

For Wade Walton and Mary Dalrymple, for supporting me unfailingly through hell and high water.

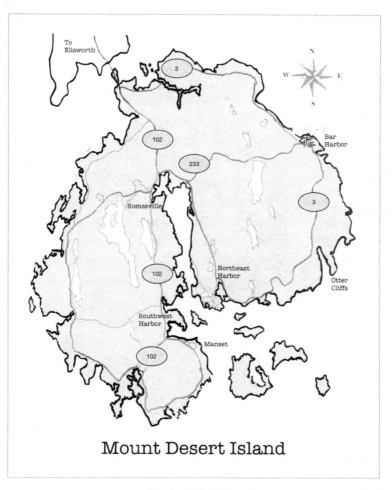

Mount Desert Island

Map by Wade Walton

Heat not a furnace for your foe so hot
That it do singe yourself.

William Shakespeare
Henry VIII

1
____

S helby Kim pulled off the road onto a well-maintained gravel drive. Pulling up to the gate, into whose decorative metalwork a discreet *BV* had been incorporated, she got out her phone and tapped a code into an app. The gate swung open. She pulled through and the gate swung shut behind her.

She passed from warm sun, a welcome change after a long stretch of cold, wet weather, into the dappled light of a wooded slope. Oaks and maples quickly gave way to pines towering over moss- and fern-covered rocks. When she glanced into her rearview mirror, she could see the occasional glint of sunlight off Bracy Cove. She returned the wave of a gardener who was preparing one of the Brookview flower beds for a spring planting.

When she reached the house, she pulled around the circular drive to the guest parking space tucked behind a giant rhododendron. She grabbed a hiking stick from the back seat, then crossed to the entrance and climbed the stone steps. She knocked and in a moment the door was opened by a young woman wearing black skinny jeans and a starched white blouse.

"Hey, Shelby, come on in." The woman stepped back to let Shelby enter. "Here for a hike with Dr. Dorn?"

"Hi, Megan," Shelby said, stepping inside. The entrance hall was an odd combination of stately and homely. Antique oil landscapes that Shelby knew were destined to hang on the walls of museums in Portland, Boston, and Philadelphia, were scattered somewhat haphazardly across the paneled walls. An intricately tiled fireplace anchored one side of the space. The other walls were lined with scratched and stained benches, under which lay a jumble of tennis shoes, badminton racquets, and kayak paddles. "We didn't have a hike scheduled, but it's such a nice day I thought we might be able to sneak one in."

"It'll be nice to get out, especially after all the rain we've been having. I'll let Dr. Dorn know you're here." Megan disappeared down one of the hallways.

Shelby shrugged out of her yellow jacket, stuffed her hat in one of the sleeves, and laid it and her hiking stick on the bench.

Megan returned a minute later. "Hey, cute outfit. As slender as you are, you should show it off, not hide it in baggy clothes."

Shelby blushed. Her brightly colored leggings and long-sleeved workout top were a far cry from the cargo pants and sweatshirt she normally wore to hike.

"Dr. Dorn says he'll be out in a minute," Megan said, then disappeared again.

A few moments later, Shelby heard purposeful footsteps, accompanied by the tick of canine toenails, approaching from one of the hallways that branched off the entrance. A woman appeared, followed by three beagles. She was reading from a small piece of paper that Shelby could tell even from across the room had the creamy texture of an expensive party invitation. The woman looked up. She was tall—just under six feet—and thin, with ash blonde hair tinged with gray scraped back into a stubby ponytail from a severe, sun-weathered face.

"Why, hello, Shelby. Here for a hike?"

"Hello, Ms. Pepperidge," said Shelby. "Yes, I hope so. It was a spur of the moment idea."

"Is Megan fetching Leo for you?"

"Yes, ma'am."

"Would you like to wait in the sitting room? It would be more comfortable."

"I'm fine waiting here. Thanks, Ms. Pepperidge."

"Well, have a nice hike," said the woman and, switching her attention back to the invitation, she passed through the entrance hall and disappeared out of sight down another hallway, followed by her canine entourage.

Shelby had to wait only a few minutes before her prospective hiking partner appeared.

Tippy Pepperidge's husband, Leo Dorn, was a couple of inches taller than his wife, with a build that could have belonged to a rugby player but a face and bearing more appropriate to a board room.

"Good morning, Shelby," he said. "I have to say I was a little surprised to hear that you were interested in a hike with me today."

"It's a perfect day for it."

"Yes, I suppose it is," he said, looking at her speculatively.

"I wanted to talk about ..." Her voice trailed off, then she continued. "About what we talked about the other day."

"You did, eh? If you could wait until tomorrow—"

"I'd rather not wait." She gave him a sheepish smile. "I got a new pair of hiking shoes I want to try out." She glanced down at her worn shoes. "Rats, I forgot to put them on. They're in the car —hold on one minute."

Before Leo had a chance to object, she slipped through the front door and hurried out to the car. She sat in the passenger seat to change her shoes, fumbling with the laces, hoping that the delay wasn't giving Leo a chance to cement his decision to postpone the hike.

When she got back to the entrance hall, he was leaning against the wall next to the fireplace, his arms folded.

"If you're really that excited about trying out a new pair of shoes, I guess I shouldn't stand in your way," he said with a smile. He pulled a jacket off a hook. "What shall it be today?"

"How about Aldrich Hill?"

"The ledge trail?"

She nodded. "The view is so nice from the top."

"Yes, I suppose it is." After a moment, he shrugged. "All right."

She patted the jacket, a slight frown creasing her forehead, until she located her hat in the pocket. She retrieved her hiking stick, then followed Leo outside.

"Do you want to talk while we walk?" he asked.

"Let's wait until we get to the top."

They crossed the drive and entered the woods on a path padded with pine needles. Birds chittered in the trees, their song occasionally drowned out by the scream of a gull that had drifted over from Eastern Way. Even when the trail would have allowed them to walk two abreast, Leo trailed a step or two behind Shelby.

After a few minutes, the trees opened up onto the first challenge of the trail: a jumble of granite boulders at the bottom of a semi-circular indentation in a sheer rock wall that rose several dozen feet above them. Leo referred to it as the Barrel, but it suggested to Shelby the jawbone of some gigantic monster, the boulders, which the millennia had heaved up to a forty-five-degree angle, like deadly teeth.

Although the day had been cloudless when Shelby arrived at Brookview, she saw that a gray overcast was beginning to move in from the west.

"I hope we finish up before it rains," she said.

"We will if we keep moving," replied Leo.

With his long legs, Leo could easily hoist himself from rock to rock, but at just over five feet tall, it was a scramble for Shelby. Collapsing her hiking stick and looping its strap over her wrist, she began the climb. She kept her eyes down on her foot placement and hand holds.

She reached the top of the stretch of rocks a little winded. From there, they followed a gentle loop through the pine woods before the path switched back and began to climb again.

They reached the Barrel again, but now Shelby was looking down at the granite boulders thirty feet below. The path ran near the edge of the drop, but on the left were bushes and small pines that, along with her hiking stick, provided opportunities to steady herself. The only potential hazard, a snarl of exposed roots that could snag an unsuspecting hiker's foot, was no hazard to someone as familiar with the path as she was. She stepped gingerly past the roots and past the stunted tree that they anchored precariously to the top of the cliff.

Finally they got to what was for Shelby the most challenging part of the climb. The path narrowed to a ledge two feet wide and two dozen feet long, bounded on the left by a barren rock wall that rose straight up to the summit and on the right by the sheer drop to the boulders below. The path tilted ever so slightly toward the drop—it was a crossing no one would make if the rocks were wet or icy. Even in weather as dry as it was now, it had taken Shelby a few hikes with Leo before she was willing to cross the ledge.

She stopped and looked back toward him. "Will you go first?"

"You've done this plenty of times before, Shelby—you shouldn't need me to take the lead anymore."

She glanced down at the rocks. "I'd feel better if you went first."

He sighed. "Fine. Come back here and we'll switch places."

She expected him to move back to where the path was wider, but when she reached him, he just turned sideways, his back pressed to the rock wall. She shuffled past, keeping her eyes averted from the drop. She flinched as he reached for her arm.

"I'm just giving you a hand," he said. "You look a little unsteady on your feet."

She stepped onto the path behind him and shrugged his hand off her arm.

He shook his head. "Ready?" he asked.

"Yes."

"One at a time?"

"Yes."

Leo started across the ledge. He moved slowly and carefully, but with an ease and assurance that Shelby would never achieve. He really did make it look like it was a stroll down a sidewalk.

Until his right foot shot to the side.

She heard his gasp. He froze, balanced on his left foot.

"Leo?" Her voice was a breathless squeak.

"Ice," he hissed.

He began to move his right foot, which was hanging over the drop, back to the ledge, but the movement made his left foot slip infinitesimally to the right.

Shelby took a step forward, then stopped.

"Not ice," he said through gritted teeth. "Not cold enough."

He slowly extended his left hand and wedged his fingers into a tiny fissure in the rock face. His left foot slipped a fraction of an inch further to the right.

"Shelby," he croaked. "Your hiking stick. Hold it out to me."

Her knees trembling, and searching in vain for a handhold

with which to anchor herself, Shelby crept onto the ledge. She dropped her eyes to the path, hyperalert for any hazards. She knew she was moving too slowly—she could sense the seconds ticking by. She tore her eyes from the ground and looked toward Leo. His left leg was starting to shake from the strain of trying to maintain his precarious position.

"Where are you?" he gasped.

He was still facing forward, unwilling to try to turn his head to watch her approach.

"I'm almost there," she said, trying to sound sure of herself, trying to convince herself that she could do what needed to be done.

He tried to tighten his grip on the fissure, but his foot slipped another inch to the right.

She took another step, and then another. "Almost there, Leo. I'm almost there."

She extended her hiking stick toward him.

He turned slowly toward her, one painful inch at a time, trying to use his uncertain grip on the fissure to steady himself.

"A little closer," he whispered, as much to himself as to her. "A little closer."

Her heart pounding, she shuffled forward on the path.

His fingers brushed the end of the stick and his features began to relax in relief.

When he fell, his cry might have been mistaken for the scream of a gull, until it was cut short when his back was broken on the granite teeth below.

2

Ann Kinnear lifted the small black dachshund off the dining room chair. It had been peering over the edge of the table at a bowl of Brussels sprouts and the dollop of butter melting on top. She placed the dog on the floor.

"Scott," she called toward the kitchen. "Ursula was checking out the dining room table again."

Scott Pate appeared in the doorway. "Again? I thought we had addressed that issue."

"Evidently the stern talking-to you gave her has worn off."

Ann's brother Mike entered the dining room carrying a roast chicken on a platter. At that moment, a gray cat with a white tuft on its chest trotted out of the living room on a direct intercept course with Mike's feet. Ann glanced at the dachshund, who was clearly torn between the need to stand watch at the table and the desire to chase the cat. Since the siren call of the dinner table seemed stronger, Ann shrugged and sat down. Mike's feet passed through the cat's semi-translucent body.

"Scooter's back," said Ann, shaking out her napkin.

"Really?" said Scott, looking around. "Where?"

"On her way to the kitchen."

"I'm surprised Ursula didn't go after her, although I suppose the Brussels sprouts won out," said Scott.

Ursula popped into the begging position next to his chair.

"Bad," said Scott mildly, and moved the bottle of wine to make room on the table for the chicken. He sat down as Mike began carving. "Any updates on when you two will be going to Maine?"

"Not yet," said Mike, "and we need to get a move on. I cleared Ann's calendar, but if things don't get going soon, I'm going to start booking engagements again." He handed a plate of chicken to Ann.

"You should come, too," she said to Scott.

"If I could get away from work, I would," said Scott, "I'd love to go back there."

"Ann has earned lifelong celebrity status on Mount Desert," said Mike. He handed Scott a plate, then put aside the carving knife and got out his phone. He scrolled, then handed the phone to Ann. "Another article about you in the *MDIslander*."

She took the phone but passed it immediately to Scott. "Can't they just let it drop?"

"Are you kidding?" said Mike. "You're the most exciting thing that's happened on Mount Desert Island since the Fire of '47."

"I understand why the production company is saying that the documentary has to be based there," said Scott, scanning the article. "I think that even outside Maine, people associate Annie with MDI now."

The phone buzzed. Mike extended his hand toward Scott.

"Sweetie, not during dinner," groaned Scott, handing over the phone.

"Speak of the devil," said Mike, reading the text. "Corey wants to meet with Ann and me at eight."

"In the morning?" asked Scott.

"No, tonight."

"Tonight?" Scott looked at his watch. "That's fifteen minutes from now."

Mike shrugged and sat down. "Eat fast," he said to Ann.

Scott shook his head. "You made the dinner. You'd think you'd want us all to have time to enjoy it."

"What's Corey in such a hurry about?" Ann asked Mike.

"I imagine he wants to talk about a possible topic."

"*Another* topic, you mean," said Scott, helping himself to Brussels sprouts.

"It's Corey's fault that it's taking so long," said Mike. "He can't come up with a reasonable topic."

"You really need to stop shooting down all the ideas that Corey suggests," said Ann. "Pretty soon he's going to get fed up and just make it a solo show: *Garrick Masser Senses Spirits*."

"Masser already knew all about every topic Corey suggested," said Mike.

"That's because as long as the backers are insisting that the documentary be based on Mount Desert, Garrick's going to know about every topic," said Ann. "He's like an MDI encyclopedia."

"He's like a world encyclopedia," said Scott.

"It's not fair," said Mike.

"It's not a competition," said Ann.

Scott leaned toward Ann. "Your brother thinks everything is a competition," he said in a stage whisper.

"That's because when you have someone like Garrick Masser who won't admit that he's become second fiddle, it *is* a competition," said Mike.

Ann rolled her eyes.

"You guys are wasting your fifteen minutes," said Scott, cutting off a piece of chicken.

After gulping down a few more bites, Ann and Mike left Scott still enjoying his dinner, and passing minuscule morsels to

Ursula. Mike detoured to the kitchen and poured his wine into a coffee mug.

"Why are you doing that?" asked Ann.

"It looks more professional."

"Hey, Corey's the one who called the meeting during dinnertime with fifteen minutes' notice. He can't very well frown upon some wine-drinking."

"You're the artiste, so wine-drinking is practically expected of you," said Mike. "I'm the business manager, so I have to pretend to be businesslike."

Ann followed him upstairs to his office.

When Mike had first escorted Ann into his home office for the unveiling of the new videoconferencing set-up, she found a sign advertising Tarot readings on the wall and a Ouija board on the table.

"Mike!" she squawked. "What the hell?"

"You don't think it will intrigue potential clients?'

"It will scare off potential clients. Or," she amended, "it will intrigue exactly the kind of clients you're always telling me you're trying to filter out."

"You don't want to give it a test run?"

"I am *not* going to—"

He held up his hands placatingly. "Okay, okay. It was supposed to be a joke."

"I told you it wasn't funny," called Scott from downstairs.

Mike had replaced the mystical props with decor he felt was more appropriate to the *Ann Kinnear Sensing* brand: vintage travel posters.

"Notice a theme?" he asked.

"Same artist?" she asked, peering at each in turn.

"No. They're all places where you've had sensing engagements."

She stepped back from a sixties-era poster featuring a TWA

jet zipping over stylized renderings of Big Ben and Westminster Abbey. "I never had an engagement in London."

"Okay, not an engagement per se, but you saw that spirit on Tower Green."

"I was seven. Plus, probably half the people who go to Tower Green see a spirit."

Now Mike settled into his chair with his mug of wine. "I wonder if Corey expects Masser to figure out how to call in to a virtual meeting," he said. "It's so twenty-first century."

"Corey told me he went over to Garrick's house and set up a computer for him so he could join the calls."

"Instead of typing comments into the chat, Masser can write them out with a quill pen and then hold the parchment up to the camera."

Ann swatted him with the back of her hand.

At the appointed time, the parties appeared on the videoconferencing screen.

Corey Duff sat in a guest room at the Bar Harbor Inn. He had relocated from his normal base of operations in Los Angeles to Mount Desert Island, Maine, a week earlier and was probably regretting his early optimism that the parties would quickly agree on a topic for the documentary he was directing. His California tan was fading to a paleness more appropriate to Maine in May. His normally wavy red hair was flattened in a bad case of hat head.

Garrick Masser sat in the waiting room in his home in Somesville, Maine, just across the hall from the office where he met with clients. Illumination appeared to be provided by a single antique lamp on a table behind him, leaving his face in shadow. However, even the dim light didn't conceal the impressive beard that Garrick was sporting.

The third picture in the gallery showed a man unfamiliar to Ann. His beard was merely a stubble, but one that looked less like the result of a skipped shave than like an intentional fashion choice. His hair was an inch shy of a pompadour, although suitably tousled to be a fitting complement to the beard, and his eyes were picturesquely accentuated with crows' feet no doubt caused by the wide smile that displayed perfect teeth. Even his lighting provided a noticeably more attractive effect than that of the other participants.

"Hello, everyone," said Corey.

"Hi, Corey. Hi, Garrick," said Ann.

Mike raised a hand in greeting.

Garrick stared stoically into the monitor.

"Garrick, can you hear us?" asked Corey.

"Of course," intoned Garrick.

"Ah, good. Before we get started, I'd like to introduce all of you to Kyle Lathey. The management at Authentic Productions has asked Kyle to join the team so that we'll have immediate access to them in case we need any resources or direction."

Mike muted the microphone and held his mug of wine to his lips to mask his mouth. "Resources or direction my ass."

Ann unmuted the mic. "Nice to meet you, Kyle."

"Likewise, Ann," said Kyle. "Pleased to meet you, too, Garrick."

"Charmed," said Garrick.

"Little hard to see you there, Garrick," said Kyle.

"Garrick, do you still have that ring light we set up?" asked Corey.

Garrick gave an audible sigh of resignation. He reached forward and a light snapped on. Now his hooked nose and jutting cheekbones were clear, although his eyes were still partially shadowed by his untamed black eyebrows.

"That's better," said Kyle heartily.

"Now that you've seen what I look like ..." said Garrick, and the light snapped off.

"Anyhow," Corey said quickly, evidently hoping to avert another exchange between Garrick and Kyle, "I have what I think is good news regarding a possible topic for the documentary. Kyle, I'm not sure how much information Authentic Productions gave you about the project, but the goal is to explore a topic that will allow Ann and Garrick to demonstrate their spirit-sensing abilities. The backers are financing the project on the condition that it be set on Mount Desert Island, since they want to capitalize on the coverage of the events at the Lynam's Point Hotel."

"Of course, I've seen the video from Lynam's Point," said Kyle. "Extraordinary stuff—over a million views last time I checked. That video is why we need Ann, Garrick, and Mount Desert all to be part of this package."

"It's unfortunate that we can't shoot at the hotel where the video was taken," said Corey, "but the new owners won't agree. However, I think we have a great alternative. Let me show you a story that hit the news just a few hours ago."

The gallery of participants' images was replaced by a screen-share from Corey's computer. It displayed the website of a Bangor news station, the video thumbnail showing a reporter standing in front of an imposing gate with a discreet *BV* worked into its decorative metalwork. Beyond the gates, a drive disappeared into a wooded property. Corey hit *Play.*

"In tragic news from Mount Desert Island," said the reporter, "we've learned that Leo Dorn, head of MDI-based Stata Mater Technology, died earlier today in a fall from a ledge on a trail on the Brookview estate, the property belonging to the family of his wife, Tippy Pepperidge."

The video of the reporter was replaced by a photo of a formally dressed couple. They were standing in front of a banner identifying the venue as a fundraiser for victims of western wildfires. Leo Dorn wore a perfectly tailored tuxedo and an easy smile. Tippy Pepperidge's hands grasped a small purse so tightly it looked like a wet cloth she was about to wring out. Her hair was pulled back in a stubby ponytail more appropriate for a workout than a black-tie gala.

"According to Stata Mater Director of Research Operations Dr. Hannah Jeskie," the reporter continued, "Dr. Dorn had been accompanied on the hike by a young Stata Mater colleague, Shelby Kim, who called 911 and led first responders to where Dorn's body lay at the bottom of the cliff."

The photo of Leo and Tippy was replaced with another, perhaps at the same event, of Leo standing on a podium, shaking the hand of a petite woman in her mid- to late-twenties, a shy smile on her face.

"We switch now to video from the news conference held at SMT headquarters in Bar Harbor earlier today."

A woman identified by the caption as *Dr. Hannah Jeskie* stood behind a lectern, on the front of which were the words *Stata Mater Technology* and a logo of a stylized flame being whisked to one side by the cool blue letters of the company's initials. Carefully casual salt-and-pepper hair framed a face whose expression was stoic despite the bloodshot eyes.

"The trail from which Dr. Dorn fell was one of his favorite hikes on MDI," said Jeskie, "one he made several times a week, weather permitting."

She pointed to someone off-camera, and the reporter's question bled through faintly on the audio: "Did the recent heavy rains play a role in the fall?"

"According to Dr. Kim, the path was completely dry. Today's rain didn't start until after Dr. Dorn's fall. Shelby said neither she nor Leo would have taken that particular trail otherwise."

A different off-camera voice asked, "Did Leo Dorn and Shelby Kim often hike together?"

"I believe they hiked at Brookview fairly regularly," said

Jeskie. "Shelby Kim is a brilliant young woman whom Leo Dorn and Tippy Pepperidge took under their wing when she joined the Stata Mater team a year ago. After first responders removed Dr. Dorn's body from Brookview, Ms. Pepperidge's concern turned to Dr. Kim's well-being. Tippy accompanied Shelby back to her apartment and ensured that she got the care she needed after such a traumatic experience." Dr. Jeskie looked down at the lectern, evidently marshaling her emotions, then looked back up at the cameras, her mouth set. "I won't comment further on the circumstances of Dr. Dorn's death, except to say that the timing of it is especially tragic in view of a planned announcement about Stata Mater's pro bono work in fire prevention and suppression technologies."

Corey ended the screen share and the videoconference participants' images displayed again.

"What kind of name is Stata Mater?" asked Kyle.

"Stata Mater is an ancient goddess to whom the Romans turned for protection against fire," said Garrick.

Kyle gave a bark of a laugh. "How in the world do you know that?"

Garrick raised an eyebrow. "How in the world do you not?"

"You know about this Stata Mater Technology?" asked Mike, clearly preparing to object to the latest proposal for the documentary subject.

Garrick sat back in his chair, rested his elbows on its arms, and steepled his fingers in front of his chest. "Dr. Leo Dorn was the husband of Elizabeth 'Tippy' Pepperidge, the granddaughter of Oliver Pepperidge of Pepperidge Realty Holdings, originally Pepperidge Land and Property. Eight years ago, Ms. Pepperidge's first husband, Frank Judd, died in a fire at his studio at the Pepperidge property on Mount Desert Island. In response to the tragedy, she established a sizable grant to establish Stata Mater Technology to do research and development work in fire prevention and suppression to then share, pro bono, with the for-profit sector. Dr. Dorn and his team—including Dr. Hannah Jeskie—won the grant. Four years later, Dr. Dorn and Ms. Pepperidge married."

"If you know so much about Stata Mater and Leo Dorn," said Mike, "I'd say this hardly qualifies as a documentary subject that will provide an even playing field."

"In the interests of the documentary as a whole," said Ann, "we should take advantage of any information anyone has about the subject. I don't mind if Garrick already has some background on the Pepperidges and Leo Dorn."

"That Kim girl is good-looking," said Kyle. "I wonder if his wing was the only thing Leo Dorn was taking her under."

"Jesus, Lathey," muttered Corey.

"What? I'm just saying—she's a good-looking girl." He leaned back and laced his fingers over a stomach that his form-fitting T-shirt showed to be washboard flat. "On the other hand, I'm betting that the Pepperidge spread is big enough that they could get up to some trouble in those woods—and not just a roll in the leaves." He glanced around the virtual table, waiting for a reaction that didn't come. He leaned forward again. "Maybe she and Dorn were screwing around, Dorn got tired of her and cut it off, and she gave him a little push."

"Based on that news photo," said Mike, "Shelby Kim is a foot shorter and a hundred pounds lighter that Leo Dorn. It's hard to imagine her pushing him to his death."

"Whether or not Leo Dorn is a viable subject for the documentary," said Garrick, "the point is moot if Ms. Pepperidge won't provide access to her property."

"I'll see if I can contact her in the next day or two to discuss it," said Corey.

"I'll come with you," said Kyle. "I can catch a red-eye tonight, be on MDI in the morning."

"I can take care of it," said Corey quickly.

"I could speak with her," said Garrick.

"You know her?" asked Corey guardedly, evidently sensing another possible barrier to Mike's agreement to the subject.

"When Mr. Judd was killed in the fire, Ms. Pepperidge hired me to try to contact him. I visited the site of the fire, but he had passed on and was not available to be contacted."

"You've worked for the widow?" asked Mike, his voice rising. "That's quite a coincidence."

"Hardly," said Garrick. "I've worked for a number of the more established families on Mount Desert Island. In fact, it seems that the more established they are, the more insistent they are about the need to contact their dead relatives."

"And the more likely it is they can afford Masser's fees," Mike muttered to Ann.

"I beg your pardon?" said Garrick blandly.

"Nothing." Mike redirected his attention to the other attendees. "If Garrick has already done work for the Pepperidges—" he began.

Ann rubbed her temple. "Mike, just stop it, okay? The whole island can't have a year-round population of more than, I don't know ..."

"Just over ten thousand," supplied Garrick.

"—just over ten thousand," she repeated. "Garrick's bound to know a lot of them."

Mike scowled. "Even if we overlook the fact that Masser already has an inside track on this topic, if he wasn't able to make contact with Frank Judd, it doesn't bode well for his ability to contact Leo Dorn. Corey, we should let Ann give it a try."

"If Dr. Dorn's spirit is available to be contacted," said Garrick, seemingly unperturbed, "I will contact him. If he has passed on, as Mr. Judd had, then neither I nor your sister will be able to make contact."

"Garrick," said Corey, "if everyone agrees to this topic, it would be great if you could talk to Ms. Pepperidge. We'll need access to her property, and I'm sure she'd be more likely to give approval to someone she knows." After a pause, he continued. "Assuming your relationship with her was not too ... prickly."

"My interactions with her were appropriate to someone who had recently lost a husband."

"Okay," said Corey, a little uncertainly. "You left on good terms, then?"

Garrick raised an eyebrow. "As I said."

Corey sighed. "Okay. I'd appreciate it if you can talk with her, Garrick. Thank you."

"I will go alone," said Garrick. "She is notoriously averse to publicity and would not appreciate a delegation arriving at her door."

"Hey," said Kyle, "this team will be doing Tippy Pepperidge and the police a favor if we're able to get in touch with Leo's spirit and find out what really happened on that trail. Be sure to tell her that."

"I shall tell her nothing of the kind," said Garrick.

"Listen, Masser—" Kyle said, his voice rising.

Corey raised a hand. "Everybody, just calm down—we're supposed to be in this together." He picked up an iPad and tapped the screen. "This is the fifth subject we've discussed, the first four having been discarded because of some direct or tangential involvement by Garrick or knowledge he had of the subject." He read from the iPad. "The Asticou Azalea Garden murder, the Manset Darling of the Docks, the St. Saviour's Tiffany window theft—"

"Oh, please, not that," said Kyle with a laugh. "Who cares?"

"—the Bangor House hotel strangling—"

"Bangor isn't on MDI," said Ann.

Corey looked up at the camera, his normal calm evidently

wearing thin. "I was having to cast my net a little wider when the MDI topics kept getting vetoed." He set the iPad aside. "Leo Dorn is an undeniably fascinating subject. I had always assumed that we would be trying to contact people who had died years ago or trying to interest viewers in a case that had disappeared from the public consciousness, but a current case will be much more gripping. More importantly, we might uncover information that would be of practical value to the friends and family of the deceased. Mike, I know you're concerned about Garrick's previous involvement with the Pepperidge family. Garrick, how long ago was it that Tippy Pepperidge hired you to try to contact Frank Judd?"

"Eight years ago."

"And have you had any contact with her since then?"

"I have not."

"Any contact with Leo Dorn?"

"No."

"With Stata Mater Technology?"

"No."

Corey sat back and shifted his gaze across the virtual meeting attendees. "If the backers are insistent on shooting the documentary on Mount Desert Island—and they are—then we can't very well reject any subject that Garrick, a long-time MDI resident, knows something about."

He paused, providing an opening for contrary views, but everyone was silent.

"As to whether the death is too recent—too fresh for Leo Dorn's loved ones—I hope that Ann and Garrick trust me to handle the topic with sensitivity." At this, he shot a look at the monitor—no doubt at Kyle—then shifted his attention to take in the whole group again. "Not to be morbid, but this is the perfect subject for us." His eyes tracked across the screen. "Thoughts?"

"Ann and I will need to talk off-camera," said Mike.

"Garrick?" asked Corey.

"I am amenable if Miss Kinnear is."

"If we're going to focus on Leo Dorn and his death as the subject of the documentary," said Corey, "we need to get started as soon as possible."

"We'll let you know tomorrow what our answer is," said Mike.

"I will await your decision with bated breath," said Garrick, and his image disappeared from the gallery.

3

I n the kitchen, Ann and Mike found Scott loading the dishwasher, Ursula standing on the open door and providing a pre-wash cycle.

"I put your plates in the oven to keep warm," said Scott.

Ann retrieved their plates, then joined Mike at the kitchen island to finish her dinner. Mike poured his wine from the coffee cup back into his wine glass and topped off their drinks.

"What was Corey's latest idea for the documentary?" asked Scott.

Mike recapped the conversation for him.

"That sounds exciting," said Scott. "A current subject will be much more interesting than a historical one."

"But Masser knows the Pepperidge family. In fact, he's done work for Tippy Pepperidge—" began Mike.

"Mike, hang it up," said Ann around a mouthful of chicken. "This will be an interesting topic, and Garrick and I might be able to actually provide some useful information about what happened to Leo Dorn."

"I'll bet all those rich families on MDI are hiring Garrick as a party game," said Mike. "You know, like kids conducting a seance at a sleepover."

"You're such an ass when it comes to Garrick," said Ann.

"That's because he thinks he's better than everyone."

"And it's especially galling to your brother when Mr. Masser acts like he's better than *you*, Annie," added Scott.

"I appreciate the thought, Mike," said Ann, "but I don't need you defending my professional honor."

"It sounds like this Kyle Lathey person is suspicious about Shelby Kim's version of events," said Scott. "If she didn't have anything to do with Dr. Dorn's fall, Annie could help clear her name, and if she did have something to do with it, Annie can help steer the police in the right direction."

Mike raised his hands. "Fine, fine. I agree it does sound interesting."

"It means you guys will have to postpone your trip to New York," said Ann.

Mike had been complaining about the lack of nightlife around West Chester, and said he was tired of the options in nearby Philadelphia, so he and Scott had tentatively planned to take the train up to New York City for a few days.

Scott waved a hand. "We can always reschedule. Plus, I'll bet you can find some fun things to do on MDI."

"You're such an optimist," said Mike.

"When I was up there with Annie," continued Scott, "I went to a place in Bar Harbor that had great jazz. Everywhere has something fun to do—you just have to look a little harder sometimes."

Mike turned to Ann. "Should we call Corey now so that he knows we discussed his proposal for a full minute, or should we wait until tomorrow?"

"Before we call Corey, I'm going to call Garrick and let him know I'm willing to do it."

"I'm sure Corey can let him know," Mike grumbled.

Ann finished her meal, then went up to the guest room that she had occupied since renting out her cabin in the Adirondacks and moving into Mike and Scott's West Chester, Pennsylvania, townhouse. She got out her phone and tapped Garrick's number.

"Yes," came the answer.

"Hey, Garrick, it's Ann."

"Yes."

"I think we should go ahead with the Leo Dorn story."

"Very well."

"Are you okay with that?"

"It seems no better or worse than any other topic Mr. Duff and his financiers might choose. I will have to rearrange some engagements to accommodate, but I believe it should be possible."

"You were smart to keep your engagements on the books until we decided on a topic. Mike cleared my calendar and I've just been killing time." In fact, she had spent the time since her last engagement quite enjoyably, taking flying lessons at Avondale Airport and studying the federal aviation regulations in preparation for her private pilot exam, which she had passed a few weeks earlier. However, she knew that Garrick viewed small planes with alarm, and so she kept the details of how she had been passing the time to herself.

"We need to ensure that the subject is kept confidential until I've had an opportunity to get approval from Ms. Pepperidge to access Brookview," said Garrick. "You may convey my provisional agreement and the condition to Mr. Duff."

"So, you know Tippy Pepperidge?"

"Yes."

"She doesn't look like a 'Tippy.'"

"Individuals don't get to choose their own nicknames."

"What did you think of Kyle Lathey?"

"He seems an unpleasant man."

"Yeah, I thought so, too, but hopefully Corey will be able to keep him in line."

"A man should be able to hear, and bear, the worst that could be said of him. I'm afraid our Mr. Lathey is likely to fail that test."

"That's good, Garrick. Did you just make that up?"

"I did not."

They wrapped up the call, then Ann called Corey to update him on their agreement to the topic and Garrick's condition. They agreed that, if possible, Ann and Mike would fly up to MDI the following day.

She ended the call, then stood and picked up her wine glass, ready to go downstairs to rejoin Mike and Scott. Then she sank back down into the chair. Was Kyle Lathey right about the number of views of the video that was driving Authentic Productions' insistence on shooting the documentary on Mount Desert Island with her and Garrick? A bit reluctantly, she got out her phone and opened YouTube, then searched on her name.

Not surprisingly, the video appeared at the top of the search results. It had been taken at the Lynam's Landing Hotel, which had stood on the western side of MDI for over a hundred years. Last Ann had heard, the hotel was in the process of being torn down by the property's new owners, who had evidently rebuffed Corey's requests to shoot the documentary there.

The video's thumbnail image was of Ann, hair darkened with blood from a gash on her head, standing with Scott Pate in the bottom of an elevator shaft. A woman, arm cradled in front of her, was propped against one wall of the shaft. Garrick's crumpled body was barely visible on the floor. The unauthorized videographer was Scott's MDI-based, jazz-loving, piercing-bedecked friend, Mace. Ann glanced at the number of views

—if anything, Kyle Lathey had understated the video's popularity.

She slipped her phone back into her pocket with a sigh. She supposed she shouldn't be surprised by the video's reach—it was an undeniably dramatic scene, one that could only have played out as it had in the presence of someone with her skill. She had never watched it herself. She didn't have to—she had lived it.

She went downstairs, where Mike and Scott were sitting on the couch watching TV. She topped off her glass from a freshly opened wine bottle on the coffee table, then sank into a chair and curled her feet under her legs.

"Garrick agreed," she said.

Mike muted the volume. "Should we call Corey?"

"I already did."

"Did Masser call him, too?"

"I conveyed the message for both of us."

Mike clicked the volume back up. "It would be nice if Masser made his own phone calls and didn't use you as his messenger."

"What are we watching?" she asked.

"It's a documentary by Authentic Productions. I realized we should check out some of their other work. I've been proceeding based on our past experience with Corey, but I didn't think to look into the outfit he's getting financing from."

"How's the show?"

"It's fascinating," said Scott. "It's about penguins. The camera work is lovely. Sort of Ken Burns but with flightless aquatic birds."

"Penguins? This project will be a bit of a departure for them if they're used to doing wildlife documentaries." She took a sip of wine. "Corey wants us to get up to Maine as soon as possible so that we're ready to go once Garrick gets Tippy's approval for access to Brookview."

Mike re-muted the TV. "I'll see if Walt is available to take us."

"Maybe I could fly us up there," she mused.

Mike raised an eyebrow. "You just got your pilot's license. Are you even allowed to do that?"

"Sure."

"No offense, but I'd be happier flying with Walt until you get a few more hours under your belt."

She sighed. "Yeah, you're probably right. But it is fun to think about."

"Pretty soon you won't even need Walt anymore," said Scott.

"I'll always need Walt," she replied.

"Do you want to bring Ursula with you?" asked Scott. "She could help keep an eye out for Leo Dorn."

"I think she'll be happier here with you," said Ann. Plus, she thought, her own sensing abilities had progressed considerably since the dachshund had helped avert a spirit-induced catastrophe at her Adirondack cabin.

"I don't think Ann needs a dog's help to spot spirits anymore," said Mike, unmuting the TV. "That's one area where we don't need someone with more hours."

4

The next morning, Scott drove Ann and Mike to Avondale Airport, where Ann's charter pilot, Walt Federman, would pick them up for the flight to Maine. Avondale was where Ann had been taking lessons, and where she now rented the flight school's Piper Warrior for solo jaunts around southeastern Pennsylvania, Delaware, and Maryland.

The day was sunny and warm, so they sat on a bench outside the airport's office while they waited for Walt to arrive.

A few minutes before the appointed time, Ann spied Walt's Piper Arrow entering the pattern. Walt eased the Arrow down onto the runway in a manner that Ann was working to emulate in the smaller Warrior, then taxied to the tie-down area. The prop spun down and Walt's wife, Helen, climbed out of the passenger seat, followed by Walt. While he got the plane secured, Helen crossed the ramp and enfolded Ann in a hug.

"Honey, it's so good to see you. We miss having you right down the road." She hugged Mike and Scott as well. "I hope you guys aren't planning to keep her here in Pennsylvania for too much longer."

"I'm thinking she might want to stay here until the Adirondacks mud season is over," said Mike with a laugh.

"Remember when you got stuck in that mud patch, Mike?" exclaimed Scott. "I thought you were going to disappear!"

"No danger of that," said Mike, "although for a minute or two, I was afraid that I was going to have to abandon my boots."

"Well, not only is the hiking less treacherous in Pennsylvania in May," said Scott, "but the shopping is better here, too. Am I right?" he asked Helen.

"Absolutely," she said. "I always look forward to our trips to King of Prussia when I can hitch a ride down here with Walt."

Walt joined them. He shook Mike and Scott's hands and gave Ann a kiss on the cheek. "Nice of you to volunteer to take Helen to the mall," he said to Scott.

"My pleasure. I have an idea about where we can have lunch, too—especially if you're in the mood for a margarita, Helen."

"Now I'm jealous," said Ann, "and I don't even like shopping."

"Plus you're going to miss your favorite," said Helen. "If Scott will make a stop at a grocery store on the way back to the townhouse, I'm going to make him my famous meatloaf for dinner." She turned to Scott. "Thank you for putting me up overnight, on top of everything else."

The fuel truck appeared from behind the hangar row, the airport's young manager, Ellis Tapscott at the wheel. Walt returned to the Arrow to oversee the fueling, and Mike and Scott wandered over as well to say hello to Ellis. Ann and Ellis exchanged waves across the ramp.

"A friend of yours?" asked Helen.

"Yup."

"Want to go say hi?"

"I get to see him all the time—I want to catch up with you."

Helen smiled. "That would be nice."

"Inside or outside?"

"Definitely outside," said Helen. "It's ten degrees warmer here than at home. I'm enjoying the sun."

They sat down on the bench.

"Do you have a goal in mind for your shopping trip or are you just browsing?" asked Ann.

"I thought I'd look around for some things for the grandkids, although who knows what teenagers want these days. Plus I desperately need a couple of pairs of jeans." She leaned toward Ann and lowered her voice, although no one was nearby. "Mine are getting a little snug, I have to admit." She straightened and laughed. "Too much meatloaf." She tried to make her expression stern. "You look like you could use a couple of servings of meatloaf."

Ann smiled. "Mike's working on fattening me up."

"Do you think you'll be coming back to Loon Pond soon?"

"I'm not sure. Among other things, I'm a lot closer to potential engagements here—we're right in the middle of the whole Boston-Washington corridor—although I know it's inconvenient for Walt to come all the way down here to fly me places."

Helen waved a hand. "Oh, he doesn't mind. Any excuse to get in the air." She smiled at Ann. "Any excuse to see you."

Ann reached over and squeezed Helen's hand. "I miss you guys. I'll be back up to the Adirondacks ... pretty soon."

Helen fiddled with the strap of her purse. "Maybe you need to sell the Loon Pond cabin and find another place—close by but ... different." Helen had been the one to try to scrub the bloodstains out of the cabin's kitchen floorboards and had charged Walt with replacing the flooring when she had been unsuccessful. She brightened. "You could upgrade the studio to be a four-season place."

Ann forced a laugh. "That would be quite an upgrade." She

shook her head. "The studio. Do you know how long it's been since I did any painting? I should just sell it."

"Don't do anything hasty," cautioned Helen.

Mike and Scott wandered back and the four of them chatted about the Mount Desert Island-based documentary while Walt went into the office to use the wi-fi to check the weather.

When he emerged, Mike grabbed his own bag and Ann's. "I'll load our stuff." He crossed the ramp to the plane, with Walt, Helen, Ann, and Scott following at a more leisurely pace.

Since Ann was a hair shorter than Mike, she had taken the less roomy back seat on previous trips. Now, though, she claimed the front passenger seat so that she could log some flight time once they were in the air.

Ann returned Scott and Helen's waves as Walt taxied to the run-up area, and followed along as he worked through his preflight checklist. Then, with Walt at the controls, they sped down the runway and rose into an almost cloudless blue sky.

As the plane climbed, Ann wondered when she would be making the trip back to the Adirondacks. The cabin still held bad memories for her, and she was sure she could sell it easily despite what had happened there—could sell it easily, she thought cynically, perhaps *because* of what had happened there. Selling the studio, which she had built a few miles away so she would have good light for her painting, might be harder, but the sensing business was doing well enough that she wouldn't need the proceeds from that to finance a purchase of a new place. She made a mental note to talk about it with Mike when they got back to Pennsylvania. It was handy to have a brother who had been a financial planner before he became the full-time business manager of *Ann Kinnear Sensing*.

She watched the houses, the cars, the ribbons of road, the rectangles of farm fields shrink below her. What she really wanted was to be able to have Mike, Scott, Helen, and Walt in one place. Ann's mother and father had died in a car crash when she and Mike were in college, and Helen and Walt had become her surrogate parents. She wanted all the people who were close to her—family by blood and by marriage, family actual and honorary—to be nearby, not a multi-hour flight apart, even if she could now make the flight herself.

When they reached seven thousand feet, Ann took the controls. Walt wouldn't let her use the autopilot, and he complimented her on her ability to maintain altitude and direction. However, her radio skills clearly weren't ideal for the busy airspace they were in: she accidentally gave a controller the identifier for the Avondale flight school Warrior rather than Walt's Arrow and stepped on other pilots' transmissions twice. She decided she wanted a little more radio practice before she tackled New York Center and turned the controls back to Walt. She spent the remainder of the flight using her iPad to investigate options for a route she could take from Chester County to Maine that would keep her out of controlled airspace.

5

Ann woke to the sounds of radio calls transferring control of the flight to Bangor Approach. The blue skies of Chester County had been replaced by a gray overcast and light rain misting the windscreen, the green fields by the innumerable rocky islands off the Maine coast. Soon she was able to pick out the runways of Hancock County-Bar Harbor Airport, just across Mount Desert Narrows from MDI.

The rain was still light when they touched down, but it must have been raining for several hours, judging by the puddles on the pavement.

"That's some pretty fancy hardware for such a little airport," Walt commented as he taxied the Arrow past the private jets parked next to the fixed base operator building, or FBO.

"The upper crust commuting to their vacation homes on MDI,'" said Mike. "One of them is probably the Pepperidge jet."

"Where are they commuting from?" asked Walt.

"Manhattan. Upstate New York. Tahoe. But based on a little research I did, I think Tippy Pepperidge spends most of her time on MDI."

Walt proceeded on to the tie-down area near the maintenance shops that was allocated to the smaller general aviation planes.

Ann climbed out of the plane and slipped on her raincoat. As she was stretching the stiffness out of her limbs, a golf cart buzzed toward them and wheeled up beside the Arrow.

"Welcome to Bar Harbor!" said the driver. "Give you a hand?"

"Ann, do you want to take the cart back to the FBO with the luggage and pick up the rental car?" asked Mike.

"Why don't you do that," said Ann, "and I'll help Walt with the plane."

"I can swing back and pick you guys up," said the young man to Ann and Walt.

"No, that's okay," said Ann. "The rain isn't bad, and I could use the walk."

"Me, too," said Walt.

Once Ann and Walt had secured the tie-downs and strapped the canvas cover over the Arrow, Walt gave the plane his traditional pat on the spinner and they started across the ramp to the FBO.

"I'm glad you're staying overnight," said Ann. "Lake Clear to Chester County to Maine is enough for one day."

"Plenty for an old codger like me, that's for sure," said Walt. "Plus, Helen's been looking forward to a night away. She always has such a good time with Scott."

"It's hard not to have a good time with Scott," Ann agreed. "Where are you staying?"

"Helen booked me a place right nearby. Said the pictures on the website looked nice."

"You know you can stay with us tonight. Corey's rented us a house. It has three bedrooms."

Walt shook his head. "I don't want to rouse someone up to cart me back out to the airport at oh-dark-thirty." He hoisted his duffle bag. "Brought along a book. I'll have an early lobster dinner, call Helen, do a little reading, then hit the sack."

She smiled. "Sounds like your kind of evening."

"Damn right."

When they reached the FBO, Ann could see Mike loading their bags into a blue Hyundai in the parking lot of the air service terminal next door.

"At least let us drop you at the lobster pound," she said to Walt.

"No thanks," said Walt. "It's practically right across the highway. I could use a little more exercise than a walk across the ramp after sitting all day."

"Okay." She gave him a kiss on the cheek, then left him to arrange the Arrow's overnight accommodation with the FBO staff.

Mike had the car running by the time she reached it, the wipers intermittently whisking droplets of rain from the windshield.

"Where to?" asked Mike.

Ann got out her phone and scrolled back through the texts. "We're staying in Manset, near Southwest Harbor." She plugged in the address, then tapped out a text letting Corey Duff know they were en route.

When they reached the highway—Route 3—they turned left. They passed landmarks familiar to Ann from her previous visit to MDI: a lobster pound, in front of which giant kettles puffed steam into the misty air, the sign promising LOBSTERS * DINNERS * ROLLS * LIVE. A little further on, a Cape Cod residence served as the office for a semi-circle of tiny white cabins with black shutters and red doors—quite possibly where Walt would be spending the night. The Bar Harbor Chamber of Commerce tourist information center displayed an OPEN sign, although its parking lot was empty. Its business would no doubt pick up in June, with the start of tourist season.

Ann was quiet until they crossed Mount Desert Narrows. "Helen asked me when I'm going back to the Adirondacks."

Mike glanced over at her, then back at the road. "What did you tell her?"

"I told her I'd be back pretty soon."

"And are you? Going to be back pretty soon?"

"I suppose. 'Pretty soon' gives a lot of leeway."

"True." The road forked and Mike bore to the right on 102. "You know you're welcome to stay with me and Scott as long as you want. We both love having you in West Chester."

"I appreciate that, Mike—I really do. I hope you guys know that. But, really, a woman in her thirties living with her brother? It's sort of pathetic."

The pines lining the road looked a bit ragged, as if they hadn't fully recovered from the Maine winter that had loosened its grip not too long before. However, occasional bursts of white and yellow blossoms in the understory indicated that spring was gaining the upper hand. A lumber store was well stocked with picnic tables and a home and garden store with bagged mulch. The road was dotted with small sheds advertising *Camp Firewood* stocked with plastic-wrapped bundles.

A few minutes later, they arrived at the address that Corey had sent Ann, a two-story house painted a cheerful yellow with a wraparound porch on two sides. Corey was seated on a tattered wicker chair on the side porch, his expression more glum than Ann expected from the normally cheerful filmmaker.

"How was the flight?" he asked as they climbed out of the car.

"Very nice," said Mike as he pulled the bags out of the trunk and handed one to Ann. "Although the clouds spoiled the view a bit."

"Yeah, it's been drizzling since this morning," said Corey. He grabbed Ann's bag. "Let me show you around."

He led them upstairs, where a bookcase-lined hallway gave access to two bedrooms and a bathroom. They dropped the bags in the bedrooms, then returned downstairs. They stepped into the living room, furnished with a sofa and loveseat that looked perfect for an evening in with a bottle of wine and a good book. It also held a baby grand piano.

"Mike," said Ann, "you can get in some practice."

"I like that ... *and* this." He crossed to shelves holding hundreds of record albums. "Look at all this vinyl." He pulled out one of the albums and held it up for Ann and Corey's inspection. "Check it out—*Saturday Night Fever!*"

The kitchen was at the back of the house. There was a small counter-height table serving as an island in the center, shelves rather than cupboards holding plates and glassware. The third bedroom opened off the kitchen.

"Wow, the kitchen is even stocked," said Ann, gesturing toward a box of Triscuits and a bag of Oreos on the counter.

"I picked up a few things," said Corey, "but don't rely on me. I'm notorious for forgetting the obvious stuff once I get to the store."

"This is great, Corey," she said. "Thanks so much for lining this up." After a beat, she asked, "How are things going?"

Just then, they heard the crunch of gravel from the driveway, the slam of a car door, and a quick tread on the porch stairs, then Kyle Lathey appeared at the glass-paned back door. He rapped briskly on the door, then stepped into the kitchen without waiting for a response. The kitchen shifted from cozy to crowded. He shook hands with Mike and surprised Ann with a kiss on the cheek.

"You got here fast," she said.

"I didn't have far to come," said Kyle. "Just around the corner from the 'production office.'" Kyle gave Corey a look as if they shared an amusing secret, although Corey didn't look particularly amused.

"I meant here to Maine. Weren't you in L.A. last night?"

"I took the red-eye, got into Bangor this morning. I went through Philly—I was surprised I didn't see you on the flight."

"Ann's charter pilot flew us up from Chester County," said Mike.

"Charter pilot, eh?" said Kyle. "Sweet."

"It's nice not to have to deal with the rigors of commercial flight," said Mike. "No hassle with parking, no security checks ... hell, we could bring a bazooka on the plane if we wanted to."

"I'm not sure Walt would allow a bazooka," said Ann, "but I do like being able to bring a Swiss Army knife and a bottle of water—"

"Of course," interrupted Kyle, "going first class takes some of the sting out of commercial."

"So," said Ann, trying to preempt an air travel pissing contest between Mike and Kyle, "how are things going here?"

Corey shot Kyle a look. "Depends on who you ask."

Ann looked from one to the other. "What do you mean?"

"There's a story on the Bangor news about the fact that Leo Dorn is the planned topic of the documentary," said Corey with a grimace.

Ann raised her eyebrows. "How did that happen? Garrick said no one could know until he got Tippy Pepperidge's okay."

Corey jerked his head toward Kyle. "Ask him."

Ann turned to Kyle. "You leaked the information?"

"It's not a leak if it comes from an official source," he said with a smug smile.

"Okay, so not a 'leak'—an outright violation of Garrick's condition."

"I made that announcement with the backers' okay."

"Lathey, you're not in charge of PR for this project," said Corey. "You are here *only* to keep the backers updated. At least that was my understanding."

"I'm here to make sure that they get their money's worth," Kyle shot back.

Corey ran his fingers through his hair. "Let's not stand around in Ann and Mike's kitchen arguing about this. I asked Garrick to meet us at the office. Let's go there." He turned to Ann and Mike. "You guys hungry?"

"I am," said Mike.

"No food service on the flight?" asked Kyle with a grin.

Walt had distributed Kit Kat bars and apple slices at the midway point, but evidently Mike agreed with Ann that this wasn't a detail to share with Kyle.

"We can stop at The Perch on the way over," said Corey. "It's a nice place, and just a couple of steps from the office. I wouldn't be surprised if it became our unofficial craft services."

"You need to get a PA on the crew to take care of stuff like ordering meals," said Kyle.

"We're not going to need a crew for long if you keep doing stuff to piss off our subject's widow," replied Corey tartly.

6

W hen they stepped outside, they found a red Tesla parked in the driveway.

"I wouldn't recommend the back seat for adults," said Kyle, "but, Ann, can I offer you a ride? Save you a walk in the rain."

"That's a rental?" asked Ann.

"Yeah. I prefer the Model S but the selection in Bangor was a little limited."

Ann glanced skyward. "The rain's tailing off, and if the office is right around the corner, I think I'll walk."

Kyle shrugged. "Suit yourself. See you in a few."

He climbed into the Tesla and peeled out of the driveway backwards.

"How far is it?" asked Mike.

"Five minutes, tops," said Corey.

"How about walking?"

"That *is* walking."

"And Lathey drove?"

Corey heaved a sigh and shrugged. "He's from L.A. Walking doesn't occur to him."

They turned right onto the two-lane state highway, then right again at the next intersection. With no traffic, they could walk abreast.

"What's the deal with Lathey?" Mike asked Corey. "I've only known him for about a minute and I already don't like him."

"Like I said, he was assigned to the project by the backers. I barely know him myself."

"Well, he's not making a good first impression by violating Tippy's condition," said Ann.

When they reached the harbor that gave Southwest its name, they turned right again onto Shore Road. The water stretched out to their left, dotted with moored boats. At the town dock, a utility truck was pulling off a miniature ferry. Across the street from the dock was a two-story shingle-sided building that would have been nondescript had it not been for its jaunty fire-engine-red door and shutters. Several picnic tables, currently unoccupied, lined the front, their umbrellas furled. A sign featuring a stylized fish identified it as The Perch. A chalkboard easel next to the front door listed the day's beers on tap, the lettering smeared in the continuing drizzle.

They stepped inside. The picnic tables might have been abandoned to the rain, but the restaurant was doing a brisk business despite the post-lunch, pre-dinner hour. Several customers were eating at the small bar, and a few more sat at tables from which they could look across the town dock's parking lot to the water beyond.

"Hey, Corey," called a man from behind the bar. He was in his mid-thirties, tall and lean, with dark, wavy hair that Ann guessed he had cut himself, perhaps without the benefit of a mirror. "I see you finally rounded up some friends to dine with."

"Yes, it looks like that documentary I told you about is finally underway. God willing," he added under his breath. "Eric, this is Ann Kinnear and her brother, Mike."

Eric shook their hands and handed out takeout menus.

"I can recommend the meatloaf," he said.

"I hate to be predictable," said Ann, "but I'd love something with lobster in it."

Eric laughed. "I can't blame you. In that case, I'd go with the lobster roll, but definitely come back for the meatloaf."

They were placing their orders—lobster rolls for Ann and Mike, meatloaf for Corey, iced teas all around—when the door opened, and Kyle stepped in.

Corey glanced out the restaurant's large front windows. "Please tell me you didn't drive here from the office."

"Parked at the office but wanted to make sure I got my order in," said Kyle.

"Lobster roll or meatloaf?" asked Corey.

"Lobster tails," replied Kyle.

"Lobster *roll* or meatloaf?" Corey repeated.

"Whatever kind of lobster they have, I guess," said Kyle.

Corey turned to Ann. "Do you think that's what Garrick will want, too?"

"I've never seen him eat anything other than bread or drink anything other than water," she said.

He laughed. "Right." He turned to Eric. "And an extra roll, hold the lobster."

Eric jotted down the order. "Going to the warehouse? I can bring it over."

"That would be great, thanks," said Corey.

As they left, Ann said, "I thought we were going to the production office."

"One and the same," said Kyle, waving toward a building just down the street.

It was a small wooden warehouse sandwiched between a prosperous-looking boatyard and a marine supply store. The sides were unadorned plywood topped with a row of dirt-smeared plexiglass windows just under the eaves. The back of the building extended over the water, supported by concrete piers. The front was covered with weathered shingles and contained two metal doors: one person-sized and another, twice the height, no doubt to accommodate boats under repair. As they approached the building, Ann could see the Tesla in the single parking space at the side of the building.

"That's the office?" she asked.

"Yeah," said Corey, a more characteristic smile lighting his face. "Don't judge until you've checked it out." He unlocked a padlock securing a hasp on the smaller of the two front doors, pushed the door open, and stood aside to let her through.

She stepped into a building that was as dilapidated inside as it was outside. Weak light leaked through the narrow windows but most of the illumination was provided by a single fluorescent fixture dangling from the rafters. A roll-up door visible at the far end of the building allowed loading directly to and from boats. The left-hand wall was stacked floor to ceiling with lobster traps. Next to the right-hand wall was a collection of heavy canvas bags and a few cases made of high impact plastic. A half dozen folding metal chairs stood around a couple of card tables in the center of the space.

But Ann's eye went to an amorphous, glowing form floating near the rafters in the far corner.

"Whoa!" she exclaimed.

"What do you see?" asked Corey eagerly.

The form was a young girl dressed in a striped T-shirt and cut-off denim shorts. Her hair was pulled back in a messy ponytail, bow-shaped plastic barrettes on either side of her head trying unsuccessfully to hold stray wisps in place. One index finger was hooked over her bottom teeth, her lips closed around the finger. She looked at them somberly.

"A little girl," said Ann.

Corey clapped his hands. "I hoped you'd see something. It must be the 'Darling of the Docks.'" He shot an amused glance at Mike. "One of the several topics that got shot down."

"What's she doing?" Mike asked Ann.

"She's just ... floating. About ten feet off the ground. She's definitely the most Casper-the-Friendly-Ghost-like spirit I've ever seen. It's sort of creepy."

"Creepy?" said Corey. "You see dead people all the time and you think a little girl is creepy?"

"I'm not used to them floating."

"What are they usually doing?"

"You know, walking around, like ... normal people. Hi, there," she said to the girl. Ann had very little interaction with children, living or dead, and was always somewhat unsure about the best way to interact with them.

The girl stared back at Ann silently.

Ann heard a car approach the warehouse, slow, then continue on.

Kyle, who was standing next to the door, cracked it open, looked out, then shut it again. "Masser."

"Where's he going?" asked Corey.

"Looking for a parking space for that land yacht of his, I guess."

"Would have been nice for you to leave the one space open for him," said Corey.

"Someone else would have taken it before he got here," said Kyle, unfazed.

A minute later, the warehouse door opened, and Garrick stepped in, ducking slightly as he did. The move was made more for effect than necessity, since even with a height of over six feet, his perennially stooped posture would have enabled him to clear the doorframe easily. He was dressed as he always was—a long black coat, black shirt open at the neck revealing a black T-shirt, black pants, and black boots. Ann wondered if he ever went swimming and, if he did, what he wore.

Garrick glanced toward the back of the warehouse. "Ah, I see you've met the Darling of the Docks."

"Why is she floating?" asked Ann.

"Why not?" replied Garrick.

"I don't know. It seems weird." She was finding the floating child surprisingly disconcerting.

Garrick raised an eyebrow but evidently felt that her comment didn't merit a response.

"What's the story with the Darling of the Docks?" she asked. "Who is she?"

"Jessica Barnwell—Jessy to her family," he said. "They used to own this warehouse. Seven-year-old Jessica was evidently assisting her grandfather with a repair to a boat, fell out of the water-access door at the rear of the building, hit her head on a rock, and drowned before she could be retrieved."

"Have you met her before?"

"I have encountered her before."

Jessy had slowly descended from the rafters and drifted to within a few feet of Garrick.

"Visually substantial but uncommunicative," he said. He turned away from the girl and toward Corey, Kyle, and Mike, who had gathered around to listen to the discussion. "Shall we get to the matter at hand?"

Corey waved them toward the card tables, which evidently constituted the team's conference room. All but Garrick pulled up folding chairs and sat.

"So ...?" prompted Garrick, Jessy floating a few feet behind him.

"He doesn't know yet?" asked Ann.

"I only found out a little while ago," said Corey. He turned to

Garrick. "Word has gotten out that Leo Dorn is the topic of the documentary."

Garrick's eyebrows pulled down ominously, further hiding his black eyes. "The news outlets have this information, regardless of the fact that I have not yet had a chance to discuss it with Ms. Pepperidge?"

Corey looked at Kyle. "You explain it," he said.

Kyle rose. "I contacted a reporter in Bangor." He leaned forward, his fisted hands on the table. "We need to strike while the iron is hot—while the public's interest in Dorn's death is high. In a couple of months—hell, in a couple of weeks—he's just going to be another rich guy who got clumsy on a walk at the family compound."

"My condition did not leave you any latitude to make decisions based on your desire to capitalize on Leo Dorn's death," said Garrick.

Kyle straightened. "If we announce the subject as a done deal, then it's going to be hard for Tippy Pepperidge to say she's not going to play along."

"Tippy Pepperidge looks to me like the kind of woman who would have no problem telling anyone she's not going to play along," said Ann. "In fact, she looks like the kind of woman who might decide not to play along on principle if she believed someone was trying to pressure her into it."

"Well," said Kyle, folding his arms, "I'm thinking you all shouldn't be as worried as you seem to be if Masser here really has the 'in' he claims to have with her."

Garrick turned and strode toward the door, Jessy scooting through the air behind him.

"Where are you going?" Kyle called after him.

Garrick reached the door and turned. "If you believed that your premature announcement of the *tentative* subject of the documentary sealed a 'done deal,' then you have very much mistaken my willingness to 'play along.' I will not be a party to trying to convince Tippy Pepperidge to give you access to Brookview. In fact, I will not be a party to this ill-run project at all."

He opened the door and almost ran into Eric, who stood outside with one hand raised to knock, the other holding two plastic bags.

"Delivery," said Eric, holding out the bags.

"I am not the recipient," said Garrick. He brushed past Eric and disappeared from view, followed by Jessy.

Eric looked uncertainly into the warehouse. "Delivery?"

Corey crossed to the door and took the bags. "Thanks, Eric."

Eric acknowledged the rest of them with a wave and closed the door.

Ann crossed her arms. "Nice going, Kyle."

Kyle sat down. "Masser will come around. He can't pass up the kind of exposure this documentary will give him."

"He doesn't need exposure," she said as Corey put the bags on one of the card tables and fell onto a folding chair. "He has a full calendar of engagements as it is. It's not as if it's a scalable business—you don't just hire more people if more prospective clients show up."

"As I keep telling you," said Mike, "we don't need Masser. Ann can carry this project on her own."

"But the backers—" began Corey.

"I know," interrupted Mike, "the backers want them both because of what happened at Lynam's Point. But think about it." He leaned forward, warming to his argument. "That was all Ann. Masser didn't contribute anything other than needing to be rescued."

"He told me what we had to do to rescue him," Ann countered as Jessy materialized through the front door. "If he hadn't been able to do that, we would never have been able to help him."

"If *you* hadn't been able to receive the message," said Mike, "we wouldn't be here today. More to the point, *he* wouldn't be here today."

"We're here today because *Garrick* has the influence we need to get the family to cooperate with us—" She shot a look toward Kyle. "—or would have, under the agreement we had."

"Per usual," said Mike, almost as an aside, "you're underselling yourself."

"'Per usual'?" said Ann, her voice rising. "What is this, a therapy session?"

"I'm telling you," said Corey, exasperated, "it's a moot point. The backers say it has to be Garrick and Ann."

Mike turned to Kyle. "You claim to be the voice of the backers in all this—do you agree? Does it *have* to be both of them?"

Kyle spread his hands and gave Mike an apologetic smile. "I'd be happy to go ahead with Ann solo, but the powers that be are insistent."

Mike flopped back in his chair. "I think you guys are making a big mistake."

They were all silent for a moment, the ghostly girl floating a dozen feet away, observing them wordlessly.

Finally, Ann said, "What are we going to do?"

Corey sighed. "I think we should give Garrick the evening to —hopefully—cool off, then check in with him again in the morning. For now, let's have our late lunch, then let Ann and Mike get settled at the house. We can reconvene for dinner, then call it a day."

Kyle clapped his hands together and stood. "Next time I have lobster, it's going to be *tails*—and that dinner's on me."

7

S helby sat at the lab table, a space cleared for her laptop among the graduated cylinders, reaction flasks, distillation columns, condensers, and crystallization tubes. The lab was no doubt its usual comfortable temperature, but she couldn't get warm. She shrugged back into her jacket, thinking that its bright yellow was hardly appropriate for her mood.

She clicked through the search results for *leo dorn death* from the past hour—friends, colleagues, even politicians expressing their shock and sorrow at his death. As she had been doing since she arrived at the Stata Mater lab hours earlier, when she got to the end of the results, she refreshed the page and scanned for any new ones.

Her eye stopped on one of the results: *L.A.-based Authentic Productions Pursuing Documentary Project on Leo Dorn's Life and Untimely Death*

Her heart thumping, she read the article.

"Leo Dorn was a mover and shaker, from his for-profit businesses to his leadership of Stata Mater Technology, a philanthropic research lab funded by his wife, Tippy

*Pepperidge," said Authentic Productions executive producer
Kyle Lathey. "His life, as well as his sudden and unexpected
death, deserves careful examination."*

*The production company is already on Mount Desert
Island—*

Shelby jumped at a light knock on the door.

"Shel?"

She turned to see Jonathan Garrido standing in the doorway.
His dark eyes were tired, his features drawn.

"I tried calling—you didn't pick up," he said, the barest
Southern drawl softening his words.

"Sorry, I must not have heard it." But the lie was a trans-
parent one since she was sure Jonathan could see her phone
lying on the desk right next to the laptop.

He crossed to the table and sank onto a stool next to her.
"What are you doing here? Nobody expects you to be working
tonight. Actually, no one expects you to be working at all. No
one else is." He glanced at the laptop screen. "You're reading
about him?"

"Someone's doing a documentary about him. And about
how he died."

"No kidding?" He leaned toward the screen and scanned the
article. "Jesus, he's barely cold."

"Yeah."

He sat back. "You shouldn't keep reading that shit, it's just
going to depress you more. Want to go out, grab dinner? Or I'll
make you dinner at my place if you don't want to go out."

"No, thanks, Jonathan. I wouldn't be very good company."

"I don't care."

She fidgeted, not meeting his eyes. "I appreciate it—I do—
but I really just want to be alone. I'm sorry."

"Don't be sorry, Shel—I just want to do whatever I can for

you. I know Leo was important to you. Hell, he was important to all of us, but I always felt like you two had a special bond." He paused, perhaps hoping she would speak, but when she remained silent, he sighed. "If it were me, I'd want to go out for a drink or three and forget about things for a while, but I know I shouldn't assume that what's good for me would be good for you." After a pause, he asked, "Do you want me to stay here with you?"

"It's sweet of you to offer, but I'd really rather be by myself, at least for now."

"Sure, sure, I understand."

"In fact," she said, and she could feel her cheeks redden, "I feel like maybe we should take a little break." She looked down at her hands.

"You mean ... a break from *us*?"

"Just for a little while."

"But ... why?" The hurt and surprise were clear in his voice.

"There's just so much going on. The preparations for the announcement, and then Leo's death."

"Shelby, when bad things happen it's not the time to take a break from the people who care about you. It's time to rely on them for support." He paused. "And maybe to offer some support to them as well."

She was silent, forcing back the tears that stung her eyes.

When he spoke again, his voice had an edge. "Maybe you have reasons for being more upset about Leo's death than I realized."

She looked up quickly. His expression was more hurt than angry. She returned her gaze to her intertwined fingers and shook her head. "It's not like that."

Finally, he heaved a sigh. "Yeah, I guess I didn't really think so." He pushed himself to his feet. "I think you're going about this all wrong, Shel. I'm heading home, so if you change your mind about wanting to talk, or just about having some company, give me a call. Or just stop by."

She attempted a wan smile. "Not going out for a drink or three?"

His mouth quirked up, but his eyes remained sad. "Not without you." He reached out and ran his hand over her hair, then dropped his hand to his side. "Don't stay too late, okay? You hanging out here doom scrolling isn't going to do anyone any good."

"Okay."

He bent as if to kiss her on the cheek, then evidently thought better of it. He turned and left the office.

She gazed toward the door as his footsteps receded down the hall. Then, pulling a damp ball of tissue out of her jacket pocket and dabbing her eyes, she turned back to the laptop and hit *Refresh* again. Nothing new.

After a brief hesitation, she added *ledge* to the search.

A new headline caught her eye: *Man Seriously Injured in Fall at Pepperidge Estate*

With a trembling finger, she clicked on the video. The reporter was back in front of the Brookview gates.

"More tragic news today from Brookview, the Pepperidge family property on Mount Desert Island. It appears that twenty-two-year-old Brian Geary entered the back of the Brookview property—without permission, according to a Pepperidge family spokesperson—and was evidently headed toward the location of Leo Dorn's fall when he himself fell from a narrow ledge. Brian Geary and his stepbrother Neal Storer host the YouTube channel *Behind the Scenes with Geary*, where they post photos and video taken by Geary of crime and accident scenes."

A photo—evidently a selfie—of a young man, a swimming pool in the background, appeared on the screen, then the view cut back to the reporter at the Brookview gate.

"Brian Geary's fall occurred at a slightly different point on the path from which Dr. Dorn fell. Although the dry weather in the period leading up to Dr. Dorn's accident means that rain was not a contributing factor in that case, it may be that the rain that began shortly after he fell had made the path slippery when Geary tried to cross it. Geary evidently lay at the base of the cliff for some time before a Brookview gardener heard his cries for help. Geary is in intensive care at Mount Desert Island Hospital in Bar Harbor. Neal Storer told us that Brian suffered damage to his spinal column, and that doctors are concerned about the possibility of paralysis."

Shelby jumped when gibberish began to pop into the search bar, then realized that her fingers had tightened into claws on the keyboard. She snatched her hands back, twisting her fingers together.

Oh, God, please, she thought, *not again.*

8

The rain had intensified through the late afternoon and early evening, and Ann and Mike passed the time at the Manset house by sampling the offerings in the upstairs bookshelves and in the living room record collection.

Around seven o'clock, Corey called to consult about dinner plans.

"You're welcome to come to Bar Harbor where Kyle and I are staying, but I wouldn't blame you if you didn't feel like heading out in this weather. I need to swing by the production office anyway—we could bring takeout to the house."

"What about the lobster tail dinner that Kyle promised us?"

"Oh, I'll make sure he delivers," said Corey. "And I'll provide the beer."

An hour later, Ann was setting a Moody Blues album on the turntable when Corey knocked on the back door. He was carrying two six-packs of Bar Harbor Real Ale, which he handed over to Ann before shrugging out of his rain-slicked jacket and hanging it on one of the pegs by the door.

"Want one now?" she asked, indicating the bottles.

"Sure, that would be great."

Ann rummaged in the kitchen drawers and, not finding a bottle opener, retrieved her Swiss Army knife from her knapsack and popped the caps off two bottles. She handed one bottle to Corey.

"Where's Mike?" he asked.

"Upstairs talking with Scott." She removed one more bottle from the cardboard carrier and left it and the knife on the kitchen island, then put the remaining beers in the fridge. "Where's Kyle?"

Corey grinned. "Picking up the promised dinners from a lobster pound down the street. I asked him to drop me off here first." He took a swallow of beer and stepped into the living room. "Hey, Moody Blues—I love this album!"

They had just sat down in the living room—Ann on the couch and Corey on the loveseat—when Ann heard Mike's tread on the stairs.

"Corey's here and he brought beer," she called.

Mike appeared in the living room doorway, phone in hand. "Scott's been following the Leo Dorn news coverage—guess what story he alerted me to?"

"Oh, God," groaned Corey, "what has Lathey done now?"

"This doesn't seem like Kyle's doing, unless he's an even bigger jerk than I thought," said Mike. "Some guy snuck onto the Pepperidge property—evidently trying to get photos of where Leo Dorn died—and fell. Looks like he might be paralyzed."

He handed his phone to Ann, with the news story open on the browser. She read, then passed the phone to Corey.

"Jesus," she said. "Even if Kyle hadn't jumped the gun on announcing the topic of the documentary, Tippy Pepperidge might not be thrilled about letting us onto the property considering all these accidents."

There was a knock on the back door and, before Ann could

rise to answer it, chilly air swirled into the house as the door opened and closed. Kyle, his rain-drenched hair somehow not completely flattened, entered with a white plastic bag in each hand.

"Lobster!" he called. "Tails this time." He put the bags on the kitchen island next to the bottle of beer. "Is that all we have? I'd fancy Champagne with lobster, but I could do with a nice Chardonnay in a pinch."

"Beer is what we've got," said Corey. "Plus, I don't think we have much to celebrate." He passed Mike's phone to Kyle.

Kyle hung his jacket over one of the kitchen stools, and a puddle immediately started to form underneath it. He took the phone from Corey, who moved Kyle's jacket to a peg by the back door.

Kyle put the phone on the island, popping the top off the beer bottle and taking a swig as he read.

"Jesus Christ," he said when he was done. He handed the phone back to Corey, who handed it to Mike.

"You can say that again," said Corey.

"We need to get an interview with that guy."

Corey opened his mouth, clamped it shut, then said, "He's in the ICU."

"Okay, well, when he's out."

"This guy's clumsiness is not the focus of our documentary."

"Like it or not, stories of people who are so committed to their jobs that they're willing to risk serious injury draw viewers."

"I doubt he was weighing the risk of paralysis when he decided to trespass on the Pepperidge property to take a photo of the place where a man died. He probably just got inattentive or unlucky and took a tumble."

"Well, I'm going to talk to him when he's out of the ICU."

Corey's voice raised a fraction—noteworthy because of its

rarity. "You're not talking to anyone. You're here to keep an eye on our progress for the backers, and that's it."

Kyle looked speculatively from Corey to Ann to Mike, then shrugged. "We can talk about it later. Let's not let the lobster get cold." He removed four Styrofoam containers from the plastic bags. "Do we have sparkling water?"

"No, Kyle," said Ann, "we have beer, which you've already opened."

"Beer's what you drink with lobster in Maine," said Mike, getting another bottle out of the fridge and popping the cap.

"That's cool," said Kyle. "When in Rome."

The kitchen island was too small to accommodate four diners comfortably, so they adjourned to the living room—Mike on the loveseat, Ann and Corey on the couch, and Kyle sitting on the floor, leaning against the couch next to Ann's legs.

Kyle regaled them with highlights of the work he had done in L.A. and New York, including a brief but, if he were to be believed, highly successful foray into feature movies. He claimed to have dated all but one of the previous year's best supporting actress nominees—a claim that Ann thought was savvy, since no one in Kyle's audience, with the possible exception of Corey, was likely to be able to fact check him. After replacing *Long Distance Voyager* with *Ellington at Newport*, leaving Corey to return the discarded album to the shelf, Kyle launched into a description of his Hollywood Hills condo. The excellent lobster dinner almost but not quite made up for the quality of the conversation.

"Kyle, you must be tired after your trip from L.A.," said Ann, nurturing a faint hope that Kyle would decide to make it an early night.

"Like I said, first class is hardly tiring. Plus, I'm still on West Coast time. Anyone feel like checking out the nightlife on Mount Desert Island, such as it is?"

"I'm kind of flagging myself," said Ann. "I'll take a pass."

"I still have some things I need to do," said Corey. "Just in case we can salvage the situation with Garrick and Tippy Pepperidge."

"Capitalize on it, you mean," said Kyle with a laugh.

Mike pushed himself off the loveseat. "I'll come with you. If it weren't for this trip to Maine, I'd be checking out the bars and bistros of the Big Apple. Let's see what MDI has to offer."

Ann raised an eyebrow at him.

Kyle slapped his hands together and rubbed them enthusiastically. "Excellent! I'm glad there's one person who isn't claiming it's past their bedtime."

Ann, Mike, and Corey collected their now-empty Styrofoam containers and carried them to the kitchen. Kyle's remained on the coffee table.

"Just leave them on the island," said Ann to Corey and Mike. "I'll see if I can find somewhere outside to get rid of them so the house doesn't smell like rotting lobsters in the morning."

"Don't you kids stay up too late," said Mike with a grin as he and Kyle donned rain gear.

They headed out, and in a moment, Ann heard the crunch of gravel in the driveway and then the squeal of the Tesla's tires.

"I guess Kyle figures if he bought and delivered dinner," said Corey, "he's off the clean-up detail." He went back to the living room and retrieved Kyle's container.

Ann and Corey made a quick dash through the rain to a metal trash container they spotted from the window, then returned to the living room with new beers.

Ann took Duke Ellington off the turntable—she had a low tolerance for jazz—and put on *The Beatles at the Hollywood Bowl*. "How did you get involved with that guy?" she asked, resuming her seat at the end of the couch. "It's like interacting with a stuck-up and socially inept teenager."

Corey took a long swallow of beer and then collapsed onto the other end of the couch. "You heard him," he said tiredly. "Making sure the backers get their money's worth."

"Not that I'm complaining, but it seems like this can't be that expensive a project. You're getting me and Garrick for free. I can't imagine the Pepperidges would expect you to pay to shoot at Brookview. It's not like there are going to be elaborate special effects—" She stopped, her beer halfway to her mouth. "Are there?"

"No, no special effects." He took another swallow of beer. "It's not just this project that they're thinking about. There could be more after this—" He rolled his eyes. "—*if* this one goes well, which seems increasingly unlikely."

"What will the other ones be about?"

"I'd love to do one about the beginnings of the steel industry in Pittsburgh. The history and future of the Maine lobster industry might be interesting." He grinned at Ann. "Now that you have your pilot's license, if you can just go ahead and get certified for aerobatics, I might be able to have my aviation-themed project after all."

She laughed. "Don't hold your breath. My goal is always to have the shiny side up and the dirty side down." She took a sip of beer. "So the backers sent Kyle out to Mount Desert Island to ..." She couldn't think of a polite way to say it.

"Babysit me, as far as I can tell," said Corey. "My concern is that if Lathey is the guy they sent out here, he must be the kind of guy they want—except with some actual video production experience—and I'm definitely not that guy."

"No, you're not," said Ann. "Thank God."

They sat in companionable silence for a while, sipping their beers and listening to the music, and to the rain drumming on the tin roof of the porch.

"I'm glad I'm not out in that," said Corey.

"I'm glad I'm not out with Kyle," said Ann.

They raised their beers and clinked bottles.

9

S helby climbed out of her car and eased the door shut. It somehow seemed important to be quiet, although the combination of the late hour and the steady rain meant that the small Otter Cliff visitor parking area was deserted.

She crossed the Park Loop Road and, by the light of her phone's flashlight app, descended the stone steps that led to the rock outcropping that was the usual place for visitors to congregate. She could hear the ringing of the bell buoy that warned ships away from the rocks known as the Spindle, a hundred yards offshore. She turned toward the sound, squinting against the raindrops that splashed her face and cooled her cheeks. She thought briefly of pulling up the hood of her jacket. She decided it was too much trouble.

She turned left and followed the Ocean Path. The light, which she kept trained on the ground, cast jittery shadows to either side of the path but left in darkness the branches that plucked at her jacket like skeletal fingers. Over the shush of rain through the needles, she thought she heard a vehicle approach and slow on the road above her. A half minute later, she heard the dull thunk of a car door closing. She tried to swallow away the tightness that suddenly gripped her throat. She had thought she might have the cliff to herself.

A few more steps brought her to another outcropping of rock. She had visited it with Jonathan only weeks before, just after the Loop Road to Otter Cliff had opened after its winter closure. It was about halfway between the popular overlook behind her and the rocks further up the coast from which climbers rappelled or top-roped. She had never done either. On the walk from Otter Point to Sand Beach, she and Jonathan had talked about taking lessons.

She had been alone on her first visit to Otter Point. It was a stormy day during her trip to Mount Desert Island to interview for the position at Stata Mater. She had read about the Spindle and visualized a dagger of stone lurking under the water, ready to impale unsuspecting ships. However, with the tide low, the rounded tops of the rocks were visible, a tiny archipelago that was periodically obscured by great fountains of spray from the incoming waves. The sight had been exhilarating. Euphoric after interviews with Leo and Hannah that she knew had gone well, she had imagined herself out there, rooted to one of those rock islands like an indomitable lighthouse as waves crashed and water swirled around her.

The water was quieter now. She could hear the muffled splash of the waves hitting the rocks at the bottom of the cliff a hundred feet below, then a long sigh as the water flowed back to the ocean. And, barely audible over this—over the ringing of the buoy and the patter of the rain—there was another sound: the crunch of feet on the path behind her.

Shelby turned off the flashlight app. She didn't want to see. She didn't want to be seen.

A cone of illumination flickered through the pines that lined the trail. The movement stopped fifty feet away and the light blinked out.

Shelby turned back toward the water. Blocking her phone from the rain as best she could, she tapped to bring up the lock screen.

It was an image of a print photograph, the glass that protected the original creating a flare of light that obscured one corner. It was a school portrait—an eighth-grade portrait, in fact —the backdrop mottled blues and greens, the subject's chin resting on her gently closed hand, every strand of glossy black hair combed carefully into place. The formality of the setting and pose made the girl's wide grin even more striking.

Not long after that photo was taken, had life dealt that girl a different hand, she would have gone on her first date—to the movies with the son of friends of her parents. But she never went on that date. Never, in fact, went on any date.

Shelby stroked her finger across the girl's now rain-splattered cheek. Water had found its way into the neck of Shelby's jacket and leaked down her back.

Out of the corner of her eye she saw the light on the path flick back on and begin to move slowly toward her.

She flinched and lost her grasp on her phone. It bounced off the rock and the screen went dark. She lunged after it and as she did her foot slipped on a rain-slicked rock and an image flashed through her mind of the Brookview trail, of the narrow ledge and those granite teeth beneath, of Leo trying to turn back to her, trying to grasp the hiking stick that would enable him to regain his balance.

She landed on her knees with a jolt. She must have bitten her tongue because she tasted blood. She began frantically running her hand over the ground. All that met her searching fingers was grit and the soft duff of pine needles.

"Stacy ... Stacy ..." she whimpered as her hands continued their fruitless search.

The light reached the edge of the rock outcropping, then

swung up to capture her in its beam, blinding her. Her heart thundering, she scrambled to her feet and edged away from the path, closer to the cliff edge.

Then the light switched off, leaving her still blinded as her eyes struggled to adjust again to the darkness. She felt a keening cry building in her chest. She wanted the phone. She wanted Stacy with her.

Shelby wondered almost idly what the cause of her death would be: the rocks a hundred feet below or the ocean. The water temperature was in the forties and the bottom of the cliff was inaccessible without ropes or a boat. If the fall didn't kill her, she wouldn't survive until help arrived, if help was summoned. And she was quite sure help would not be summoned.

She turned her head slightly toward where she had last seen the light, then turned resolutely back toward the water. She thought she heard a slight intake of breath from behind her.

The rocks or the ocean. She hoped it was not the ocean.

But at least it would not be fire.

10

Ann was waiting impatiently for the coffee maker to burble the final drops of coffee into the carafe when Mike appeared in the kitchen in a sweatshirt and sweatpants, his feet bare. He ran his fingers through his hair, leaving it sticking straight up, and got a mug from one of the shelves over the counter.

"Make enough for two?" he asked.

"Yup." She filled her mug then his. They sat down at the small kitchen island. "How was your night out with your new best friend, Kyle Lathey?"

He shrugged. "He's not that bad."

"Not that bad?" She took a sip of coffee. "I guess it depends on who you compare him to."

He grinned. "Well, I must admit, if you compare him to *your* new best friend, Corey Duff—"

"Corey's not my new best friend."

"Oh, yeah? What is he?"

"He's an old friend."

"I think he wants to be more than an 'old friend.' He

wouldn't have spent so much time in West Chester talking to you about the documentary if he didn't."

"He was doing what he needed to do to get me on board," said Ann. "You heard him—the requirement was Garrick and me on MDI."

Mike shook his head. "I'm telling you, he's interested in you other than just as a documentary subject. And I'm not the only one. Scott's the one who told me to give you and Corey some time alone together."

Ann rolled her eyes. "Scott, the perennial matchmaker."

"Corey is a nice guy. Good looking. And, maybe most importantly, he knows about your ability and doesn't care." He raised a finger. "Correction. He knows about your ability and he does care, but in a good way." He took a sip of coffee. "So what did you kids get up to?"

"We drank beer and listened to records."

"My sister, the wanton woman."

"That's me." She took a sip of coffee. "So you really took one for the team and went out for a night on the town with Kyle just to give me time alone with Corey?"

"Well ..."

"Mike," she said balefully.

"I don't know why he and Corey are being so stubborn about needing to have Masser on the project. The backers may be saying that they need both of you now, but has either Kyle or Corey made an argument for another approach? I doubt Corey has."

"Why not?" asked Ann testily. "You were singing his praises a minute ago."

"He's the creative one, but Lathey's the ballsy one. You heard him—he's here to make sure the backers get their money's worth. Well, I think they'll get more than their money's worth if they focus the documentary on you."

"And you used your outing to try to convince Kyle of that?"

"I did."

"And how did that work out for you?"

Mike sighed. "I don't think he was buying it." He yawned. "I need some breakfast."

"Maybe you can go into Southwest Harbor and pick up some groceries. Corey stocked us up with bagels and cream cheese, but no orange juice. I also wouldn't mind a supply of bananas."

"All right. Coming along?"

"Can't. Corey and I are going to Somesville to see if we can talk Garrick back onto the project."

"When's that?"

"He'll be here any minute. Did I mention that it was going to be Corey and me going to Somesville? *Just* Corey and me?"

"Hey, I—"

"You're just going to antagonize Garrick if you're there."

"He's the one doing the antagonizing."

"I can't entirely disagree, but the idea is to get Garrick involved again, not to give him a reason to dig in his heels. If you're there, he's likely to stick with his plan to sit it out just to annoy you."

"Annoy me? I'm thrilled that he bowed out."

Corey arrived a few minutes later, armed with two cups of coffee enclosed in cardboard sleeves bearing the stylized fish logo of The Perch. He and Ann left Mike sulking in the kitchen. They climbed into Corey's Chevy Suburban and headed for Somesville.

The day was sunny but windy, small whitecaps visible in the harbor, the boats rocking at their moorings. As they reached Somesville, Ann noticed for the first time that Garrick lived just down the street from a funeral home. She wondered if the funeral home's clients ever asked him to try to mediate one last communication with their dead friends or relatives.

Garrick lived in a nineteenth-century Federal-style home. The only sign that it housed his business was a small brass sign next to the front door: *Garrick Masser, Consulting.*

"Does he know we're coming?" Ann asked as they climbed the steps to the porch.

"Yes. I didn't want to risk being left standing out here if he refused to let us in."

He knocked and after half a minute the door opened. Garrick glared out at them from the entrance hall.

"Hi, Garrick," said Ann.

"Hey, Garrick," said Corey.

Garrick turned, walked down the hall, and disappeared into his office.

Ann and Corey exchanged a look and shrugged. They stepped inside and, as Ann passed the room that Garrick used as a waiting room, she caught a glimpse of the videoconferencing set-up that Corey had installed. It was the only visible nod to modern technology that Ann had seen in the home.

They entered Garrick's office. To the right, facing the center of the room, was a large desk, two well-worn leather wing chairs facing it. Against the far wall was an unlit fireplace flanked by windows overlooking the side yard. Except for another pair of windows overlooking the front, all the other wall space was lined with floor-to-ceiling bookshelves, the upper shelves accessible via a wheeled ladder attached to a brass rail above the top shelf.

Garrick waved toward the guest chairs and took a seat behind the desk.

"As I told you on the phone, Mr. Duff," said Garrick, "I can't imagine that I can make my position any clearer than I did yesterday."

"Garrick," said Corey, "I would feel terrible if the ill-informed action of one person derailed the project. I still believe that Leo Dorn is not only a fascinating subject, but that the situation could benefit in a very practical way from your special skill. A conversation with Leo Dorn might be the only way to find out what really happened at Brookview."

"You have Miss Kinnear to pursue such information, should she wish to do so."

The *ah-OO-gah* of a submarine dive alarm emanated from Corey's jacket pocket.

Garrick raised his eyebrows. "What in the world?"

"It's just a call from Kyle." Corey reached into the pocket and silenced the phone. "But you're the one with the connection to Tippy Pepperidge, which I think will be vital for us to get the access we need."

The dive alarm sounded again.

"Good heavens," muttered Garrick.

"Jeez, Lathey, give it a rest," said Corey as he again silenced the phone, then turned his attention back to Garrick. "On top of that, there's now been the incident with the trespasser at Brookview. Of course, it could have been an accident, like the reports are claiming, but if Leo is still at that location, he might have seen the guy fall and could confirm exactly what happened."

"As I understand it," replied Garrick, "the trespasser is still alive, if not well. You can ask him what happened when he is discharged from the hospital, although I myself do not find it hard to imagine that it was anything other than a case of ill-advised foot placement."

"Danger, Will Robinson!" a mechanical voice exclaimed from Corey's pocket.

"Now he's texting me," sighed Corey. He pulled out his phone again and glanced at the screen, his expression shifting from annoyance to concern. "Shelby Kim is missing."

Ann and Garrick exchanged glances.

Corey tapped the phone and held it to his ear. After a moment, he said, "Lathey, what's going on?" He listened for a moment, then said, "Hold on, I'm going to put you on speaker."

"Took you long enough to pick up," Kyle's voice boomed from the phone. Corey adjusted the volume. "I'm at Stata Mater Technology with Hannah Jeskie, the Number Two. Well, I guess she's Number One now that Dorn is ..." His voice trailed off, and they could hear a female voice in the background, its reproving tone clear even over the phone. "—now that Dr. Dorn is no longer with us," said Kyle. "Here, I'll let her tell you."

Kyle must have put his phone on speaker as well, because now the female voice was clear.

"Hello, this is Hannah Jeskie—I'm the Director of Research Operations at Stata Mater. I stopped by Shelby Kim's apartment this morning on my way to work. She was so devastated by Leo's death that I wanted to check up on her. When she didn't answer the door, I assumed I'd find her at work, but she's not here. None of the staff have seen her this morning. In fact, the last time anyone saw her here was last night. Jonathan Garrido said he spoke with her in the lab around six o'clock. Jonathan and I have both tried calling her on her cell phone but she's not picking up. I was able to get in touch with her landlord and talked him into checking her apartment. He confirmed that she's not there. Jonathan is calling around to Shelby's friends and going to some of the places he knows she frequented."

"Does she have family nearby?" asked Corey.

"In Connecticut, I believe," said Hannah. "We'll have emergency contact information for her in the SMT files—her parents, no doubt. I hate to worry them unnecessarily, but it wouldn't be like her to take time off from work without letting us know."

"Even two days after her friend Leo Dorn died?" asked Kyle.

"Yes, even two days after Dr. Dorn passed away. Shelby is extremely committed to the work she does at SMT."

"What is that work?" asked Kyle.

"She is one of our most talented researchers," said Hannah. "In fact, she has developed a breakthrough technology that we had planned to announce very soon, had it not been for Dr. Dorn's death."

"Maybe one of your competitors had something to do with her disappearance—and with Dorn's death," said Kyle.

"If Shelby Kim said that Leo slipped and fell, then he slipped and fell," said Hannah, her tone clipped. "And Stata Mater doesn't have competitors—we have beneficiaries. We do pro bono work. Our inventions benefit all organizations in the fire prevention and suppression industries. In any case, whatever the reason for Shelby's disappearance, Jonathan and I are very worried about her."

"It sounds like you're doing everything you can," said Ann.

"Who is that?" asked Hannah.

"That was Ann Kinnear," said Corey, "and I'm Corey Duff. We're here in Garrick Masser's office in Somesville."

"Ah, yes, I'm familiar with Mr. Masser from his work with Ms. Pepperidge in the past."

"Did Kyle explain to you about the documentary we're working on?" asked Corey.

"Very briefly. I understand there's interest in bringing Mr. Masser's skills to bear in the current situation."

Corey glanced at Ann and Garrick. "Yes, something like that, but I'd like to discuss it with you in more detail ... at a more appropriate time."

"Yes, of course," she said. "But now I really must be going."

"I'm going to help these guys take a look around for Shelby Kim," said Kyle.

Corey grimaced. "Kyle ..."

They heard Hannah sigh. "I suppose an extra set of eyes and legs can't hurt."

"Good luck, Dr. Jeskie," said Corey. He stabbed off the call. "If Kyle screws it up with SMT as well as with Tippy Pepperidge, I'll push him off a ledge myself."

"I'm sure that situation would be most annoying for you," said Garrick. "Now if you have nothing else for me ..."

"Garrick, if Shelby Kim is missing, it should be even more incentive for you to come back to the project. If she's dead and you could contact her spirit—"

"I would caution you not to jump to conclusions," said Garrick. "Dr. Kim might be seeking some privacy in a coffee shop or ..." This evidently exhausted the places Garrick could think of where someone would seek privacy. "Or grocery shopping," he concluded.

"If she's missing," Corey said, "she might be distraught and in need of help. If she was as close to Leo Dorn as folks have suggested, he might be able to help us find her and get her help. If she was so distraught that she killed herself, we should know that. It would keep us from following a lot of—forgive the phrase—dead ends. If someone else killed her, then others might be in danger, and speaking with Shelby or Leo might save lives. It's not only for selfish reasons that I'm asking you to return to the project."

"But you have Miss Kinnear," said Garrick.

Ann felt that little flush of pride that any hint of a compliment from Garrick brought on. She glanced at Corey, curious to see how he would answer that.

"And I'm glad to have her," said Corey, "but I think this is a case of 'all sensing hands on deck.'"

Garrick stood. "I am unconvinced that my involvement is

necessary, and my objection to Mr. Lathey has not been diminished by our most recent conversation with him." He extended his arm toward the door. "I'm afraid you will have to soldier on without me."

11

A s Ann and Corey climbed into Corey's car, Ann called Mike to update him on the situation.

"Did you eat breakfast yet?" she asked when she was done.

"I just finished my shower and was about to head over to Southwest to grab something," said Mike.

"We're going to strategize over brunch—want to come?"

"You're inviting me to sit at the grown-up table?"

"Don't be a whiner."

"Okay. Where are we going?"

She put Mike on speaker. "Corey, does The Perch serve brunch?" she asked.

"I don't think so, but I don't want to go there anyway," he said. "I'm afraid we'd run into Kyle, just in case he gets bored with the search for Shelby. Mike, can you meet us in Somesville? You can leave your car at the Selectmen's Building and we can drive into Bar Harbor."

"Sure thing—I'll be there in fifteen minutes."

Corey and Ann drove the short distance to the rendezvous point: a tiny white clapboard building set next to an arched wooden bridge over a wind-rippled stream. Ann snapped a few pictures and texted them to Scott, then she and Corey crossed the road to enjoy the view across a pond and past the diminutive library to the Somesville harbor beyond. When Mike arrived, they transferred to Corey's Suburban for the drive to Bar Harbor.

They parked at the Bar Harbor Inn, where Corey was staying. The branches of the trees that dotted the property were bright with buds, and daffodils bloomed in beds lining the drive.

"I know a good place on Cottage Street," said Corey. "Definitely not Kyle's kind of place."

George's Restaurant was clearly a destination for locals as well as visitors, based on the animated conversations going on between the servers and some of the diners. The three slid into a booth, Ann and Mike on one side, Corey on the other. An aproned woman came by, coffee pot in hand, and took their orders: a veggie omelet for Ann, a meat-lover's omelet for Mike, and pancakes and sausage for Corey.

"So," said Mike, "what's everyone's theory about this latest development?"

"Maybe Shelby Kim and Leo Dorn *were* romantically involved," said Corey, "and she killed herself out of grief at his death."

"His accidental death?" asked Ann.

"Sure. Why?"

"Because another possibility is that Shelby pushed Leo off the path and then killed herself out of remorse."

"I still find that hard to believe," said Mike. "According to those pictures they showed on the news, he's so much bigger than her, I can't imagine how she could overpower him like that."

"So what's your theory?" asked Ann.

"Two of the shining lights of Stata Mater Technology dying

in suspicious circumstances? The other possibility is that it has nothing to do with romance and everything to do with money. Maybe one of their competitors is picking off SMT staff."

"Kyle suggested that when we were talking with Hannah Jeskie, but she pointed out that the last thing anyone in the industry would want to do is disrupt Stata Mater's operations because they're basically giving away their R&D work."

Mike shrugged. "Okay, so maybe it's not a financial incentive. Maybe someone is jealous of their achievements. I'm just saying, it could be for a reason other than a love affair gone wrong."

Corey sat back with a sigh. "All this is just navel-gazing if we're really done with the documentary."

"Assuming Kyle doesn't mess up the Stata Mater angle," said Ann, "I do see the benefit of continuing with the project, especially in view of Shelby Kim's disappearance. We could possibly find out some information that would help locate her. But I would still prefer to do it with Garrick. Isn't there any way to get rid of Kyle? It seems that if he were gone, Garrick would be much more likely to come back, especially if we find out Shelby is dead."

"Hey, I'd be the first to show Kyle the door if I felt I could, but you heard him—he has an assignment from the people holding the purse strings."

"It seems like he's overstepping his assignment," said Ann.

"I can't disagree with that," said Corey. "Unless he has assignments beyond what he's told me."

"If Lathey's not removable," said Mike, "and Masser won't participate unless he's gone, then I would think that the backers would rather have the documentary proceed as a solo project with Ann—"

Ann and Corey both turned to him, exasperated, when they were interrupted by Corey's phone announcing, "Danger, Will Robinson!"

Corey pulled out his phone and read the message that Kyle had sent. "Jonathan Garrido found Shelby Kim's car at Otter Cliff." He glanced up. "That's not far from here, is it?"

Ann tapped her phone's map app. "South of here, along the coast. About twenty minutes away."

"Kyle says he and Hannah are going to check it out. I think I should probably go out there, try to curb his enthusiasm."

"Hope you have a baseball bat in the back of your car," said Mike.

"Do you guys want to stay and have your brunch? I can swing back and pick you up after I see what's up at Otter Cliff."

"No way," said Mike. "We're coming with you."

Corey raised his hand, trying to catch the server's eye. "Okay. I'll ask if we can get our food boxed up to go."

"Want us to go get the car while you do that?" asked Ann.

"That would be great." Corey handed Ann the key to the Suburban.

Mike got up and Ann slid out of the booth after him.

"We'll pick you up out front," she said.

When they stepped outside and onto the sidewalk, Ann stopped and turned to Mike. "Mike, you need to back off. This campaign to try to talk Corey and Kyle into doing the documentary just with me isn't doing anyone any good—least of all me."

A woman carrying a Hannaford shopping bag edged past them.

"I'm just trying to—" Mike began.

"I know what you're trying to do. I know you're trying to look out for my best interests, but I don't want to do the documentary myself."

"Why not?"

"Because, like it or not, Garrick is the better senser." Mike opened his mouth and she held up a hand. "Yes, I'm improving, but I'm not as good as he is. Not only will a documentary including Garrick make a better show, but I feel like I can learn a lot from him. You need to cool it."

He crossed his arms, looking very much like a six-year-old Mike after having been told by his seven-year-old sister that she didn't need him to defend her from playground bullies.

"And you've got to lay off Garrick, too," she continued. "You baiting him is definitely not doing anyone any good."

He heaved a sigh. "Okay, fine."

"Let's get the car," she said. "I agree with Corey—we don't want to leave Kyle unsupervised for long."

12

Ann, Corey, and Mike headed south from Bar Harbor on Route 3. Shortly after leaving the town proper, they passed a complex of brick buildings.

"Hey," said Ann, turning in her seat as the buildings receded behind them. "I saw a sign for Stata Mater back there. It's huge!"

"I think they rent space in one of the buildings," said Corey. "Even Tippy Pepperidge doesn't have that much money."

They passed into Acadia National Park, the road now lined with pines and birches. The view to the right opened up to a pond that Ann's GPS identified only as The Tarn, backed by the mass of Dorr Mountain. Along the shoulder of the road, tight-suited bikers readied themselves for their rides and parents herded children toward trail heads.

They turned left to follow Otter Cliff Road, passing occasional private homes. Some were tidy, even elegant, some decrepit, some on lots so large that the residence was a mere hint beyond the trees. The road became rougher, Corey slowing for potholes and cracks in the pavement—no doubt results of the harsh Maine winter.

They reached the Park Loop Road and turned right, and now

Ann could catch peeks of the ocean through the pines. Blocks of granite protected the drivers on the two-lane, one-way road from the drop-off to the left.

Just before the road forked into two single lanes, Corey turned into a small parking area on the right. He pulled the Suburban in beside the red Tesla and they climbed out. Kyle was speaking with a distraught-looking man about Ann's age and a woman Ann recognized from the news conference announcing Leo Dorn's death as Hannah Jeskie.

Kyle, who was in a high state of excitement, introduced the young man as Jonathan Garrido.

"Who are you?" asked Jonathan, clearly rattled.

"These are the other people who are working on the documentary about Leo Dorn that I told you about," said Kyle.

"Jonathan is the one who found Shelby's car," said Hannah. She laid a hand on Jonathan's shoulder. "It's possible that Shelby is just out for a walk on the shore path."

"I already checked the path to the right of the overlook," said Jonathan. "We should check between here and Sand Beach."

Hannah glanced toward Corey's SUV. "Perhaps someone could drive that vehicle to Sand Beach and meet us there so we don't have to hike all the way back. It's about two miles, and I wouldn't want to get all the way there and be without a vehicle."

There was an awkward silence, no one wanting to miss out on the excitement of the search.

"Kyle?" Corey asked, apparently without much hope.

"No way."

"I don't want to send Ann," said Corey, not voicing what everyone except Jonathan likely knew or suspected was his reason: if Shelby Kim was dead, he wanted Ann with the search party to keep an eye out for the young woman's spirit.

Mike sighed. "I'll do it," he said, holding his hand out to Corey for the keys.

"The Park Loop Road is one-way," said Hannah, "so you're going to have to go all the way around. It'll take you about half an hour."

"Jesus," groaned Mike, "it would be faster to just back up to Sand Beach."

As Mike pulled the Suburban out of the small parking lot and onto the Park Loop Road, the rest of the group—Jonathan, Kyle, Corey, and Ann, with Hannah bringing up the rear—crossed the road. They descended the steps to the overlook, where tourists were standing on the rocks, gazing out at the vista or snapping pictures of each other with the ocean as the backdrop. The view, however, was not as expansive as it might have been. A fog bank drifted just beyond the spot where the water boiled around a rock formation a hundred yards offshore. Ann could hear the muffled clang of a buoy emanating from the fog.

The group turned left and followed the Ocean Path through a stand of pine trees. The road above them was out of sight, but Ann could hear cars passing. After a dozen yards, the trees opened up onto an outcropping of rock stretching to the right of the path.

Jonathan stopped, the others accordioning to a stop behind him. He looked across the short stretch of stone, toward where Ann could hear waves crashing on the rocks far below. Then he turned back toward the path and walked on. Kyle and Corey followed.

Ann hesitated, then stepped onto the outcropping. To the left and slightly below where she stood was a rocky plateau, on top of which stood a group of people wearing helmets and harnesses. Ropes snaked off the rock and, as she watched, one of the climbers disappeared over the edge.

"I never tire of this view," came a voice from behind Ann. She turned to see that Hannah Jeskie had also stopped. Hannah stepped up beside Ann and pointed toward a thin stripe of palest buff between the navy blue of the water beneath and the verdant green of the hills above. "Sand Beach." She pointed to the right, where the land turned east to meet the fog bank. "Great Head." She turned to Ann. "Is this your first visit to MDI?"

"I've been to MDI before, but never to Otter Cliff."

After a moment, Hannah said, "I understand that you have the same ability as Mr. Masser."

"Yes."

"You're looking for Shelby in a ... professional capacity?"

Ann wasn't sure whether to read skepticism or curiosity in Hannah's question. "Right now I'm just another pair of eyes and legs."

Hannah sighed. "I am hoping that the ability to see the dead isn't needed in this case, but I must admit that I'm concerned."

"No reason to assume the worst unless we have to," said Ann.

Hannah scanned the vista again, dropped her head, then turned and started back across the rock outcropping to the path.

Ann was about to follow when a flicker caught her eye. She turned back, thinking that it was sunlight glinting off the water a hundred feet below. Then she realized that not only was it coming from a direction in which the fog had almost reached the shore but was much closer than she had thought. Was, in fact, almost next to her.

She stepped toward it: a space that was not a flicker of light, but a flicker of darkness, a space which was missing something, hovering near the edge of the cliff.

Hannah had reached the path but turned around when she realized Ann wasn't following. "Be careful there," she called.

"I will," Ann called back.

"What is it?"

"I'm not sure. Do you see ..." Ann waved her hand toward the space that held nothing where something should be. "...that?"

"The Spindle?" Hannah asked, looking toward the offshore rocks.

Not in the mood to try to explain something she herself didn't understand, Ann didn't respond. She inched cautiously toward the space. "Shelby Kim?"

"Do you see Shelby?" asked Hannah, her voice rising. She hurried across the rock to where Ann stood.

Ann realized that Hannah thought Ann had seen Shelby Kim on the rocks below the cliff.

"No," she said hurriedly. "It's ..."

But what was it? It certainly wasn't Shelby Kim's spirit—no more than a hand-shaped depression in concrete was the hand that had made it. But she wasn't going to try to explain that to Hannah.

"It's nothing," said Ann—a statement that was not only convenient but true.

She shifted slightly, trying to put something other than the fog behind the space, in case a different backdrop would reveal different characteristics, when her eye caught something very much of this world: a cell phone lying almost hidden beneath the still-soft needles of a pine sapling.

Hannah followed her gaze. When she saw the phone, her hand went to her throat. "Oh, no."

"Do you know if it's Shelby's?" Ann asked, her voice dropping almost to a whisper.

"I'm not sure. Jonathan would know." said Hannah. "If it is her phone, I hate to think what that might mean."

Ann didn't have to ask her to explain. There were only a few reasons she could think of that would result in the phone of an evidently distraught woman lying at a cliff edge, and none of them was good.

She glanced over Hannah's shoulder and saw Jonathan, Kyle, and Corey backtracking down the path.

"Find something?" called Kyle.

"Ann found a phone," said Hannah.

Jonathan hurried across the outcropping to where Ann and Hannah stood and scooped up the phone. He tapped, bringing up the lock screen image, and his face blanched.

"Is it Shelby's?" asked Hannah quietly.

"Yes." His voice was barely a croak.

"You're sure?" asked Kyle.

"Yes," said Jonathan. "I recognize the picture." He turned the phone so they could see it.

"That's Shelby?" asked Ann uncertainly. She supposed the photo could be of the person they had seen on the news reports, shaking hands with Leo Dorn in the archive photo, but how many people used a childhood picture of themselves as their lock screen image?

"No, it's her sister, Stacy." He turned the phone back to gaze at the photo. "It was the last formal photo that was taken before a fire burned down the Kims' home. Stacy was thirteen years old."

"Did she die in the fire?" asked Ann, her voice soft.

"No. But she was badly burned."

The group was silent for a moment, then Corey said, "We need to let the authorities know that we found Shelby's phone."

"I'll call 911," said Ann, slipping her own phone out of her pocket.

"You shouldn't have picked it up," said Kyle to Jonathan. "You've messed up any evidence the police could have gotten from it."

Jonathan's eyes widened, and he shifted the phone in his hands so that he was holding it by the very edge.

"It won't make any difference at this point," Kyle said. He turned to Corey. "Can you get a videographer up here?"

Although the fog, which had now almost reached them, had

dampened the sound even of the buoy tolling offshore, it obviously didn't keep Jonathan from hearing Kyle's question.

"A videographer?" he said, his voice rising. "What the hell do you think you're doing?"

Kyle held up his hands in what he obviously thought was a conciliating gesture. "I told you we were doing a documentary, Jon. I just want to make sure we capture all the relevant material."

"*Relevant material*? We just found Shelby's phone next to the cliff and you're talking about *relevant material*?"

Hannah laid her hand on Jonathan's shoulder. "We're not going to let anyone take advantage of this situation, Jonathan."

"I have to say—" began Kyle.

"Not now," said Hannah. "Whatever you have to say, you can say it later."

Ann's call went through, and she heard, in a pronounced Maine accent, "911. What's your emergency?"

13

After Ann had provided the dispatcher with the information about their discovery of the phone, she called Mike to let him know that it was no longer necessary for him to wait for them at Sand Beach. He completed the circuit of the Park Loop Road and arrived back at Otter Cliff shortly before police and National Park Service rangers arrived in response to Ann's call to 911. The group now stood in the parking lot, officers and rangers interviewing each person in the party individually.

"How did you know Miss Kim?" asked the officer interviewing Ann. She seemed to be a few years younger than Ann, with lovely blue eyes and a glossy ponytail of auburn hair that hung half-way down her back. Her name tag read *Finney*.

"I didn't know her," said Ann, not bothering to correct Finney's reference to *Miss* rather than *Dr.* Kim, since it might call into question Ann's claim not to have known her. "I came up here to participate in a documentary about Leo Dorn."

Officer Finney looked at her expectantly.

"His life and death," Ann added.

Finney gave a lopsided but pleasant smile. "Not much to say

about his death, from what I hear. Didn't watch his footing and took a tumble."

"Yes, it sounds that way."

"And with Miss Kim out of touch, no one to say otherwise. Guess we'll never know." She scrunched up her nose. "Unless ..."

Ann steeled herself.

Finney looked down at her notes. "You're *that* Ann Kinnear?"

Not sure if this was going to count in her favor or against her, Ann cautiously replied, "Yes."

Finney glanced around to where other interviews were in progress, then leaned toward Ann. "So, you know Garrick Masser?"

"Yes," said Ann, still hoping she was racking up social credit, not debit.

The woman shook her head. "Man, what happened with you two at Lynam's Point—that was really something." She looked at her notes again. "So you're the one who found Shelby Kim's phone?"

"Yes."

"Can you show me where?"

Ann and Officer Finney walked back down the Ocean Path and Ann pointed out the location where she had found it.

"Did you touch it?" asked Finney.

"No." Since Ann had seen Jonathan hand Shelby's phone to a latex-gloved officer, she felt she didn't need to mention Jonathan's investigative faux pas to Finney.

"It's quite a bit off the main path. How did you happen to see it there?"

Ann considered her options. Finney seemed personally intrigued by the likes of Ann and Garrick, but she was an officer of the law. Ann didn't fancy having a spirit-sensing experience that she herself was still trying to understand be immortalized in the official record. "It seemed possible that Shelby might have fallen," she said. "I was seeing if I could get close enough to the edge of the cliff—safely, of course—to see down to the rocks at the bottom."

Finney jotted a note, then got out her phone and took a couple of photos of the area Ann had indicated. "Not safe to take those kinds of chances near a cliff edge."

"Yes, I realize that now," said Ann, hoping she sounded appropriately chastened. "I suppose the police will be searching the rocks? And the water? Assuming Shelby doesn't show up, of course."

Finney tucked her notepad into her pocket. "Yes, we'll send climbers down to check the rocks, and the Coast Guard will check the water." She shaded her eyes and looked south, across the now fog-free water. "In fact, I think that's the Coasties now."

Ann followed Finney's gaze and saw a white boat with an angled red stripe across its hull approaching.

When they returned to the parking area, Finney said, "That's all for now, Miss Kinnear. We'll be in touch if we have any more questions." She crossed the parking lot to where one of her colleagues was standing next to an annoyed-looking Kyle.

Mike, whose interview was evidently also complete, joined Ann.

"The police want Hannah and Jonathan to go back to the police station for a chat. Kyle and Corey, too," he said, "but they said we could go."

"I understand why they'd want to talk with Jonathan and Hannah, since they know Shelby, but why Corey and Kyle?"

"Because Kyle was being a pain in the ass, and I think they figured they didn't want to let him off the hook too easily. I think Corey got dinged by association. Plus," Mike added, "I dropped Masser's name and that seemed to generate some goodwill for me."

"Yeah, I noticed that I won points by knowing Garrick, too," said Ann, "but you're such a hypocrite to throw around Garrick's name when it benefits you."

Mike grinned. "It's not his clout that I object to. It's him personally."

Since Corey's summons to the police station left Ann and Mike carless, Officer Finney drove them back to Somesville to pick up the Hyundai from the Selectmen's Building, not so subtly pumping Ann for information about Garrick on the way. After retrieving the car, Ann and Mike stopped at the Southwest Harbor Food Mart and picked up supplies.

It was six o'clock by the time they arrived back at Manset. Ann was starving. With their boxed-up brunches no doubt congealing in the back of Corey's Suburban, she hadn't yet had anything to eat. Mike heated up a can of New England clam chowder, toasted some bread, and steamed two ears of corn on the cob. They ate at the kitchen island, hashing through various theories, although they found that the discovery of Shelby's car and phone had only slightly changed their thinking since their discussion with Corey that morning.

Still hungry when she had finished her dinner, Ann started in on the Oreos. After cleaning up the dishes, she popped her head into the living room, where Mike was listening to Fleetwood Mac.

"I'm going to run back up to Somesville and let Garrick know what happened at Otter Cliff," she said.

"Why bother?" asked Mike. "He made it clear that he wants nothing to do with the documentary."

"It's different now. I'm betting Shelby Kim is dead. The phone lying there by the cliff edge like that—it seems like someone might lay their phone aside if they jumped."

"Or drop it if someone pushed them."

"Or if they slipped and fell. But the point is that this has gotten even bigger than the project since we talked with Garrick this morning."

Mike shrugged and downed a slug of wine. "I'm guessing you don't want company."

"I'm guessing you'd rather stay here anyway."

"Can't say I'd object." He took the keys to the Hyundai out of his pocket and handed them to her, then pulled out his phone. "I'll give Scott a call. Anything for me to report about a budding romance?"

"No, Mike. Having us all worried about some young woman being dead really isn't conducive to romance."

"You treating Corey like he's your brother really isn't conducive to romance."

"He's my back-up brother," she called from the back door, "just in case you prove to be too annoying."

14

Ann parked in Garrick's driveway, climbed the steps to the porch, and tapped the door with the heavy brass knocker. In a minute the door opened, Garrick silhouetted against the dim light of the entrance hall.

"Miss Kinnear," he said.

"Hi, Garrick. Can I come in?"

He stepped aside, then closed the door behind her. "How may I help you?"

"There have been some interesting developments."

"With the documentary?"

"Not necessarily."

He glowered at her for a moment, then turned and stalked into his office. Ann followed.

Garrick sank into his desk chair and waved her into one of the guest chairs facing it. She glanced around the office as she took off her jacket and hung it over the back of the chair. A fire crackled cozily in the fireplace and a steaming mug of what she assumed was hot water sat on Garrick's desk next to a closed book, from which a tasseled bookmark extended. She stepped toward the desk and read the title.

"*Historic Ghosts and Ghost Hunters* by H. Addington Bruce. What's it about?"

"An early twentieth century examination of how the work of psychopathologists, investigators of abnormal mental life, and psychical researchers, explorers of the supernormal in human experience, can be plumbed to illuminate the nature of human personality."

After a moment, Ann asked, "How is it?"

"Sententious."

"Good to know. I'll give it a miss." She dropped into the chair and stifled a yawn. She hadn't realized how tired she was.

Garrick raised his eyebrows expectantly.

She updated him on the events of the day—Jonathan Garrido's discovery of Shelby Kim's car at Otter Cliff, the subsequent discovery of Shelby's phone near the cliff edge, the police continuing their interviews of Corey, Kyle, Hannah, and Jonathan at the station.

When she was done, she paused, hoping that he would come to the conclusion himself that he owed it not to the documentary team but to Leo Dorn and Shelby Kim to re-engage in the efforts to contact them. Instead, he was looking at her speculatively.

"Explain again how you came to find Dr. Kim's mobile phone," he said.

"I thought I saw something near the cliff edge. I thought at first it might have been Shelby's spirit and I was trying to get a better angle on it, trying to tell what it was, when I saw the phone."

"And what was it that had initially caught your attention?"

"I don't know," she said slowly. "At first I thought it was an effect that was similar to how it used to be for me when a spirit was present. Just a flicker, a bit of light where there shouldn't be light or a movement where there shouldn't be movement. But this wasn't light or movement, it was … the absence of light or movement."

"A spirit negative."

"Like a photograph? I suppose …"

"Not like a photograph. Like a mold."

"Yes," she said, surprised. "Exactly."

"It is what is left behind when a person's spirit departs their body."

Ann sat forward. "So someone killed Shelby Kim at the cliff top?"

"It's possible. Or she killed herself."

"But if she jumped, then she would have been alive until she hit the rocks. Or the water." Ann suppressed a shiver. "In which case, I can imagine her spirit might have migrated from the rocks to the top of the cliff. But would the same be true of a spirit negative?"

Garrick steepled his fingers in front of his chest. "If a person knows he or she is going to die, the spirit may leave the body before the physical life force departs. The spirit may be else-where, but its negative is left behind. Imagine if you had an air-filled balloon underwater and pricked it with a pin. For a frac-tion of a second, the water would retain the shape of the balloon before it rushed in to fill that void. That is the manifestation of a spirit negative. It's possible that is what you saw."

"And in your analogy, the balloon is her spirit?"

"Well, to be precise, the air in the balloon is her spirit. If one were to extend the metaphor, the balloon itself might be consid-ered the body that contained that spirit."

"So her spirit could still be at Otter Cliff?"

"It could be."

"Her spirit left because she knew she was going to die …"

"Yes. Either by her own hand, or by the act of another person."

"What do you think happened?"

"I have no idea. It's quite possible that there is a non-criminal explanation for the circumstances, although I believe the Stata Mater staff would be well advised to stay away from scenic overlooks for the time being."

Ann sat forward. "That's just it. The stakes are much higher than just whether Corey and Kyle can get the documentary made. People's lives might be at risk, and Leo Dorn and Shelby Kim might have information that could prevent that."

"So you should attempt to contact them."

She sat back. "Shelby Kim, yes. I can try to contact her. But I think you'll have better luck with Leo Dorn. Among other considerations, you're more likely to get permission from Tippy Pepperidge to get access to Brookview than Corey or Kyle or I would."

At the mention of Kyle's name, Garrick's eyebrows drew together. "What an odious man."

"I agree, but Corey can't help that he's been saddled with a jerk, and Corey will be in just as much trouble as Kyle will if the documentary gets derailed."

"You are more concerned about Mr. Duff than about Mr. Lathey?"

"Aren't you?"

He raised an eyebrow. "I'm not particularly concerned with either one of them." He heaved a sigh. "Very well. I agree that the stakes are high, and that my personal reservations must be set aside for the greater good. You may notify Mr. Duff that I agree to rejoin the project."

Ann smiled. "That's great news. But it looks like you can notify Corey yourself, since I see a Mac power cord plugged into the wall behind your desk. Since it looks like you're not the Luddite you claim to be, maybe you can drop Corey an email."

Garrick glared at her.

She raised her hand. "Okay, okay, I'll let him know."

15

Four Weeks Earlier

From across the Stata Mater conference room table, Shelby Kim looked from Leo Dorn to Hannah Jeskie and back, her hands twisting in her lap in eager anticipation. They were slowly turning the pages of the reports she had assembled, stopping to examine a graph here, a chemical analysis there.

"A form of clean agent," said Leo. He glanced at Hannah. "Not a breakthrough in itself."

"No," said Hannah slowly, "but look at the composition—it would be so much easier and less expensive to manufacture than what's available today, and that means affordable to more organizations."

"And much easier to deploy," said Shelby. "A simple nozzle attachment and it could be injected into water from a pumper truck or hydrant, doubling or even tripling the effectiveness in terms of fire suppression. And it's adaptable. Tweak it a bit and it could take on the properties of a lubricant. That might lend itself to other applications, where the materials that are currently available build up over time and degrade equipment performance."

"A better suppressant that retains all the benefits of clean agents," said Leo. "Noncorrosive, nonconductive, environmentally friendly."

"No toxins. No residue left behind at all," said Shelby.

"Nothing left behind," echoed Hannah.

Shelby nodded vigorously. "Leave no trace."

Leo smiled. "Like on the hiking trails." He looked again to Hannah. "The data seem to bear that out. Do you concur?"

Hannah carefully flipped the pages back into place. She looked up at Shelby, her face impassive. "I do." A smile broke over her face. "This is extraordinary, Shelby. Really quite extraordinary. Well done."

Shelby had been sure of the results, but to hear Leo and Hannah confirm them—she could barely stay in her seat for the excitement.

Leo stood and, evidently feeling the same excitement as Shelby, strode to the window. "Imagine what this will mean for firefighting—and, more importantly, for the people who might otherwise become victims of fires." He shook his head. "Wait until Tippy finds out." He turned and smiled at Shelby. "And you must be the one to tell her."

16

Ann stepped out onto the porch of the Manset house, her morning coffee in an insulated mug she had found on the kitchen shelves. She judged the temperature to be in the low fifties with high, wispy clouds periodically dimming the weak sunshine. On the theory that she might be returning to Otter Cliff to continue the search for Shelby Kim, she had put on jeans, a long-sleeved cotton T-shirt under a light wool sweater, and her hiking boots. If she brought her raincoat, she should be ready for whatever conditions were likely to develop.

She stepped back into the kitchen and topped off her coffee. She pulled on her raincoat, then popped her head into the living room, where Mike was noodling away on the baby grand.

"I'm heading over to the office."

"The warehouse, you mean."

"Don't be grumpy."

"I can't believe you're banning me from the office."

"I thought it was just a warehouse."

"You say potato," he said, plinking out a few notes of the song.

"It's going to be tricky enough keeping things going smoothly—or at least as smoothly as possible—between Garrick and Kyle," she said. "I don't need you there irritating Garrick as well. You should take a hike. An actual hike," she amended quickly.

Mike switched to *The Ants Go Marching*.

Ann shook her head, grabbed the thermal mug, and headed out the door.

She reached the production office, where Kyle's Tesla once again occupied the one parking space at the side of the building, just as Garrick coasted by in his black Cadillac Fleetwood and then crept down the street to park by the side of the road. No one would ever accuse Garrick Masser of having a heavy foot on the accelerator. She waited at the door as he unfolded himself from the driver's seat and made his way toward her.

"Hey, Garrick," she said.

"Miss Kinnear," he said with a nod, and preceded her into the building.

Jessy Barnwell floated near the rafters, although when Garrick entered, she descended and hovered near his shoulder.

He gave the girl a brief nod, then folded his arms and stood stoically near the door, as if ready to beat a hasty retreat.

Corey and Kyle stood near one of the card tables, which held bagels and spreads, a plastic carton of orange juice, a thermos, and small stacks of disposable cups, utensils, plates, and napkins.

"Hey, Corey. Hey, Kyle," said Ann, crossing to the table. "Thanks to whoever provided the breakfast spread."

"That would be me," said Corey.

"There's a lot of carbs on that table," said Kyle. "I think I'll grab some sashimi later."

"Good luck with that," said Corey, taking a seat at the other card table with his coffee and bagel.

Ann, who had drunk some of her coffee on the walk over, unscrewed the lid of the thermos.

"That's hot water," called Corey from the other table.

Ann scanned the table. "I don't see tea bags."

"It's not for tea—it's for Garrick." He turned to Garrick. "Hot water, Garrick?"

"No. Thank you."

Ann recapped the thermos, grabbed a plain bagel, spread it with cream cheese, poured herself a cup of juice, and took a seat next to Corey.

Kyle took the third chair, and Ann was relieved when Garrick lowered himself somewhat reluctantly onto the fourth.

"Garrick," said Corey, "I just want to say how much I appreciate you putting aside your reservations to return to the project."

"I can't disagree that pursuing communication with Dr. Dorn and Dr. Kim may yield practical benefits," said Garrick.

Corey nodded. "I propose that you try to contact Leo Dorn at Brookview and, Ann, that you try to contact Shelby Kim at Otter Cliff."

"Maybe Dorn would be more likely to make an appearance if we send in an attractive woman," said Kyle, directing a smile toward Ann.

"This isn't a dating game," said Corey with some irritation. "I'm sure it won't be easy to convince Tippy Pepperidge to let us shoot at Brookview, and I'm assuming she'll be more likely to agree to it if Garrick is our point person for that assignment. As for Shelby Kim—if she is in fact dead—her spirit may be more likely to communicate with someone who isn't quite as forbidding-looking as Garrick."

Garrick looked vaguely pleased.

"I suppose it's your call," Kyle said to Corey, "but if one of them can't make contact, we shouldn't just assume it's because there's no ghost there to be contacted. We need to factor in that the ghost might just be put off by that individual. Maybe Dorn really would rather communicate with a good-looking woman. Maybe Kim has a thing for spooky-looking guys."

Garrick looked miffed.

Kyle turned to Ann. "Am I right?"

"Based on my experience, a spirit's preferences are usually the same as when they were alive. If Shelby preferred a certain look, or a certain personality, she probably still would."

"If either Garrick or Ann is unable to make contact," said Corey, "then the other will have an opportunity to try."

"It still sounds like a competition," said Ann.

"That's not the intent," said Corey.

"I don't know what the problem is with a little competition," said Kyle. "That's really going to draw in the viewers." He grinned. "We'll have hashtag *TeamAnn* and hashtag *TeamGarrick*."

Before Garrick could comment—although the V'd angle of his eyebrows was comment enough—Corey jumped in. "No teams, no hashtags. We're in this together, and my goal is *not* to turn Ann and Garrick into the sensing community's social media influencers." He turned to Garrick. "How would you like to go about approaching Tippy Pepperidge about getting access to the property? The sooner we can pin that down, the better."

Shifting his glare from Kyle to Corey, Garrick said, "I will go to Brookview and speak with her as soon as this meeting is adjourned."

"That's great," said Corey.

He put his coffee cup and plate on the floor next to his chair and gestured for Ann to do the same. Picking up a long tube of paper that had been leaning against the table, he slid off the rubber band that encircled it and unrolled it on the table. He held down two edges and Ann held down the other two.

"Keeping a happy thought that Ms. Pepperidge will give us permission to shoot at Brookview," he said, "I got this topographic map of the area where Leo Dorn fell. That's where we'll want to set up for the shoot." He laid his finger on the map. "Here's the drive to the house." He moved his finger across the map to where the elevation lines merged, indicating steep—even vertical—terrain. "And as far as I can tell, this is where he fell."

"Ah. Interesting," said Garrick.

"Are you familiar with the property?" asked Corey.

"Not with that portion of it. The Brookview property is quite extensive. The area I visited to attempt contact with Mr. Judd was some distance away, near a road accessing the back of the property."

"How big is the property?" asked Kyle.

"Approximately one thousand acres," said Garrick.

Kyle let out a whistle. "You've got to have some bucks to afford a spread that big on this island."

Garrick turned to Corey. "There appears to be some distance, and a significant increase in elevation, between the house and the location of Dr. Dorn's death."

"That a problem, Masser?" asked Kyle.

Garrick ignored him. "Might it not pose a challenge to transport the video equipment to that location?"

"I've schlepped that stuff further and into worse terrain than that," said Corey. "We'll get it done."

"It may perhaps be preferable to have Miss Kinnear be the one to try to contact Dr. Dorn—" An uncharacteristic look of panic was starting to creep across Garrick's face.

"Don't be a prima donna, Masser," said Kyle. "We can't very well bring Dorn to you. A little walk in the woods might cheer you up."

But Ann realized why Garrick was hedging: a weak heart,

which had been further weakened by the events that had taken place during her last visit to Mount Desert Island. The distance from the drive to the location where Leo had fallen and those close-packed elevation lines must have looked alarming to Garrick.

"I'm sure you can get the equipment there," she said to Corey, "but why bother if you don't have to?" She scanned the map and pointed to a location closer to the house, accessible via a gentler grade. "Maybe next to this stream. That would make a nice location, wouldn't it? Why don't I go out there and see if Leo's around? If he is, I can ask him if he can move away from the location where he died, closer to the drive."

"He might be able to move around?" asked Kyle, surprised.

"Sometimes," said Ann. "Plus, if I'm the one to contact Leo to make the arrangements, it means that his first interaction with Garrick won't happen until we have the equipment and crew there. You'd want to catch the first encounter between the interviewer and interviewee on video, right, Corey?" She snuck a look at Garrick.

Looking relieved, he said, "Quite."

"Good thought about having the first contact happen on camera," said Corey. "Plus, we don't want to be painted with the same brush as the guy from *Behind the Scenes with Geary* and seem to be using the location of Dorn's death in an insensitive way. Let's go with Ann's proposal." He rolled up the map. "Garrick, why don't you and Ann go to Brookview and see if you can talk to Tippy. If Tippy gives the okay, Ann could hike to the site of Leo's death and see if she can make contact."

Garrick stood and started for the door. Ann stuffed the last piece of bagel into her mouth, picked up her coffee mug, and trotted after him. Kyle followed.

"What are you doing?" asked Ann around the bagel.

"I'm coming along."

She swallowed. "No you're not."

He grinned at her. "And you're going to stop me how?"

"If you come along, I'm going to pretend I don't see Leo even if he's there."

His grin faded. "That's not playing fair."

"Hey, if it's TeamAnn and TeamKyle, I'd guess that the spectators like it when every player makes the best use of their advantage."

Garrick opened the door, then turned back to Kyle. "It's primo uomo."

"What?"

"If it's a man, it's not prima donna, it's primo uomo."

Ann followed Garrick out of the warehouse and pulled the door closed on Corey's laugh.

17

S ince Garrick hated to drive and seized any opportunity to be driven, Ann took the wheel of the Fleetwood for the trip to Brookview.

They drove up and over the top of Somes Sound and down the eastern side. They passed the venerable Asticou Inn and skirted the boat-dotted water of Northeast Harbor.

About a mile further on, Garrick said, "Just up here."

Ann pulled the big car carefully off the road. The drive Garrick had directed her to was blocked by the decorative metal gates she had seen on the news reports, as well as by a stocky man in chinos, black collared shirt, and black windbreaker. He raised his hand to signal them to stop, then stepped to the driver's window as Ann pulled up next to him. She buzzed down the window.

"Ms. Pepperidge isn't taking any visitors nor giving any interviews," he said, in a tone that suggested he had repeated the same message a dozen times that day already.

Garrick leaned over from the passenger seat. "Good afternoon, Mr. Durgin."

Durgin leaned forward and peered into the car. "Why, hello,

Mr. Masser. Sorry, didn't see it was you. Trying to keep the snoops away." He shook his head. "Wish I had been able to keep away that guy who fell off Aldrich Hill, but he snuck in the back of the property. Sounds like he won't be doing much sneaking anytime soon." His voice was sad but resigned. "Haven't seen you here at Brookview for a while."

"We should consider it fortunate that Ms. Pepperidge has not had need of my services for so long."

"That's for sure. She know you're coming?"

"Not as of yet, but if you could ask her if she might see me and my ..." There was a slight hesitation, and Ann waited anxiously to find out how he would complete the sentence. "... colleague, Ann Kinnear, we would be grateful."

Colleague. Ann turned her face toward the window so Garrick wouldn't see her smile.

"Sure," said Durgin. "I'll check. Hold on one minute."

He stepped away from the car and spoke quietly into a cell phone. There was a wait of a few minutes, during which time he waved away another car, then he spoke into the phone again, nodded, and approached the Fleetwood.

"She gave the okay. Megan will meet you at the front door. Nice to meet you, Miss Kinnear. Nice seeing you, Mr. Masser. Wish it were under happier circumstances."

Durgin tapped his phone and the metal gate swung open. Ann rolled up the drive.

As they wound through the woods, Ann expected the view to open out to a vista that would display the Pepperidge manse to best advantage, but when the drive widened to a carefully groomed gravel parking area, it took her a moment to realize that they had reached the house. It was a relatively modestly sized and unadorned building, so closely surrounded by trees and plantings that it was hard to get a sense of its architecture.

A young woman wearing black skinny jeans and a starched

white blouse was waiting by the porch stairs. She directed them into a parking space behind a giant rhododendron.

"Hello, Mr. Masser, Miss Kinnear," she said as they got out of the Fleetwood. "I'm Megan. If you'll follow me, please."

She led them inside and down a hallway to a sitting room. Rough beams supported a high, coffered ceiling, another beam forming the mantel over the laid but unlit fire. Directly in front of the fireplace was a tattered plaid blanket covered with dog fur. To one side of the blanket was a couch covered in cracked leather; on the other, two chairs upholstered in an outdated blue and yellow fabric. The wooden floors were softened by faded Persian rugs. Glass doors gave a view across a small but lush lawn leading to an irregularly shaped pool lined in granite.

"Please make yourself comfortable. Ms. Pepperidge will be with you shortly." Megan said, then disappeared down the hallway.

Ann wandered over to the glass doors. "I'm not usually a big fan of residential swimming pools," she said, "but that one is nice—it fits in with the surroundings." She turned back to see Garrick examining the painting hanging over the fireplace mantel, a riot of purples, yellows, oranges, and reds depicting a pathway between a grove of trees and a walled garden.

"Georges Braque," he said.

"Colorful," said Ann.

He raised an eyebrow at her. "Indeed."

A few minutes later, they heard footsteps—human and canine—and Tippy Pepperidge entered the room, followed by Megan and three beagles. The imposing personality Ann had sensed from the archive photo used in the news coverage of Leo Dorn's death was borne out by the woman's presence in person: eyes that assessed as well as observed, a thin-lipped mouth that was hard to imagine parted in laughter, a pointed chin thrust forward like the prow of a ship cutting through rough seas.

"Ms. Pepperidge," said Garrick.

"Garrick," she replied, extending her hand to shake his. "It's been a long time."

"May I introduce my colleague, Ann Kinnear."

Tippy extended her hand. "How do you do."

Ann shook Tippy's hand. "Pleased to meet you."

Tippy gestured them toward the seats near the fireplace.

Ann and Garrick took the upholstered chairs and Tippy Pepperidge sat on the couch. The beagles arranged themselves on the plaid blanket.

"Coffee or tea?" she asked. She gave Garrick a slight smile. "Hot water?"

"No, thank you," said Garrick.

"I'm fine, thanks," said Ann.

"Thank you, Megan," said Tippy, and the young woman nodded and disappeared down the hallway.

Tippy turned to Garrick. "What can I do for you, Garrick?"

"I first wish to express my condolences on the death of Dr. Dorn."

She dipped her head almost imperceptibly. "Thank you."

"Might I save you the discourtesy of meaningless pleasantries?"

"Of course."

"I have been asked to participate in a documentary exploring my spirit-sensing ability, and that of Miss Kinnear. The people responsible for the documentary require it to be set on Mount Desert Island. They have considered and, for their own reasons, discarded several possible topics."

"And they want you to try to communicate with Leo," Tippy interjected.

"Yes. They believe that any communication I might have with Dr. Dorn would not only be of interest to potential viewers of the documentary but might also shed light on the circumstances of his death, especially in view of Dr. Kim's disappearance."

"They wonder if Shelby had anything to do with it."

"Perhaps. The timing of her disappearance, so soon after Dr. Dorn's death, is noteworthy."

"It is certainly worrisome. I considered asking Max Durgin to look into it, although I don't want to seem to be intruding on the police investigation. One must tread carefully in such circumstances."

"'The better part of valor is discretion.'"

Tippy gave a slight smile. "Just so." She took in a deep breath. "Shelby Kim is a talented young woman who is deeply committed to her work. I consider her one of Stata Mater's most promising hires." Her gaze shifted to Ann for a moment, and then back to Garrick. "And not someone I would suspect of pushing my husband off a trail to his death."

"The mechanics of it alone would seem to argue against it," said Garrick, "Dr. Kim being a woman of slight stature and Dr. Dorn much taller and heavier."

"More importantly," said Tippy, "Shelby Kim is no murderer."

"Are you aware that Miss Kinnear found Dr. Kim's phone near the edge of Otter Cliff?"

Tippy looked down at her hands, then back up at Garrick. "Yes. The police let me know."

"The fact that Dr. Kim has disappeared, and the circumstances of her disappearance, may suggest that something other than mere carelessness on a hiking trail was responsible for Dr. Dorn's death and Dr. Kim's disappearance."

Tippy rose from the couch and went to the glass doors. She reached a long-fingered hand to her forehead and squeezed her temples. "The accident at the ledge involving that young man— Brian Geary—is also a consideration. The lawyers have advised me to make no public comments about that incident and to let the authorities sort it out. We mustn't drag that topic into the mix."

"I see no reason we should need to," replied Garrick.

Tippy raised her eyes again to look out across the landscaped lawn. She was silent for a few moments, then she spoke.

"I very much admire Shelby Kim. In her young life, she has faced down tragedy—tragedy that put her on the path that brought her to Stata Mater."

"The fire that injured her sister?" asked Ann.

Tippy turned from the window. "You know about that?"

"Jonathan Garrido mentioned it when we found Shelby's phone at Otter Cliff."

"Ah, yes. Jonathan. I believe they were dating." Tippy returned to the couch and sat. "Shelby's inventions have been extraordinary for one so young, and we were just on the brink of announcing the latest when Leo died. An invention that will revolutionize firefighting, and that will save countless people from unnecessary suffering and death. An invention that might have saved Shelby's sister had it been available at that time. An invention that might have saved Frank." She glanced toward Ann. "My first husband." She returned her gaze to Garrick. "You believe some good could come of speaking with Leo?"

"He might be able to provide some information that would help us find out what happened to Dr. Kim."

"And what happened to him as well."

"Perhaps."

Tippy was silent and Ann became aware of the sounds of a ticking clock filtering in from the hallway and the gentle snoring of the dogs.

Finally, Tippy nodded. "Very well. You may try to contact Leo to get information that might shed light on what happened to

Shelby. And, of course, what happened to him if it wasn't an accident." She smiled humorlessly. "I assume Leo dead will be as closemouthed about his activities as Leo alive, but he would certainly want us to know if Shelby Kim pushed him off Aldrich Hill." She glanced at Ann and then back to Garrick. "But I'm giving this permission on the condition that you not share any information you might learn from Leo, except what might help Shelby, or might bring her to justice in the unlikely event that she was in fact responsible for Leo's death and is alive and on the run."

"It seems to me to be a reasonable condition," said Garrick.

"I'm not sure Corey would agree," said Ann.

"We've already seen evidence of a lack of discretion on the part of the documentary producers," said Tippy. "I'm not happy that a presumptive announcement was made about the project's topic. I don't want information unrelated to Leo's death or to Shelby Kim's disappearance or death to become fodder for the media. I trust you, Garrick, but I don't trust the people running this project." Ann got the impression that Tippy was working hard not to glance at her again. "I would like Hannah Jeskie to be present for any activities related to the project that take place here at Brookview."

"To the extent it is in my power to agree to terms, I do. As Miss Kinnear points out, the documentary producers obviously will also need to confirm their compliance."

"All these conditions seem unfair to Corey Duff, who as far as I know is the one responsible for the actual content of the documentary," said Ann, who was beginning to get annoyed at Tippy apparently lumping Corey, not to mention Ann herself, in with the likes of Kyle Lathey. "He isn't the one who leaked the information."

"Fair or not," said Tippy briskly, "those are the terms. And if the producers agree to the terms and then choose not to abide by them, I have the resources to make the lives of those associated with the documentary very difficult."

"I feel quite confident," said Garrick, "that if we can obtain information that will shed light on the death of your husband or on Dr. Kim's situation, that should be sufficient fodder for Mr. Duff's project."

Tippy turned her gaze to Ann. "Miss Kinnear?"

"If the conditions are acceptable to Garrick and to the producers, then I agree to abide by them as well."

"Very good," said Tippy.

"Since the producers are anxious to start the project," said Garrick, "might Miss Kinnear go out to the trail where Dr. Dorn and Dr. Kim were hiking to ascertain if it will be possible to speak with him?"

"Yes, I can take her there." Tippy stood. "Will you be accompanying us, Garrick?"

"I will remain here if that's acceptable."

"Certainly. Can I get you anything while you wait?"

"Just water. Thank you."

Tippy nodded, then, leaving Garrick to return to his examination of the Braque painting, preceded Ann to the entrance hall. She slipped off a pair of felt clogs and pulled a pair of hiking boots out from the jumble under the benches. As she was lacing them on, Megan appeared.

"Megan, can you take Mr. Masser some hot water?" Tippy asked.

"Did something spill?" asked Megan.

Tippy stood. "It's not for cleaning up. That's what he likes to drink." She looked toward Ann. "At least that's what he liked to drink the last time I saw him."

"That's still what he likes to drink," said Ann.

Tippy nodded to Megan, who shrugged and disappeared down the hall toward the back of the house.

Ann followed Tippy outside, then across the gravel drive. "They took the Aldrich trail," said Tippy. "This way."

The clouds had continued to build, creating a patchwork of light and dark gray lowering over the trees, and the temperature had dipped a few degrees while she and Garrick were in the house. Ann zipped up her jacket and hurried after Tippy.

They followed a well-maintained dirt path through the woods, and after a few minutes Ann began to understand how it had been possible for Brian Geary not to have been found for some time after his fall. Brookview was not just a large residential property; it was a small nature preserve.

She guessed that Tippy Pepperidge hiked the property as often as her husband had. Ann considered herself to be in fairly good shape, and she was two decades younger than Tippy Pepperidge, but she had to work to keep up with the older woman.

They came to the stream that Ann has proposed as a possible site for Garrick's interview with Leo. It was crossed by a picturesque wooden bridge. Tippy stepped onto the bridge and nodded upstream.

"It's just up there," she said. "I'd prefer not to accompany you all the way to the rocks, if you don't mind."

"Of course." Ann hesitated. "Is there anything you'd like me to ask Leo if I contact him?"

"Not that I can think of but thank you for asking." Tippy looked skyward. "I don't know how far up the path you intend to go, but if it rains, don't try crossing the ledge—it's treacherous when it's wet. It's where the young man fell. If you get further than the ledge and the rain starts, please call Garrick and I'll have someone come out and get you."

"I don't know Garrick's cell phone number," said Ann. "I'm not even sure he has a cell phone."

Tippy nodded. "Good point. You can call Megan."

Ann entered the number Tippy gave her into her phone, then Tippy turned back toward the house and strode away.

Ann watched her disappear among the pines and wondered what had made Tippy Pepperidge so committed to maintaining contact with her first husband's spirit when she seemed so committed to avoiding an encounter with her second.

nn continued up the rapidly steepening path. In a few minutes, she reached the spot where Leo Dorn must have met his death: a tilted series of granite steps beneath a curving rock face. She scanned the cliff above the rocks and noticed a bit of yellow crime scene tape fluttering from a tree that leaned vertiginously over the drop.

She was wondering whether or not she would need to climb the rock steps when she caught sight of a flicker toward their top. After a moment, the flicker consolidated and resolved itself into a man she recognized from the news reports.

"Leo Dorn?" she called up to him.

He stopped and looked down at her, the surprise on his face clear even at this distance. "You can see me?" His voice was as forceful as it must have been in life.

"Yes. My name's Ann Kinnear. I'm a colleague of Garrick Masser."

"Ah, yes. Garrick Masser." He began to descend the canted rocks toward her, his form solidifying further as he approached. "My wife was a client of his, although it was before I met her."

He stopped a dozen feet away. "And will Mr. Masser be visiting Brookview as well?"

"That's what I've come to talk with you about," she said. "There's a filmmaker named Corey Duff who wants to do a documentary about you, and they'd like to video your conversation with Garrick."

Leo gave a rueful smile. "I'm not going to flatter myself that the documentary was planned before my death. I may live at Brookview—have lived at Brookview—but I'm no Pepperidge."

"Corey has been looking for a subject that would lend itself to an exploration of spirit sensing—one based on Mount Desert Island—and then ..."

"Then I fell and became the perfect subject."

"Well ... yes."

"No chance of letting the dead rest in peace?"

"Of course, it's entirely up to you, but there are some extenuating circumstances that would make it especially helpful for Garrick to speak with you as soon as possible."

Leo gave a short laugh. "I've never been one to shy away from free publicity, but I have to say that is an offer that I never anticipated. What would we talk about?"

"For one thing, Garrick would ask you about your fall."

Leo considered for a moment, then sat down on one of the rocks. Ann climbed onto the stepped granite and found a spot where she could sit facing him.

"I actually don't remember much about the fall," he said. "What theories are the authorities discussing?"

"I'd rather not say. Corey wants you to have the conversation with Garrick, and it should be fresh when you tell him—not something you've already told someone else."

"Why aren't Corey Duff and Garrick Masser here now?"

"It seemed sensible to make sure that we could contact you first."

"And Tippy is on board with this?"

"As long as we comply with certain conditions."

"And what are those conditions?"

"That the conversation is focused on certain topics, and that we not share information beyond certain agreed-upon parameters. I'd rather not say more than that."

"And if you can communicate with me, is it a guarantee that Masser will be able to as well?"

"Oh, yes."

"He couldn't communicate with Frank Judd—Tippy's first husband."

"I feel certain that that was because Mr. Judd wasn't there to be communicated with."

Leo shifted his gaze in the direction of the house. "I have to admit that I always assumed Masser was a charlatan. I was surprised when I learned that Tippy had hired him. It didn't seem like the kind of thing that my usually practical wife would go in for." He paused. "But I obviously need to rethink my position in view of this conversation." He leaned back against the rock behind him. "However, any conversation I had with Garrick Masser would be quite a short one if all he wants to ask me about is my fall and the only answer I can give is that I don't remember much about it."

"There are some other things he'd like to talk with you about as well."

Leo raised an eyebrow. "Things that I gather you can't tell me about so that it's *fresh* when Masser asks me."

"That's the idea."

He crossed his arms. "I'm sorry, I never gave interviews during my life unless I knew what questions were going to be asked of me, and I can't see a reason to change that policy now that I'm dead."

"Why not? Your circumstances are quite different now. What

could happen as a result of a conversation with Garrick that would impact you in any meaningful way?"

"Because no man is an island, even in death. Exercising a little care in the information I shared with strangers protected the people and the institutions I cared about when I was alive. I don't see why that should change now that I'm dead."

"You still care about them?"

"Of course. Why wouldn't I?"

"It's not always the way."

He looked at her expectantly, but she realized that her conversation with Leo Dorn had already gone on longer than Corey would have preferred. "Does this mean you're refusing the interview?"

"Yes, unless I have more background information."

Ann's eyes drifted back to the yellow tape fluttering from the tree above them. Leo's request was a reasonable one—she had to give him a little more incentive to speak with Garrick. "Shelby Kim has disappeared."

He uncrossed his arms and sat forward. "She has?"

"You might be able to share information that would help us find out what's happened to her."

"I don't have any information." He gave a harsh laugh. "I've been dead."

"You might have a piece of information that you don't even realize is related to her disappearance that could help us find out what happened to her."

He rubbed his chin. "If you won't tell me what people are saying about my death, I'm assuming you won't tell me what they are saying about Shelby's disappearance."

"I'd rather not."

His gaze held hers as he ticked through some internal calculation. After a half minute, he shook his head. "No. Regardless of what people are saying about her disappearance, I can't think of any information I have that might help. You'll be able to get better information from people who are still around: Hannah Jeskie or Jonathan Garrido at Stata Mater Technology. My wife. Even our assistant, Megan. Perhaps Shelby's family."

Ann nodded. "I'm sure the authorities are following up with those people, but I'll check to make sure." After a pause, she continued. "So, the interview ..."

"You say Tippy gave the okay for Masser to talk to me as long as he stuck to some agreed-upon topics, and he and the other people involved in the project didn't share any information beyond those topics. Once he starts asking questions, what's to keep him from going off-script?"

"Your wife asked that Hannah Jeskie be present for the shoot to make sure that we adhere to the conditions."

"Ah, good. Hannah will be an excellent person in that role—she'll take care of things." He considered for a moment. "Very well. I agree to the interview."

"Thank you."

"And the shoot will take place here at the rocks? It seems a bit morbid."

Ann was grateful that Leo had given her an alternative to *Garrick can't make it this far* to explain her next request.

"Yes, I agree it would be morbid. Plus, it would be tough to get the equipment all the way out here. Do you know if you can move away from this spot?"

"It seems I can move some distance from the rocks. I've walked to the back of the property, but I can't go as far as the drive or the house."

"How about the bridge over the stream that's between here and the house?"

"Yes, that's about as far as I can go in that direction."

It struck Ann as odd that Leo Dorn could range around the Pepperidge property as far as he said he could, but not reach the house. She would have guessed that his connection to the residence would be stronger than his connection to the grounds. Despite his evident enjoyment of hiking, he seemed like a man more in tune with the comforts of an elegant home. However, this, too, could be a topic for Garrick's conversation with Leo, assuming Hannah Jeskie believed it fit within the parameters set out by Tippy.

"I'll tell the documentary crew that that's where we'll meet up," she said.

"When will you be back?"

"They're in quite a hurry, but I doubt they would be able to pull everything together today. How about tomorrow morning?"

"Certainly." He gave a wry smile. "It's not like I have anywhere else to be."

"I appreciate it, Dr. Dorn."

They both stood up.

"I'll keep thinking about anything I might be able to offer to help out with the search for Shelby," he said.

"That would be great. I'll see you tomorrow, then."

She was about to start back down the path, but Leo held up his hand. "Before you go, there's something you may be able to help me with."

"What's that?"

"I believe someone has hidden something at the top of Aldrich Hill. However, it's in a compartment, and in my current state, I don't seem to be able to open it."

"I'd be happy to help," said Ann.

He gestured back the way he had come—up the rock steps. "After you."

"Don't you want to lead the way? I don't know where I'm going."

"There's only one path to the top."

Ann shrugged and began to clamber up the rocks, feeling the expected waft of cold air as she passed Leo.

nn was breathing heavily by the time they got to the level portion of the path at the top of the rock steps. They came to the scraggly tree from whose branches the strip of yellow tape fluttered. It must mark the place from which Leo or Brian Geary had fallen. The path did run relatively close to the edge of the cliff, but the tree and a few stunted bushes stood between the path and the edge.

She looked back at Leo. "Quite a drop."

"Indeed."

"I can see where it would be easy to get your feet tangled in the roots."

"Yes. When Shelby and I would hike this trail, I would always remind her to be careful." He gave a harsh laugh. "Ironic."

She waited to see if he would say more, but then realized that once again she was broaching a topic that Corey would want to save for the camera. She turned back to the path, stepping gingerly over the roots.

She continued on, following the path along the concave curve of the rock, until she saw that ahead of her it squeezed down to a narrow ledge. On the left was a sheer wall. On the right was nothing but space between the path and the granite steps below.

She turned back to Leo again.

"We need to cross this?"

"Yes."

She examined the ledge. It wasn't its width—about two feet —that bothered her as much as the fact that the rock angled ever so slightly toward the drop.

"Afraid of heights?" asked Leo.

"Not especially." Not, for example, in a plane, where her well-being didn't rely on careful footwork—except in the last seconds before a landing in a squirrelly cross-wind.

She realized that if Brian Geary had entered the back of the Pepperidge property, he might well have come this way, and would have encountered this portion of the trail before he reached the spot from where it seemed that Leo had fallen.

Remembering Corey's comment that Geary's fall would not be the focus of the documentary, she asked, "Someone snuck onto the property after you fell, evidently to try to take pictures or video of where it happened. Is this the place where he fell?"

"I wouldn't be surprised," replied Leo.

"You didn't see it happen?"

"I don't think so." He shook his head. "I know that sounds odd—you'd think the question of whether you'd seen someone fall off a hiking trail would be a clear yes or no—but it was a confused time. I think it took me a while to come to grips with what had happened to me, let alone come to grips with what had happened to another person."

He appeared ready to elaborate, but Ann felt that perhaps this was information that Corey *would* want to capture during the next day's shoot. She held up a hand. "Better save it for the camera." She turned back to the ledge. "Man, if someone was going to fall, this would be the place."

The statement slipped out before she realized how tactless it sounded, as if Leo's fall from the portion of the path marked with the yellow tape was somehow less excusable.

"But the place where you fell was tricky, too," she added hastily. "Easy to get your foot caught in those roots."

She glanced back, embarrassed, expecting Leo Dorn to look angry, or at least irritated, but she caught a glimpse of some other emotion—surprise?—before it morphed into a rueful smile. "Yes. No one ever accused me of doing the expected."

She kept her eyes on him for several more seconds to see if she could see a flicker of that expression again, but it was gone.

He gestured toward the ledge. "It's no danger on a dry day like today."

"I understand that it was dry when you fell."

"It hadn't rained for some time."

She hesitated. She knew she shouldn't ask, but suddenly she was uncomfortable having Leo Dorn between her and the Brookview house. "What made you fall?"

He crossed his arms and raised an eyebrow. "I thought we were supposed to wait for the cameras to be rolling before I answered that."

She mustered a smile. "I won't tell if you won't."

He shrugged. "Like I said, I don't remember much about the fall."

"Sometimes seeing the scene from a different perspective helps bring it back," she said, improvising. "Seeing it from the bottom of the cliff, for example."

"I've seen it from that perspective, as you know. It didn't help."

"And you've been as far back toward the house as the stream?"

"Yes."

"And evidently to the top of the hill, since there's something there you want to show me."

His expression shaded toward impatience. "Yes, there as well."

"But not as far as the house."

"No."

Suddenly Ann wondered if Leo Dorn's spirit could get as far as Otter Cliff, several miles away.

She looked down at the rocks below the ledge and almost yelped when she heard Leo's voice only a few feet behind her.

"It doesn't get easier the longer you think about it," he said.

"Did you and Shelby Kim ever hike at Otter Point?" she asked, flailing for some clue as to what was going on in Leo Dorn's head.

"The Ocean Path is a little too crowded for my taste." He looked skyward. The clouds had been building as they walked and were now billowing upward like the aftermath of an explosion. "If we're going to get to the top of the hill before it rains, we need to get moving."

"How will we get back down?"

"For you, there's a road just over the top of the hill. And I'm not particularly concerned about falling—at least not anymore."

Ann took a deep breath. "Okay, just give me a little space. I don't want to feel like I'm being crowded."

Leo held up his hands, then turned and retreated down the path. He turned back to her. "Enough space?"

"Sure." She contemplated the ledge again. Leo was right, it didn't get easier the longer she thought about it. She turned sideways and, with her back to the rock wall, shuffled sideways onto the ledge.

Leo laughed. "I have to say that in all the years I've been

hiking this trail, I've never seen anyone use that approach." He took a step forward.

"Stay there until I'm off the ledge," said Ann sharply.

He held up his hands again and stepped back.

She kept her eyes on the ledge, watching for any unevenness in the surface that might catch her boot, while monitoring Leo in her peripheral vision. He crossed his arms and examined the sky.

She felt her heartbeat slow as the path widened. A comforting fringe of pines now stood between her and the drop.

"Can I come over now?" called Leo.

"Yes. Thanks."

She turned and continued up the path and was well into the pine woods when he caught up with her.

"Not a bad idea," he said, "crossing that way. As long as you don't mind facing the drop."

"Better to face it than to let it take you by surprise."

They continued climbing, the ascent now more gradual, and soon reached the top of the hill. Ann paused to look out at the view across the pine-covered hills—most of which must be Pepperidge property—to the blue-gray expanse of the ocean beyond. She could see a demarcation in the water that she suspected indicated where the rain had begun to fall.

"Not much further," said Leo, and gestured for her to continue up the path.

When he said, "Here we are," it took Ann a moment to realize what he was referring to. Then she saw the blackened pit —clearly the remains of a building's foundation and basement —and the evidence of a long-ago fire: chunks of rubble that might have been part of a fireplace, the dull shine of a piece of copper pipe.

"What is that?" she asked. "Or what *was* it?"

"That was Frank Judd's studio. What I want to show you is in the basement."

Ann followed him to the edge of the pit and saw that a flight of stone steps led to the bottom. Just as she started carefully down the steps behind Leo, the rain began to fall in drops so fat that Ann felt as if she could hear the discrete plop of each one hitting the ground.

"Frank was trapped in his darkroom in the basement when the fire broke out," Leo said. He reached the bottom of the steps and turned back toward Ann. "Any sign of him?"

Ann scanned the basement. "No. But sometimes time of day or other factors play a part in whether or when a spirit makes an appearance, assuming they're still around."

Leo nodded. "I didn't sense anyone here either ... but maybe I wouldn't. This is a whole new world to figure out. What I wanted to show you is over here."

She followed him to the stone foundation that supported the stairs. The stones bore signs of the fire that had killed Frank Judd, the mortar between them crumbling.

"That one," said Leo, pointing.

One of the stones was out of alignment from the others, the mortar surrounding it completely gone.

"There's a hiding place behind it,'" said Leo. "I discovered it when I was poking around up here one day. I found a stash of pot—Frank's recreational drug of choice, I suppose. The stone was fitted in more tightly then, and it had protected the stash from the fire. Pot doesn't have much appeal to me, but I do enjoy an occasional cigar. My wife doesn't approve, so I'd store them in there, then sneak away to enjoy them in peace." He gestured toward the stone. "But you can see that someone has disturbed it. I was curious to see if the cigars were still there, but I can't move the stone. Can you look?"

Ann hesitated, still a bit spooked from the episode at the

ledge. Then she realized that if Leo couldn't affect the stone physically, he very likely couldn't affect her either. And if he intended her harm, the few feet he had retreated down the path back at the ledge would hardly have kept him from rushing out and trying to frighten her into an ill-advised step off the edge.

She bent and worked her fingers between the stone and its neighbors. She pulled, bracing herself for its weight when it dropped, but it wasn't as heavy as she had expected. Someone had chipped away the back portion, no doubt to make room for the hiding space. She lowered the stone carefully to the ground and peered into the hole.

"There's something in there." She got out her phone, opened the flashlight app, and shone it inside. "I can't see what it is."

"Can you get it out?"

Ann reached in and pulled out a canteen. She peered into the hole again, then reached in and pulled out a wooden box. She held the canteen and the box out for Leo's inspection.

Leo gestured toward the box. "Those are the cigars. Take them if you want."

"No, thanks." She put the cigar box back in the compartment. "Is the canteen yours?"

"No."

"How did it get there?" she asked.

"I don't know. Is there anything in it?"

She shook it. "A little bit of liquid, I think."

She grasped the cap, but Leo said, "Don't open it."

She dropped her hand. "Okay."

"I'd be curious to find out what's in it."

"My guess would be water."

"But wouldn't it be interesting if it was something else?"

"Like what?"

"I wouldn't want to speculate. Plus," he added, "your director might want to capture the reveal about its contents 'fresh,' as you say."

Ann thought that a canteen containing a mysterious liquid that was buried at the site of a fatal fire in a secret compartment that had contained the victim's pot stash sounded like an angle more up Kyle's alley than Corey's.

"Who else knows about the hiding place?" she asked. "Tippy?"

"Not as far as I know. She wouldn't have been as forgiving of my bad habit as of Frank's. If she knew about it, she would have mentioned it. Shelby did catch me up here one time when she was out on a solo hike." He smiled. "We had a laugh over the fact that the problem with a bad habit that produces a distinctive aroma is that it's harder to keep it a secret."

"Might she have told Tippy about the hiding place?"

"I doubt it. She's not the tattling kind."

Suddenly the image of Jonathan picking up Shelby's phone at Otter Cliff popped into her mind. "Should I be worried that I'm tampering with evidence?"

"Oh, I don't think so," he said. "I'm really just asking you to humor my curiosity. Can you have the contents analyzed? There are a couple of labs in Bangor."

After a pause, she slung the canteen's strap over her shoulder somewhat reluctantly. "I'll see what I can do."

She heard the rumble of distant thunder. "I should go. You said there's a road nearby …?"

"Yes. I'll show you."

He led her back up the basement steps and to a cracked drive, at the end of which Ann could see a road.

"I think this is where the young man who fell parked," said Leo. "There was a car and then later it was gone."

"Might he have put the canteen there?" asked Ann.

"Why would he?"

"Why would anyone?"

He sighed. "True."

When they came to the end of the drive, Ann caught a glimpse of a vast expanse of slate roof and innumerable brick chimneys through the trees on the other side of the narrow road.

She gestured toward the building. "Summer cottage?" she asked, only half joking.

"Hilltop. It has belonged to the Aldrich family, for whom Aldrich Hill was named, for generations. There's a rotating roster of Aldriches in residence at any one time. It's used year-round."

"I was surprised that the Brookview house isn't more ostentatious," she said. "I mean that as a compliment."

He gave a half-smile that didn't reach his eyes. "Yes, 'thou shalt not be ostentatious' would be the eleventh Commandment as far as the Pepperidges are concerned."

Ann looked around. "Are we still on Pepperidge property?"

"Yes, right up to the road. It's the biggest piece of private property on MDI." He leaned toward her conspiratorially. "Although of course we would never say that in polite company."

Ann laughed.

She looked to her left, toward where the road sloped down before curving out of sight in the pines. "That way?"

"If you followed the road, you'd get to the bottom of the drive to Brookview eventually, but it would be a long, wet walk. I'd recommend calling Tippy or Megan."

"Tippy gave me Megan's number—I'll call her."

Leo nodded. "Very good."

"Is there any message you'd like me to take back to Tippy?" Ann asked.

"Did she ask you to ask me for a message?"

Ann hesitated. "Not specifically."

His features tightened for a moment, then he said, "I

suppose that if you tried to contact one dead husband and it didn't pan out, perhaps it would dampen your enthusiasm to try again."

His tone was so noncommittal that Ann couldn't tell whether he was being sincere or sarcastic.

He must have sensed her uncertainty. "I must admit that the opportunity to send a post-mortem message is not one I ever spent much time considering. Let me give it some thought. I'll let you know next time I see you."

"Will I need to find you to let you know when the documentary crew arrives tomorrow?" she asked.

"No, I'll meet you at the bridge." He gazed at her for a moment, then shook his head with a laugh. "I must thank you for making the trip out here to look for me. I thought my days of conversation were past." He raised his hand in farewell, then turned and walked back down the drive.

Ann got out her phone and tapped Megan's number.

"Hey, Megan—it's Ann Kinnear."

"We're glad to hear from you," said Megan. "We got a little worried when the rain started."

"I'm at the back of the property, by Frank Judd's studio. I'd rather not come back on the same path and have to cross the ledge now that it's wet."

"That's smart. I know where you are. I'll pick you up—be there in a jiff."

They ended the call and Ann sat down on a rock partially protected by a large pine from the rain, which had settled into a steady downpour. She thought back to the look of surprise she had caught on Leo Dorn's face when she referred to the location of his fall. Had Shelby Kim pointed the authorities to the wrong location? Ann could imagine the young woman being distraught and confused, could imagine her waving from the base of the cliff to a point on the path above and having the police make the wrong assumption about where she was pointing.

But if Shelby had lied to the police, what reason would she have to do so? And what reason would Leo Dorn have to cover for her?

20

Megan arrived a few minutes after Ann's call, driving a notably unostentatious Volvo station wagon that smelled like it was mainly used to transport wet beagles.

"Bad timing with the rain," said Megan sympathetically as she executed a U-turn. "You were smart not to try to get back on foot. No one hikes up Aldrich Hill after a rain."

"But it wasn't wet when Dr. Dorn fell?"

Megan's expression softened toward sadness. "No—dry as a bone, at least until after he had fallen." She glanced at the canteen slung over Ann's shoulder. "I don't remember you having a canteen with you."

"I found it." After a pause, Ann asked, "Does it look familiar to you?"

Without bothering to look again, Megan said, "I don't know anyone who uses a canteen rather than a water bottle these days."

They rolled down the hill, the wipers slapping a soothing rhythm on the windshield.

"I saw the remains of Frank Judd's studio," said Ann. "He was a painter?"

"A photographer. He had a darkroom in the basement, and I understand that he would sometimes hold exhibits of works of other photographers he admired. He'd invite friends and family." She smiled. "I'm guessing that every photographer for a hundred miles around dreamed of having Frank Judd become a patron of their work."

Megan turned the Volvo onto a road that Ann recognized from her own drive to Brookview with Garrick. A minute later the decorative metal gates came into view and opened in response to Megan tapping an app on her phone. They started up the drive.

"How well do you know Shelby Kim?" Ann asked.

Megan glanced over at Ann, then returned her eyes to the rain-slick road. "I talk to her when she stops by the house—I don't pal around with her or anything like that." After a moment, she continued. "She's a nice kid." She laughed. "Listen to me. She's my age, but she's the kind of person who seemed like a 'kid.' Sweet, you know?"

"Naive?"

After a moment, Megan said, "Maybe," then followed up with an overly hearty, "Here we are!" as she pulled up to the entrance. "I'll drop you off here—I'm going to take the car back to the garage."

Ann found Tippy Pepperidge and Garrick in the sitting room, seated in front of the now-lit fire. They stood when she entered.

"I didn't expect the rain to start so soon," said Tippy. "It's good you were dressed for the conditions." She glanced at the canteen slung over Ann's shoulder. "Although I don't remember you being quite that thoroughly prepared."

Ann suddenly wished she hadn't asked Megan about the

canteen, and that she had put it in Garrick's car before coming into the house. Tippy would have every right to claim it since it had been recovered on Pepperidge property. Leo had told Ann to take it to a lab, not to his wife.

"I found it near the road," said Ann.

"It looks a bit worse for wear." Tippy extended her hand. "If you'd like me to dispose of it—"

"No," Ann said quickly. "I think I'll see if I can clean it up."

Tippy dropped her hand. "Certainly." After a pause, she continued. "Was your outing a success?"

"Yes, I was able to contact Dr. Dorn."

There was a silence, during which Ann wondered if Tippy would ask what her dead husband might have had to say to Ann, but it was Garrick who broke the silence.

"With that accomplished, I believe we can be on our way." He turned to Tippy. "Thank you for your hospitality and your cooperation, Ms. Pepperidge."

Tippy followed them to the entrance, then pulled an umbrella from a basket containing a half dozen and held it out. "Garrick, I don't know that you're quite as prepared for the conditions as Miss Kinnear is. You can use this."

Garrick inclined his head in thanks but didn't reach for the umbrella. Ann took it.

"I'll drop it off when we come back for the shoot," said Ann.

Ann ended up holding the umbrella over Garrick's head as they made their way to the car. After escorting him to the passenger side, she ran to the driver's side and tossed the umbrella and the canteen in the back before dropping into the driver's seat. She started up the Fleetwood, turned the wipers to high, and backed out of the parking space.

"I can update you on what happened on the way back to Somesville," she said as she started down the drive.

"No conversation while driving," said Garrick, "especially in treacherous weather. You can update me when we get to the house."

Ann complied with Garrick's *no talking while driving* rule during the ride, although her mind was largely occupied with mulling over her meeting with Leo Dorn.

When they reached Garrick's house, Ann pulled up to the detached garage and looked over at Garrick expectantly. He looked stoically forward. With a sigh, she climbed out of the car, ran to the garage, and hoisted open the door.

She hurried back to the car and dropped into the driver's seat. "You should get an automatic garage door opener."

"I rarely go out in bad weather," he said.

"I'm guessing you rarely go out at all," she said as she eased the Fleetwood into the garage.

Ann handed the umbrella to Garrick, then got the canteen out of the back. During their brief walk from the garage to the back door, Garrick held the umbrella so far over their heads that she would likely have stayed drier if she had made the dash without it. Garrick unlocked the back door and led her quickly through the kitchen to the hallway. Was he afraid that she would notice an Alexa on the table or a Keurig on the counter? As far as she could tell, he didn't even have a microwave.

They hung their coats and the umbrella on pegs near the front door, then Ann followed Garrick into the office. Garrick went to the fireplace, where a fire was already laid, and lit the kindling with a long match from a holder on the mantel. He gestured toward one of the guest chairs and lowered himself into the desk chair.

"It would save me some time to be able to update you and Corey at the same time," said Ann. "Is it okay if I loop him in via phone?"

"Very well."

Ann got out her phone, opened the contacts, and tapped

Corey's name. It rang to voicemail. "Hey, Corey, I'm in Somesville with Garrick and was just calling to tell you about our trip to Brookview. Give me a call." She slipped her phone back into her pocket, then turned her chair to face the fire a little more directly and stretched out her legs. "Leo Dorn says he can move around the property quite a bit. He can get to the back of the property and to the stream but can't reach the house. Does that seem odd to you?"

"No."

"You'd think he'd have more incentive to visit his wife than to visit the ruins of Frank Judd's studio."

Garrick raised an eyebrow.

"How well do you know Tippy Pepperidge?" she asked.

"She was a client."

"And you never met Leo Dorn?"

"No."

"Do you have any sense of what sort of relationship they had?"

"No."

"It seems like maybe when Leo died they had some sort of ... unfinished business."

"Unfinished business?"

"Don't you think it's weird that neither one of them had a message they wanted to send to the other?"

After a pause, Garrick said, "Not particularly."

"Well, trust me on this—if two people have been married for years, it would be normal for them to seize the opportunity to send a message after the death of one of them."

"And you know this from personal experience?"

"Well, no, not *personal* experience—"

Ann's phone buzzed. She tapped it to speaker. "Hi, Corey."

"How did it go?" he asked.

"We made contact with Leo Dorn. He says he can meet us at

the stream. It's very picturesque—I think it will make a nice setting for his interview with Garrick. We can do the interview tomorrow morning, if we can get ready that quickly."

"Yes, we should be able to do that. That's great news, Ann, thanks," said Corey, not sounding quite as enthusiastic as Ann had expected. "Maybe we can do something visually interesting with the running water as a representation of SMT's fire suppression work." After a beat, he continued. "I've got some news to report, too—although not as positive as yours. Searchers found a piece of yellow cloth stuck in the rocks at the base of Otter Cliff, and Jonathan Garrido has confirmed that it looks like a piece of the jacket Shelby Kim was wearing the last time he saw her. I think it's safe to assume that Shelby went off that cliff, either by accident or on purpose—her own purpose or someone else's."

Kyle's voice came faintly over the call. "Are you talking to Ann and Masser? Put that on speaker." When he spoke next, his voice was clear. "We need to get back to Brookview. We need to confront Tippy Pepperidge with this information, and if Ann can communicate with Leo, we need to see his reaction to the news as well."

"Absolutely not," said Corey. "We need to approach this carefully. The last thing we need is for Ms. Pepperidge not only to withdraw her permission for us to shoot at Brookview, but to sic her lawyers on us for harassment."

"Then we need to get Ann out to Otter Cliff," said Kyle.

Ann turned toward the window of Garrick's office. Rain was running down the glass, blurring the shapes outside. "I'm not going anywhere in this weather," she said. She thought back to the ledge on Aldrich Hill. "And I'm certainly not going out in this looking for a spirit on the edge of a cliff."

"Leo Dorn agreed to talk to us tomorrow," said Corey. "That's soon enough. It looks like we're not going to be able to use anything we learn to save Shelby Kim."

They ended the call and Ann called Mike for a ride from Somesville back to Manset. When he arrived, she made the dash to the car without bothering to deploy the umbrella she had retrieved from the entrance hall.

"So, what's up?" Mike asked as soon as she dropped into the passenger seat.

"Let's wait until we get back to the house," she said. "It'll be more fun over a glass of wine."

Mike gave a huff of exasperation.

"What have you been up to?" she asked.

"I picked up some supplies, including a nice Cab from the wine shop in Southwest Harbor. I did take a hike—Eagle Lake Carriage Road—until the rain started. Then I did a little research into Shelby Kim."

"Oh, yeah? What did you find out?"

"Impressive CV. She got her undergraduate degree from MIT when she was twenty, got her master's degree when she was twenty-two, and defended her PhD dissertation two years ago, when she was twenty-five."

"No wonder Tippy Pepperidge described her as one of Stata Mater's most promising hires."

When they reached Manset, Mike poured two glasses of the Cab and they settled into the couch and loveseat in the living room.

Ann updated him on Tippy's approval for the video shoot to proceed under certain conditions, Ann's meeting with Leo, and the news about the discovery of the scrap of yellow cloth at the base of Otter Cliff.

"Jesus," Mike said with a shake of his head. "When you found her phone at the cliff, it seemed ominous, but I hoped there was some benign explanation. But finding a piece of her jacket on the rocks? I guess it's pretty clear she jumped."

"Pretty clear that she went over the edge, but not what the circumstances were," said Ann. "Here's another oddity." She returned to the kitchen and came back with the canteen. "Leo Dorn led me to this. It was in a secret compartment in the basement of what used to be Frank Judd's studio at the back of the Pepperidge property. Leo said only he and Shelby know about the compartment, although he thinks Brian Geary parked near the studio."

"Geary brought a canteen to Brookview and then hid it in the basement of a burned-out building?"

"Him or somebody else. Leo asked me to get the contents analyzed."

"Why?"

"I haven't any idea—but it can't hurt, right?"

"Hey, if the dead guy says to get the contents analyzed, I'm all over it."

"He said there are places in Bangor that could do it." She handed him the canteen. "Can you look into that?"

"Sure, since I'm banned from all the other activities."

"He says not to open it before handing it over to the lab."

Ann's phone pinged with a text and she read the message. "Corey wants to know if we want to grab some dinner with the crew."

"Sure."

She looked out the window. "The weather is awful."

"Don't be a baby."

She sighed. "Okay." She tapped out a response.

"Are you going to tell Corey about the canteen?" asked Mike.

"I would, but it seems like Kyle has ears everywhere and I'd hate for him to find out before we know what the deal is. Let's keep it between the two of us for now."

21

The rain had moderated to a drizzle when Ann and Mike arrived at the Back Street Grill in Bar Harbor to meet up with Corey and the rest of the crew. There were a few couples seated at tables, a group of college-aged guys cheering on a sporting event on the TV over the bar, and a group of twenty-something women arguing loudly but cheerfully about what songs to play on the jukebox.

Ann spotted Corey and Kyle at a table in the corner with two other men. Corey introduced them as Chet and Marty, the videographer and the grip he had hired for the shoot. After introductions had been made, they pulled up another table to accommodate Ann and Mike.

Ann took a seat and Mike was about to sit down next to her when Kyle slipped past him and into the chair.

"You get to talk with her all the time, Mike," said Kyle, directing a smile toward Ann. "Why don't you give someone else a chance to chat with your sister."

"Smooth move, Lathey," said Corey.

"Got an issue with hiring women, Duff?" asked Kyle. "Ann's

going to start feeling lonely as the only woman. Who's she going to powder her nose with?"

"I can say without fear of contradiction," said Ann, "that I have never considered a trip to the restroom to be a group event."

"It's true," said Mike. "She's very independent in that way."

"Tomorrow the male-to-female ratio will change slightly," said Corey. "I hired a female PA."

"What's a PA?" asked Mike.

"Production assistant." He looked at Ann with a grin. "Someone you know. Someone local."

"I don't know anyone around here other than Garrick," she said.

"Your circle of acquaintances on MDI is larger than you're giving yourself credit for."

She considered. "Megan?" she asked uncertainly.

"I'm pretty sure that the way to get back in Tippy Pepperidge's good graces is not to hire away the Brookview staff," said Corey. "You'll see the person I'm talking about tomorrow. I'm curious if you'll recognize her."

"I hate surprises."

"I think you'll enjoy this one." He addressed the group. "First round's on me. What does everyone want?"

They all chose various types of beer and Corey went to the bar to put in their order.

"So, Marty," said Mike, "what exactly is it that a grip does?"

Ann was curious herself, but Kyle turned toward her and rested his arm across the back of her chair.

"Ever been to L.A., Ann?"

"Nope."

"You know what the temperatures were today?"

"Nope."

"High of seventy-five and low of sixty."

"Sounds nice."

"You can eat al fresco any time of the year—barely any rain from April through October—and L.A. has some of the best restaurants in the world. Of course, it's nice to get away to San Francisco and the wine country for some variety. An hour-and-a-half away," he gave her an unctuous smile, "even if you don't have a charter pilot." He adjusted his arm so that it was resting against her shoulder blades. "And then the cooler temperatures at night—perfect for curling up in front of a fire."

She glanced at the intruding arm. "Kyle, do you mind?"

He shifted his arm so that at least it was no longer against her back.

She tried to turn her chair, and her attention, toward the rest of the party. She had missed the explanation for what a grip did, but now Chet and Marty were recounting stories from recent video production gigs.

"Where do you like to travel?" asked Kyle, shifting his chair to keep him in her line of sight.

After a moment's thought, she said, "London." Since London was often cold and wet, and wasn't widely known for its gourmet restaurants, she hoped it wouldn't be of interest to Kyle.

"Love London!" he exclaimed. "The history. The architecture."

"I saw a headless guy at the Tower when I was seven."

"An exhibit?"

"No, an actual headless guy."

"Really? That's ..."

Ann was gratified that this response was one which Kyle's experience had evidently not equipped him to address. She caught a bit of the conversation from the rest of the group.

"Don't you want to hear Chet and Marty's story about shooting the Stonington Lobster Boat Races?" she asked.

"Sure. Sounds fascinating," he said with a sigh, evidently abandoning his attempt to keep her attention.

Within a few minutes, everyone had finished their first beers.

Kyle, his good humor evidently revived, slapped his hands together. "Next round's on me. Same all around?"

"If you're buying," said Mike, "I'm changing my order. Maybe a Scotch ..."

As Mike debated what brand and age of Scotch he was going to put on Kyle's tab, Ann's gaze wandered to the bar. The young women, having resolved the issue of jukebox selection—Taylor Swift—had migrated to the bar and were chatting and laughing. One had a glossy auburn ponytail hanging halfway down her back.

"Hey," said Ann, "isn't that Officer Finney?"

Kyle's gaze followed Ann's. "The woman who was interviewing you at Otter Cliff?"

"Yeah."

"I do believe you're right," he said. "Mike, why don't you stick with beer, and switch it up for the next round."

Before Mike could reply, Kyle stood and headed for the bar. A minute later, he was talking and laughing with the group of women.

"Oh, God, what's he doing?" groaned Corey.

"Looking for some action of one kind or another is my guess," said Mike.

A few minutes later, Kyle returned to their table with their beers on a tray. "Here you go, kids," he said, handing around the drinks. "After this, you're on your own, because I'm going to accompany Officer Finney—Sarah Jane—and her friends to another bar they assure me is *the* best place on MDI."

"Kyle—" began Corey, sounding as menacing as it was possible for him to sound.

Kyle clapped him on the shoulder. "Not to worry, my friend. I promise to be bright-eyed and bushy-tailed by call time tomorrow."

Kyle returned to the group at the bar. He spoke to Finney, who looked toward the table and gave Ann a friendly wave. Then he followed Finney and her friends to the entrance, hurrying ahead when they reached it to open the door for them.

"This can't be good," said Corey.

"You know what would make you feel better?" said Mike. "Pizza. How about one large meat-lover's and one large veggie. That should make everyone happy."

Corey went to the bar to put in the pizza order. When he came back, he sat down in the chair Kyle had vacated.

"Sorry about Kyle being such a jerk," he said.

"He is kind of a pain in the ass," said Ann. "Are you sure you can't get rid of him?"

Corey swallowed a slug of beer. "Haven't figured out how to yet." He grinned. "But if he really annoys you, let me know and I'll pop him in the nose."

She laughed. "You're about the last person I can imagine popping someone in the nose just for being annoying."

He put his hand over his heart. "You cut me to the quick. I'm not that much of a milquetoast, am I?"

She smiled, but she could tell she had hurt his feelings. "I'm sure if the motivation was sufficient, you'd be a nose-popping fiend."

"Tell me more about your meeting with Leo Dorn," he said.

She relayed some of the details of the meeting, and recounted Garrick's position—or lack thereof—about Leo and Tippy's seeming lack of interest in communicating with each other.

"Do *you* think it's weird?" she asked.

"It does seem a little weird, especially knowing that she had hired Garrick to try to communicate with her first husband."

"On the other hand," mused Ann, "it was clear when we were talking to Tippy that she trusts Garrick more than she trusts me. Maybe if Garrick was the one going out to talk with Leo, she would have asked him to mediate a conversation, or at least sent a message."

"I think it's better for us that she didn't ask you to," said Corey. "We want to be recording when we hear whatever it is Leo has to say. Or," he amended, "when you and Garrick hear it."

Ann nodded and took a sip of beer. She had left out only the discovery of the canteen. She was still afraid that Kyle would somehow find out about it and consider it fodder for another leak to the media. She'd wait until Mike had gotten the analysis done before deciding if it was worth telling Corey. After all, there was no point getting him excited about something that might be a tablespoon of water.

22

After the pizza and another round of beers—this one on Ann's tab—the Authentic Productions team adjourned to a back room where Corey had discovered a pool table. Chet cadged a quarter from Marty to play the jukebox, and in a moment *Thunder Road* filled the room.

"God almighty," said Marty, "don't you ever play anything else?"

Ann got a yearning for chocolate ice cream and went to the bar to investigate options. She discovered that the closest the restaurant could offer was a shot of chocolate liqueur, which seemed excessive after her three beers, especially since she was already smothering yawns.

She returned to the back room just as Mike pocketed the eight ball to win a match from Chet. She climbed back onto one of the stools at the high top from which she had been watching the game. Mike came over to reward himself with a swallow of beer.

"Are you about ready to go?" she asked.

"Are you kidding? I'm the defending champion. Corey's my next victim."

Corey joined them in time to hear Mike's boast and downed a slug of his own beer as Ann pulled her phone out of her pocket.

"I wonder if they have ride shares on MDI ..." she said.

"If you're okay to drive," said Corey, "you can take the car you and Mike came in and I'll drive your baby brother home after I've knocked some humility into him."

"That okay with you?" Ann asked Mike.

"Sure thing," said Mike, digging the car keys out of his pocket and dropping them into her hand. "After I beat Corey, we can use the ride back to Manset for me to give him some pointers." He went to the table to rack the balls.

Ann shook her head. "Before we came up here," she said to Corey, "while we were all debating about the documentary topic, Mike and Scott had planned to take the train up to New York for some wining and dining. I guess he feels like he's going to enjoy some nightlife even though that trip got cancelled." She shrugged into her jacket. "Thanks for playing chauffeur, Corey."

Corey chalked his cue. "No problem. I don't plan to stay much longer myself, considering we need to be at Brookview in the morning."

Ann waved to Chet and Marty, who were passing the time at the dart board until their turn at the pool table. When she stepped out of the restaurant, she found that the rain had tapered off, but the temperature was dropping. She zipped up her jacket and headed up the street to where Mike had parked the Hyundai.

She drove west out of Bar Harbor, then turned south on 102. As she approached Southwest Harbor, the sight of the Food Mart sign reminded her of her chocolate ice cream craving.

The parking lot was deserted, but the *Open* sign by the entrance was lit. She glanced at the clock on the Hyundai's dashboard: she guessed she had three minutes to obtain her ice cream. She parked the car and hurried into the store.

A young man sweeping the floor near the registers glanced up with a look of annoyance. "We're just about to close."

"Won't be a minute—really," she said, and jogged toward the frozen food section.

She grabbed the ice cream, paid the young man—who was somewhat mollified by the fact that she had actually concluded her shopping trip within the promised minute—and headed back into the parking lot.

There was another car in the lot now: a red hatchback. It was hard to tell the make and model, since it was outside the pool of illumination cast by the parking lot lights, but it looked like a Volkswagen Jetta. Its headlights were off but the sound of its engine running was clear in the quiet evening air. She couldn't see the driver, but guessed it was a female based on the silhouette. She thought briefly of alerting the driver that the store was closing, but as far as she knew, it could be the checker's girlfriend waiting to pick him up.

She climbed into the Hyundai, started it up, and headed for the exit. The headlights of the red hatchback came on. It also headed for the exit.

Ann turned left onto the highway.

The hatchback—definitely a Jetta— turned left as well. It closed the distance between it and the Hyundai, then dropped back to about fifty yards.

Her heart thumping, Ann slowed at the main intersection in town, then turned left onto Clark Point Road.

The Jetta followed, maintaining its distance.

Praying that her memory of the town's streets was accurate, she turned left on Herrick, which bore to the left and took her back to 102.

She turned right and headed north.

She was hardly surprised when the Jetta did the same.

She thought of Leo Dorn, who had died in a fall from a bone-dry path he had hiked dozens, if not hundreds, of times. She thought of his statement that he had been confused in the time after his fall. Perhaps he was confused about the circumstances of his fall as well. And she thought of that scrap of yellow fabric that suggested that they were unlikely to find Shelby Kim alive.

Against these alarming thoughts was the knowledge that she had gained a certain notoriety on Mount Desert Island. It wouldn't be the first time that someone had recognized and followed her to ask for help contacting a dead friend or relative, to ask for an autograph, or, on one memorable occasion, to ask for a lock of her hair.

She glanced back. The Jetta was still there, about fifty yards back.

She fumbled her phone out of her pocket and tapped Mike's number.

"Hey there," he said loudly over the strains of *Thunder Road* in the background. "Are you back in Manset?"

She pictured Mike, and no doubt Corey, Chet, and Marty as well, speeding to Southwest Harbor to come to her rescue—a rescue that she wasn't sure was even needed.

"Nope. Got as far as Southwest," she said. "Based on the soundtrack, am I right that you're still at the Back Street Grill?"

"Yup. I think this is the fifth rendition of *Thunder Road*," said Mike. "Someone better cut off Chet's supply of quarters soon. What are you doing in Southwest?"

"I decided I want another beer after all. I'm coming back to Bar Harbor."

"Okay," he said. "If it's just beer you want, there's some in the fridge at Manset, but if you come back, I'll add you to my tally of victims at the pool table."

When she reached Bar Harbor, the Jetta was still trailing her at the same distance. She pulled into a parking space right in front of the restaurant. The Jetta slowed, then turned at the intersection behind her and disappeared from sight.

She hurried into the restaurant, then stood in a small vestibule behind its glass-paned door, watching to see if the Jetta would circle the block, but after a couple of minutes, there was still no sign of it.

When she stepped into the restaurant, she spotted Mike, Corey, Chet, and Marty seated at the bar.

"I tried to keep the pool table for you," said Mike, "but there was starting to be a line, so we called it quits. We just put in an order for another round—what do you want?"

"That's okay, I don't really want a beer. I think someone's following me."

She glanced toward the front window and, as she did so, saw the Jetta roll past.

"That's it!" she exclaimed. "That's the car that was following me."

"Are you okay?" asked Corey.

"Yes, I'm fine. But that car was in the parking lot of the Food Mart, then it followed me to Southwest Harbor and back here."

"Stay here," said Mike. He jumped off his stool and headed for the door.

"No, Mike—" she said.

"Wait for me," said Corey to Mike.

"Corey, I don't think—"

Chet and Marty were also standing and looked ready to follow Mike as well, but Corey said, "Stay here with Ann," then hurried outside after Mike.

Ann, Chet, and Marty went to the restaurant's large front windows and looked out, but they couldn't see far up or down the street, and there was no sign of the Jetta or of Mike or Corey.

She had almost talked Chet and Marty into accompanying her in search of Mike and Corey when they re-entered the restaurant, both breathing heavily.

"Did you catch up with it?" she asked.

"No, we should have split up," said Corey. "We picked the wrong direction. But we did see it from a distance on one of the side streets. It pulled away before we could get to it, but we got a look at the license: a Maine plate starting with *ZP*. We should call the cops."

"And tell them what?" asked Ann.

"That someone was following you."

"It's not a crime."

"No, but in view of what's been happening on MDI in the last few days, I think they'd want to know."

"I'd call Sarah Jane Finney, but I think she's otherwise occupied," said Ann. "Plus, I'd rather not let Kyle know about ... whatever this is."

"I totally agree," said Corey. He got out his wallet and pulled out a card. "This is the cop I talked to at Otter Cliff, and back at the police station. Let's give him a call."

"Okay, but let's not call him from the bar," said Ann. "I don't think that will make the right impression."

They agreed that Ann and Mike would head back to Manset, and that Ann would make the call en route. The round of drinks arrived at that moment and Corey settled up the tab. Chet and Marty, saying that there was no point in letting the drinks go to waste, volunteered to finish them up before heading back to the Bar Harbor Inn.

Ann, Mike, and Corey stepped outside, Ann glancing nervously up and down the nearly deserted street.

"Give me a minute to get the Suburban," said Corey, "and I'll follow you."

"That's not necessary," said Ann, beginning to feel self-conscious about the situation.

"Maybe not," he said, "but I'd feel better doing it."

"New best friend," Mike whispered with a waggle of his eyebrows as he passed her on his way to the driver's door.

23

Three Weeks Earlier

Shelby scanned the other cars as Jonathan pulled into the parking lot of Blackwood's restaurant. They were all cars she was used to seeing in the Stata Mater lot.

"Looks like everyone's here," he said. His voice was a little more subdued than usual.

She glanced over at him, trying to hide a pleased smile. "Yes."

She pulled down the sun visor and examined her makeup—a nod to the occasion—and was pleased with the result. As Jonathan got out of the car, she got out the lipstick that she had bought that morning and touched up her lips. She hadn't wanted to do it while they were driving for fear the car would hit a pothole and she'd arrive at the restaurant with a smear of Marvelous Moxy across her face.

Jonathan opened her door. "Lookin' good, Shel. I'm going to have to take you out to fancy restaurants more often."

The words were right, but the tone was still muted. She hoped that Jonathan's mood didn't spring from jealousy. He had been pursuing the same research track as she had and would have gotten to the same destination eventually. She had just gotten there first. She had briefly thought of discussing the situation with him but decided against it. They hadn't been dating that long, and it seemed too early for a conversation that serious. Plus, she thought, she didn't want to ruin her own mood.

She assessed the path from the car to the front door. The remains of a slushy April snow still covered unpaved, shaded ground but she was relieved to see that the parking lot had been thoroughly cleared. She was glad she didn't have to worry about splashing slush on her new cream-colored wool pants or ruining her new burgundy velvet shoes.

"I could carry you there," said Jonathan with a mischievous twinkle in his eye.

She laughed. That sounded more like the Jonathan she was used to.

"I think I can make it," she said, "although after an evening in heels, you might need to carry me back."

"After an evening of champagne toasts, I might have to carry you back," he said cheerfully, offering his crooked arm.

They stepped into the entry of the restaurant, a room created out of the porch of the residence the building had once been. They could hear the buzz of conversation beyond the door that separated the entry from the dining room.

"Dr. Kim?" asked a young man as he stepped out from behind the host station.

"Yes."

"Good evening, I'm Troy and we're so pleased to have you with us tonight. If there's anything you need, please let me know. Your party is waiting for you. May I take your coats?"

As they shrugged out of their coats, Shelby tried to peer through the glass panes of the door that separated the entry from the dining room. "Where are they?"

Troy's smile broadened. "You won't have trouble finding them—Ms. Pepperidge reserved the entire restaurant for the evening. If you'll wait for just a moment."

With their coats draped over his arm, he slipped through the door. Before it closed behind him, Shelby caught a glimpse of what was normally the dining room, now cleared of tables, and a number of people chatting and laughing.

"The whole restaurant!" she whispered to Jonathan.

"They're really rolling out the red carpet for you."

A minute later the door opened again—now the buzz had quieted—and Troy said, "Right this way."

Jonathan swept out his hand. "After you."

Troy opened the door and stood aside, and Shelby stepped into the dining room.

She was met by a dozen pairs of eyes—Tippy Pepperidge, Leo Dorn, Hannah Jeskie, and the rest of the Stata Mater research staff.

"The guest of honor," said Tippy, beaming at her. "Bravo!" she said and began an enthusiastic clapping.

There was a chorus of *bravos*, and the other guests joined Tippy in applause.

Shelby thought she might faint from happiness.

When the applause died down, Tippy stepped forward and clasped Shelby's hand in both her own.

"Shelby, I am so proud of what you've accomplished."

Two servers began circulating with trays of champagne glasses. Troy appeared at Shelby's elbow with glasses for her and Jonathan.

Shelby's colleagues gathered around and added their compliments to Tippy's. Having already downed his champagne, Jonathan went to a bar set up in a corner of the room to get a beer, then detoured to where Leo and Hannah were chatting nearby. Servers circulated with trays of hors d'oeuvres, which Shelby was too excited to eat. They also periodically topped off her champagne, which she was evidently not too excited to drink.

Conversations passed in a happy blur. When Troy cleared his throat to catch the guests' attention, Shelby was surprised to see that an hour had elapsed.

"Dinner will be served shortly if you'd like to adjourn to the next room," Troy announced.

Servers directed the guests into a separate room, where individual four-tops had been rearranged into one long, linen-covered banquet table. Troy led Shelby to a chair at the head of the table, with Jonathan to one side and Leo to the other. Tippy took a seat at the other end of the table.

When the guests were settled, the servers returned to top off their glasses once again. When they had retired, Tippy stood and cleared her throat. The room quieted.

"Shelby, I arranged this celebration because I wanted to thank you personally for all the incredible hard work you've done for Stata Mater Technology since you joined a year ago, and for the tremendous advance that work has achieved. The improved clean agent you've developed, and its lower production costs, will make this technology more accessible to fire departments across the country—in fact, around the world. Its increased effectiveness means that firefighters will be able to control fires far larger than they have been able to in the past. And I understand from Leo and Hannah that this is just the beginning of what we might be able to achieve with this adaptable new substance. It's an extraordinary contribution to the cause we are all working toward." She glanced down at her glass, then back up at Shelby, tears sparkling in her eyes, although not falling. "I feel certain that if this technology had been available eight years ago, my late husband might still be alive today. You can be so proud knowing that your work will save countless lives that otherwise would have been taken by fire and will prevent untold suffering." She raised her glass. "To Shelby Kim."

The others in the room raised their glasses. "To Shelby Kim."

Tippy looked toward Leo. "Leo, is there anything you'd like to add?"

He stood. "I think you've expressed our gratitude to Shelby admirably, Tippy. I only want to add that we've named the agent that Shelby developed, and our records now reflect that as," he smiled at Shelby, "SK-1." Smiles and nods greeted this. Shelby's face flamed with pride. "Now, of course," Leo continued, "we're all anxious to see what SK-2 will be." The guests laughed and Shelby joined in, nodding ruefully. Leo raised his glass. "Many thanks for a job well done."

The guests raised their glasses and drank again. Leo sat.

"Speech!" called Amory, one of the researchers in the fire prevention lab. Others took up the call.

Jonathan nudged Shelby's elbow. "Go on, Shel," he whispered. "They want to hear from you."

Tippy resumed her seat. Shelby stood, twisting her napkin in her hands.

"I'm so grateful to Ms. Pepperidge for hosting this event. I'm so grateful to Dr. Dorn and Dr. Jeskie for all the support they've provided to me since the first day I joined Stata Mater. I'm so grateful to have all of you as colleagues—I couldn't have done what I did without your knowledge and your help. Thank you."

She sat down to another round of applause.

"Before they serve dinner," said Tippy, "I'd like to use the opportunity of having you all here to sound a cautionary note. This development is very recent, and we need to proceed carefully. Extensive testing will obviously be needed to confirm what we all believe to be true. Since Stata Mater is a non-profit organization, we're worried less about competitors getting access to our research—in fact, once proven out in tests, we will of course be sharing our findings with those in the for-profit fire suppression industry—but we must nonetheless plan our announcement deliberately. For one thing, as with any scientific advance, this technology could be turned to less praiseworthy purposes. There's no telling how people will twist a technical development to their own ends, and we must be prepared for those negative results as well as the positive ones. For another thing, although this is good news for many in the fire suppression industry, the manufacturers of the clean agents that Shelby's invention will likely supplant may be less enthusiastic. We need to consider our response to their concerns. I'm asking all of you to keep Shelby's invention confidential for the time being, until we've had a chance to do our due diligence."

There was a murmur of assent from the guests.

Tippy gave a nod to Troy and a moment later servers began arriving with bowls of lobster bisque.

Leo turned to Hannah, who was seated next to him, for some shop talk.

Jonathan leaned toward Shelby. "That was quite a speech from Tippy," he whispered. "I never thought I'd have an opportunity to refer to her as 'effusive.'"

"Do you mind?" Shelby asked.

He smiled at her. "I can't deny I'm little bit jealous. But you deserve it, Shel."

She slipped her hand into his and gave it a squeeze.

24

When Ann looked out of her bedroom window the next morning, she found that the day had dawned sunny, everything washed fresh by the rain. With no updates from the MDI police about the car that Ann had reported as having followed her the previous evening, Mike insisted on driving her to the production office. As they passed The Perch, they saw Eric wiping down the picnic tables in anticipation of customers who were willing to brave the cool temperatures for some time in the sun. He gave them a wave, and Ann's distaste for her unsought celebrity didn't keep her from feeling that little thrill of being recognized in a place that wasn't one's home, and for a reason other than her unusual ability.

When they reached the warehouse, Chet and Marty were loading equipment into a van that was double-parked in front—Kyle's Tesla once again occupying the one parking space at the side of the building. Ann grabbed Tippy Pepperidge's loaner umbrella out of the back seat, then gave Mike a wave as he headed off to a chemical analysis lab in Bangor with the canteen from Brookview.

Inside, she found Hannah Jeskie checking out the stack of

lobster traps that lined one wall, and Corey and Kyle sitting at one of the card tables. A young woman was arranging a continental breakfast on the other card table a short distance away.

"I say we go to Otter Cliff and see if Ann can contact Shelby Kim," Kyle said as Ann approached. "Tell Tippy Pepperidge that we'll be at Brookview tomorrow."

Ann sat down at the table.

"Want some coffee?" Corey asked. "Something to wake you up after a boring night out in Bar Harbor?"

She hoped this was his way of telegraphing that he hadn't shared the excitement of the previous evening with Kyle.

"Sure," she said, and began to stand, but Corey waved her back into the chair.

"Our new PA can bring you some," he said with a grin. He nodded to the young woman, then turned back to Kyle. "I'm not jerking Tippy Pepperidge around and risk having her rethink her willingness to let us shoot on her property. Plus, we might need to line up a boat if Shelby's spirit is near the rocks rather than at the clifftop. We'll go to Otter Cliff tomorrow."

"Maybe she'll be gone by then," said Kyle. He turned to Ann. "She might be there today but gone tomorrow, right?"

"It's possible. But I agree with Corey about not wanting to jerk Tippy around. We're already skating on thin ice based on your premature announcement of the documentary topic."

"I have to concur," said Hannah, joining them at the table. "Tippy Pepperidge is not a woman who appreciates sudden changes of plans."

Kyle threw up his hands. "Okay. Fine."

"We want to do everything we can to keep Ms. Pepperidge happy and show our gratitude for her cooperation," said Corey. "For example, we don't want a convoy of cars showing up at Brookview, so we're going to take just two vehicles over—I'll take most of us in the Suburban, and Chet, Marty, and," he shot an amused look at Ann, "our new PA can follow in the van."

The young woman appeared at the table with a steaming cardboard cup of coffee, along with a few packets of sugar and creamer.

"Thank you," said Ann, taking the coffee cup.

The PA looked at her, smiling tentatively.

"Do you recognize your old buddy?" Corey asked Ann, suppressing a laugh.

Ann was racking her brain, although she was certain she hadn't met this woman before, when something about the shy enthusiasm rang a bell.

"Mace?" she asked, astounded. The black crewcut that the young woman had had the last time Ann had seen her had been replaced by shoulder-length blond hair, the dark eyeliner by a scrubbed-clean look, the frayed denim jacket and combat boots by bell bottoms and a T-shirt with *The Crew* neatly hand-embroidered on the front. The ear studs, nose rings, and lip rings were gone. "I didn't recognize you."

The young woman grinned. "Quite a change, right?" If her clearer speech were any indication, the tongue post was gone as well.

"The new look suits you," said Ann.

"Yeah, my mom likes it better, too. And she's super excited about me getting the PA job. She made the T-shirt. Made ones for Chet and Marty, too."

"I like it," Chet called from across the warehouse. "I don't think I've ever had a *Crew* T-shirt before."

"Do you want one?" the young woman asked Ann eagerly. "My mom can whip one up in no time."

"Ann's not *The Crew*," said Kyle. "She's the talent. So what's the backstory about the two of you?" he asked, clearly irritated at being left out of the joke.

"Mace worked at the inn where Scott and I stayed in South-west Harbor," said Ann. "And she was with Scott when he showed up at Lynam's Point Hotel."

"You're the one who took the video?" Kyle asked the young woman, his interest clearly piqued.

She blushed. "Yeah, that was me." She turned to Ann. "Sorry if that caused you problems."

Ann shrugged. She would have preferred that the video had not hit the internet, but it was water under the bridge. "No problem. Just no unauthorized video on this project."

Mace shook her head vigorously.

"We already have that as a condition of *Maisie's* employment by Authentic Productions," said Corey.

"Maisie?" asked Ann.

"Yeah, *Mace* was part of the whole Goth thing," said the young woman. "It was just a phase."

Ann suppressed a smile. Maisie looked like she was barely out of her teens, and Ann suspected she had many such phases ahead of her.

Corey glanced at his watch. "If we leave soon, we can be at Brookview at the time Leo Dorn fell." He glanced toward Ann. "That will be helpful, right?"

"It can't hurt. It'll also be about the same time I encountered him there."

Corey and Maisie went to help Chet and Marty finish loading the equipment and Kyle wandered to a corner of the warehouse to take a phone call, leaving Ann at the table with Hannah.

"Do you know if there have been any developments since they found the piece of Shelby's jacket?" asked Ann.

"Not that I've heard," said Hannah, "and the authorities promised to keep me and Ms. Pepperidge apprised of any developments."

Ann and Hannah chatted about the history of the Manset waterfront and the best dish at The Perch—Hannah recommended the meatloaf—until Corey announced it was time to head out.

"Maisie," he said, "why don't you ride in the equipment van with Chet and Marty. The rest of us will take the Suburban."

"How about the food that's left?" asked Maisie.

Kyle, who was topping up his coffee, said, "Leave it. We'll order more if we need it."

Maisie shrugged and trotted across the warehouse to the door.

Ann went to the table and grabbed a danish.

"It seems a shame to waste perfectly good food," said Hannah. She began pulling plastic wrap over the tray of pastries. "We should take this with us in case anyone gets hungry later on."

When the food was packed up, they went down the street to where Corey's Suburban was parked. Since Hannah was carrying the tray of pastries, Ann ceded the roomier front seat to her and got in back with Kyle.

"Where's Garrick?" asked Ann.

"He declined the carpool request," said Corey.

"I guess he hates driving less than he hates being in a car with other people," she said.

"We'd save ourselves a lot of headaches if we were working just with Ann," said Kyle, and gave a *but what can you do?* shrug.

As they drove north on 102, Ann turned around to check for the Jetta, but couldn't see past the equipment van behind them. When Corey made the right turn onto Route 3, she turned again and scanned the traffic behind the van, which appeared to be gratifyingly free of red hatchbacks.

When they got to the entrance of Brookview, Max Durgin

was waiting for them at the gate. Corey rolled down the window and Durgin stepped to the driver's door.

"Mr. Duff?" asked Durgin, then saw the other passengers. "Hey, Dr. Jeskie. Hey, Miss Kinnear. How're you doing?"

"Fine, Max," said Hannah. "How are you?"

"Well as can be expected," he said. His eyes went to Kyle. "And you're Kyle Lathey?"

Kyle buzzed his window down. "In the flesh."

He stuck out a hand and Durgin gave it a peremptory shake.

"The rest of the crew is in the van behind us," said Corey.

"Very good," said Durgin. He pulled out his phone and tapped. The gate swung open. "Megan will meet you at the house and show you where to park."

"Has Garrick Masser gotten here yet?" asked Corey.

"Not yet, but I'll send him up when he does."

The Suburban and the equipment van passed through the gate and wended their way up the drive.

"Quite a spread," said Kyle, gazing around appreciatively.

He revised his opinion when they got to the top of the drive. "You'd think that if they have the cash for the property, they could do better with the house."

Megan was waiting for them on the porch, a puffy black jacket over her uniform of black skinny jeans and starched white shirt. She ventured down the stairs to the drive to wave the Suburban and the van into the parking area behind the giant rhododendron, then returned to the porch.

When they climbed out, Hannah said, "Let me bring Megan over and make introductions." She crossed the drive, spoke briefly with Megan, then the two of them came to where the vehicles were parked.

Hannah introduced Megan to Chet, Marty, and Maisie—whom Corey was now referring to as the Crew—then introduced Corey and Kyle.

"*Very* pleased to meet you," said Kyle with a blinding smile as he took Megan's hand.

Ann wondered if Sarah Jane Finney was expecting a call from Kyle ... and whether she would get one.

"And I believe you already know Ann Kinnear," said Hannah to Megan.

"Yes. Hi," said Megan, not meeting Ann's eyes.

Megan seemed more distracted than she had on Ann and Garrick's visit the previous day. Ann wondered if it was due to Kyle: either Megan was so impressed that she didn't have eyes for anyone else, or she was so put off by his manner that she was hoping to disengage herself from the whole group. Ann hoped for Megan's sake that it was the second.

"Looks like you'll have a nice day for filming," Megan said. "We've set up a couple of chairs from the house on the bridge like Maisie requested. We weren't sure if you'd want one or two ..." She laughed weakly. "Arranging seating for a ghost is new to me. We also brought out some chairs for the crew."

"That's great—we really appreciate it," said Corey. "Can you send Garrick Masser along when he arrives?"

"Sure. I'll wait here, as long as you can get to the bridge on your own."

Her gaze flickered to Ann, then slid off.

Ann considered another possible reason for Megan's changed demeanor. Maybe she considered Ann to be a rival for Kyle's attention. Ann could have set Megan's mind at ease on that front.

"No problem," said Ann. "Oh," she added, "hold on, I have something for you." She jogged back to the Suburban, retrieved the umbrella from the back seat, and brought it back to where the group was standing. "Thanks for the loan," she said, handing the umbrella to Megan.

"That wasn't necessary," said Megan, "but thanks."

The Crew finished getting the van unloaded and Corey pulled a laptop bag from the back of the Suburban. Then the group started down the path that Ann had followed the previous day.

When they got to the stream, they found two venerable wing chairs arranged on the bridge, and a half dozen stackable plastic patio chairs to one side of the path.

Hannah seemed a little winded from the walk and plopped down on one of the wing chairs. "My goodness, I guess walking the halls of Stata Mater doesn't really count as exercise."

The overnight rains had raised the level of the stream considerably and Corey began a conversation with Chet about how to handle the sound of the water in the audio recording. Marty and Maisie began setting up equipment.

Ann wandered onto the bridge and looked up and down the stream. Birds twittered in the trees and sunlight sparkled off beads of moisture in the branches. It was certainly the prettiest day they had had since arriving on MDI—although maybe not the somber atmosphere that Corey might have preferred for a discussion with a dead man.

Marty arrived on the bridge and began setting up the cameras.

Corey joined them a moment later, carrying the laptop bag and trailed by Kyle.

"Where's Masser?" asked Kyle irritably. "We have to get going."

"It'll take us a little bit to set up," said Corey. "We don't need him here yet."

"We're making a lot of allowances for him," said Kyle. "I don't like it." He strode away, evidently to oversee something that Marty and Maisie were doing.

"I hope to God the backers don't plan on having Kyle be my minder for the follow-on projects we're discussing," muttered

Corey to Ann. He pulled a laptop out of the case. "Of course, we're only going to be able to capture Garrick's side of the conversation, but it would be great to have a record of what Leo's saying. Would you mind taking some notes?"

She took the laptop from him. "Sure, no problem."

A few minutes later, Marty had gotten the camera and some reflectors set up and trained on the wing chairs.

Hannah braced her hands on the arms of the chair, ready to relinquish her seat, but Marty waved her back. "You can be our stand-in for Garrick," he said. "Although your coloring isn't quite right."

"Looks like my height isn't quite right either," she said, gesturing down the path. "Here comes Mr. Masser now."

Garrick was walking slowly up the path toward them, his fingers massaging his neck to one side of his Adam's apple—the carotid massage that Ann knew he used to quiet his heart. His escort wasn't Megan, but Tippy Pepperidge. She was following him, seeming to let Garrick set the pace, and Ann wondered if she knew about Garrick's weak heart.

However, as they approached, Ann revised her explanation for the pair's slow pace. Tippy glanced around the area with what Ann would have called, in any other person, nervousness, then said emphatically, "Well, there they are," and turned and hurried back down the path. It seemed more likely that she was regretting her decision to accompany Garrick to the site of a planned conversation with her dead husband.

Hannah relocated to one of the plastic patio chairs and the Crew got Garrick settled in one of the wing chairs on the bridge and made the required adjustments to the reflectors and camera position.

Ann pulled a chair over near the bridge, outside of camera range but within earshot.

"Garrick," said Corey, "as much as possible, try to repeat

what Leo has to say. Obviously, we don't have any way of capturing his side of the conversation, but Ann is going to be taking notes, so it will be helpful for you to repeat it for the camera."

"Very well."

"Sort of like when a speaker with a mic is taking questions from the audience and repeats them for the benefit of people who might not have heard them."

"Yes, I understand the concept," said Garrick irritably.

"And if you need to say something to me while we're shooting—"

"I can't imagine that that will be necessary."

Corey sighed. "Fine."

"Here comes Leo," called Ann.

"Places, everyone," said Corey.

25

G arrick stood as Leo Dorn descended the path toward the bridge. Ann thought Leo looked, if possible, even more substantial than he had the previous day. Hannah rose from her chair, scanning the area in which Ann and Garrick were looking.

Leo paused on the path and looked over the group. He gave Ann a nod, then his gaze rested on Hannah for a moment, perhaps wondering if she sensed his presence. When Hannah's uncertain expression didn't change, he resumed his walk to the bridge.

"Garrick Masser, I presume," he said.

"Dr. Dorn," said Garrick. He waved Leo into one of the chairs and both the men sat.

Leo crossed his legs and looked around at the assembled equipment and crew. "This is certainly unlike any interview I've ever done before."

Garrick was silent for a moment, then said, "So you say that this is certainly unlike any interview you've ever done before."

Leo smiled politely. "Exactly."

After another pause, Garrick said, "So you concur that this is exactly that."

"Garrick," called Corey from behind the camera, "you don't have to repeat *everything* Leo says."

"And which parts would you want me to repeat?" said Garrick, although it was a bit hard to understand him since he was evidently trying to move his lips as little as possible.

"Just the parts that are germane to the topic. Also, you can talk normally if you need to say something to me—we'll just edit out those parts."

"You might have explained that more clearly before we started," said Garrick in his normal voice. Leo was trying unsuccessfully to hide his amusement—although he needed to worry about its impact only on Garrick and Ann.

Garrick crossed his legs, now looking a bit more comfortable, and returned his attention to Leo. "Allow me to jump immediately to the topic at hand, Dr. Dorn. Can you describe the circumstances of your fall?"

Leo's amused expression faded. He glanced toward Hannah, who had lowered herself back onto her chair, then returned his attention to Garrick. "It's all a bit of a blur. One moment I was on the path, then next I was ... well, on the rocks, but obviously not merely injured. Many years ago, I had a minor medical procedure and recall coming out of anesthesia, gradually becoming aware of my surroundings. The experience was very similar." He paused. "Is that common?"

Garrick repeated Leo's response for the benefit of the audio recording, then said, "Based on the experiences of those spirits with whom I have communicated, I believe it is common. I understand Shelby Kim was with you when you fell?"

"She had stopped by Brookview on the spur of the moment to ask me if I would like to go for a hike. It was such a nice day—

dry and clear after a cold, rainy stretch—that I was happy to say yes."

Garrick continued to repeat Leo's responses.

"Do you recall where she was, exactly, when you fell?" Garrick asked.

Leo glanced again at Hannah, then looked back at Garrick, his gaze speculative. "I suspect you—or at least the police—would have a better sense of that than I would, since, as I mentioned, my recollection of the event is hazy. I assume Shelby would have provided a statement after the event. What does she say happened?"

"I'm afraid I'm not privy to the information she shared with the police." Changing topics, Garrick asked, "Are you aware that a young man entered the Brookview property without permission and fell from a narrow ledge not far from where yourself fell?"

"Yes, I was aware of that but, again, that was a confused time for me. I knew there was a person on the path, I was vaguely aware that something bad had happened to him. I understand he survived?"

"He survived but was badly injured."

"I'm very sorry to hear that."

"His name was Brian Geary. Do you know him?"

"No. If he was a member of the media, Hannah Jeskie might be a better source of information. She handled all of Stata Mater's media relations."

When Garrick conveyed Leo's suggestion, Ann glanced up from her transcription duties to steal a glance at Hannah. Hannah was perched on the edge of the chair, her hands folded so tightly in her lap that her knuckles were white. She looked very much like most of the clients Ann had worked for—eager to believe that the dead could be contacted but alarmed when the contact occurred.

"I would call Mr. Geary a member of the media in only the most imprecise sense," said Garrick. "I understand that he posts content on YouTube."

"Ah. I have to say that YouTube is not one of the media outlets that SMT focused on," said Leo with a smile.

Garrick re-crossed his legs. "As I believe my colleague Miss Kinnear told you, Shelby Kim has disappeared."

Leo's smile faded. "Yes, she did tell me that."

"Miss Kinnear discovered Dr. Kim's cell phone at the top of Otter Cliff."

"She did? That I didn't know. Does anyone know how it got there?"

"Not definitively. But since then, authorities have discovered a piece of cloth thought to be from Dr. Kim's jacket in the rocks at the base of the cliff."

Leo's eyes widened. He looked down at his clasped hands, then back up at Garrick. "That is very bad news indeed."

"Do you have any insight into what might have happened to her?"

"Well, certainly the discovery of her phone at the top of the cliff and a piece of her clothing in the rocks at the bottom suggests that she fell. I suppose she might have slipped and dropped the phone as she was trying to regain her balance ..."

"Or as she was trying to fend off an attacker."

Leo sat forward. "Do you have evidence of that?"

"No. I am merely speculating about possible scenarios."

"Why would someone attack Shelby?"

"That is one of the questions upon which we were hoping you might shed some light."

"I have no idea."

"Another possibility," continued Garrick, "is that Dr. Kim placed the phone there before jumping from the cliff."

Leo sat back in his chair. "Good lord."

"Do you have any reason to suspect that Dr. Kim might take her own life?"

"Absolutely not."

"Might Dr. Kim have been so distraught at your death that she was driven to suicide?"

"I can't imagine that. Shelby and I were very fond of each other, but that reaction would seem excessive. Even seeing a friend fall to his death, traumatic as I'm sure that was for her ..." His eyes narrowed. "And friends is all we were. Friends and colleagues. My wife is a friend to her as well. I hope you're not suggesting some inappropriate relationship between me and Shelby Kim."

"Merely exploring some of the various theories that are springing up to explain these events."

"Well, you can put that theory to rest."

Garrick nodded. "Very well." He rearranged his long legs again. "I understand from the news conference Dr. Jeskie held after your death that Stata Mater was preparing to announce a major advance in your research. Might there be a connection among your death, Dr. Kim's disappearance, and the planned announcement?"

Leo appeared to relax a bit. "Not that I can imagine. Not wanting to speculate on conversations related to the announcement that may have occurred after my death, I would refer you to Dr. Jeskie for more information. In fact," he said, glancing toward Hannah, "might we involve Dr. Jeskie in our conversation?"

Garrick restated Leo's request for Corey's benefit.

"Absolutely," said Kyle.

Corey shot an angry look at Kyle. "One director on the set, Lathey," he said. He turned to Hannah. "Would you be willing to participate?" he asked.

Hannah, who was looking a bit flustered by the proceedings,

nodded, stood, and patted her hair. "If you think it will be useful."

Ann flexed her fingers, grateful for a temporary reprieve from typing.

Corey looked toward Maisie. "Can we get another chair out here?"

With a slight smile, Leo rose from his chair. "I can stand."

There was a brief break while Chet and Marty adjusted the cameras and reflectors to accommodate Hannah, then recording resumed.

"Perhaps you could ask Hannah if she believes these events are related to the upcoming SMT announcement," suggested Leo.

Garrick posed the question to Hannah.

"I can't imagine they would be," she said. "We've never had an announcement of a new technical development that was greeted by anything other than enthusiasm."

"There is no one in the fire prevention and suppression industries who would feel otherwise?" asked Garrick.

"Well ..." Hannah looked around uncertainly, perhaps disconcerted by Leo Dorn's invisible presence.

"There might be those who would be less enthused?" pressed Garrick. "It seems that every scientific advance is likely to prove a disruption to those established in that sector. And disruptions are rarely welcomed."

"Shelby Kim had improved upon an existing technology," said Hannah.

"And would the manufacturers of that technology welcome Dr. Kim's improvement?" asked Garrick.

"They will need to retool their operations a bit, but they'll have access to all the data they need to enable them to take advantage of the new development. They may experience a temporary disruption, but the result will be products that are far superior to what they and their competitors can offer today."

Garrick probed the topic a bit, but neither Hannah nor Leo would move from their position that the ultimate benefits to the industry far outweighed any short-term negative impacts, and that others in the fire prevention and suppression industry would recognize this.

Garrick then ran through the various other theories espoused by members of the documentary team and hinted at in the news reports, including an illicit affair gone wrong and a revenge killing by a thwarted lover. Leo and Hannah dismissed them for all the reasons others had: the height and weight difference between Shelby and Leo that would have made an attack on Aldrich Hill an unlikely cause of Leo's fall, Tippy Pepperidge's obvious fondness for Shelby Kim.

Just as it appeared that Garrick had exhausted his supply of questions, a voice came from off-camera: "There's another twist to all this."

Cast and crew turned toward Kyle.

"Lathey," said Corey, "you may be the babysitter for this production, but you're not the subject. Stow it."

"Bear with me, Duff—you're going to like this." Kyle stepped toward the chairs where Garrick and Hannah sat, and where Leo Dorn stood.

Chet glanced toward Corey, who threw up his hands, then nodded and dropped heavily onto the chair that Hannah had vacated. Chet reframed the shot to include Kyle.

"I've gotten some interesting information from sources close to the investigation," said Kyle.

Ann thought back to Kyle's departure from the restaurant with Sarah Jane Finney and had a pretty good idea who the source was.

"When the police contacted Shelby Kim's parents,"

continued Kyle, "they learned that the family's bakery burned down the night after Leo fell to his death and the same night that it seems that Shelby disappeared. The preliminary investigation suggests that the fire might have been accidentally set off by the younger Kim daughter, Stacy. The police say that if Shelby is alive, they want to speak with her about these events."

"I don't believe that this has any bearing—" began Hannah.

Kyle ignored her and continued. "It turns out that before Hannah and I got to Otter Cliff the morning when the search for Shelby began, Jonathan Garrido, who has a key to Shelby Kim's car, searched her car, ostensibly looking for a clue as to her whereabouts."

"What is this—?" began Hannah again.

"He says he found a flash drive in the car. Then, after we found Shelby's phone near the cliff edge, and after we had all given our statements at the police station, he went home and checked the contents of the drive. He returned to the police station and turned it over to them. Not realizing that it belonged to Shelby and not to Jonathan, they opened the file it contained." He looked around expectantly, clearly enjoying playing out the suspense.

"And what did they find?" asked Hannah, her brow furrowing.

"A video of a man going into a building that blows up shortly after he enters it."

"Oscar?" asked Hannah, her face relaxing into surprise.

"What?" said Kyle, evidently not expecting this response.

"Oscar Sanz?"

Kyle crossed his arms. "Who's Oscar Sanz?"

"Oscar Sanz was a consultant who worked with Stata Mater a couple of years ago," she replied. "Some time after he had left SMT, he was killed in an explosion in Mexico while on another consulting engagement, as I recall. There was an investigation, and it was determined to be an accident—a gas leak that was most likely ignited when Oscar lit a cigarette." She shook her head. "I recall that he did take a great many smoke breaks."

"Ironic that an SMT consultant happened to die in a building explosion," said Kyle.

"*Former* SMT consultant at the time of his death."

"Still."

"Just because an occurrence is ironic does not necessarily mean it is suspicious." Hannah's initial alarm at Kyle's unscripted intrusion was moderating into annoyance that she had been alarmed needlessly. "If you're interested, I can put you in touch with the investigators."

Kyle rallied. "Why would Shelby Kim have a flash drive with video of the explosion in her car—assuming that is, in fact, where it came from?"

"News of the explosion was the primary topic at the SMT water cooler for some time," said Hannah, "although that was before Shelby joined us. Perhaps someone at SMT had downloaded the video, which was available on the internet, to one of the servers and Shelby found it there. Maybe someone mentioned it and she was curious and downloaded it herself. Researchers in fire prevention and suppression have a legitimate professional interest in studying those types of video resources."

"But why would she have it on a flash drive in her car?" pressed Kyle.

"I really have no idea, Mr. Lathey," said Hannah, her patience evidently exhausted. "But I would caution you not to pursue your inquiry further with SMT staff or we'll consider it harassment."

"Shelby Kim was already studying fire technology when that explosion occurred," said Kyle. "Maybe she—"

"Lathey," said Corey. "Stand down."

Everyone turned to Corey. His mouth was pressed into a thin line, his expression stormy, his hands balled into fists.

"Chet, stop rolling," he said.

Chet flipped a switch, and the glowing red indicator went dark.

"Ladies and gentlemen," said Corey, "we're done here."

When Corey told Kyle to wait for the rest of them back at the Brookview house, Ann was relieved that Kyle had the sense not to argue. As the Crew began to strike equipment and wrap cables, the rest of them congregated on the bridge.

"I would like to apologize for that," said Corey to Hannah. "Obviously we can't have Kyle Lathey on location while we're shooting. I'll do my best to make sure that will be the case going forward. If I can ensure his absence, I hope you'll be willing to put in a good word with Ms. Pepperidge to allow us to come back to Brookview another day to continue our conversation with Dr. Dorn, and I hope you'll be willing to participate."

Hannah looked with irritation toward Kyle's retreating form. "If we can ensure his absence, I would consider it."

"Thank you." Corey scanned the area, his gaze passing through the space where Leo stood next to Hannah's chair. "And Dr. Dorn ...?"

"Yes, I would consider it as well," said Leo.

Garrick conveyed Leo's response to Corey.

Corey turned to Ann. "If we can get approval for a return

visit, can you come back to Brookview and let Dr. Dorn know when we'll be shooting again?"

"Sure."

"Okay, thanks everybody. Let's get packed up," said Corey.

He went to help the Crew, while Garrick retired a little way down the path, his hands clasped behind him. Ann, Hannah, and Leo remained on the bridge.

"I hope the police aren't looking at Jonathan as a suspect in Shelby's disappearance," said Leo. "He's been with SMT for years, and his record—professionally and personally—is exemplary. We run thorough background checks on anyone we're considering hiring."

Ann repeated his words for Hannah's benefit.

Hannah nodded. "I will certainly vouch for Jonathan with the authorities." She sighed. "It's upsetting that Mr. Lathey seems both to be implicating Jonathan and to be continuing to propagate this rumor about Shelby and Leo. I wish we could nip that in the bud. It's not like she was looking around for a boyfriend. I believe she and Jonathan had been dating for several months. She was always friendly to everyone—was well liked by her fellow researchers—but she was closest to Jonathan. If she were sharing personal information with anyone, it would be with him, and he says he's unaware of anything that would shed light on her disappearance."

"Yes, if anyone could share useful information with the authorities, it would be Jonathan," said Leo, "although I don't doubt that he's shared as much as he knows with them. If the authorities are suspicious of him in any way, that must be rubbing salt in the wound. Hannah, will you make sure he's taken care of?"

When Ann had conveyed Leo's request, Hannah nodded. "Of course."

"Let's hope that there's some alternative explanation for

Shelby's disappearance than that she fell from the cliff," said
Leo. "Her inner strength and resolve far exceed her size—we
shouldn't count her out until we have more definitive evidence
than a scrap of cloth. However, she would no doubt be traumatized by what she's been through. Take care of her as well,
Hannah, if she's found."

"Yes, I will."

Leo and Hannah exchanged farewells through Ann, then
Hannah wandered over to where the last of the equipment was
being packed up.

Leo beckoned Ann to follow him as he began climbing the
path toward the rock steps.

"I don't suppose you've had a chance to get the contents of
the canteen analyzed yet?"

"No. My brother took it to a lab in Bangor today, but I haven't
heard anything from him yet." She was silent for a moment,
then asked, "Did you think of any message you'd like me to
convey to Tippy?"

He stopped. "Ah, yes, a message." He gazed back down the
path, as if to look through the pine woods to where Tippy
Pepperidge no doubt waited at the house for the video crew to
announce the completion of their work. "It can't be easy for her,
having lost two husbands, especially because Frank Judd was
someone she had known since she was a child. Although it
pains me to say it, he was her true soul mate. I know she was
devastated that Garrick Masser couldn't contact him. Part of me
thinks that carrying on some sort of mediated conversation with
me now might reopen that wound." He sighed. "I think it might
be best just to tell her that I love her, I miss her, and I wish her
the best." He turned his gaze back to Ann. "Even if Tippy isn't
willing to continue with the documentary, I assume I'll see you
again, once you have the lab results from the canteen back. If
she hasn't given permission for the documentary team to be on

the property, I could meet you at the studio—no one's likely to see you there."

"I'd rather not be sneaking around behind Tippy's back," said Ann. "Plus, I imagine Max Durgin is going to be a little more diligent about patrolling the grounds after what happened with Brian Geary."

"Then let's hope that Corey is successful in convincing her to continue with the project—and that he's successful in getting rid of Lathey."

"Yes, let's hope," replied Ann.

Leo nodded, then turned and disappeared up the path.

When Ann got back to the bridge, the Crew and most of the equipment were gone, and Corey was straightening from zipping the one remaining canvas case. He surveyed the area. "I need to let Megan know that the chairs can be returned to the house."

"I can let her know," said Hannah. "I want to stop at the house anyway. I live practically right around the corner, and I'm thinking of asking Megan to give me a ride home. I'll make some arrangements to retrieve the car I left in Manset. It will save me another tedious roundtrip today."

Ann was pretty sure it was Kyle Lathey and not a tedious roundtrip that Hannah wanted to avoid. The idea was appealing to her as well. She went over to where Garrick stood.

"Can I hitch a ride back to Manset with you?" she asked.

He drew down his brows.

"I'll drive," she said.

He appeared slightly mollified. "Very well."

"Can we take Hannah, too? It would save her having to arrange to pick up her car in Manset."

"I thought she arrived with you, Mr. Duff, and Mr. Lathey."

"I don't think she wants to drive back with Kyle."

"So you would prefer to allow Mr. Duff and Mr. Lathey to

travel back to Manset together? Alone?"

"Well ... yes. Maybe Corey will seize the opportunity to chew out Kyle."

"How selfless of you to give Mr. Duff that opportunity."

"I'm not claiming it's selfless. I just don't want to ride back with Kyle."

Garrick looked put out again, then gave a theatrical sigh. "Very well."

"Thanks, Garrick—I'll let Hannah know we can give her a ride."

Hannah had started down the path toward Brookview with Corey. Ann trotted to catch up with them.

"Garrick is going to drive me back to Manset," she said, "and he offered to take you, too, Hannah."

"That would be perfect," said Hannah, sounding relieved. "Thank you so much. I'll go ahead and let Megan know about the chairs before we leave."

After Hannah was a little distance ahead, Corey turned to Ann.

"Coward," he said with a tired smile.

"Let me know if he annoys you and I'll pop him in the nose next time I see him," she said.

His smile lightened a bit, then his expression sobered. "Garrick's taking you right to the Manset house?"

"As far as I know. Why?"

"Did you ever hear back from the police about the car that was following you last night?"

She pulled her phone out of her pocket to check for messages or texts. "No ... but I'm not sure I would expect them to report back to me."

"Still, I think you should be careful. Make sure Garrick drops you off right at the house, or that you have someone with you if you're out and about."

They waited for Garrick to catch up with them, then made their way at a sedate pace back to the drive. Hannah was chatting with Megan on the front steps. As they approached the pair, Megan slipped inside.

"Megan will arrange for the chairs to be brought back to the house," said Hannah.

"Great—thanks," Corey said, then peeled off to help the Crew load the van.

Garrick handed Ann the car keys, then stepped to the back door of the Fleetwood, which was parked near the entrance.

"I can sit in back," said Hannah.

"Nonsense," Garrick said and lowered himself into the car.

"He likes sitting back there," said Ann to Hannah. "It makes him feel like he's being chauffeured."

Hannah shrugged cheerfully. "No argument from me," she said, getting in the front passenger seat.

Ann gave a wave as they passed Corey and the Crew. She could see Kyle in the passenger seat of the Suburban, talking on his phone.

They rolled down the drive toward the front gate, Ann driving slower than she normally would in deference to Garrick's general distrust of all things automotive.

"That was quite an experience," said Hannah.

"You can say that again," replied Ann.

"I'm grateful that Corey put a stop to it."

"I would have loved it if he could have put a stop to Kyle Lathey before now," said Ann, "but I think the reprieve might be short-lived. Evidently Kyle is the backers' golden boy."

They rode in silence for a few moments, then Hannah said, "Leo seemed genuinely concerned about what might have happened to Shelby. Do the dead always continue to be interested in or care about what's happening in the ..." She hesitated. "... 'real world'?"

"I guess it's still the 'real world' to them," said Ann.

"You'd think they'd have other things on their minds," said Hannah.

"Such as?" asked Garrick.

"The larger questions of life and death."

"The very fact of their continued existence in this sphere suggests that they are not prepared to face the larger questions of life and death, the answers to which might enable them to move on."

"A lot of times they stay behind because they still have a stake in this world," said Ann.

"Just so," said Garrick. "Now please pay attention to the road."

"Garrick, you know it is possible for a person to talk and drive safely at the same time," said Ann.

"It's ill-advised."

They completed the rest of the trip to Manset in silence.

"My car's right up there," said Hannah, pointing to a sedate-looking BMW parked at the side of the road a dozen yards from the warehouse.

As Ann pulled up to it, Garrick said, "By the way, where is your brother?"

"He drove up to Bangor to take care of something," said Ann.

"For you?"

"Yes."

"Running your errands?"

"Well, I suppose you could say that." She glanced in the rearview mirror and noted that the news seemed to have cheered him up.

"I appreciate the detour, Garrick," said Ann as they all climbed out of the Fleetwood.

"Yes, thank you very much," said Hannah.

"Certainly," he said, tilting a slight bow toward the women.

He lowered himself into the driver's seat and, after making a tiny but time-consuming adjustment to the rear view mirror, coasted majestically down the road.

Hannah's eyes followed the car as it rolled to an extended stop at the intersection then turned toward Seawall Road and rolled slowly out of sight.

"He's certainly a cautious driver," she said. She turned to Ann with a smile. "And a nervous passenger."

"It makes me crazy to be in the car with him if he's driving," said Ann. "It's better all-around if I drive."

"Of course, I know what happened to the two of you at Lynam's Point," said Hannah. "Everyone on MDI does, but had you known each other before that?"

"A few years—we actually met during the shooting of another documentary Corey made called *The Sense of Death*."

"And it sounds like he knows your brother as well?"

"Yes, my brother Mike. He's my business manager."

"I'm guessing that, based on Garrick's pleasure at the news that Mike was out running errands for you, the two of them are not close friends?"

"That's putting it mildly. Garrick thinks Mike is a disrespectful upstart and Mike thinks Garrick is a pompous ass."

Hannah laughed. "And is there any truth in either of those accusations?"

Ann nodded, laughing as well. "Oh, yes. Both."

"So I suppose I'll see you again if Corey is able to arrange a return visit to Brookview," said Hannah.

"Do you want to come by the house where Mike and I are staying?" asked Ann. "We could stop by The Perch and pick up some beer." Ann glanced at her watch. "And we could get some takeout if you're hungry."

Hannah looked pleased. "That would be lovely. Thank you."

27

Ann and Hannah stopped at The Perch for beer and lobster rolls. With her brother in mind, Ann added a second six-pack and a third lobster roll. When Eric handed over the bill along with the food and drink, Hannah snagged it.

"That's not necessary," said Ann. "It's mostly stuff for me and Mike."

"Consider it my thank you for saving me from the inconvenience of trying to get back to Manset without a car," said Hannah, "or the aggravation of having to ride back with Kyle Lathey."

With dinner supplies in hand, they walked the couple of blocks to the house. There was no car in the driveway, and no one in the house.

"I'm surprised Mike isn't here," said Ann.

She pulled out her phone and tapped out a text: *Back in Manset—you?*

In a moment, his response came back. *Having dinner out—care to join?*

I'm in for the evening ... have fun

"My brother, the social butterfly," she said to Hannah. "Looks like it'll just be the two of us."

She put Mike's lobster roll in the refrigerator and got out plates for herself and Hannah.

When she reached for a glass on one of the kitchen shelves, Hannah said, "No need for a glass for me. I'm a beer-in-the-bottle girl."

Ann thought that the sofa and love seat would be more comfortable than stools at the kitchen island, so she led Hannah into the living room. Ann sat down on the couch and Hannah put her plate and beer bottle on an end table next to the loveseat.

"This is a darling house," said Hannah. She went to the shelves of albums and began flipping through them. "Oh, Joni Mitchell! I love Joni." She pulled out an album. "*Clouds*. That was my favorite."

"Want to put it on?"

Hannah laughed and slipped the album back onto the shelf. "If you did, you'd never get rid of me. I'd want to listen to the whole Joni Mitchell canon." She flipped through a few more albums. "And it looks like they have it."

She sat down and took a sip of beer. "I have to admit that when I first learned, years ago, that Tippy had hired Garrick Masser when her first husband died, I was surprised—shocked, even. She seemed like such a practical woman," she looked at Ann with a somewhat sheepish expression, "and it seemed like such an impractical pursuit. But when Leo and I won the Stata Mater grant and I got to know her better and grew to respect her, I reconsidered my position. Today, I didn't find myself questioning the information you and Garrick said you were learning from Leo." She laughed. "No one is that good an actor." She shook her head. "Quite an experience. For me, at least. I suppose it's not as noteworthy for you."

"It's not as unique for me as it is for most people, but it's not every day that I speak with a dead person, and certainly not every day that I get to see Garrick do it." She took a sip of beer. "And not every day that I get to see Corey lay into someone."

"He seems like the kind of man who would be slow to get riled up."

"That's for sure."

"Slow to simmer down as well?"

Ann laughed. "No, I think he's fast to simmer down—otherwise I wouldn't have trusted him alone with Kyle for the ride back."

Hannah laughed and took a bite of lobster roll. "I saw you were taking notes during the conversation," she said, dabbing her mouth delicately with one of the handful of napkins Eric had added to the takeout bag.

Ann shrugged. "I was the only person available who could take dictation."

"You were able to capture it all?"

"Most of it. I'm a fast typist."

"Will Corey use your transcript in the documentary?"

"I'm actually not sure how he's planning to use it. Obviously, a video of Garrick talking to thin air won't be particularly compelling, even though Garrick was conveying what Leo said."

"I'm curious—when you find yourself in that type of situation, having to mediate a conversation between a living person and a dead person—do you relay the words verbatim, or do you summarize?"

"I think Garrick and I both try to relay the words verbatim, because you never know when a rewording that seems innocent will change the meaning that the spirit intends to convey. For the transcript, I couldn't catch it all, so that's more of an approximation."

Hannah set aside her roll and sat forward. "As the person

responsible for looking out for the interests of Tippy Pepperidge and Stata Mater, I feel that I should review the transcript to confirm there isn't any information in there that would violate Tippy's conditions."

"You'd have to talk with Corey about that," said Ann. "I'm sure you have plenty of time—it's not like he's going to air the documentary tomorrow, especially after today's dust-up. Maybe you can talk to him about having a chance to review all the material before it's finalized."

"Your notes are on your laptop?"

"They're on Corey's laptop."

"And that's being kept in a secure location?"

"As far as I know, but we can check with him to make sure."

"I hate to be distrustful," said Hannah, "but I'm specifically wondering if it's accessible to Kyle Lathey."

Ann smiled grimly. "Ah, yes, I see where you're going. It's a good point. I could text Corey and ask him about it."

"Could you? As I say, I hate to be distrustful, but I would feel better if I knew that only Corey—and you—had access to it."

Ann put her beer aside, got out her phone, and tapped out a message to Corey. She and Hannah chatted about Joni Mitchell until a text pinged into Ann's phone. She checked the message.

"He said that the laptop is with him and that he'll be sure to keep it in a secure location."

"I appreciate that. Please thank him for me."

Ann tapped back a response, then slipped the phone back into her pocket.

"Did you know Shelby Kim well?" Ann asked. She sighed. "I suppose I should say 'do you know,' although I have to say I'm not holding out much hope that she's alive."

Hannah sank back against the cushions of the loveseat. "Yes, I agree." She was silent for a few moments, then continued. "She was really a charming young lady. So committed to the work

Stata Mater did. She was very often the last person to leave the office at night."

"Working late ... with Leo Dorn?"

Hannah gave a sad laugh. "Not only is Leo Dorn not one to burn the midnight oil, but I truly think there was nothing going on between the two of them. Shelby idolized Leo, but she idolized Tippy, too, and she isn't someone to betray a person she idolizes. I've certainly never seen anything to suggest that Tippy is suspicious or jealous of Shelby."

"I'm surprised that Tippy doesn't seem interested in speaking with Leo, especially since she tried to contact her first husband through Garrick."

"Tippy and Leo weren't a particularly demonstrative couple."

Ann waited, but Hannah just sipped her beer.

"What was driving Shelby to burn the midnight oil?" asked Ann.

Hannah gazed toward the wall of albums. After a few moments, she said, "When Shelby was sixteen, there was a fire at her home. She and her mother got out of the house with minor injuries, but her father was hospitalized—smoke inhalation, suffered when he ran back into the building to try to rescue her sister, Stacy, who was thirteen at the time. Stacy survived, but was badly burned. She still lives with her parents and works in the bakery."

"The bakery that burned?"

Hannah nodded sadly. "Yes. The bakery that burned."

"It does seem like a stretch that it would be a coincidence."

"Although I hate to say it, I can't disagree." She dabbed her lips with the napkin again. "Because of my work with Stata Mater, I have contacts with fire investigators across the country. I believe I know the person who would be in charge of an investigation in the Kim family's hometown—might even have been in charge of the investigation of the fire at their home all those years ago. If you can give me a few minutes, I might be able to find out what they've learned."

"Of course."

To give Hannah some privacy, and because she needed another beer, Ann went to the kitchen. She popped the top off another bottle then, almost guiltily, got out her phone, opened the browser, and typed in *oscar sanz explosion*. She clicked the first result.

A video thumbnail displayed black letters on a white background: *WARNING: Some viewers may find the following video disturbing. Viewer discretion is advised.* After a brief pause, she clicked *Play*.

The video showed sand-colored commercial buildings on a sand-colored city street, the occasional dusty car passing by. After a few seconds, a middle-aged man appeared, walking down the sidewalk. He stopped at the door of one of the buildings, drew something out of his pocket—evidently a ring of keys —then opened the door and stepped inside. For a moment, he was visible through the glass-enclosed entrance relocking the door, then he turned and moved out of view.

Based on what Kyle and Hannah had said at the Brookview shoot, she knew what was going to happen, but she jumped nonetheless when the building disappeared in a soundless brown cloud of dirt and debris, which began raining down around the camera a few seconds later. As the dust cleared, she could see flames shooting up from the rubble. It was hard to imagine that anyone had found Oscar Sanz in that rubble, much less the cigarette that authorities evidently thought he had lit. She let the video play to the end—only a few more seconds— then slipped the phone back into her pocket.

When she heard Hannah wrapping up her conversation, she got a beer out of the fridge for Hannah and rejoined her in the living room.

"According to my contact," said Hannah, her face grave, "it appears that Stacy had been working late at the bakery the night of the fire and left the coffee maker plugged in. They suspect that's what started the fire."

"Jesus," said Ann, "that family can't catch a break when it comes to fire."

Hannah suddenly looked alarmed. "I'm speaking out of turn. I intended for that to be off-the-record with regard to the documentary."

Ann handed the beer to Hannah and sat down on the couch. "It's information that Corey would want to know—and no doubt will find out eventually as he does more research on the subjects of the documentary."

Hannah sighed. "I suppose so. I'll talk to him about that tomorrow when I ask him about access to the transcript. He seems like a reasonable young man." She smiled at Ann. "A nice young man, too."

"Yes, very nice."

"And good-looking."

Ann raised an eyebrow.

"Unless young men aren't your thing," said Hannah quickly.

Ann laughed. "No, it's not that. It just—" She stopped to consider what, in fact, it was, then continued. "It's awkward to go on a date when you might be enjoying a conversation in a nice restaurant and see a dead guy over your date's shoulder."

Hannah laughed. "Would that really happen?"

Ann smiled ruefully. "It did happen."

"What did you do?"

"I tried to ignore him."

"Your date?"

Ann laughed. "No, the dead guy."

"Why didn't you just tell your date what you had seen?"

"He didn't know about my ability."

Hannah looked surprised.

"It was before I was more well-known," said Ann. "Before all the ruckus about me and Garrick at the Lynam's Point Hotel."

Hannah sat forward. "But that doesn't explain why he didn't know. Why didn't you tell him about your ability?"

Ann took a long pull of beer. "Because some people think it's cool, but some people just think I'm crazy. Or lying."

"You'll never know unless you try."

Ann's voice hardened. "I did try. Once."

Hannah sat back. "Ah."

"Anyway," said Ann, her voice unnaturally cheerful, "you don't need to listen to my dating woes."

Hannah smiled. "I'm known as the Den Mother of SMT—behind my back, of course—so if you ever need a sympathetic ear, one can be had for a beer. In fact," she said, getting out her phone, "let me send you my contact information."

The conversation drifted back to Joni Mitchell while they finished their beers, then Hannah said, "I really should be going. Thank you for the beer—and for the conversation." She stood. "Do you have any idea what the next steps will be?"

"I suppose Corey will want to follow up on the piece of Shelby's clothing that was found at Otter Cliff. I'm not sure what his plan for that is."

"I imagine Tippy will expect me to be there as well if there will be videotaping. I'll mention that to Corey as well when I talk to him tomorrow."

Hannah put on her coat and they stepped out onto the porch. The temperature had dropped markedly while they had been inside

"Hold on," said Ann, "let me grab my jacket and I'll walk over to the production office with you."

"That's not necessary," said Hannah.

"I'd feel better," said Ann, "with all the weird stuff that's going on. In fact, I'll need to ask you to drop me back here because Corey didn't want me out and about by myself. I think someone followed me last night."

"Really?" said Hannah, looking alarmed. "Do you have any idea who it was?"

"No. Someone in a red Volkswagen Jetta, but I never got a good look at them."

"Oh," said Hannah, looking somewhat relieved. "You were near Brookview?"

"No, they followed me around Southwest Harbor then back to Bar Harbor," said Ann.

Hannah's expression morphed again, to one of confusion. "Really? That's odd."

"Why's that?"

"Because it sounds like Megan's car."

28

Three Weeks Earlier

Shelby groaned as the other Stata Mater staff speculated about what the dessert course would bring. The entrees had been scallops, filet mignon, or miso risotto, depending on the diner's preference.

"I don't think I can do it," she said to Jonathan. "I'm *stuffed*."

"It's up to you to set a good example," he said. "Clean plate and all that."

Troy entered, carrying three bottles of wine in one hand and three wine glasses in the other, and whispered something to Tippy Pepperidge. She said something in reply and gestured toward Leo. Troy nodded and walked down the table to where Leo sat.

"Dr. Dorn, we unfortunately don't have the wine that we had planned to serve with dessert, but we do have several excellent alternatives. Ms. Pepperidge said that you would be the right person to select the replacement."

Leo sat back. "Certainly. I'm afraid that wine connoisseurship is not an interest that my wife shares."

Troy smiled and arranged the glasses and two of the bottles in front of Leo. He opened the third bottle.

"This is a California Cabernet Sauvignon," Troy said as he poured, "that would go well with the chocolate and berries."

A server who looked like she couldn't have been out of high school reached between Leo and Hannah to refill Hannah's water glass. Just as Leo brought the wine glass to his mouth, her water pitcher connected with his arm hard enough to slosh most of the ruby red liquid out of the glass, across the tablecloth, and onto his white shirt.

"Beverly!" gasped Troy, blanching.

"Oh, God," squawked Beverly, attracting the attention of all the guests. "I'm so sorry, Mr. Pepperidge!"

Troy's face achieved a paler shade of whiteness. "Go get *Dr. Dorn* a wet towel," he said through clenched teeth.

Beverly fled from the now-silent dining room.

Leo placed his glass with exaggerated care on the table.

"Dr. Dorn," said Troy, "my deepest apologies—" He grabbed a clean napkin from a nearby server station and held it out to Leo.

Leo ignored it and stood. "I can take care of clean-up on my own, thank you," he muttered and stalked out of the dining room.

There was a moment of tense silence, then Tippy said, "Let's go with that one. It smells delicious."

A wave a relieved laughter rippled around the table.

"Very good, Ms. Pepperidge," said Troy, and scuttled out of the room behind Beverly and Leo.

As conversation resumed, Tippy also rose from the table and left the room.

"Shel," said Jonathan, "watch out—"

Shelby looked down just in time to see a thin trickle of wine leave the table and splash on the leg of her cream-colored pants.

"Oh, no," she groaned.

Jonathan dipped his napkin in his water glass and handed it to her. "Sorry I didn't see it a second earlier," he said, contrite.

"No problem," said Shelby with a sigh. "I think it's going to take more than a wet napkin, though. I'll be right back."

When she stood, she decided that, should the dessert wine actually get served, she would decline it. She had already had a lot more champagne and wine than she was used to. She steadied herself on the back of her chair for a moment. Then, under Jonathan's amused gaze, she made her way purposefully across the dining room.

The restrooms were located between the main room, where the champagne and hors d'oeuvres had been served, and a third dining room, which had not been used for the evening's festivities. Shelby wet a paper towel and, as she dabbed at the stain on her pants, she became aware of the sounds of a conversation taking place in the unused room.

"Good heavens, it's only a shirt. Just clean it up as best you can and stop making Troy suffer for Beverly's awkwardness." Tippy.

"I think you know that I don't care about a ruined shirt." Leo.

"The mix-up with the name? You can't let it bother you, Leo. For every time you get called 'Mr. Pepperidge,' I get called 'Mrs. Dorn.'"

"Not in this restaurant, you don't. Not in Bar Harbor. Not on MDI. Not anywhere where they know you're a Pepperidge."

"This is a ridiculous discussion. One in a string of ridiculous discussions that we've had over the last few days."

Shelby, starting to feel guilty for eavesdropping, had unlocked the door to the restroom and was about to step out when she heard Leo's response.

"Oh, my thoughts about Shelby's invention are ridiculous?"

Shelby eased the door shut, relocked it, and leaned toward the wall.

"Certainly not worth discussing," said Tippy.

"You're the one who brought it up."

"Which I regret."

"We're passing up a unique opportunity with this invention."

"No, Leo, we're following the path that I set Stata Mater on when I established it as a *not-for-profit* concern, and the path it was on when you applied to head it. Once we have done our due diligence, we will share Shelby's invention with others who have the capacity to conduct further tests and to productionize it. That has always been our goal and I don't intend to change it just because we now have this incredible resource to share. *Especially* not now that we have this incredible resource to share."

"That's easy for you to say. You've got the Pepperidge millions behind you."

Tippy's voice turned hard. "And it was the Pepperidge millions that made this invention possible."

"You don't have businesses—for-profit businesses—with bills to pay, equipment and raw materials to purchase, salaries to cover."

"I would argue that I have all those things with Stata Mater, save the profit motive."

"But you don't have creditors breathing down your neck."

"That is certainly true. Perhaps you should divest yourself of those businesses if profit is their goal and if they are not proving profitable."

"It's not that easy. No one wants to buy unprofitable businesses."

"I didn't say it was easy."

Shelby knew she shouldn't be overhearing this conversation, but she couldn't tear herself away.

"If profit is your ultimate motive," continued Tippy, "why did you apply for the Stata Mater grant when you knew it was for a non-profit effort?"

"My other businesses were doing well at the time. I had time and energy to devote to other pursuits."

"Or perhaps you saw it as a way of gaining access to the Pepperidge name. Money. Influence. Status. Is that what drew you to SMT? Is it what drew you to me?"

"Tippy, don't be ridiculous. I believed in Stata Mater's goals, I had the scientific background to help, and I was in a position to enlist others in the field—like Hannah—who I knew could do good work in pursuit of those goals."

"*Believed* in the goals? Meaning you no longer believe in them?"

"Other matters are demanding my attention right now."

"Then by all means, feel free to direct your full attention to those matters. I'll take over management of Stata Mater if you are no longer motivated to do so—or capable of doing so."

"Tippy," Leo's voice was tinged with a pleading tone, "I'm getting in too deep. I have creditors who are getting less and less patient with me."

"Leo, our pre-nuptial agreement says that what you brought to the marriage stays yours, and what I brought to the marriage stays mine." Her voice was icy. "I see no reason to reconsider that agreement now."

Shelby heard steps approaching from the direction of the room where the dinner was being held, and then Troy's voice.

"Ms. Pepperidge. Dr. Dorn. I just wanted to let you know that we've served dessert."

"Thank you, Troy," said Tippy. "We'll be right in."

Troy's footsteps receded toward the dining room.

"I'd suggest calling Megan and asking her to bring you a fresh shirt," said Tippy, "but I don't think we'll be staying much longer." Then her steps followed Troy's.

Shelby pressed her ear against the wall but could hear nothing. She tried to imagine what Leo must be doing, what he must be feeling. A minute ticked by, but there was still no sound from the other side of the wall. Had he returned to the dining room with Tippy, his stride matching hers so that it sounded like a single set of steps?

Shelby almost yelped at a tentative knock on the door.

"Uh ... anyone in there?" asked a female voice.

"Oh, sorry! One minute!" Shelby ran the water for a few seconds then opened the door to find Gretchen, one of the other researchers, standing outside.

"Sorry, didn't mean to rush you," said Gretchen.

"No problem, no problem," Shelby said with a nervous laugh. She slipped by Gretchen and hurried to the dining room.

Tippy had resumed her seat at one end of the table, chatting with one of the researchers seated beside her, her expression bearing no hint of the conversation Shelby had overheard.

Leo entered a few minutes later, stone-faced, and returned to his seat.

"Any luck getting the stain out?" Hannah asked him.

"I decided I'd do more harm than good if I tried," said Leo, with a laugh that perhaps only Shelby noticed was a bit strained.

"Well, it's too bad they wasted any of the wine on your shirt and on the tablecloth," said Hannah, lifting her glass. "It's wonderful with the dessert."

"I'd rather have drunk it than worn it," said Leo. He tried for a joking tone, but this time even Hannah seemed to notice that the tone didn't match his dark mood.

29

Ann woke the next morning to cheerful sunshine and a temperature warmer than she had encountered yet on MDI. She showered, dressed, made a breakfast of coffee, a banana, and a bagel, and was paging through a copy of *Down East Magazine* when her phone rang.

"Hey, Corey," she answered. "Did I miss a crew call?"

"Nope, I'm still sorting things out. I'm at the production office and thought I might find you or Mike here, although I don't know how you'd get past the padlock on the door," he said. "Why's your rental car parked down here?"

She glanced out the window and confirmed that there was, in fact, no Hyundai in the driveway. "I have no idea. I'm pretty sure Mike's upstairs. I heard him come in late last night. Hold on."

She went upstairs and didn't even have to press her ear to the door to hear Mike snoring.

"In his bedroom and out like a light," she told Corey as she returned to the kitchen. "I'll find out what the scoop is when he emerges."

"Did you ever hear from the Mount Desert police about the car that was following you?" he asked.

"No, but I have an idea who it might have been." She topped off her mug, then settled down at the kitchen island to tell Corey about Hannah's visit to the Manset house the previous night, and Hannah's comment that Megan drove the same make and model of car.

"Red Jettas aren't all that unusual," he said slowly, "but it does seem like quite a coincidence."

"You know," said Ann, "as I think back to our trip to Brookview yesterday, Megan was acting kind of weird. Not that we're best buddies, but she was much more friendly when she drove me back to the house after my conversation with Leo. Yesterday it felt like she was going out of her way to avoid me— or going out of her way to avoid talking to me when she couldn't avoid me."

"Maybe it was her in the Jetta, and she knows you know it was her, and she's embarrassed. We know the plate started with ZP—we could check Megan's plate."

"How? I don't know her last name to look up her home address, and I haven't seen a red Jetta at Brookview. I don't much feel like sneaking around trying to find where she parks or staking out the entrance to watch her drive by if Max Durgin is on gatekeeper duty."

"Are you going to talk with her about it? Or Tippy?"

Ann sighed. "I can't imagine that accusing Megan of following me around MDI would improve our standing with either one of them."

"You shouldn't let that keep you from asking them about it."

"It would be embarrassing if it turns out it was someone else. I'll wait to see if I hear back from the police, and I'll keep an eye out. If I see the Jetta again, I'll say something to Megan."

They ended the call and a few minutes later Ann heard steps

descending the stairs, then Mike shuffled into the kitchen. She had been itching to find out what if anything he had learned about the contents of the canteen, but his appearance—pajama-clad and barefoot, his hair askew, bloodshot eyes squinted against the morning light filtering through the kitchen curtains —demanded an explanation.

"Wild night?" she asked.

"Wilder than I expected." He got a mug off the shelf and poured the last of the coffee from the carafe.

"Hey, I was planning on drinking that."

"I'll make more in a minute," he said, sitting down at the kitchen island.

"What time did you get home?"

"A little after midnight."

"Lightweight."

"It's possible to do quite a bit of drinking before midnight if you put your mind to it. Plus, I couldn't resist the siren call of having a designated driver."

"Who were you out with?"

"Kyle."

Her mug halted half-way to her mouth. "Kyle?"

"Yeah. He's actually not so bad one-on-one."

She put her mug on the island. "Is he the one who instigated the boys' night out?"

"Yes."

"When?"

"I don't know—yesterday around four?"

"Damn."

"What?"

"The shoot turned into quite a fiasco, thanks to your new best buddy, Kyle. He must have called you right after Corey shut it down."

"What happened?"

Ann gave him a rundown of the events at the shoot, including the logistical challenges posed by the fact that they had carpooled to Brookview but then no one had wanted to ride back to Manset with Kyle.

"Masser *carpooled*?" asked Mike.

"Well, no, he came separately. Good thing, too, because he gave Hannah and me a ride back."

"Masser *drove you*?"

"Well, no, I drove—but it was his car."

"Actually, Kyle didn't carpool back either," said Mike. "I picked him up at Brookview and then drove him back to the production office to get his car. We took the Tesla for our wild night in Ellsworth," he added with a chagrined look.

"What did you do in Ellsworth?"

"Drank."

"Too bad we didn't run into you in Manset," she said sourly. "I might have been able to keep you from getting in with a bad crowd."

Mike took a contemplative sip of coffee. "Lathey did mention that Garrick was pretty tough in his questioning of Leo Dorn. His description made me feel almost fond of the old vulture."

"But Kyle conveniently left out the part where he himself stepped onto center stage?"

"Yeah, he did leave out that part."

"Well, he's on Corey's shit list now. What did he want from you?"

"Why would he necessarily want something from me?"

"Because Kyle Lathey doesn't seem like the kind of guy who pals around with someone unless he plans to get something out of it. What did you talk about?"

Mike hesitated. "This and that."

"This and that?"

"Oh, you know ..."

"Mike, you did *not* ask Kyle Lathey to do the project with just me again, did you?"

"I might have."

"I swear to God—"

Ann's phone rang. She glanced at the caller ID, held up her finger to Mike, and hit *Accept*.

"It appears that Kyle has been at it again," said Corey without preamble.

"What now?" asked Ann, glaring at Mike.

"I just checked the news, and the morning reports are all about Jonathan Garrido having been the one who found the flash drive in Shelby Kim's car. One theory is that he planted the drive there."

"Why would he do that?" asked Ann, exasperated. "Everyone says they were dating—and everyone implies they were happy."

"A new theory is that the two of them were responsible for the explosion that killed Oscar Sanz."

"Seriously? It was before Shelby even worked at SMT!"

"Believe me, the people churning out these theories aren't deterred by logic."

Ann rubbed her forehead. "Any others?"

"The jilted lover theory is still out there—that Jonathan pushed Leo off the ledge."

"And Leo wouldn't remember that?"

"You said that he told you he was confused right after he fell."

"He'd have to be pretty damn confused to have missed that. And if Jonathan pushed Leo, why would Shelby cover for him?"

"He threatened her?"

"And then what happened to Shelby?"

"Lover's quarrel at Otter Cliff?"

"You must be kidding me!"

"Hey, don't yell at me, I'm just the messenger. And it just

keeps getting better. Garrick got a visit from the cops this morning, wanting information about the documentary and the rumors about Jonathan Garrido."

Ann groaned. "Oh, great."

"That's not all. After the cops left, Hannah arrived at Garrick's house to convey Tippy's displeasure with Kyle's latest infraction."

"Why didn't she just complain directly to Kyle?"

"Doesn't know where to find him, I guess."

"Well, when I find him, I'm going to kill him."

"Only if you find him before I do. Anyhow, Garrick wants us in Somesville pronto," said Corey.

"What's going on?" asked Mike, who had evidently shaken off his grogginess as he followed Ann's side of the conversation.

"Corey, hold on one sec," she said, and gave Mike a quick update on the situation. "Garrick wants us to go to his house to discuss the situation."

"Summoning the minions?" he said.

"Mike, just stop," she said, then switched her attention to the phone. "Corey, can you pick me up?"

"Sure. I'll be there in just a couple of minutes," said Corey, just as Mike said, "You don't need him to pick you up—we have a car."

"Thanks, Corey," she said, and ended the call.

"Hey!" said Mike.

"Why don't you get some fresh air by walking over to the production office and picking up the car while Corey and I go try to smooth Garrick's ruffled feathers. Again."

"I want to come along."

"Look at you," said Ann. "You're a mess. You can't be ready to go by the time Corey gets here, and you certainly wouldn't be in the right frame of mind to deal with Garrick."

"Watch me," said Mike, putting his now-empty coffee mug on the counter and heading for his bedroom.

Just as Corey pulled into the driveway, Mike reappeared, clothed and tidied, with sunglasses over his bloodshot eyes. "Oh, ye of little faith," he said to Ann.

Corey knocked on the door and Ann opened it for him.

"Mike's insisting on going," she said. "We'll pick up our car at the production office and meet up with you in Somesville, if that's okay."

"Sure, no problem," said Corey. "See you at Garrick's." He returned to the Suburban and backed out of the driveway.

"Don't make me regret letting you tag along," Ann said to Mike.

"Let me just brew another pot of coffee before we go," said Mike.

"Mike!"

"Won't take a minute."

"You are barely less annoying than you were a quarter of a century ago."

nn and Mike arrived at Garrick's house almost half an hour later. They found an antsy Corey waiting on the porch.

"You didn't have to wait outside for us," said Ann.

"Are you kidding? I wasn't going to face the music alone."

Ann knocked on the door and, in a few moments, Garrick opened it.

"Gracious of you to come," he said, and turned and stalked into his office.

Hannah was seated in one of the two guest chairs facing Garrick's desk. Corey waved Ann toward the other one. For a moment she considered offering it to Mike, who even in the muted light of Garrick's office hadn't taken off his sunglasses, but she realized that Mike would kill her if she created an opening for Garrick to offer some pithy observations about his hangover. She sat down.

Hannah gave Ann a sympathetic smile.

"I left Lathey a message to meet us here," said Corey. "No word from him, I guess?"

"No," said Garrick.

"I believe we need to have him involved in this discussion," said Hannah, "since I feel quite sure that he had a hand in this latest unfortunate development."

Tight-lipped, Corey pulled his phone out of his pocket and tapped. After a few moments, he said, "Where are you? Did you get my message?" Then, after too short a time for Kyle to have answered, he continued. "Hold on. I'm putting you on speaker."

He propped the phone up on Garrick's desk.

"Kyle," he continued, "I'm here with Hannah, Garrick, Ann, and Mike, and I can tell you it's a pretty unhappy group."

"Unhappy, eh?" Ann thought she heard a grin in Kyle's voice.

"Are you responsible for the rumors floating around about Jonathan Garrido?" Corey asked.

"I'm just helping the press think through all the possibilities," replied Kyle. "That flash drive that Garrido claimed he found in Kim's car—the possibility of a lover's triangle—"

"I resent these accusations," Hannah burst out. "Tippy Pepperidge has asked me to take her out to Otter Point so that she can pay her respects to Shelby Kim. She would hardly do that for a young woman she suspected of having an affair with her husband."

"Sure, but if they did have an affair, there's no guarantee the wife would know about it."

"This is completely unacceptable," spluttered Hannah.

"I quite agree with Dr. Jeskie," said Garrick. "I regret that I reversed my earlier decision to leave the project. I reinstate that decision now, and I will not change my mind again."

"Masser," said Kyle, "you signed a contract. There are steps we can take if you withdraw—steps that will hit you in the wallet—and we won't hesitate to use them."

"You are welcome to try," said Garrick. "I will be interested—although only mildly interested—to observe the results." He reached over and tapped the phone's screen.

There was a moment of silence, then Kyle said. "Listen, you pompous bastard—"

Garrick tapped the phone's screen again. "How do you hang this thing up," he muttered.

"Are you hanging up on me—?" Kyle got out before Ann reached over and ended the call.

They were all silent, then Corey puffed out a lungful of air. "Crap."

"Corey," said Mike, "let's get out of here and discuss options."

"There are no options," said Corey.

"There's no reason the project has to end—"

"There is a reason it has to end, Mike," said Corey angrily. "The backers have said it has to be Ann and Garrick right from the start, and they're not likely to change their minds now."

"I'm surprised you would insist that your sister continue in what appears to be an untenable situation," said Garrick to Mike.

"Untenable for you, maybe—" retorted Mike.

Hannah broke in. "I believe that discussion of continuation of the project is moot. I feel certain that Tippy will agree with me and Garrick that the project must come to a halt, and if we are going to pit her attorneys against attorneys representing Authentic Productions, I know who I would put my money on."

Garrick stood. "Mr. Duff, I regret that it has come to this. I agreed to participate in this project because I found our earlier collaboration to be not entirely distasteful. It is only Mr. Lathey's behavior that has led us to this impasse. I regret that your project will be brought down by his unethical behavior. Good day to you."

Mike opened his mouth but then caught Ann's glare and clamped it shut again.

Ann, Mike, and Corey trudged down the hall to the front

door, like students dismissed from the principal's office after having been roped into the school troublemaker's antics.

Ann closed Garrick's front door behind her a little more forcefully than she intended, then she wheeled on Mike.

"Mike, what the hell? I'd chalk up your behavior to you being hung over except that you've been acting like an idiot when it comes to anything related to Garrick since we got here —since before we got here!"

Mike took off his sunglasses, thought better of it, and put them back on. "Ann, I'm almost not surprised that you think you can't carry this project without Masser." He turned to Corey. "But, Corey, I am surprised that you don't see this as an opportunity to explore the spirit-sensing topic without Masser's showboating. How come he thinks he doesn't have to comply with the request to carpool to the Pepperidge property? How come he couldn't make the effort to go to the actual location of Leo Dorn's death? It would have made much better—"

"Mike."

Ann's stony tone stopped Mike's rant.

"I think it would be best if you went back to Pennsylvania," she said.

Mike looked from Ann to Corey and back to Ann.

Corey shifted uneasily.

"You're ... sending me home?" asked Mike.

"Yes," said Ann.

Mike looked so nonplussed as his hangover-addled brain considered and discarded responses that Ann almost—not quite, but almost—felt sorry for him.

Finally he said, "How are you going to get back to Manset?"

"I'm sure Corey will give me a ride."

Mike took off his sunglasses, grimaced, pinched the bridge of his nose, and put the glasses back on. "Fine. Fine."

Ann and Corey watched from the porch as Mike crossed the

street to where the Hyundai was parked, eliciting a honk from an oncoming vehicle, did a three-point turn to reverse direction, and accelerated back toward Manset.

Corey turned to Ann. "Well, this is quite the cluster."

She looked down the road, although Mike had disappeared around a curve. "Yeah."

"Would lobster make it better?"

She gave him a wan smile. "Worth a try."

31

Ann and Corey decided to go back to George's Restaurant, where they and Mike had ordered breakfasts three days earlier—breakfasts that Corey admitted had sat forgotten in the back of the Suburban until the trip to Brookview. On the way to Bar Harbor, Ann placed a call.

"Officer Kessling," came the answer.

"Hi, this is Ann Kinnear. I called you the day before yesterday about someone who was following me in a red Jetta. I was wondering if you had been able to get any information about who it might be based on the description and the partial license plate number."

"Nothing to report yet. We'll be in touch if we have anything for you."

She thanked him and ended the call. "No news."

"How many red Jettas with a Maine plate that starts with *ZP* can there be?" Corey said, irritated.

When they got to the restaurant, Ann scanned the menu and decided that lobster was, in fact, a pretty good idea. She ordered lobster mac and cheese and Corey ordered a burger. They both asked for coffee.

As the server filled their cups, Ann gave an exclamation. "Rats!"

"Everything okay, hon?" asked the server.

"Yes—sorry—I was thinking of something else."

When the server stepped away, Corey asked, "Everything okay?"

"I just thought of something I should have asked Mike before I sent him packing."

She described the discovery of the canteen at Brookview, and Mike's assignment to get the contents analyzed. She figured that under the current circumstances, the risk of any information she shared with Corey making its way to Kyle was minimal.

"I never got to ask Mike what the results were," she concluded.

"Want to call him and ask now?"

"I don't think the timing would be great."

"You could try calling the lab yourself."

"That's true."

An online search indicated that there were two places in Bangor to which Mike might have taken the canteen. Ann's call to the first one went to voicemail. At the second, she reached a woman who admitted to the fact that Mike Kinnear had dropped off an item to be analyzed.

"Can you tell me what the results were?" Ann asked. "I'm Mr. Kinnear's assistant."

"No, I'm sorry, he only authorized us to release the results to himself or his sister, Ann."

Ann sighed. "I'm Ann."

"I thought you were his assistant."

After switching from phone call to video, and after an online image search had confirmed Ann's identity, the woman said, "After all that, I'm afraid you'll be disappointed by the results—or lack of results. We couldn't get any substance to test. There was definitely some liquid in the canteen when we received it—we could hear it in there—but when we went to take the sample, it was gone. Evaporated, I guess. We only had the canteen open for a few minutes. We were really surprised that any liquid could evaporate that quickly."

"And there was no residue to test?"

"Nothing."

"Do you still have the canteen?"

"No, your brother took it with him."

Ann thanked the woman and disconnected.

"No joy, I gather," said Corey.

"Nope." She recounted what the woman had told her.

Their food arrived. By unspoken agreement they suspended their discussion of the project debacle while they ate, switching instead to a discussion of the Maine trivia documented on the paper placemats. When the server had cleared their dishes and topped off their coffees, Corey leaned back.

"I can hardly blame Garrick for withdrawing—I'm tempted to quit the project myself." He rubbed his hands down his face. "What a mess."

"What the hell is it with Kyle? Why is he even involved in the project?"

Corey slumped forward over his coffee. "I don't know, but my guess is that the backers liked my creative approach and technical skills but felt I was too much of a nice guy."

"Nice guy is a problem?"

"I gather that they thought that *The Sense of Death* documentary would have been better if I had staged it as a competition—as they clearly still believe with the current project. I figured I could work around it, but maybe they put Kyle on the project to try to make sure I didn't."

"Can't you just get other backers?"

He gave a wan smile. "There aren't folks lining up to fund a project about people who talk with the dead."

"Well, Kyle's clearly doing more than monitoring the situation and reporting back. Yesterday after he left Brookview, he got together with Mike and wined and dined him."

Corey's eyebrows rose. "Why?"

"To pump him for information is my guess. Evidently Kyle never bothered to mention to Mike that he had tried to take over the interview with Leo."

Corey shook his head. "What an asshole."

"What are you going to do?"

He took a sip of coffee then gazed into the mug. "I don't know. If I back out of the project, I'd be blacklisted for any other projects—by them and by anyone whose ear they can bend. But I also don't want to get between Authentic Production's lawyers and Tippy's, if it comes to that."

"I don't want to sound like I'm unsympathetic to the bad situation you're in," said Ann, "but there's a bigger problem than the documentary. We still don't know what happened to Shelby, and whether her disappearance is connected to what happened to Leo. And if the death of this former SMT consultant and the burning of the Kim family's bakery are related to what's happening on MDI, I think that gives credence to the idea that someone in the industry sees SMT as a threat in some way. I doubt someone blew up Oscar Sanz in Mexico or burned down Shelby's parents' bakery in Connecticut because Shelby was having an affair with Leo, or because she was suicidal from unrequited love."

"Makes sense."

"We should still go out to Otter Cliff and see if I can get in touch with Shelby."

"We can drive out there now if you want."

Ann shook her head. "I don't think she's at the cliff top. I saw something there—something Garrick called a 'spirit negative'—that makes me think her actual spirit is going to be somewhere else. I think if we're going to find her, it's going to be by the rocks at the bottom of the cliff, or further out in the water, depending …" Her voice trailed off.

"On whether the fall killed her, or the water did," he finished.

"Yeah."

Corey shuddered. After a moment, he said, "The top of the cliff I can get you to, but we'll obviously need a boat—and a skipper—to check out the rocks and the water. I had been talking to some people in Manset about taking the talent and crew out there before the shit hit the fan, but I'm afraid if we leave from there, Kyle will find out. Plus," he added grimly, "if this isn't on the production company's expense account, I'm not sure I can afford it."

"I think that Hannah Jeskie might have a boat."

Corey raised his eyebrows.

"Remember when we were in Garrick's office, Hannah said that she was going to take Tippy out to Otter Point to pay her respects to Shelby?"

"Yeah."

"Tippy doesn't strike me as the kind of woman who would need someone to drive her out there. She'd only ask Hannah to help her out if she needed to get there by boat."

"I don't know that Hannah Jeskie is going to be so excited to help us out after our dressing-down in Garrick's office."

"She's angry with Kyle, not with us. Plus, she and I had a nice conversation when we got back to Manset after the video shoot."

"I don't know if you should be talking to her separate from the documentary production—" He trailed off as he saw Ann's expression. He took a morose sip of coffee. "You're right. Doesn't much matter in the scheme of things."

"Hannah actually had a couple of things she wanted to talk with you about—wanting to see the notes I took of Leo's side of the conversation and some additional background on Shelby Kim."

"What's the deal with Shelby Kim?"

Ann pulled her phone out of her pocket. "Let's see if Hannah does have a boat ... and if she does, and we can win her over, she can tell you herself on the way to Otter Cliff."

32

Several hours later, Ann, Corey, and Hannah were motoring toward Otter Point in Hannah's 1963 Thompson runabout, *Mariposa*. Hannah captained the boat from a sparsely equipped panel that looked very much like a 1960s automobile dashboard. Ann and Corey were seated in swivel seats behind her.

"It looks like we'll get to Otter Point when the tide's coming in." Hannah looked back at Ann. "There are rocks that are exposed at low tide that will be covered now. Is that desirable? I'm not sure what we're looking for. Or where."

"I'm not sure either, but since we're likely not looking for a body, I can't imagine it matters."

"Not looking for a body?" Hannah said uncertainly.

"Well, at least not a physical body—I'm sure that search and rescue is better equipped to do that than we are—and I'm not sure that tides are going to matter to a spirit."

"Ah, I understand." Hannah glanced toward some dark clouds hovering offshore. "We can't stay out for long—that's heading our way. *Mariposa* would normally be a river or lake boat, not an ocean boat, but I just fell in love with her when I saw her. I would have proposed delaying our trip, but if we can find out some useful information from Shelby, maybe it will help nip this whole fiasco in the bud—or at least bring it to a head. We want to be back at the marina before that storm reaches us."

Ann also hoped to be back at the marina before the bad weather caught up with them. Hannah was wearing a knee-length rain slicker and Corey had on an oilskin jacket, but she had dressed for the sunny skies and warm temperatures she had encountered in Manset that morning.

As they motored toward Otter Point, Hannah recapped for Corey her conversation with Ann of the previous evening.

"I appreciate you sharing the information about the fire at the Kims' home with me," said Corey. "And if by some miracle we do get to proceed with the documentary, I don't see any reason not to show you Ann's notes from Garrick and Leo's conversation, but at the moment that seems like a long shot."

As they approached the jutting headland, Ann could hear the clang of the bell buoy and see a roil of white water churning about a hundred yards from the shore. A fleck of yellow was visible at the center of the disturbance. As they drew nearer, it resolved itself into the form of a young woman, submerged below the waist in the roiling water.

Ann pointed. "I think I see her."

Hannah looked alarmed. "In the water?"

"No, on the rocks. Well, where I imagine the rocks are."

"You see a body on the Spindle?" Hannah asked, her voice rising.

"No, sorry," said Ann hastily. "I think I see Shelby's spirit."

As they drew closer, it was clear that this was in fact the same young woman shown shaking Leo Dorn's hand in the archive photo used in the news coverage of his death. However, if some tiny part of Ann's brain had harbored any hope that the young woman had been waiting on the rocks to be rescued for the last four days, in full view of any observers on the cliffs, her appearance would have dashed those hopes. Although the force of the swirling water would have knocked even the sturdiest person off their feet, Shelby's steady stance was unaffected. Although spray from the larger waves shot a dozen feet in the air, her hair appeared as dry as it had in the news photo.

Shelby might no longer need to worry about hypothermia, but seeing the young woman standing waist-deep in the frigid water gave Ann a vicarious shiver. She flashed to the reports she had read—assigned to her by her flight instructor, Russo—about the Miracle on the Hudson. She guessed that that river's January temperature of the low forties was not much colder than the ocean off MDI in May. How long could a living person have lasted in water that cold—five minutes? Ten?

"Can you get us closer?" asked Ann.

"A little closer," said Hannah, "but not too close. With the tide covering the rocks, I'm having to estimate where they are, and I don't want to be proven wrong, especially with the wind picking up. There's not a lot of margin for error."

Hannah edged the boat closer to the Spindle, dividing her attention between the roiling water and the bank of clouds that was quickly moving in their direction. Ann noticed that although their activity was being observed by a growing contingent of onlookers on the cliffs, Shelby herself kept her gaze averted from the boat. Her expression was pensive—not the expression of a person, living or dead, who is happy to see approaching rescuers.

When *Mariposa* was a few dozen feet from where Shelby stood, Hannah said, "That's the best I can do."

Ann cupped her hands around her mouth. "Hello," she said, intentionally avoiding using the young woman's name, since she was quite sure the conversation would carry to the people on the cliffs. She didn't want to feed Kyle's media fire by calling out the name of the woman who had disappeared from this area. Let the observers think what they liked about her inexplicable behavior. "My name is Ann."

Shelby's ocean-ward gaze didn't move.

"Can you hear me?"

A faint *yes, we can hear you* drifted across the water, evidently from someone on the cliff who thought that the question was aimed at them.

"Great," muttered Ann. "Person on the rocks, can you hear me?" she called.

The responding *yes!* from the cliffs was a little more strident this time.

She heard a muffled laugh from Corey.

"Person on the Spindle," she clarified, "can you hear me?"

This time there was no answer from the cliffs, but equally no answer from Shelby Kim. Ann decided that eliciting a response from Shelby trumped discretion.

"Shelby, we want to know what happened to you at Otter Cliff. Can you tell me?"

She sensed more than saw cell phones coming out of pockets along the clifftop.

Shelby turned her face away from Ann and toward the freshening breeze from the oncoming storm.

Ann spent a few more minutes trying to get a response from Shelby, even asking Hannah to move the boat in the direction in which Shelby was looking, but the only response was that Shelby shifted her gaze to another quadrant. Ann invoked Leo's name, Jonathan's name. She offered to mediate a conversation with Hannah. She asked about Stata Mater.

"Anything?" asked Corey eventually.

Ann shook her head. "No."

"Nothing at all?" asked Hannah.

"Nope."

Hannah glanced nervously toward the storm. "I'm sorry, Ann, but we really need to get going. We can come back when the weather's better."

As if to punctuate her message, a larger wave jogged the little boat, and Ann grabbed for the back of Hannah's seat to keep her balance.

"All right," said Ann, and lowered herself into one of the passenger seats.

Corey sat as well, and Hannah throttled up the engine and turned the boat back toward Northeast Harbor.

They didn't speak much on the trip back. Hannah concentrated on piloting *Mariposa* through the increasingly choppy water. Ann and Corey concentrated on remaining in their seats as the rising wind buffeted the small boat, the oncoming line of rain visible as it advanced across the water toward them.

It caught up with them before they reached the marina, drops denting the water like hammer blows on soft metal. Ann was quickly soaked to the skin.

Ann and Corey helped Hannah get the boat tied up. By the time they trudged toward the parking area, where they had left their vehicles, the day was already darkening even though the sun wouldn't set for a few hours.

Corey unlocked the Suburban and Ann scrambled in out of the rain. Hannah stood outside, water running off the hood of her slicker.

"I suppose that your sighting at the Spindle makes it clear that Shelby is dead," she said somberly.

"Yes, I think we can assume that now," replied Ann.

"I need to give Tippy an update," said Hannah. "If we can agree that the focus should be on trying to contact Leo and Shelby to see if they can share any information that might help us get to the bottom of this, and if we all agree to turn our attention away from the documentary, at least for now, I'll ask her about letting Ann go back to Brookview to contact Leo again. Maybe he will have thought of something that could help."

Corey nodded, raindrops falling from the end of his nose. "I think that's a sensible plan."

"And we should try to get back to the Spindle as soon as possible," said Ann. "I'd like to give it another try when we have more time."

"I think the two of you need to change into dry clothes before we do anything else," said Hannah, "and I wouldn't mind putting on a pair of dry socks. Why don't we all get changed and then meet up at the production office to firm up our plan." She glanced at her watch. "It's six o'clock now. Should we say eight o'clock to reconvene? That would give you time to grab dinner as well."

"That sounds good t-to me," said Ann, her teeth starting to chatter.

"You poor dear," said Hannah, shaking her head. She unlocked her car, which was parked next to the Suburban, and got a heavy quilted jacket out of the back. "Here, take this with you—it will help keep you warm."

Ann was loath to take off her light jacket, wet though it was, so she pulled Hannah's jacket on over her own. "Thanks."

"If I could make one more suggestion ...?" said Hannah.

"Sure," said Corey.

"Corey, are you staying in Bar Harbor?"

"Yes—the Bar Harbor Inn."

"If that jacket keeps Ann warm enough, you'll save yourself quite a drive if you stop in Bar Harbor first for you to change and then go on to Manset. The Inn has a nice bar, a neat whiskey should warm you up, and the food in the restaurant is decent."

"That's a good idea," said Ann. She pictured the lobster claw that Mount Desert Island resembled, the eastern and western pincers separated by Somes Sound running north to south up the middle of the island. It meant that although Northeast Harbor on the southern tip of the eastern pincer and Southwest Harbor and Manset near the southern tip of the western pincer were only about a mile-and-a-half apart as the crow—or gull— flies, the trip was almost half an hour by car. "I'm already feeling warmer. Thanks, Hannah."

Hannah got in her car and Corey climbed into the Suburban.

"Are you sure you don't want to go to Manset first?" asked Corey.

"No, I'm good."

"Too bad we didn't think to ask Hannah to drop you at the Manset dock when we were still on the boat," said Corey, starting the engine and cranking the heat to high. "It probably would have gotten you into dry clothes a lot faster."

33

Ann and Corey drove north through Acadia, then turned east on Eagle Lake Road. When Corey pulled into the parking lot of the Bar Harbor Inn, Ann was still shivering despite the hot air blasting from the Suburban's vents.

"Look at you," said Corey self-reprovingly. "I should have taken you to Manset first."

"No, I'm good," said Ann, although the clacking of her teeth suggested otherwise.

"Your problem is not enough insulation," he said. "A lot of body fat—that's the ticket. Come on in and I'll loan you something dry to wear."

She followed Corey to his room, which no doubt had a lovely view across Frenchman Bay to the Porcupine Islands in brighter and clearer conditions. He sorted through a tangle of clothes in one of the dresser drawers. "Don't let the state of disorganization fool you—it's all clean. Jeans ... T-shirt ... sweatshirt ... socks. That ought to hold you until we get to Manset." He handed the stack of clothes to her.

"Thanks, Corey." She looked around the room.

"You can change in the bathroom. I'll change out here."

She went into the bathroom, shed her sodden clothes, and pulled on the dry ones. Since she was half a foot shorter than Corey, the result was comical but warm. She waited until she hadn't heard the opening and closing of dresser drawers for a minute, then knocked on the inside of the door.

"Okay to come out?" she called.

"I'm decent when you are," he said.

He was laying out his wet clothes on the bed to dry.

"There's a washer and dryer at the Manset house," she said. "Want to take those along and we can put them through the dryer?"

"Yeah, great," he said, gathering up the clothes and stuffing them into a plastic Hannaford supermarket bag. He found another bag for Ann's wet clothes.

She glanced at her watch. "We'll need to kill some time if we're not meeting up with Hannah until eight."

"I like the idea of a whiskey, and the food at the hotel's restaurant is pretty good," said Corey.

They went to the lobby and had started toward the restaurant when a tall, thin figure rose from one of the chairs in the lobby. Tippy Pepperidge.

"Tippy," said Ann, "I didn't expect to see you here."

"Hannah called to give me an update and said she thought you were headed here. I was wondering if I could speak with you for a moment." She glanced at Corey. "Privately, if possible."

"Of course. I'll get us a table," said Corey. "Would you like to join us, Ms. Pepperidge—after you've spoken with Ann?"

"No, thank you. I need to be getting back to Brookview. Also, I noticed that Kyle Lathey is dining in the restaurant."

"Ah. Then perhaps I'll wait ..." Corey glanced around the lobby, no doubt looking for a location to which he could retire to give Tippy and Ann privacy.

"If you'd like to wait here," said Tippy, "the manager was kind enough to make a conference room available for me. We won't be a moment."

Tippy turned and walked briskly toward one of the hallways leading off the lobby. Ann gave Corey a *who knows?* shrug and followed.

Ann mulled over possible explanations for Tippy's appearance in Bar Harbor. Had Tippy ventured into the rain to surprise the two of them at the inn because she felt that Garrick's scolding, perhaps as described to her by Hannah, was insufficient? If that was the reason, why wasn't Corey included in the discussion? Was only Ann going to be held responsible for Kyle's behavior? By the time they reached the small conference room, Ann was already formulating her response to any complaints Tippy might have.

Tippy closed the door behind them and turned to Ann. "I understand that you saw someone following you the night before last."

"That's right," replied Ann, surprised.

"Hannah mentioned it to me." Tippy took a deep breath. "That was Megan."

"Really? How do you know?"

"Because she was following you at my request."

Ann raised her eyebrows. "Why?"

Tippy was silent for a few moments, then gestured to the chairs drawn up to the conference table.

They sat, and Tippy placed her hands, fingers laced together, on the table. "When I heard that you had been able to communicate with Leo that day that you and Garrick came to Brookview, I started thinking that perhaps you would be able to contact my late husband." She looked down at her hands. "My *first* late husband." She raised her eyes to Ann's. "As you know, I hired Garrick to try to contact Frank not long after he died, and

Garrick reported that Frank was not there to be contacted—that he must have passed on to whatever lies beyond—but I thought that, as with any profession, perhaps another person would have a different experience, obtain a different result."

"If Garrick said that Frank wasn't—" Ann began, but Tippy held up a hand.

"Please, let me finish. I was anxious to try one more time to make contact with Frank, and I thought you might succeed where Garrick had failed. However, as you know, I have been less than pleased about Kyle Lathey's behavior, and I wanted to better understand your relationship with him before I made the request. I didn't want Frank's death to become part of the Authentic Productions' project. I asked Megan to follow you to see if she could find out—for example, if you spent time with him outside of the production activities and, if you did, if your relationship seemed ... more than professional."

"Ah," said Ann.

Tippy looked back down at her hands. "I shouldn't have subjected you to that treatment, and I shouldn't have asked Megan to do that." She heaved a sigh. "I suppose the loss of a loved one makes people do things they would never ordinarily do. However, that's no excuse. I have apologized to Megan, and I apologize to you as well. Not only was it a violation of your privacy, but I realize that, with everything going on, seeing a car following you must have been alarming."

"Thank you for letting me know."

"Hannah tells me that you're no fan of Kyle Lathey. Is she correct?"

"Yes. Corey and I are as upset by the things he's been doing as you are."

"Then I'd like to ask you if you would be willing to try to contact Frank when the current furor over Leo's death and Shelby's disappearance settles down." She attempted a smile. "It's been eight years. I'm thinking that another few days or weeks won't make much difference."

"Yes, a spirit can still be present after that long, but ..." Ann hesitated. "When I was waiting for Megan to pick me up at the back of the Brookview property after I contacted Leo, I saw where Frank's studio was. I didn't see him there."

"But you couldn't have been there for more than a few minutes, correct?"

"That's right."

"I'd like you to go back. Give it more time."

"I don't believe I'll be able to contact a spirit that Garrick says isn't there to be contacted. But if you'd like, I'll try."

"Yes, I would appreciate that. Thank you."

They stood.

"I understand from Hannah that you saw Shelby at the Spindle, and that her appearance there indicates that she must be dead."

"Yes, I believe so."

Tippy took a deep breath and let it out slowly. "Not what I had hoped for, certainly." After a pause, she continued. "I also understand that she wasn't very communicative."

"That's right. We're hoping to try again when the weather's better."

"You're on your way back to Manset now?" asked Tippy.

"Yes, to get some dry clothes—" Ann looked down at the jeans that, even cuffed, bagged around her ankles. "—that fit."

Ann followed Tippy back to the lobby, where Corey was leaning against the wall, partially obscured by a bushy ficus, checking his phone. Tippy shook his hand, then Ann's, then headed off into the rain.

"What do you want to do about dinner?" asked Corey, clearly itching to ask Ann about her conversation with Tippy.

"Let's go to The Perch," said Ann. "Everyone keeps raving

about it, but I've only gotten beer and a takeout lobster roll from there. I'll update you on the way."

"Sounds good," said Corey. "And since The Perch is right down the street from the office, if Hannah is running late, we can watch for her from the restaurant."

"She seems more like the type to be running early," said Ann.

As they drove, Ann told Corey about the explanation for the mysterious red Jetta, although not her promise to Tippy to try to contact Frank Judd.

"So it wasn't my imagination that Megan seemed a little weird when we were at Brookview for the shoot," she said. "I'm guessing that covert tailing is not her usual assignment."

"I'll bet the cops tied the car to Megan and Megan to Tippy Pepperidge but didn't want to let on," he said. "Status does have its privileges."

When they got to Manset, they made a stop at the house, where Ann ran in to put the wet clothes in the dryer. She detoured upstairs and swapped Corey's jeans for a pair of her own, but she felt so snug in the over-large sweatshirt that she kept it on. Since the rain was still sheeting down, they drove rather than walked to The Perch. They detoured past the production office in case Hannah was ahead of schedule, but the single space was empty.

There were only a few patrons in The Perch, so they were able to get a table by the window, although they found that the rapidly descending darkness and the rain kept them from seeing much beyond the town dock's parking lot across the street.

Eric arrived at their table and took their orders. They both ordered meatloaf and beers, whiskey not being on offer.

"So," said Corey when Eric had left, "what's your take on the situation with Shelby?"

"I don't know. It wasn't a matter of her trying to communicate with me and being unable to, or of me being unable to receive a communication. She clearly just didn't want to talk with me."

"Or with Hannah, it sounds like."

"At least not with me as the intermediary."

"Is there a different approach we could try?"

"The only thing I can think of at the moment is that she might be more willing to talk to me as I become more familiar to her. Although I'm not thrilled about the idea of having to make trip after trip out to the Spindle with a bunch of people taking photos and videos of me seeming to talk to myself."

Eric arrived with their beers. "How's the warehouse working out for you?" he asked Corey.

"Eric owns the warehouse," Corey said to Ann, then turned back to Eric. "It's working out great. Hey, I forgot to tell you, Ann saw the Darling of the Docks."

"No kidding!" Eric turned to Ann with a grin. "That's cool. Have you talked to her?"

"No," said Ann. "She doesn't seem very interested." She hoped it wasn't a trend—having spirits be unwilling to communicate with her would put a real crimp in the *Ann Kinnear Sensing* business.

"Yeah, I've heard people say she didn't talk much when she was alive, unless she was around her grandfather," said Eric, "in which case you evidently couldn't shut her up."

"She was helping her grandfather out at the warehouse when she died, right?"

"Yeah. The grandfather was devastated—blamed himself for not keeping a close enough eye on her—and started drinking. He went off the Park Loop Road near Kebo Brook a couple years later, although some say it wasn't an accident."

"That's a sad story," said Ann.

"Yeah. I imagine you hear a lot of sad stories in your line of work."

Ann nodded. It didn't seem the right moment to share that, although some of her interactions with the dead were sad, some were inspiring, some were annoying, some were boring, some were funny—just like her interactions with the living.

As Eric returned to the bar, she thought back to her attempts to engage Jessy Barnwell in conversation. Garrick had seemed to establish at least a tenuous connection with the little girl. "Maybe we should ask Garrick to try with Shelby."

Corey laughed. "You're always deferring to Garrick. What would Mike say if he were here?"

She wondered what Mike was up to. He could be back in West Chester by now. Maybe he and Scott were packing for their postponed trip to New York.

She mustered a smile. "He would tell me I can carry the show on my own."

34

They passed the time until quarter to eight at The Perch. By the time they left, the rain was beginning to tail off. They hopped in the Suburban to drive the short distance down the street to the warehouse.

"I'll drop you off and park up the road so that Hannah can use the parking spot next to the office," said Corey. He dug in his pocket and handed over a key. "That's to the padlock on the door."

Ann hopped out of the vehicle, unlocked and removed the padlock, and stepped inside. The interior was dark, except for a somewhat indistinct glow near the rafters that Ann surmised was Jessy Barnwell. Ann groped along the wall next to the door until she found the light switch. She flipped it and the fluorescent fixture flickered to life, illuminating the ersatz conference area but leaving most of the space in darkness. The video equipment was back under its tarp, having evidently been unloaded after the Brookview shoot.

Ann sat down on one of the folding metal chairs at the card table and dropped the padlock on the table. The glow resolved itself into Jessy, who gazed solemnly at Ann from near the top of the stack of lobster traps.

Ann realized she was more tired than she should be at eight in the evening. She was considering returning to The Perch for a takeout cup of coffee when she heard a vehicle approaching at a faster clip than she would have expected from Hannah Jeskie. It braked to a stop when it reached the warehouse, and she heard the crunch of gravel from the parking space at the side of the building. A moment later the door opened. Rather than Hannah, Kyle Lathey stood in the door.

"Hi, Kyle," she said unenthusiastically.

He strode across the warehouse to where she sat. "Where have you guys been?"

"Why do you want to know?"

"Because anything having to do with this project is my business."

"It doesn't have anything to do with the project," said Ann, a statement which might have been misleading but was, as far as she understood, true.

He sat down on one of the chairs. "I find that hard to believe, considering you, Duff, and Jeskie were evidently summoning spirits at Otter Point." He got out his phone, tapped, and held it out to her.

It was a video taken by one of the onlookers on the cliff, Hannah maneuvering *Mariposa*, Corey looking over Ann's shoulder toward the water roiling over the Spindle. Ann's calls to Shelby came through faintly on the audio.

She sighed and handed Kyle's phone back to him.

"It doesn't have anything to do with the project," she said again. "That was the agreement we had with Hannah to get her to take us out there."

"Then what does it have to do with?"

"With trying to find out what happened to Shelby."

"What are you wearing?"

"What?"

With a grin, Kyle gestured to the overlarge sweatshirt. "Unless you and Duff both went to Pitt, I'm guessing those are his clothes."

Ann was debating whether or not to answer, imagining the ribbing that an unrehearsed explanation could provoke, when Corey came through the door, shaking rain from his coat.

"Took the executive parking space again, I see," he said to Kyle. "What are you doing here?"

"I couldn't get in touch with you. You weren't in your room at the inn, you weren't at Ann's place." He turned a knowing grin toward Ann. "Although I certainly wouldn't have interrupted if I had seen the Suburban in the driveway." He turned back to Corey. "I thought I'd check here."

The door opened again, and Hannah stepped in. "Ah, Mr. Lathey," she said, with obvious distaste.

"Well, this is convenient," said Kyle. "The gang's all here."

Hannah crossed to the table and sat down. "There is no 'gang.' We have agreed that it is time to put the documentary on hold while we focus on understanding what happened to Leo and Shelby."

"Oh," said Kyle, "you've agreed to that, have you?"

"Yes, we have," said Corey.

"Well, you guys might think that the right thing do to is to go out and have a little chat with Shelby Kim," he tapped open the video again and watched it play as he spoke, "although from what I can see, it wasn't a very interactive chat, and not a very long one." He slipped the phone back in his pocket. "I think the angle to take is Jonathan Garrido. He's the one who can tie all these events together." He stood and paced the cracked concrete floor. "He got jealous of Shelby Kim's relationship with Leo Dorn and pushed Dorn to his death. Shelby still cared enough about Garrido to cover for him, but the trauma of her boyfriend killing her lover was too much and she committed suicide at Otter Cliff."

"And the fire at the Kims' bakery?" asked Hannah.

"Garrido getting his revenge on Shelby through her family."

"And the explosion that killed the SMT consultant," asked Ann.

"Maybe professional jealousy. The first time Garrido decided murder was the answer to a problem ... or was it the first?"

"You can't possibly—" began Hannah.

"Maybe professional jealousy, maybe something personal," continued Kyle. "Garrido's a student of fire and explosions. It would be easy for him to rig an explosion to look like an accident."

"It would be easy for any of us on the research staff of Stata Mater to rig an explosion to look like an accident," said Hannah tiredly.

Kyle slapped his hands together and rubbed them. "Exactly! Makes for pretty meaty content. But my money's on Garrido."

"More and more," said Hannah, "this is feeling like a witch-hunt, with Jonathan being the hunted."

"Well," replied Kyle, "you have to admit, it's plausible he was behind everything that has happened."

"I have to admit nothing of the kind. When we returned from our visit to Otter Point, I called Jonathan and told him that Ann had seen Shelby's spirit. His reaction was not one that I would expect from a cold-blooded murderer." She stood. "As Shelby's close friend, he deserved to know. A bunch of morbidly curious reality TV addicts—evidently the audience that you are catering to, Mr. Lathey—does not deserve to know. If you insist on pursuing this despite Ms. Pepperidge's objections, then this will become a matter for the attorneys." She turned to Corey and Ann. "I'll be in touch in the morning." She crossed to the door and slammed it behind her.

The three were silent for a moment, then Kyle turned to Corey. "If Pepperidge is going to pull out the big legal guns to interfere with the documentary, we need to talk with the guys back in L.A."

"Can't argue with you there," said Corey, his voice tight, "although what I want to talk with them about might be a little different than what you want to talk with them about." He pulled out his cell phone.

"What are you doing?" asked Kyle.

"Calling the 'guys back in L.A.'"

"Not from here. I want this meeting to be on video—I like looking these guys in the eyes when I'm talking to them—and I don't want them seeing what we've been using as a production office. It's not exactly the image I want to project. Let's head back to Bar Harbor. I'm sure the hotel has a conference room we can use. Plus," he glanced at Ann, then back at Corey, "privacy."

Corey stuffed his phone back in his pocket. "Fine."

Kyle pulled his own phone out as he turned toward the door. "Can you drive? I have a couple of calls I want to make en route." He stepped outside.

"Kill me now," groaned Corey.

"You wouldn't be my preferred victim," said Ann.

"Can you stand a two-minute drive with him? We can drop you off at the house on the way."

"That's okay, the rain's stopped. Plus, I'd like to see if I can strike up a conversation with the Darling of the Docks." Ann glanced up to where the girl still hovered near the top of the stack of lobster traps. Maybe some progress with Jessy would give her an idea about how to approach Shelby Kim. She stood and walked with Corey to the door.

"We'll also need to resume our conversation with Hannah tomorrow," he said. He hesitated at the door. "You'll be okay getting back yourself?"

"Yeah—now that we know who was in that red Jetta, and why."

35

Ann returned to the card table and resumed her seat, then leaned back and considered the small form floating near the rafters. Garrick had said that he had encountered but not spoken with Jessy Barnwell. The little girl had seemed more interested in him than she had in anyone else who had visited the warehouse. Maybe Garrick's ability to perceive Jessy made him more interesting than most of the people who must pass through the building—although it didn't seem to be counting in Ann's favor—but his forbidding presence counted against him. Much as she hated to agree with Kyle Lathey about anything, it was true that, just as with the living, spirits had their preferences about the people with whom they interacted.

"Hi, there," she said. "I'm Ann."

Jessy stuck her finger in her mouth and stared down at Ann.

"I understand you're Jessy Barnwell."

Nothing.

"I like your barrettes."

Jessy touched one of the plastic bows but otherwise seemed unimpressed.

It seemed apparent to Ann that her lack of experience interacting with young children, a lack she suspected Garrick shared, was not helping her cause. She wished Scott Pate, who could strike up a conversation with anyone, was there to coach her. Or Helen Federman. Or even Hannah Jeskie.

"Did you spend a lot of time at the warehouse before ... you know ..." She trailed off. She rarely felt uncomfortable referring to death when talking with spirits, but her conversations were rarely with someone so young. Would Jessy be more sensitive about the topic? Or frightened by it?

Jessy crossed her arms and began to look peevish.

Maybe more information about Jessy and her history would help. Ann got out her phone, opened the browser app, and tapped in *jessica barnwell manset*. After a bit of scrolling she found a database of newspaper archives that contained a story about Jessy's death. It included a photo of the warehouse but none of Jessy.

It did, however, reference her grandfather, Clarence Barnwell. Ann searched on his name and quickly found his obituary, which included a photograph.

Ann enlarged the photo. If you darkened his beard and mustache, subtracted a couple dozen pounds, and gave him a more dour expression, he could have been Garrick's older brother.

She turned the phone toward the little girl. "Your grandfather reminds me of my friend, Garrick. Does he remind you of Garrick?"

Jessy drifted a little closer to examine the photo.

"I understand that you helped your granddad out around the warehouse," Ann continued. "I'll bet that meant a lot to him."

Jessy drifted upward.

"Do you ever go anywhere other than the warehouse?"

Jessy's upward drift continued, and she passed through the warehouse's wooden rafters and disappeared through the ceiling.

Ann sighed. Maybe she should volunteer to watch some of Mike and Scott's friends' kids from time to time to improve her adult-to-child communication skills. She considered it for a moment and decided that a better option would be to tell Mike to restrict her sensing engagements to those involving adults.

Her phone buzzed. She pulled it out and checked the caller ID: *Mike*. She hit Accept.

"Hey," she said.

"Hey," said Mike. "How are things going?"

"About as well as you would expect with Kyle Lathey in the mix. Was Walt able to fly you home?"

"We worked it out."

"How was the trip?"

"Uneventful. Listen, I got a call from Jonathan Garrido—he left a message on the *Ann Kinnear Sensing* number. He wants to talk to you. Is it okay if I give him your cell number?"

"Sure."

"Okay. That was it."

"Hey, I spoke with someone at the lab in Bangor and, once I convinced them that I was your sister, they told me there was no trace of anything in the canteen. It sounds like whatever was in there had evaporated by the time they tried to take a sample. Sorry to send you on a wild goose chase."

"It wasn't you—it was Leo Dorn—but in any case, it's no problem."

"Whatever happened to the canteen?"

There was a pause at the other end. "I have it with me," said Mike. After another pause, he added, "I can get it back to you if you need it."

"I guess there's no reason to have it here if there's nothing in it. Thanks for doing that."

"Sure."

She sighed. "Okay, I better get going."

"Okay."

"Give my love to Scott."

"Will do."

They disconnected. She was beginning to regret having sent Mike home—among other things, even he was more comfortable talking with children than she was.

She noticed that Jessy had descended through the ceiling and was once again floating near the top of the stack of traps. Perhaps it would be better if she stayed silent and let the little girl approach her on her own terms. She settled back in the chair, wondering if eye contact was desirable.

Ann was beginning to tire of the exercise, which was devolving into a staring contest, when her phone buzzed, displaying a Bar Harbor origin.

"Hello?" she answered.

"Ann Kinnear?" asked the Texas-tinged voice she remembered from when she had met Jonathan Garrido at Otter Cliff.

"Hi, Jonathan."

"I appreciate you letting your brother give me your number."

"No problem."

"I talked to Hannah Jeskie earlier this evening. I understand that you saw Shelby at the Spindle."

"Yes."

"I'd love to hear about it."

"I wouldn't have much to tell you. I was able to see her but not to communicate with her."

"I'd still like to hear about it."

She stifled a sigh. "Okay. I'm free any time tomorrow after, say, nine o'clock."

"If it wouldn't be too much trouble, it would mean a lot to me to be able to talk with you tonight. I—" His voice caught, and he cleared his throat. "After they found the scrap of her jacket in the rocks, I never thought I'd have a chance to talk with someone who had seen her—and of course it would never have occurred to me that I'd have a chance to talk with someone who had seen her after she was dead." He cleared his throat again. "It's obvious that Hannah Jeskie believes you. If you could just talk about the experience, tell me how Shelby looked ..."

Ann considered. She didn't want to overreact, especially because she was feeling a little self-conscious about the fuss over the red Jetta. However, she had only met Jonathan Garrido once, and he seemed to be the frontrunner in public sentiment as the person most likely to have had a hand in the deaths of Leo Dorn and Shelby Kim. He seemed like a nice guy—one who had been genuinely aghast at the discovery of Shelby's phone near the cliff edge—but under the circumstances she didn't want to count on her first impression.

"Jonathan," she said, "can I call you right back? I have a call coming in I need to take."

"Right back?" he pressed.

"I promise."

"All right, I'll be waiting."

Ann ended the call, then opened her contact list and tapped Hannah's number.

"Hello?" Hannah must have been on the road, since Ann could hear what sounded like car sounds in the background.

"Hey, Hannah, it's Ann. Sorry to bother you, but I got a call from Jonathan Garrido and he wants to meet up with me. He wants to talk about our sighting of Shelby at the Spindle."

Hannah sighed. "Poor boy. He really is broken up by this—understandably so."

"How well do you know him?"

"Jonathan? I've worked with him for three years at Stata Mater—in fact, I'm the person who brought him on. He's a skilled researcher and someone I like very much personally. Why?"

"I'm still at the production office and I'm just wondering if he's the kind of guy I should have a late-night meeting at a waterfront warehouse with."

Hannah laughed. "You make it sound very noir. Aren't Corey and Kyle there?"

"No, they drove over to Bar Harbor for a videoconference with Authentic Productions management."

"Well, I would meet Jonathan Garrido in a dark alley at midnight—" Her voice hardened. "—but then I'm in the pro-Jonathan camp, unlike Kyle Lathey."

As far as Ann was concerned, the reminder that Kyle seemed to have it out for Jonathan counted as a point in Jonathan's favor.

"If you're nervous," continued Hannah, "you could always have someone on the phone with you while you're with him."

"That's a good idea." Ann paused. "Could you be the one on the phone?"

"I'm afraid not," said Hannah. "There's some Stata Mater business I need to take care of—I've been woefully neglecting my duties over the last week."

"That's okay—I'll think of someone else. Thanks, Hannah."

They ended the call.

She gazed at Jessy, who was floating a few inches above the topmost row of lobster traps, then tapped Jonathan's number.

"Sorry about that," she said. "I'm at the video production office in Manset. Can you come here?"

"Sure."

She gave him the address. "Don't expect anything fancy—it's a warehouse. When do you think you'll be here?"

"About half an hour."

"Don't rush, especially because the roads might be slick because of the rain." The last thing Stata Mater—or anyone else, for that matter—needed was another of their researchers coming to grief.

"I'll be careful. I really appreciate this, Ann—thanks."

She passed the time trying to look approachable for Jessy's benefit—to no effect—and thinking that she would have been more comfortable waiting in the Manset house. However, from a safety point of view, the warehouse was probably a better bet. There were more people at the waterfront than there would be on Seawall Road—she assumed there were people coming and going from The Perch, just down the street, and she could hear some activity from the marina next door.

When fifteen minutes had passed, she got out her phone and tapped Mike's number. It rang a few times and went to voicemail. She had just talked to him—why wouldn't he be answering now?

She disconnected and tapped Scott's number. He picked up almost immediately.

"Hey, Scott."

"Hey, Annie! What are you up to?"

"Trying to get in touch with Mike. Is he there at the house?"

"No, he went out a little while ago. I decided to bake cookies and didn't have any vanilla, so he volunteered to get some. He was probably driving when you called. I'll ask him to call you when he gets home."

"What kind of cookies are you baking?" asked Ann.

They were debating whether saltiness was a desirable characteristic for chocolate chip cookies when the door of the warehouse opened, and Jonathan Garrido stepped in.

Ann glanced at her watch: twenty minutes. Evidently Jonathan hadn't heeded her advice not to rush.

She briefly tried to figure out a way she could seem to end

her call with Scott while in reality keeping the line open. However, she couldn't think of a way to signal to Scott not to hang up without indicating to Jonathan that she, too, found him suspicious enough that she felt the need for a chaperone for their meeting. Plus, if the look of misery on his face was contrived, then he had a career as an actor awaiting him if the research gig didn't work out.

"Scott, I've got to go—it was great talking to you. No need for Mike to call me back."

"You're sure?"

"Yup, I'm sure. Bye." She ended the call and slipped the phone into her pocket.

"Thank you so much for seeing me tonight," said Jonathan. "I think I'd have gone crazy if I had to wait until tomorrow to find out what you saw at the Spindle."

She waved him toward a chair at the table, and he sat.

"How are you doing?" she asked.

He ran his fingers through his hair. "The police called me and said they wanted to put me under protection, just in case this theory that someone in the industry has it out for SMT staff is true." He shook his head. "It's ridiculous! Why would anyone want to interfere with Stata Mater's work? We're giving away our inventions, for God's sake."

"Wouldn't that mean putting everyone at Stata Mater under protection?"

"There aren't that many of us—fewer than a dozen on the research team."

"I just talked with Hannah and she didn't say anything about them contacting her."

Jonathan pulled out his phone. "I just got the call not long ago. Maybe the police are working through a list and hadn't gotten to Hannah yet." He tapped and put the phone to his ear and, after a moment, said, "Hey, Hannah, it's Jonathan. I'm here with Ann Kinnear. Okay if I put you on speaker?" After a moment, he tapped the speaker on.

"Hello, Jonathan. Hello again, Ann," said Hannah. Ann could still hear what sounded like traffic noise in the background.

"Have you gotten a call about being put under police protection?" Jonathan asked Hannah.

"Yes, just a couple of minutes ago. I gathered that they haven't been able to determine whether Shelby jumped or was pushed from Otter Cliff, and with it looking like there might have been foul play, they're relooking at Leo's death as well. I guess they want to play it safe."

"They think it's me," groaned Jonathan. "I just know it."

"Don't be silly," Hannah said briskly. "They're just considering every possibility."

"If they're pursuing every possibility," said Jonathan, "they should put Ann and Garrick under protection, too. They're the only ones who could talk with the victims and find out what really happened."

After a pause, Hannah said, "Yes, I suppose that's true ... although I'm not sure the authorities would see it that way."

"I can't imagine Garrick being excited about police protection," said Ann, "especially if it meant having a cop staying in his house with him."

"I do see the benefit of being extra careful," said Hannah, "just until we have a better handle on what's going on. I imagine the MDI police are stretched quite thin with all this unusual activity and it would be better for them if they didn't have to assign one officer to each of us. I would invite the two of you to stay at my place, but I only have two bedrooms."

"If this is really necessary," said Ann, "the two of you are welcome to stay at the house in Manset. It has three bedrooms, and two of them are available. That would be more convenient for me anyway because I don't have a car."

"That sounds like an excellent idea," said Hannah, sounding relieved. "Jonathan, what do you think?"

"Better than staying home alone and jumping at every noise."

"Very good," said Hannah. "Let me pack up an overnight bag and I'll meet you at the production office. And I'll call the police and let them know what our plan is."

They ended the call. Jonathan slipped his phone into his pocket, then leaned forward, his elbows on the table. "So you saw Shelby at the Spindle."

"Yes, I saw her standing on the rocks. I tried talking to her, but I didn't get any response."

"How did she look? You know ..." Jonathan grimaced and made a vague gesture toward his face.

"She looked like I imagine she did when she was alive. Not like her body would look now. Even her clothes looked like they must have when she went off the cliff. For example, no tears in her jacket, as far as I could see."

"How did she seem?"

Ann hesitated. "She seemed like she didn't want us there."

Jonathan looked surprised. "Really? Why do you think that was?"

"I don't know. If someone pushed her, I would think she would want us to know who it was. If she fell, I would think that she would want us to know that there was no foul play involved. If she jumped ... I don't know. Maybe she was embarrassed or regretted doing it."

He ran his fingers through his hair, leaned back in his chair, and shifted his gaze to the ceiling. "Based on what Shelby told me about her family, I don't know if they could stand it if they knew she killed herself. If the question of what happened at Otter Cliff is never answered, they can hang onto the possibility that she died accidentally during a hike, doing something she loved."

"In the middle of the night?" Ann asked with raised eyebrows.

Jonathan slumped forward again. "People can convince themselves of some pretty crazy shit if the alternative is too painful." He hesitated, then continued. "Maybe Shelby would be more talkative if I was there."

"Maybe."

"Would you go back and try again?"

"We can ask Hannah if she'd be up for another run as water taxi—"

"I can take us. I have a boat—bigger than Hannah's, so weather wouldn't be so much of an issue."

"I do believe bigger would be better. Let's check the weather in the morning and see how it's looking."

"If I'm lucky," said Jonathan, "a big storm will hit and distract everyone's attention from the rumor mill. Now people think that I somehow pushed Leo off the path. Most of them probably think that I pushed Shelby off Otter Cliff. And Kyle Lathey is fanning the flames."

Ann heard a sound, like the rattle of a doorknob, from the vicinity of the front door. Was it Hannah arriving for the impromptu sleepover at the Manset house? Corey and Kyle back already from their meeting with Authentic Productions? Eric checking to see why there was still a light burning at his warehouse? The noises from the marina had stopped a few minutes before. Maybe whoever had been working there had decided to check on the unexpected late-night activity at the warehouse. But the door remained closed.

"Did you hear something?" she asked Jonathan.

"No. Did you?"

"I thought so, but maybe I was wrong."

Jessy drifted toward the front of the building and disappeared through the wall. Ann wondered in any of the denizens of Manset ever caught a glimpse of a little girl materializing through a wall or door. Few had a sensing skill as advanced as hers and Garrick's, but she suspected that many had a hint of the ability.

She turned back to Jonathan. "I understand from Hannah that you and Shelby were close." She wanted to make it clear to Jonathan that she, unlike Kyle, wasn't digging for dirt on him.

"Yes. We had been dating for a couple of months. But she had just broken up with me."

"Really?" said Ann, surprised. "I hadn't heard about that. When did that happen?"

"The day after Leo died."

"No kidding," she said, suddenly wishing she had kept Scott on the line.

He sighed. "She was really upset about his death. I can understand why. Not only was she close to him—" He shot a look at Ann. "—strictly professionally, I would bet my life on it — but she was right there when it happened. Watched him fall and hit the rocks."

"Did she talk about it with you?"

Jonathan smiled sadly and drew his fingers across his mouth, ending with a little twist. "She wasn't one to talk about things like that, things that upset her. I didn't ask. I figured she'd tell me if and when she wanted to." He picked up the padlock from the table and turned it in his fingers. After a moment, he continued. "I was surprised when she broke things off between us. I thought things were going well."

As Ann considered this information, she caught a movement out of the corner of her eye and turned to see Jessy materializing through the front wall. Jessy drifted toward the table where Ann and Jonathan sat, then removed her finger from her mouth and hooked her index fingers together like links in a chain. Was this her indication that she finally wanted to connect? Ann wished Jessy had come to that conclusion half an hour ago.

"Not right now," Ann murmured under her breath to the little girl.

"Pardon?" said Jonathan.

"Nothing." After a pause, she continued in a carefully neutral voice. "I understand you had a key to Shelby's car."

"Yeah. We both liked hiking but didn't like to do out-and-backs, so we would take both our cars, leave one at one end of the trail and the other at the other end, and then we could hike through. It was easier if we had keys to each other's cars."

"You found the flash drive in her car."

"Yeah." He tossed the padlock back on the table and leaned back in the chair. "Another tidbit from Kyle Lathey?"

She nodded.

"It was just sitting right there on the passenger seat. When I saw what was on it, I couldn't believe it."

"You were surprised?"

He sat forward, angry. "Of course I was surprised. Why should Shelby have a video of a former SMT guy getting blown up? She wasn't even at SMT when it happened, and after the initial excitement died down, people tended not to talk about it much." He laughed bitterly. "The first victim of the Stata Mater curse, I guess. I should have just kept quiet about it, but I made the mistake of taking it to the police."

"It was the right thing to do."

He jumped to his feet and began pacing. "What if the police aren't really interested in providing protection for us against some competitor's hit man? What if they're just using it as an excuse to keep me under surveillance?"

"If they wanted to keep you under surveillance, I'm guessing they could do that without having to have an excuse." Ann was suddenly anxious to change the topic, at least until Hannah joined them and they were comfortably ensconced in the Manset house. She crossed her arms. "I wish the building was a little better heated. I feel like I'm never going to get warm."

Jonathan sat back down at the table and pulled the padlock toward him, turning it in nervous fingers. "Who was that you were talking to when I showed up?"

"My brother-in-law." She mustered a smile. "We were having an in-depth conversation about cookies. Chocolate chip."

He gazed down at the padlock. After a moment, he said, "Shelby liked shortbread."

She sniffed. "Do you smell that?"

He raised his eyebrows. "Shortbread?"

She sat forward and scanned the warehouse. "No. It smells like something's burning."

36

Jonathan looked around, alarm registering on his face. "Smoke?"

"It's faint," said Ann. "Maybe it's coming from next door."

A movement from near the table caught Ann's eye, and she saw Jessy shaking her head.

"Not from next door?" asked Ann. "From this building?"

The girl nodded.

Jonathan evidently thought Ann was answering her own question, not talking to a spirit, since he stood and scanned the warehouse.

Ann thought back to the video on the flash drive Jonathan had claimed he found in Shelby Kim's car: Oscar Sanz walking into the building that blew up seconds later. She jumped up from the table. "Let's get out of here." As she grabbed her knapsack, she saw the flicker of flames at the base of the wall opposite the lobster traps. "There!" she said, pointing.

They ran for the front door. Ann grabbed the knob and pulled, but the door stayed shut. She braced one arm against the doorjamb and pulled again. Nothing.

"Let me try," said Jonathan.

She stepped aside and Jonathan heaved on the door. It remained closed.

Jessy had followed them to the door. "I think it's padlocked on the outside." Ann turned to the girl and linked her fingers together as she had seen Jessy do. "That's what you meant by this, isn't it?"

Jessy nodded.

"What are you talking about?" asked Jonathan.

"There's a spirit in the warehouse, a little girl. She says there's a padlock on the outside of the door."

"But the padlock on the table—"

"Was on the outside of this door when I got here," said Ann.

"Someone locked us in while we were sitting there talking?" said Jonathan, his voice spiking.

Ann glanced toward the metal double-height door on the front wall, but she didn't need Jessy to tell her that that was padlocked shut on the inside. A quick scan of the area didn't reveal a convenient key hanging on a nearby nail.

"I think there's a door in back," said Ann.

They dashed across the warehouse. Fingers of flame were now creeping up the right-hand wall, licking around the wooden supports in what looked like gentle caresses. Ann could hear a quiet hiss emanating from the wood.

The light from the ceiling fixture didn't reach to the back of the warehouse and Ann was groping for the handle of the roll-up door she remembered seeing when a light—Jonathan's flashlight app—hit the door, revealing another padlock.

"Shit!" hissed Jonathan.

"Try kicking it open," said Ann. "I'm calling 911."

Jonathan raised a foot and slammed it into the door. The wood shook but didn't give.

Ann stabbed the controls on her phone.

Jonathan slammed his foot into the door again, with the same result.

Ann heard the ring of the call going through.

Jonathan slammed his foot into the door a third time. Nothing.

"I don't think we're going to have any better luck with the door in front," he said. "It's metal—and it opens in."

"Maybe we can break through a wall. Let's try the front—maybe someone will hear us and help."

They ran again to the front of the building, Ann with the phone held to her ear. The ringing continued.

Jonathan kicked at the front wall between the two doors.

"No one's picking up," said Ann.

"That's because they're all—" *Bang!* "—guarding Stata Mater staff," said Jonathan through clenched teeth.

Ann contributed a few kicks to the wall. "It's tougher than it looks," she gasped. She could feel the heat from the fire tingling on her exposed skin.

"Still no answer?" he asked.

She shook her head.

"Emergency services close down for the night?" he said, his voice tight with frustration. He stepped back from the wall. "Maybe there's something in here we can use that will work better than our feet."

They scanned the warehouse but, as far as Ann could see, except for the card tables, the folding chairs, and the pile of video equipment, it was completely empty.

Jonathan took a step toward the pile. "Maybe something in there?"

Ann mentally ran through the equipment she had seen deployed at Brookview for the shoot—flimsy reflector stands, cameras that were heavy but would take too long to remove from their carrying cases, especially because the fire was beginning to lick at the corner of the tarp under which they lay.

"Nothing I can think of," she said.

Just then, the call went through. "I'm calling to report a fire —" she began.

"Hello! This is Hannah Jeskie. I can't answer your call right now—"

"Damn it!" she exclaimed.

"What?"

She stabbed off the call. "I accidentally redialed Hannah."

"I'm going to try one of the chairs," said Jonathan. He ran to the conference area and grabbed one of the folding chairs, then brought it back and began swinging it at the wall. The chair had little more effect than their feet had. Jonathan tossed the chair aside and it hit the floor with a clang.

Ann was about to try again to put in the emergency call when her eyes drifted to the small plexiglass-covered windows near the ceiling

"Jonathan, call 911."

The fire on the right-hand side of the warehouse had continued to spread, and it no longer looked gentle—it reminded Ann of a snake consuming its prey, the old, splintered wood of the supports gradually being enveloped by flames and smoke, the earlier hiss now morphing to a screech.

"I'm calling to report a fire," she heard Jonathan say. "The Manset waterfront. We're trapped inside the warehouse."

Ann jogged to the stack of lobster traps and upended her knapsack onto the floor. Jonathan appeared at her side, still talking to the dispatcher, as she scrabbled through the contents. She found her Swiss Army knife and slipped it into her pocket.

"What are you doing?" he asked, his voice unsteady.

"I'm going to see if I can get one of the windows open."

She grasped the slats of one of the lobster traps. She was

surprised that it was metal, not wood, which she counted as a blessing—the less flammable material in the building the better.

The heat pressed against her back and she could sense a canopy of smoke beginning to collect in the rafters.

She wedged the toe of her boot into one of the narrow openings between the slats, then pulled herself off the ground. She half expected the entire stack to come down on top of her, but someone must have secured it to the wall, although whoever had done the securing had not anticipated that a person would try to use it as a climbing wall. The stack shivered, and she sensed Jonathan next to her, trying to steady it.

Ann remembered driving by the Southwest Harbor Fire Department on her trips up and down Route 102. It was just on the other side of the town center, not five minutes away. She recalled reading that fire crews could turn out in less than two minutes.

She didn't think they had seven minutes.

She shifted her hand up for a higher purchase, extracted her toe from its original position, and pulled herself up.

Out of the corner of her eye she could see that flames had reached the top of the opposite wall and were crawling across the rafters toward her. The crackle of the burning wood might have sounded cheerful in other circumstances—seated around the fire pit in Mike and Scott's back yard, for example—but she could only imagine each crack as a split in the wood that supported the roof. The pall of smoke was descending lower each second, and although the densest part of it had not yet reached the top of the stack, the air scraped her throat as she climbed. She pulled her shirt up to cover her nose and mouth.

She hauled herself onto the top of the precarious platform. A security light from the neighboring building cast a stark glow through the dirt-streaked plexiglass and she could see that the panes were secured by a few screws. She tried banging on the window—to dislodge it or to attract the attention of any passersby—but the window merely vibrated with a dull thunk. Furthermore, her weight shift sent a tremor through the stack of traps and, over the rising sound of the flames, she thought she heard the snap of a rope breaking. The stack swayed nauseatingly, then thudded back against the wall. She risked a glance down and could make out Jonathan's figure, his back braced against the stack.

She turned back to the windows. The plexiglass rested against an exterior wooden frame—there was no way she would be able to push it out without unfastening the screws.

Her lungs screamed for air but she tried to keep her breathing shallow. Her head felt so hot she had a dizzying image of her hair bursting into flame.

She fumbled the Swiss Army knife out of her pocket. The choking smoke not only made it painful to breathe but had brought tears to her eyes that nearly blinded her. She began pulling tools out of the knife's handle—a corkscrew, a tiny scissors, something that she guessed was a can opener. Did it even have a screwdriver?

She yelped as a blade sliced her finger and a fit of coughing gripped her. She'd use the knife. By feel, she slotted the end of the blade into one of the screw heads and began to turn. Within a few seconds, the blade was wet—no doubt with blood—and she wiped her hand across the front of the sweatshirt. She returned to the screw, alternating between turning the blade and trying to wipe her hand dry. A half a minute must have ticked by before the screw came loose and disappeared between the stack of traps and the wall.

Ann's head was pounding, and now the smoke was starting to block the illumination from the security light. She ran her hand around the edge of the piece of plexiglass. Three more screws.

She twisted to check the progress of the fire. Flames were now dancing along the rafters, and the smoke was roiling down from the ceiling like an angry storm cloud. Then, as she watched, the smoke swirled and, for a moment, cleared. She almost laughed with relief—until she realized that the cause of the momentary reprieve was that the fire had burned through the roof. At that moment, she felt a vibration travel through the structure and one of the braces at the back of the warehouse gave way and crashed to the floor.

She reversed the knife in her hand and jammed it into the wooden window frame. The tip of the knife buried itself in the wood and the stack swayed. Either Jonathan had moved away from the stack, or her climb to the top had shifted the center of gravity high enough that he couldn't exert much stabilizing force. She forced the knife out, twisting it as she pulled, bringing the stack tight against the wall as she did so. She ran her fingers over the space where the knife had hit—the wood was spongy, and it felt as if a piece of wood had come out with the knife.

She plunged the knife into the frame again. The stack shuddered and tilted away from the wall.

She twisted and pulled the knife out. The stack swayed upright again.

She plunged and pulled, plunged and pulled, expecting at any moment that the stack would overbalance and send her crashing to the concrete floor, but each time her pull brought her and the stack back to the wall. She was now completely blind, the smoke building once again and ripping choking coughs from her with each breath.

After half a minute, she groped at the space and found that she had dug a finger's-width divot in the wood. She worked her fingers between the wood and the plexiglass, barely feeling the splinters that rasped into her knuckles. She gave a wrench, then a second, a third, and the panel separated from the frame.

A cool, fresh breeze swirled past her. She gulped in air.

She couldn't turn the pane to fit it out the window. She pulled it toward her, then tried to balance it on top of the stack of traps, but it slipped off the edge. She was grateful that the crash she heard dimly over the mounting roar of the fire sounded more like plexiglass hitting concrete than like plexiglass hitting Jonathan. She pulled her head and shoulders out the opening.

She could hear people yelling, evidently clustered near the front door. She heard the dull ring of metal on metal and guessed that someone was using an ax on the door. Then she heard and felt a thunk and guessed that now they had turned their attention to the door frame.

"Help!" she tried to yell, but it came out as a croak.

She sucked in fresh outside air, then shimmied around so that her head and shoulders were inside again. She shifted on her precarious perch and managed to swing her legs out the window. She wanted to call down to Jonathan that he would be out soon, but she didn't want to lower the shirt from her face or take the lungful of air she would need to do it.

She realized that she should have taken a better look out the window to see where she was going to land, but it was too late now—she couldn't turn her head to look, and she doubted she could have climbed back into the building, even if she had wanted to. She was steeling herself to make the drop blind when she heard more yelling.

"Someone's climbing out the window! Over here!"

Out of the corner of her eye, she saw several forms appear around the corner of the building.

"Hold on, miss!" she heard, then the voices were below her. "Can you hang by your hands? Then we can reach your feet."

Dreading losing her hold, she managed to shift so that her hands were braced on the rotting wood of the window frame.

Regretting that her usual exercise regimen of hiking and walking didn't do much for arm strength, she tried to lower herself but lost her grip almost immediately.

She tumbled down, but hands grabbed her as she fell. She hit the ground awkwardly but upright, surrounded by several men, including Eric.

"Are you okay?" he asked, his face flushed, his eyes wide.

She nodded, trying to summon the breath to talk.

"Is anyone else in there?" asked another one.

"Yes," she said, already hobbling toward the front of the warehouse. "One person."

When she got to the front, one of the men was, in fact, working on the doorframe with an ax that looked woefully unequal to the task. She could see that a padlock was looped through the hasp on the door.

"Somebody replaced the lock," said Eric. "That padlock isn't mine."

Just then two fire engines rolled up, followed by a police cruiser.

"There's someone inside," yelled one of the men as the first responders swarmed out of the vehicles.

As one of the firefighters retrieved a crowbar from the truck, the police officer began herding onlookers away from the building.

The crowbar made quick work of the hasp to which the padlock was secured. Firefighters stood at the open door, scanning an interior that was painted a dirty orange by the blaze.

Ann slipped past the officer and hobbled toward door.

"He's to the left," she yelled. "Next to a pile of traps."

One of the firefighters gave her a thumbs up and disappeared into the building.

The police officer appeared beside her.

"You need to step back, ma'am."

"But I might be able to help—"

"They know what they're doing. The best help is to give them room to do their jobs."

She was trying to marshal other arguments when a movement from the other side of the street caught her eye. Hannah was waving to her from the group of onlookers.

Ann hobbled over to her, followed by the officer.

"I just got here," said Hannah when Ann reached her. "What in the world happened? Where's Jonathan?"

Ann decided that the answer to the first question could wait. "He's still in there," she said grimly.

She watched with a growing sense of dread—had Jonathan moved away from the stack of traps?—when finally the firefighter emerged, leading Jonathan behind him. An EMT escorted Jonathan to an ambulance. Hannah hurried over to him, Ann following as quickly as her aching ankle would allow.

When they reached the ambulance, the EMT was trying to coax Jonathan into the back.

"Jonathan, are you all right?" Hannah asked.

He nodded, tried to speak, and was overcome by a paroxysm of coughing.

"It's best if you get checked up at the hospital, sir," the EMT said.

"No, I'm fine," Jonathan croaked, then had to pause to let another bout of coughing pass. He pointed at Ann. "She's bleeding."

She looked down and realized that her cut finger had left a gory mess across the front of Corey's sweatshirt.

As one team of firefighters began pumping water on the warehouse and another began hosing down the roof of the marine supply store, the EMTs tended to Ann and Jonathan. They draped mylar emergency blankets around their shoulders, then one of them cleaned and bandaged Ann's finger.

The EMTs continued to argue the benefits of a trip to the hospital with Jonathan, who seemed as averse to the idea as Ann was. Hannah leaned toward Ann.

"Do you really not want to go?" she whispered.

"I don't think I need to—and I'm a big fan of avoiding trips to hospitals if at all possible."

Hannah addressed the EMTs. "My name is Dr. Hannah Jeskie. I'm a friend of these two, and I can keep an eye on them. I'll be sure to get them to the emergency department if their situation warrants."

The EMTs exchanged looks and shrugs, then turned their attention to the fire.

Hannah smiled at Ann and whispered, "Sometimes it doesn't pay to be too specific about one's field of research."

A few minutes later, there was a shotgun-like crack from the warehouse. Then the roof collapsed with a roar, sending a billow of sparks and smoke into the sky.

"Oh, God," groaned Ann, "all of Corey's equipment."

"And your car, I'm afraid, miss." It was one of the men who had caught her when she fell.

"What?"

"Your Tesla, miss. I'm afraid it's getting a little ... melty."

She looked at him for a moment and then surprised him and the other bystanders with a rasping laugh.

37

Ann sat on the couch in the living room of the Manset house, now dressed in her own clothes, an extra-large glass of red wine at her side. She would likely still be in the shower if Jonathan hadn't been waiting his turn. She hoped that the hot water held out for him.

Corey's sweatshirt was soaking in the kitchen sink, although Ann didn't hold out much hope of getting out the bloodstains. The rest of the smoke-tainted clothes were sloshing in the basement washing machine, and the arrival of a still stunned Eric with a supply of clean clothes for Jonathan eliminated the need for her to pass on Corey's clothes to another needy recipient.

From the kitchen, she could hear Hannah chatting with Officer Damczyk, who had been assigned as their protection detail. The smell of soup wafted into the living room and Ann's stomach growled.

Hannah came into the living room, carrying a bowl and an empty wine glass, a bottle of red wine tucked under her arm. She put the bowl down on the coffee table. "Chicken noodle, courtesy of The Perch." She topped off Ann's glass, filled her own, and sat down on the loveseat. "Officer Damczyk says that they sent someone over to Garrick's house, but Garrick wouldn't let him in, so the officer is parked in Garrick's driveway."

Ann sat up. "Corey and Kyle ... I should have thought to tell the police—"

"The police got in touch with them in Bar Harbor—they're fine. I imagine they'll be along here any minute."

Headlights swept across the living room wall and Hannah stepped to the window.

"In fact, I believe that's them now. Officer," Hannah called toward the kitchen, "that's Mr. Duff and Mr. Lathey arriving."

She returned to the kitchen and in a moment, Ann heard conversation—including one voice she hadn't expected to hear.

Mike stepped into the living room. "Holy hell, are you okay?"

"How did you get here so fast?" she asked, amazed.

"I didn't have far to come. I've been at the Bar Harbor Inn. I ran into Corey and Kyle."

She put down her glass and levered herself off the couch with a wince. She hadn't gotten away from the warehouse unscathed, but it appeared to be nothing worse than the cut finger, a twinge-y back muscle, a slightly twisted ankle, and noticeably reddened cheeks, ears, and hands.

They met in the middle of the room and hugged, although Mike must have noticed her wince because his hug was gentle.

"I hung around in case you needed me," he said as Corey and Kyle came into the room. "But obviously that didn't do much good. *Are* you okay?"

Corey hovered behind Mike, concerned eyes on Ann.

"You don't look too much the worse for wear," said Kyle cheerfully.

"Nothing that a good night's sleep and more wine won't cure," said Ann, addressing her response to Mike.

"Well, sit back down," said Mike. "Can I get you anything?"

"No, thanks. Hannah's been taking care of us."

Hannah returned from the kitchen with more glasses and a freshly opened bottle of wine. "We're enjoying the therapeutic benefits of Cabernet Sauvignon," she said. "May I pour for you gentlemen?"

Mike and Kyle accepted. Corey declined. Mike managed to beat Kyle to a seat beside Ann on the couch, so Kyle detoured to the loveseat. Corey pulled out the piano bench for Hannah to sit on, then propped himself against the piano.

"So, what happened?" he asked.

Ann ran through the events at the warehouse, including the padlocked front door that had trapped her and Jonathan. "Eric said the padlock's not his—in fact, I brought the padlock that I took off the front door inside with me. I think I might have heard when whoever it was put it on the door."

"I know this is a long shot, but any chance it was an accident?" asked Corey. "Someone locking the warehouse thinking that it was empty?"

"And then, coincidentally, having it catch fire?" said Mike.

"And who would just happen to lock the door other than someone on the project or Eric?" added Ann.

"Yeah, you're right," said Corey, running his fingers through his hair. "I just can't believe someone tried to burn down the warehouse with you guys in it."

"I suppose it's possible we weren't the targets," said Ann uncertainly. "Maybe someone has a vendetta against Eric."

Kyle snorted. "That's a little hard to believe, with all the stuff going on that ties in with Stata Mater."

"Good thing you have an alibi, Kyle," grumbled Mike. "Otherwise I might be tempted to think that you had staged the ultimate photo and video op."

Kyle's face creased with irritation. "That's a shitty thing to say."

"Well, if anyone still suspected Jonathan of any involvement in all this, I hope that this erases any suspicions," said Hannah. "Not only would he have been unlikely to try to burn the warehouse down with himself in it, but he obviously wasn't in a position to put the padlock on the door after he entered."

They heard a slow tread descending the steps from the second floor and Jonathan appeared in the living room door. He was wearing a sweatshirt emblazoned with The Perch's stylized fish logo and the message *Pull up a stool and perch a while!* The back of his neck was bright red and his hair looked a bit frizzled, but otherwise he also looked relatively unscathed. As he greeted the party, Hannah poured him a large glass of wine and offered him her seat on the piano bench, which he declined.

"Any expert opinion on the fire, Jonathan?" Mike asked.

"I'm afraid I wasn't observing it with my usual scientific detachment, but the way the flames spread, it wouldn't be like any accidental fire I've ever seen."

Ann turned to Corey. "I've got to imagine that the video equipment is a total loss."

He sighed. "I don't see us having a use for it anytime soon in any case."

"And, Kyle, I think your car's a goner, too," she said.

He shrugged. "It's a rental. Not my problem."

She took a sip of wine, somewhat disappointed. She had to admit that she had hoped that Kyle Lathey would be a little more upset about the "melty" Tesla.

After a few more minutes discussing open questions, unsatisfying answers, and unsubstantiated theories, Ann smothered a yawn.

"You look beat," said Mike. "We should let you get some rest." He stood. "What's the plan for accommodations for tonight?"

She pushed herself off the couch. "Hannah and Jonathan are going to stay here. We figured it would be easier for the police to have us all in one place." She gave him an apologetic smile. "Sorry I gave your room away—I thought you were in Pennsylvania."

"No problem. I'll go back to the Bar Harbor Inn. In the morning we can see what the authorities have come up with for the cause of the fire."

They filtered through to the kitchen. As the others headed for the back door, Ann called Corey back. She waved toward the sweatshirt soaking in the sink. "I don't think the sweatshirt is salvageable. I owe you a replacement."

"Don't worry about it," he said. He held her gaze for a moment. "God, I was so worried about you when I heard about the fire. If something had happened to you because of your involvement in the project—" He clamped his lips shut and dropped his eyes to the floor.

"I'm fine," she said. "Plus, if you can get Tippy's okay to continue with the documentary, think what an exciting segment the fire will be. I'll bet someone got it on video."

He met her eyes and raised an eyebrow. "Now you're starting to sound like Kyle." His reproving tone didn't completely hide his relieved smile.

She smiled back. "Heaven forbid."

"Duff, you coming?" called Kyle from the back door.

"See you tomorrow," Corey said to Ann.

She followed them to the door. As Mike stepped outside, she put a hand on his arm.

"Mike, thank you for staying on MDI. It means a lot to me."

He grinned. "Those also serve who only stand and wait." He turned and followed Corey and Kyle to the car.

38

Two Weeks Earlier

S helby knocked lightly on the door of Leo's office. She didn't really expect to get an answer, since it was seven o'clock in the morning—several hours before Leo normally arrived at the lab. When she was met with the expected silence, she tapped the passcode into the digital lock and stepped into the office.

She had spoken to Leo the previous day about some data she needed for her final tests of the new clean agent. He had told her it was in a notebook in his office and to help herself.

She pulled open the drawer where he usually kept the tablet containing the ELN—electronic laboratory notebook—where he documented his research, but the drawer was empty. She sighed and slid it shut. There was little on the desk that might hide a tablet: a framed photo of Tippy, a docking station, a phone, a wire tray for the rare paper mail or hard copy documents he had to deal with. She glanced around the office, but the rest of it was not so neat, and she didn't feel like searching for the tablet. She would wait until Leo arrived at the lab.

She was about to leave the office when her gaze drifted back to the wire tray. It held a blue notebook, a pen clipped to its spiral binding.

She didn't recall Leo ever using a paper notebook—in fact, she couldn't remember ever seeing him write anything by hand —but he hadn't specified that the notebook was of the electronic variety.

She picked up the notebook and flipped it open. It was filled with precise block lettering that wouldn't have been out of place on an architectural drawing. It was just the kind of writing she would have expected from Leo Dorn. She paged through several sheets. Yes, this was clearly related to her research.

She looked around for something to leave a note on but, true to Leo's normally paperless operations, she couldn't see anything. She tore a corner off the last page of the notebook and jotted a note.

Leo, I borrowed the notebook, let me know when you need it back. Shelby

She anchored the note with the photo of Tippy, then strolled back to the lab, turning pages as she went. Yes, this was definitely material related to her research, although there were some unexpected entries, some notes regarding unfamiliar results. She reached the lab and settled down at the table to examine it more closely.

An hour later, her surprise had morphed into shock.

She sensed more than heard the lab door open behind her and turned to see Leo Dorn standing in the doorway.

"I see you found the notebook," he said.

"What is this?"

He stepped into the lab and closed the door. "What do you think it is?"

"It's clearly based on my work. There are similarities

between this substance and mine—mainly that it leaves no residue."

He came to the lab table and sat down on the stool next to her. "Did you not expect that we would explore variations of your invention? It's the greatest compliment a researcher can receive—to have others build on his or her work."

"Of course—to improve the desired effect. But this isn't a fire suppressant. It's an accelerant, one that would prove almost impossible to extinguish with commonly-used firefighting techniques."

"Sometimes modifications yield unexpected results."

"This isn't a modification that would be an accidental result. You'd have to be intentionally pursuing accelerant behavior to get this result."

He shrugged. "Sometimes pursuing the behavior opposite of the desired one can prove valuable. It can provide insights that can improve the ability to achieve the desired behavior."

"I don't believe it. You're taking what I created and twisting it. There's no good that could come out of creating this substance. There's no purpose for it."

"There's a purpose for any invention. It just depends on what one's goals are."

She crossed her arms. "So what are your goals?"

He stood and walked to the window, hands in his pockets. "You know that I have business interests beyond just Stata Mater, correct?"

"Yes."

"For-profit businesses." He smiled grimly. "At least, theoretically."

Shelby remembered the argument between Leo and Tippy that she had overheard at the restaurant. "You're earning money with this variant?"

He turned to look at her but didn't answer.

"Who would buy an accelerant?" she asked.

"I think you know the answer to that, Shelby."

"You're selling this to arsonists?" she asked, aghast.

He returned to the lab table and resumed his seat next to her.

"There are people who are out there sitting on useless properties, unsellable properties, whose problems would be solved by a hot-burning, fast-moving fire. A fire that would have done its work by the time the firefighters arrived. A fire that would have progressed so far that no firefighter would need to risk his or her life trying to stop it. A fire that occurred in an unoccupied building so that no firefighter would need to risk his or her life by entering it."

Her voice shot up. "You're telling me that you developed an accelerant to graciously help other people out of their financial troubles? An accelerant so good that it would save the lives of firefighters? I don't believe that for a minute—and I can't believe that you've fooled yourself into believing it." She stopped, hoping he would explain, would clarify how this was not at all what she seemed to think, but he was silent. "The fact that you kept your notes in an actual notebook, not in an ELN, makes it look like you were trying to hide what you're doing. No one is likely to look in a paper notebook. I certainly wouldn't have unless I had thought it was the one you intended for me." She paused. "It wasn't intended for me, was it?"

"No, I ... had forgotten that I left it on the desk." He watched her for a moment, impassive, then pulled in a deep breath. "It's just business, Shelby."

"So you *are* selling the accelerant to arsonists." She felt tears fill her eyes and willed them not to fall.

"It's not a product-for-purchase scenario. It's a ..." He hesitated, choosing his words with care. "It's a partnership. My partners learn of properties belonging to cash-strapped owners—

properties that are, as I said, uninhabited, that are a distance from the nearest fire station, that have no redeeming historical value—and make the needed arrangements. I provide the product. We divide the insurance proceeds with the owner. No residue, so nothing to suggest to an investigator anything other than an accidental fire."

"You think you're providing a service," she said, disgusted.

"We *are* providing a service. And we're very careful to make sure that no one is hurt."

"Except the insurance companies."

He smiled slightly. "Well, yes, except for them. I myself can't drum up much moral outrage over that." He leaned forward. "Shelby, I know you would never want to be directly involved in something like this, but if you could see your way to forgetting what you read in that notebook, forgetting this conversation—"

She jumped to her feet. "You're asking me to cover this up? You're asking me to do that even knowing what happened to my sister? You're crazy!"

He stood as well. "Now, Shelby —"

"I'm going to tell Hannah what you're doing."

He raised a hand. "Now, Shelby, let's not drag Hannah into this."

"I'm going to tell Tippy."

His expression darkened. "I wouldn't do that if I were you."

"Why not?" She tried to sound defiant, but her voice trembled.

He pulled something out of his pocket and handed it to her. It was a flash drive.

"There's a video on it. Watch it."

It took her three tries to get the drive plugged into her laptop. There was only one file on it. She clicked it open.

The video showed a street, a man entering the frame, walking to one of the commercial buildings, unlocking the door, stepping inside a glass-enclosed entrance, relocking the door behind him, then moving away from the door and out of view.

"Who is that?" asked Shelby.

"His name might be familiar to you," said Leo, "but it's unimportant."

Unsure what she was supposed to be watching for, Shelby leaned toward the laptop's display.

When the building exploded, she jumped back so suddenly that she would have fallen if Leo hadn't grabbed her arm.

"Who was that?" Shelby croaked.

"That was Oscar Sanz. Not long before that explosion occurred, he had been doing consulting work for Stata Mater. He, too, happened upon some information he shouldn't have seen. He, too, threatened to report that information to my wife."

"How come I never heard of him?"

"By the time of the explosion, he had left Stata Mater and moved on to other work in Mexico. When he told me what he had found in the Stata Mater records, he had seemed more amenable to an accommodation than you seem to be at the moment. I was working out the details when I heard from a source that Mr. Sanz was rethinking his position."

"Didn't anyone investigate the explosion?"

"They did. It was deemed to be an accident. There had been a rash of similar incidents in the area—"

Shelby gasped. "You didn't—?"

Leo raised his hand. "Those other explosions weren't caused by anything other than unfortunate circumstances ... at least as far as I know. They did, however, ensure that there was not too much incentive to do more than a cursory investigation of this explosion."

He gestured to Shelby's stool. She lowered herself onto the edge. He sat on the other.

"Shelby, I never wanted you to get involved in any of this.

And I realize that this all seems even worse to you than it would to someone else because of what happened to your sister. But I need to make sure that no one ever learns of this. It's not just me who would be put in jeopardy—it's all the people I've worked with as well. If they knew that you had found that notebook, I feel pretty certain what action they would take."

Shelby's eyes drifted to the video, which showed a crowd beginning to gather near the now-burning building.

"That's right, Shelby. And it's not only you who would pay the price. They would wreak their revenge on those close to you. Jonathan Garrido. Your parents." He paused. "Your sister."

Shelby covered her mouth with her hand and hiccupped back a sob.

Leo leaned toward her. "Shelby, they never need to know that you found that notebook. But if they *do* find out, I can't be responsible for what they do."

She buried her face in her hands.

"Do you want to take that chance, not only for yourself, but for the people you love?"

After a long moment, and without moving her hands from her face, she shook her head.

She flinched as she felt his hand on her shoulder.

"I didn't think so."

39

Ann woke up to the welcome smell of coffee brewing. She had slept in the bedroom adjoining the kitchen, leaving the upstairs bedrooms for Hannah and Jonathan, and she could hear the murmur of voices from the next room. She struggled into jeans and a sweatshirt, her back and ankle having stiffened up overnight, and opened the door.

Mike and Officer Damczyk were seated at the kitchen island, each with a mug of coffee in front of him, each absorbed in his phone.

"Morning, Miss Kinnear," said Damczyk, rising from his stool. "Here, have a seat. I need to check in with the station anyway."

As Damczyk retired to the living room, Mike also stood.

"How are you feeling?" he asked.

"Not bad. Nothing that some coffee won't fix."

She reached for a mug on one of the kitchen shelves, but Mike beat her to it. "I can get it for you."

"Gee, thanks, I'm not sure I could have managed it myself," she teased as she sat down on Damczyk's vacated stool.

"Smart ass," said Mike as he poured her coffee and handed over the mug.

Her phone buzzed with a text.

She read the message. "Corey's going over to the warehouse and shoot some video."

"With what?" asked Mike, resuming his seat. "We drove by there last night and it didn't look to me like there was going to be much left to salvage."

She tapped and, in a moment, reported Corey's response. "He's using his cell phone."

Mike sipped his coffee. "High tech."

"Officer Damczyk," Ann called to the next room. "Is it okay if we go over to the warehouse and check it out?"

Damczyk appeared at the kitchen door. "I can't have some of you here at the house by yourselves and some of you at the warehouse."

"I imagine Hannah and Jonathan will want to see it, too," she said. "Maybe we can all go over there when they're up."

The two came downstairs a few minutes later and, despite Ann's protests, Hannah insisted on making them a breakfast of bacon, eggs, and toast from supplies that Mike had picked up that morning on his way from Bar Harbor. After breakfast, the group set off for the warehouse.

The day was sunny, the sky cloudless, a light breeze blowing in from the water. They passed The Perch, where Eric was sitting on one of the picnic tables, feet on the bench, chin resting in his cupped hands. He was watching the buzz of activity around the warehouse site, his expression morose.

"Any news?" asked Ann as they came up to him.

"Nothing official," he said, "but of course everyone's assuming it was ..." He glanced toward Damczyk. "... not an accident."

The officer nodded noncommittally.

"I would just like to say for the record that I really liked that warehouse," said Eric.

"Unless you have some connection to Stata Mater that you haven't shared," said Mike, "I'm guessing you're in the clear. Except, you know, for a burned-down building."

"My only connection was selling beer, meatloaf, and lobster rolls to the documentary team." Eric sighed. "I guess I'll take some more bottled water over to the firefighters." He climbed down from the table and hoisted a pack of bottles that had been sitting on the bench, then joined the group as they continued toward where the warehouse had stood.

Smoke still rose from the ruins. A few men in protective gear were poking around in the debris. The neighboring buildings showed some charring on the sides that had faced the warehouse, but otherwise appeared undamaged. A tow truck was loading the remains of the Tesla onto its flatbed.

Ann saw Corey walking slowly along behind the barriers that had been erected around the site, videoing with his phone. Kyle followed him, his commentary just audible over the buzz of activity. Ann hoped that Corey wasn't recording audio.

Eric went to the barrier and handed the pack of water bottles over to a grandfatherly man wearing a *Southwest Harbor Fire Department* T-shirt, who began transferring the bottles to a cooler next to one of the fire trucks. Behind the man floated Jessy Barnwell. She was chatting away, punctuating her monologue with extravagant gestures. Although the man was probably not consciously aware of her presence, he had a wistful smile on his face that didn't seem tied to the task at hand. If one had darkened his almost-white beard and mustache and subtracted a dozen pounds, he could have been Clarence Barnwell.

"Do you know who that is?" Ann asked Damczyk, gesturing toward the man.

"Fred Barnwell. Retired firefighter, but he still helps out at the fire scenes."

"Any relation to Clarence Barnwell?"

"Yeah, Clarence was Fred's brother."

"Could I ask him something? I think he might," she hesitated, considering how to position the request with Damczyk, "have access to some important information."

Damczyk looked skeptical, but after a moment he nodded. Maybe he had been told to humor MDI's second most famous spirit senser. "You guys stay here," he said to Hannah, Jonathan, and Mike, then led Ann to the barrier.

"Hey, Fred!" he yelled.

Fred Barnwell turned from where he was putting the now-empty water bottle container into the back of a dirty yellow pickup. Jessy turned as well, looking irritated that her monologue had been interrupted.

"Have a minute?" called Damczyk to Fred.

"Sure thing," Fred called back and ambled toward them, followed by Jessy.

"Fred, this is Ann Kinnear," said Damczyk when Fred reached the barrier. "Ann, Fred Barnwell."

"*The* Ann Kinnear?" asked Fred.

"That's me," she said with a smile. As in her conversation with Officer Finney at Otter Cliff, Ann hoped that this would count in her favor.

Fred grinned. "No kidding. Pleased to meet you."

"Miss Kinnear thinks you might have access to," Damczyk shot a look at Ann, "some important information."

"Don't know what it would be, but I'm happy to help if I can," said Fred.

"Mr. Barnwell, I'm going to ask you some questions that may seem strange or silly, but if you can just play along with me for a minute, I'll explain."

"Well, now I'm curious," said Fred, crossing his arms. "Sure, I'll play along."

"I imagine that as a firefighter, you're unhappy that the warehouse burned down."

Jessy looked back toward the ruins, her expression sad.

"I sure am," said Fred. "And not just for that reason. That warehouse used to belong to my brother."

"So I'm sure you'd be interested in any information that might help us find out who set the fire."

"Of course."

Ann glanced at Jessy. The girl had turned her attention from the warehouse to the conversation.

"And if someone had that type of information," Ann said to Fred, "I imagine that you would want them to share it. Is that true?"

"I would hope they would."

"And to share it with me, specifically."

"Sure. With whoever could make some use out of it."

Jessy turned her eyes to Ann and, after a few seconds of consideration, nodded.

"Your brother's granddaughter, Jessy, is here," Ann said to Fred.

Fred glanced around. "Where?"

"Right beside you."

Fred started and looked to his right.

"Other side," said Ann.

He scanned the area to his left. Jessy grinned at him.

"Jessy," said Ann, turning her attention to the girl, "did you see anyone outside the warehouse after I showed up last night?"

Jessy shook her head.

"Did you see anything unusual going on outside the warehouse last night?"

Jessy perked up and hooked her fingers together.

"Anything other than the padlock on the door?"

Jessy's expression fell and she shook her head again.

"Did you see anyone unusual at the warehouse any time yesterday?"

Jessy tentatively pointed to Ann.

"Other than me?"

Jessy pointed toward where Mike, Hannah, and Jonathan stood.

"Anyone other than the people you've seen me talking with in the warehouse?"

Jessy shook her head.

Damczyk was looking studiously toward the activity around the site and appeared to be trying not to laugh.

"Are you, uh, getting any info?" asked Fred, scanning the area toward which Ann was looking.

"I got the information I was looking for," said Ann, "although not what I was hoping for. I saw Jessy following you. She was chatting away at you—the first time I've seen her talking to someone. She wouldn't talk to me at all. I thought if you vouched for me, it might help. It did."

Fred's eyes were still scanning through the area where Jessy floated, and the slight smile Ann had noticed before had returned.

"Have you been back to the warehouse since your brother died?" she asked Fred.

"Couple of times," he said, distracted.

"Did you sense anything during those visits? Get any impressions?"

"Can't say I did ..." he began. He paused, then continued. "Well, I did feel sort of ... happy. Can't say why."

"I think it's because Jessy was there," said Ann.

"Can't say I ever knew that little girl all that well—I was

living out of state for most of the time she was alive—but she was the apple of my brother's eye."

"She's staying around here for a reason," said Ann. She turned back to Jessy. "Jessy, why are you still here at the warehouse?"

Looking for Grandpa, Jessy said in a voice so faint, Ann could barely catch it.

"Do you know what happened to your grandpa?" asked Ann.

He went away and didn't come back.

Ann considered for a long moment, then, hoping she was choosing the right approach, she said, "Your grandpa's dead."

Jessy looked surprised, although not particularly traumatized.

"He died near Kebo Brook," said Ann. "Off the Park Loop Road. I think you might find him there."

Now Jessy looked stricken. *I know Kebo Brook but I don't know how to get there.*

"If your Great-Uncle Fred drove there, could you follow him?"

Jessy nodded vigorously.

Ann turned to Fred. "Fred, would you mind driving to where your brother died?"

"Uh ... sure." He scanned the area again. "Jessy's coming along?"

"Yes. She just needs to be able to follow you to get there."

"Do I ...." Fred glanced toward Damczyk and then back at Ann. "Do I need to bring her back here afterwards?"

"I don't think so. I'm hoping she'll find what she's looking for there, but I'll check later to make sure." She turned to Jessy. "How does that sound?"

Jessy grinned. *Sounds good.*

"Good luck, Jessy."

Thanks, Miss Kinnear.

Looking a little dazed, and with a few glances toward where Jessy floated behind him, Fred climbed into the pickup and started it up. Jessy positioned herself over the truck bed. Fred looked back and Ann gave him a thumbs up. He rolled away slowly, Jessy maintaining her position over the bed. At the intersection, the pickup—and Jessy—turned toward Seawall Road and disappeared from sight.

"Everyone gone?" asked Damczyk. He looked a bit more somber than he had a minute before.

"Yup. Just us now," Ann said and, feeling more cheered than she had in days, returned to where Mike, Hannah, and Jonathan stood, followed by Damczyk.

Ann noticed that while she had been talking with Fred and Jessy, Kyle had abandoned Corey in favor of Eric. Kyle gestured down the road toward the town dock and Eric shook his head. Kyle indicated the marina next door to the former warehouse and Eric shrugged. The one-sided conversation continued for another minute, then Eric extracted himself and started back to The Perch, waving to Ann and the rest of the group as he passed.

They watched the activity at the site for a few more minutes, then Ann said, "Well, that's enough for me. Anyone else ready to head back?"

"I am," said Jonathan.

"Me, too," said Mike.

"I'd like to stay," said Hannah. "I might be able to get a lead on what the cause was or where it started."

"If Dr. Jeskie is going to check out the site," said Damczyk, "she should have some official escort. I can stay with her, but that means there isn't anyone to go back to the house with the rest of you."

"We'll be fine," said Ann. "We'll stick together."

"You guys are going right back to the house?" he asked.

"Yup," said Ann.

Mike and Jonathan nodded their agreement.

Damczyk considered for a moment, then said, "Okay." He turned to Hannah. "After you, Dr. Jeskie."

Damczyk and Hannah started toward the smoking ruins as Ann, Mike, and Jonathan turned back toward the house.

Eric was now sweeping The Perch's patio.

"Hey, what was Kyle Lathey bending your ear about back there?" asked Ann.

Eric stopped sweeping and leaned on the broom. "Looking to rent a boat."

"Why?" she asked, although she had a pretty good idea.

"Said he wanted to go out to the Spindle."

"What did you tell him?" asked Jonathan, his voice tight.

"Not much. I've given Corey my contacts for boat charters. I figure if he wants Kyle to have that information, he'll give it to him."

Ann smiled gratefully. "Thanks."

They returned to the house, where Mike wandered into the living room and started plunking out *Smoke Gets in Your Eyes* on the piano. Ann started another pot of coffee. When it had brewed, she filled her mug, then two more for Mike and Jonathan.

She found Jonathan gazing out one of the living room windows, his hands jammed in his pockets.

"Thanks," he said as he took the mug. He turned from the window. "There's only one reason Lathey would want to go to the Spindle—to take video if he thinks he's continuing with the documentary."

"Yeah," said Ann. "But unless he has me or Garrick with him, there's not much he's going to be able to do other than shoot the scenery."

"Maybe he's enlisted Garrick."

"Kyle Lathey is clearly one of Garrick's least favorite people."

"Maybe Lathey offered him enough money to get him to go."

"I don't see Garrick being swayed by offers of money."

"But you don't know for sure."

Ann sighed and got out her phone. She opened her contacts and tapped Garrick's number. In a moment, he answered.

"Yes."

"Garrick, it's Ann. Can I put you on speaker? Mike and Jonathan are here."

Heavy sigh. "If you must."

She switched to speaker. "Did Kyle Lathey approach you about going out to the Spindle to try to communicate with Shelby Kim?"

"Yes."

"Did you tell him you would do it?"

There was silence for a moment, then Garrick said, "I will ascribe your willingness to ask such a ridiculous question to the evident trauma of the events of last night. Good day."

He hung up.

Ann raised an eyebrow at Jonathan and slipped the phone back in her pocket.

"Okay, fine," he said. "But Lathey still might want to go, and it won't be that hard for him to find someone who will take him. I'm afraid that even if he can't communicate with Shelby, he'll scare her away."

"We can ask Officer Damczyk about going out there when he and Hannah get back."

"I don't think we should wait."

"But we told him we'd stay at the house."

"No, you told him we'd stick together," said Jonathan with a slight smile. "The three of us can go to the Spindle together."

Ann and Mike exchanged glances.

"I think we need to go right now," continued Jonathan, "before Lathey lines up a boat and captain. Plus, don't you think

Shelby might be more likely to speak if someone she knows, like me, is there?"

"Hannah was there when we went to the Spindle the first time and it didn't help," said Ann.

"But Hannah was just a work colleague," said Jonathan. "I was ... more than that." He set his coffee cup aside. "We need to talk with her. I think Shelby might be the only person who can set us on the right track about what really happened to her. And to Leo. Not to mention the warehouse. Assuming she's still at the Spindle when we get there."

Ann looked at Jonathan for a long moment. There was anger in his face—no doubt the anger of someone who felt himself unjustly accused of a crime—but also the sadness of someone who has lost someone he cared deeply about.

"You said you have a boat?" asked Ann.

"Hey," said Mike, "I don't think we should be using Ann's unintentionally vague promise to Damczyk as an excuse to go running off on our own investigative mission."

"It is true that Shelby may be more likely to talk with Jonathan there—" she shot Jonathan a look. "—assuming there are no bad feelings."

He nodded. "There weren't. It's true she said she wanted a little break, but it was on friendly terms."

Mike raised his eyebrows. "You guys had broken up?"

"He told me that last night, Mike," said Ann. "And he's right that Kyle's arrival at the Spindle might drive her away. Finding a way to communicate with Shelby is probably the best way of finding out what's really going on. None of the theories we've come up with seems to fit all the different events. There may be a completely different thread—one none of us have thought of —connecting Leo and Shelby's deaths, which might have been just unfortunate accidents, and the fire at the warehouse."

"And the fire at Shelby's parents' bakery," said Mike.

"True," she said. "Not to mention the explosion that killed that Stata Mater consultant. But I don't think we're going to figure out what it is sitting here. I say we go."

Mike looked from Ann to Jonathan and back. Evidently what he saw deterred him from arguing. He sighed. "Okay, fine. I have the feeling you guys are going in any case, and I don't feel like staying here by myself and getting chewed out by Damczyk when he gets back. Plus," he said, glancing out the window, "it is a nice day for a boat ride."

40

M ike drove them to Seal Harbor, where Jonathan's boat was moored.

Jonathan's *Hotshot* would have been far better suited to the previous day's outing than Hannah's delicate *Mariposa*. As Jonathan rowed them out to the mooring, readied the boat for the trip, and handed around life vests, he told Ann and Mike that *Hotshot* had been built in Southwest Harbor as a working lobster boat and later outfitted for pleasure use. After the previous day's bumpy ride, Ann was glad to be venturing out in such a sturdy- and stable-looking craft, although the continuing sunny weather suggested the boat wouldn't face anything more threatening than gentle swells.

As they motored out of the harbor and turned east, Ann cast occasional glances behind them, but she saw no sign of a boat following. It was possible that if Kyle had found a willing captain in Manset, he could have beaten them to their destination, but as they neared Otter Point, she saw no sign of a boat by the rocks. As before, however, she did see a figure in the midst of the white froth that marked the Spindle.

"Jonathan, do you have binoculars?"

"Sure. Why—do you see her?"

"I think so."

"That's great," he said, his voice excited. "Can someone hold the wheel for a minute?"

Mike took the wheel so that Ann could keep her eyes on the figure on the rocks, and Jonathan retrieved the binoculars from below deck.

As before, the rocks were submerged, but now the water reached only to Shelby's thighs. Also as before, her face was turned away from the approaching boat, although Ann sensed that Shelby might be stealing glances at *Hotshot* through the curtain of her dark hair.

"She's on the rocks," she said to Jonathan. "Get as close as you can."

As Jonathan goosed the throttle to bring the boat closer, Ann gave an internal sigh—the nicer weather was providing an even larger crowd on Otter Cliff than during her previous visit.

When the boat was about two dozen feet from the rocks, she called over. "Shelby, can you hear me? I'm here with Jonathan."

The young woman didn't respond.

"Shelby, last night someone tried to burn down a building that Jonathan and I were in."

Shelby seemed to draw in a quick breath, and her eyes flicked to the boat, then away.

"Obviously we were able to get out, but it seems clear that someone set the fire intentionally. There are so many theories floating around about who could be doing these things, and why, the police don't know where to look first. If you could tell us what happened to you—if you could confirm what happened to Leo—it would be a huge help. It could very possibly save lives. It could save Jonathan's life."

Shelby's eyes drifted up to Jonathan, who was doing his best to focus on keeping the boat off the rocks, then dropped again.

Ann and Jonathan tried various tactics to engage Shelby, but she was no more responsive than she had been on Ann's earlier visit.

Finally Ann shook her head. "No luck. Jonathan, can you think of any other approach we should try?"

"No," he said, looking mournfully toward the rocks. "Shel," he called, "anything you can tell us—anything—might help."

Shelby dropped her head, as if engrossed in the water swirling around her legs.

Jonathan glanced at Ann, who shook her head.

"I don't know what else to do," she said. "It's conceivable that she would be more likely to talk if I were alone—I could try coming out in a kayak—but I doubt it." She hesitated. "You might want to ask Garrick to give it a try."

Jonathan sighed. "I suppose it can't hurt."

Ann wondered what the chances were that Jonathan could talk Garrick into it. Considering the way Garrick felt about cars and small planes, she was pretty sure a trip to a rocky outcropping, even in a boat the size of *Hotshot*, would be a hard no.

"I'll come back, Shel," Jonathan called to the rocks, "in case you decide you have something you want to tell us." He took the wheel and turned back toward Seal Harbor.

The boat was just completing the turn and Jonathan was throttling up when a movement from the Spindle attracted Ann's attention. Shelby Kim was raising her hand to her mouth. Ann snatched up the binoculars and pointed them at the young woman.

Shelby was facing them now, looking after the boat. As Ann watched, Shelby made the motion again: she drew her fingers across her lips, then gave a twist—every child's mime for a secret to be kept, for words that could not be uttered.

"Go back!" she yelled to Jonathan.

"What?" he called over the noise of the engine.

"Go back to the Spindle!"

Jonathan cranked the wheel around and as the boat turned, the wheelhouse momentarily blocked Ann's view of the rocks.

When she could see it again, it was empty.

"Damn!"

"What?" asked Mike.

"She's not there anymore. But I saw her move." She mimicked the sealing-the-lips motion Shelby had made. She turned to Jonathan. "Actually, I saw you do that—when we were talking at the warehouse before the fire and you told me Shelby didn't like to talk about things that upset her. What does it mean?"

Jonathan killed the engine and let the boat drift lazily toward the Spindle.

"It's something she did—I picked it up from her." He gazed toward the rocks. "We had been dating for a little while, and I asked her about her family. At first, she just told me she wasn't in touch with them, but eventually she told me about what had led her to Stata Mater—what had led her to study fire."

"The fire at her house when she was a child?" asked Ann.

He sat down heavily on the captain's chair. Ann and Mike lowered themselves onto the bench on the back deck.

"You know about the fire?" Jonathan asked.

"You mentioned it when we found Shelby's phone at Otter Cliff, and Kyle talked about it at the shoot at Brookview, but he didn't go into any details."

"Shelby was sixteen. When the fire started, she managed to climb out of the window of her second-floor bedroom onto the porch roof and then jump from there into some bushes. She got a bad cut on her leg—she still has the scar." He sighed. "*Had* the scar. Her parents' bedroom was on the first floor, and they were able to get out through the back door. But her sister, Stacy ..." His voice trailed off, and he rubbed his forehead with a trembling hand. "Stacy was trapped in her bedroom. Her dad tried to go back into the house for her—in fact, he got back in the house before the firefighters dragged him out."

"But Stacy survived, right?" asked Ann.

"Yes, she survived, but she was badly burned."

No one said anything for several moments, then Ann said, "I'm sorry, but I don't understand how that relates to what I saw Shelby do on the Spindle." She once again mimicked the sealing-the-lips motion. "Does it mean she never talked about her sister?"

"It did mean that, but it meant more than that." He gazed toward where the water frothed over the rocks. "Shelby was responsible for the fire. A friend had given her a candle and she loved the scent. Vanilla. Her mother didn't like it, but she let Shelby burn it because she loved it so much. Shelby told me that she accidentally left the candle burning on the kitchen counter. The window was open, and the breeze must have blown the curtains into the candle."

Mike puffed out a breath. "Jesus. What a thing to live with."

Jonathan nodded. "There's more. The investigators came to the hospital to tell her mother what they thought had happened. Shelby and her mom were dividing their time between Stacy, who was in the ICU, and her dad, who was being treated for smoke inhalation." He paused. "Her mom told the investigators that she was the one who had left the candle burning. Shelby tried to tell them what had really happened—that she had forgotten to put the candle out before she went to bed—but her mom gave a little shake of her head and made that motion." He, too, drew his fingers across his lips, then twisted shut the invisible lock.

They all turned their gaze back to the still-empty rock.

"She's telling us that someone is lying to protect her?" asked Mike.

"Or just that she can't talk to us," said Ann. "Maybe that she's been warned not to talk to us?"

"Or maybe just that someone is lying about their role in what's happening," said Jonathan.

"We hardly need a spirit to tell us that," said Mike. "Seems like a dead end if we can't get her to talk with Ann."

Jonathan stood, his face anguished. "But are we even going to have another chance?" He looked to Ann. "You said she wasn't there anymore."

Ann shook her head. "I don't know, Jonathan. She may reappear. She may not. We'll just have to keep checking." She sighed. "I think we might as well head back. Maybe Hannah will have found something at the warehouse that will tell us how the fire started."

With a last, forlorn look back toward the Spindle, Jonathan re-started the engine and spun the wheel to point the boat toward Seal Harbor.

A few minutes later, Ann spotted a boat approaching them. At first, she thought that Kyle must have found his ride, but when she looked through the binoculars, she recognized the boat. "I think that's Hannah," she said.

Jonathan cut the power, and in a few minutes, *Mariposa* pulled up beside them.

"Nicer day for an outing than when you and I went out, Ann," called Hannah.

"That's for sure."

Jonathan dropped a couple of fenders over the side and grabbed the line that Hannah tossed him.

"Corey was trying to get in touch with the three of you but couldn't get through," said Hannah, "and when I found you weren't in the Manset house, I thought I knew where you might be. I told him I'd come and get you."

"What's up?" asked Ann.

"He wants you to come back to Manset—we've found something."

"What did you find?"

"He asked me not to tell you because he wants to do a video segment and he wants to record your reaction when you hear what it is. Corey sounded like he was anxious for you to get there."

"Okay," said Ann, "we'll meet you at Manset."

"I need to stop by my house first," she said. "Corey needed a couple of things ..." She reached down and picked up a vintage boom box from the deck. "... including this. He needed something to play a cassette on and didn't have a cassette player. I told him I had one he could borrow." She passed it across to Jonathan. "He needed a couple of other things as well, but I didn't have time to find them before I came out here. I'll meet up with you in Manset as soon as I do that."

"You guys found a cassette tape in the warehouse?" asked Ann. "How could a cassette tape survive that fire?"

Hannah gave a pleased smile. "I didn't say that what Corey had found was at the warehouse."

Ann smiled back. "Very mysterious."

"Were you at the Spindle?" asked Hannah.

"Yes. We saw her again."

"Any luck communicating with her?"

"Not yet."

Hannah sighed. "We may need to look elsewhere to figure out what's going on." She tossed the line back to Jonathan. "I'll see you back in Manset." She spun the wheel of *Mariposa* and motored away.

Jonathan put the cassette player on the deck next to the captain's chair, coiled the rope, and pulled in the fenders, then Ann and Mike sat down again as he fired up the engine and followed in Hannah's wake.

"A cassette tape," said Mike. "I wonder what that's all about."

"I don't know," said Ann. "I can't imagine either Shelby Kim or Leo Dorn leaving a message on a cassette tape—although there is something sort of *Mission Impossible* about it."

"Maybe something in the Stata Mater records?" said Mike uncertainly. "SMT's been around for a while—I guess it's possible they used to keep records on cassette."

"SMT hasn't been around *that* long," said Jonathan. "Even when it was first established, cassette tapes would have been outdated technology."

Ann got out her phone and glanced at the screen. "Did Hannah say that Corey tried to call us?" she asked.

"She said he was trying to get in touch with us and couldn't get through," said Mike. "Why?"

"Because I'm getting a strong cell signal. Why didn't he just call?"

She opened her contacts and hit Corey's number. In a moment, he answered.

"Hey, Corey, it's Ann."

"Hey, Ann. What's up?"

"Were you trying to get in touch with us?"

"No. Why?"

Ann stood, steadying herself on the side of the boat, her eyes on the boom box that sat on the deck near Jonathan's feet. "Were you looking for a way to play a cassette tape?"

He laughed. "Not for the last couple of decades. Why?"

That view of Shelby Kim on the Spindle, drawing her fingers across her lips—the sign that something was not as it should be —flashed into her mind.

She lunged for the boom box, her phone falling from her hand and skittering across the deck.

"What is it?" exclaimed Mike.

Jonathan, surprised, pulled the power back and the boat slowed and settled.

Ann grabbed the boom box and heaved it as far from the boat as she could.

Jonathan's eyebrows rose as he watched the box bob on the waves. "What are you doing?"

"Get us out of here!" yelled Ann.

Jonathan's eyes widened and he turned back to the wheel and hit the throttle.

Then the ocean exploded.

41

The water was so cold, it was like a simultaneous punch to every part of her body. Ann gasped at the shock and sucked in frigid water before her life vest brought her to the surface. She thrashed her arms, rotating her body, looking desperately for the boat.

It was about a hundred feet away, probably carried forward by its momentum, and maybe by the explosion itself. She couldn't see any damage above the water line, but it was sinking at the stern, the waves already lapping at the green-and-gold letters spelling out *Hotshot* on the transom.

She couldn't see either of the men.

"Mike! Jonathan!" She meant it to be a scream, but it came out as only a croak.

She saw a head appear over the side of the boat—Jonathan pulling himself up from the deck, looking stunned and disoriented. Blood coursed down one side of his face.

"Jonathan!" she yelled again.

His eyes found her. "Jesus, Ann, hold on!" He grabbed a life ring from the cabin and began looking frantically around the cockpit. "I need to find some line."

"Mike! Where's Mike?" she gasped. She could feel herself beginning to hyperventilate. She tried to take a deep breath, tried to get her breathing under control, but she couldn't control her body's response to the stunning cold.

"He's here!" yelled Jonathan. He dropped the life ring and knelt, disappearing from Ann's view.

She thought of that article Russo had assigned her as homework between flying lessons—of the Miracle on the Hudson and the frigid water that could have claimed the lives that Sully Sullenberger had saved with his astounding landing—and a mental timer began ticking down the minutes that she could expect to stay conscious in the forty-degree water.

She tried to dog paddle toward the boat, but her arms wouldn't obey her mental commands and the life vest kept trying to turn her onto her back.

"Mike!" She struggled over on her stomach so she could see the boat.

Jonathan's head appeared again as he tried to stand, but the angle of the deck was becoming steeper, and he lost his footing and fell out of sight with a squawked *Shit!*

Ann allowed the vest to flip her over, her back to the boat, and tried kicking her legs. They felt like inanimate weights. She labored for what seemed like a minute but was probably no more than a few seconds. The scant insulation her clothes had initially provided was gone, and her waterlogged pants were dragging her legs down. She was about to roll over to see if she was making any progress toward the boat, when something cracked into her head, sending her under the waves for a moment, and sending another mouthful of water down her throat. Stars sparkled in front of her eyes.

When her vision cleared, she saw a life ring floating a few feet from her.

"Sorry about that," yelled Jonathan. "Grab the ring!"

She flailed toward the ring. "Is Mike okay?"

Ann heard the sound of Mike's voice but couldn't make out the words.

"He says he's fine," yelled Jonathan.

She grabbed the ring and Jonathan began hauling her toward the boat.

The life vest continued its job of keeping her face-up, and she ended up being towed backwards toward the boat. She wanted to curl herself around the ring, as if that would conserve some of her rapidly dissipating body heat, but her back muscles were contracting with the cold.

A half minute later, her head thumped into the side of the boat, momentarily reigniting the lights behind her eyelids.

"Jesus, sorry," Jonathan muttered above her.

She heaved one arm up, expecting Jonathan to grab it. When she felt nothing, she thrashed around to face the boat.

Jonathan, one side of his face a watery red where blood continued to flow from a gash near his temple, was standing up to his knees in water, trying to steady himself on the bench at the back of the boat. His hand was stretched out to her, but it was a yard away. It might as well have been a mile.

But she realized that she was going to find no respite aboard *Hotshot*. The water washing across the cockpit had almost reached the bench's seat. She could see Mike as well. He gripped the frame of the door to the cabin with one hand, trying to keep himself from sliding into the water in which Jonathan stood. His other arm was held awkwardly across his body. His face was a pasty white.

"I thought you said you were okay!" croaked Ann, trying to control the chattering of her teeth.

"I am okay," said Mike, sounding as if he were trying to convince himself. "We need to get you out of the water."

"Looks like you're going to be in here with me in a minute," she mumbled through numbed lips.

She heard the blast of a boat horn.

Jonathan looked up. "Oh, thank God. Someone's coming."

Ann turned to see a lobster boat barreling toward them. It slowed as it neared, its bow settling into the water, and approached carefully so as not to further swamp *Hotshot*. Behind the lobster boat, Ann could see other boats heading their way.

There were two men on the boat—*Lisa Jane*, according to the faded letters on the bow. The older of the two was at the helm, tweaking the controls to sidle *Lisa Jane* up against *Hotshot*. The younger one was in the back, dropping fenders over the side. Jonathan threw a line and the younger man caught it and pulled *Hotshot* toward *Lisa Jane*, although Ann noticed he didn't tie the line from the sinking boat to a cleat.

"Get her out of the water," Mike called to the younger man, his voice thready with pain.

Jonathan pulled the life ring, with Ann clinging to it, toward the back of *Hotshot*. He must have passed the line to the young man on *Lisa Jane* because in a moment Ann fetched up against the side of the lobster boat. She tried to reach her arms up, but she couldn't move them. The younger man leaned over the gunwale, grabbed the collar of her life vest, and hauled her into the boat, dumping her unceremoniously onto the deck.

"Him next," she heard Jonathan say.

The older man was now holding the line connecting the two boats. The younger man reached across to *Hotshot*, to where Jonathan had gotten Mike propped up against the gunwale.

"Watch his—" Ann tried to say with numbed lips.

She heard a shout of pain.

"—arm," she mumbled.

Ann managed to prop herself up on one side of the boat, and

the older man got Mike arranged against the other side. The younger one helped Jonathan cross from *Hotshot*, then disappeared into the cabin and emerged with three moth-eaten blankets. Jonathan cocooned himself in one. The older lobsterman carefully wrapped another around Mike. The younger one draped the third blanket around Ann, whose shaking was now more like a seizure than a shiver.

He disappeared into the cabin again and emerged with a thermos. He unscrewed the cap and poured a steaming stream of coffee into it. He knelt by Ann.

"Drink this," he said. "It'll warm you up."

Ann reached for the cup, but her hands were shaking so badly that she knocked the cup out of the young man's hands and onto the deck.

He poured another cup and held it to her lips. It was obviously instant, with a faint metallic tang. She had never tasted anything so good.

He glanced over her head. "Here comes the cavalry," he said. "Coast Guard out of Southwest."

"Tell them—" her voice caught, and she gave a watery cough. "Tell them they need to find Hannah Jeskie."

42

Ann sat in one of the curtained cubicles in the emergency room, cocooned in a warming blanket, a cardboard cup of hot tea cradled in her hands. In the cubicle to the right, Mike was having a cast applied to his broken arm. In the cubicle to the left, Jonathan was having the gash on his head stitched up.

The curtain leading to Ann's cubicle parted and the nurse who had been attending to the three of them looked in.

"You have a visitor," she said. "Your husband is here."

"I don't—"

Corey appeared behind the nurse.

"Sweetheart," he said, "thank heavens you're all right. It's a good thing we're married, otherwise they wouldn't let me back here."

The nurse rolled her eyes and withdrew.

"Husband, eh?" said Ann.

He grinned and shrugged.

"My better half," she said.

"That's me."

"The old ball and chain."

Corey raised an eyebrow. "I think that's usually the wife."

"Don't mind her," Mike called from the next cubicle. "She's still a little disoriented, I think."

"Am not," said Ann sullenly.

"She made me stop making jokes about 'boom boxes.'"

Corey tweaked back the curtain separating Ann's cubicle from Mike's. "It is sort of irresistible. How are you doing?"

"Better now that they pumped me full of pain killers," said Mike.

"I was disoriented when we first got here," said Ann, "but I'm feeling better now. He, evidently, was alert when we first got here but is getting increasingly disoriented as the drugs kick in, so in a few minutes, he'll have nothing on me."

"How about Jonathan?"

"No painkillers but disoriented nonetheless," came a voice from the left-hand cubicle. "Plus, I've got a killer headache."

"Well," said Corey, "I can't tell you how relieved I was when I heard you were all okay, relatively speaking. I wish I had your call from the boat on voicemail—it would make your hair stand on end. I can't wait to hear the whole story—"

Ann opened her mouth, but he raised his hand.

"—but not right now. Right now you just need to warm up." He directed his voice toward the right-hand cubicle. "And *you*, Mike, need to be enjoying your meds." He directed his voice to the left-hand cubicle. "And *you*, Jonathan, need to talk someone into giving you some."

"Hear, hear," said Jonathan.

Just as Corey sat down on a chair next to Ann's bed, the curtain parted again. "You have another visitor," said the nurse.

"Who is it now?" asked Ann.

"Your other husband," she said tiredly.

Ann glanced at Corey. "Kyle?"

Corey stood. "She definitely does not have another husband."

The nurse nodded. "The early bird gets the worm, I guess," she said. She pulled the curtain closed and her steps moved away from the cubicle.

A moment later they heard her raised voice. "Sir! I asked you to wait outside."

"But my wife—" they heard Kyle's voice approaching.

"Oh, God," groaned Ann.

Kyle appeared at the cubicle, a highly irate nurse at his side. "Darling," he said with a grin.

"I beat you to it," said Corey.

"Which one do you want here?" the nurse asked Ann.

"The first one," she said.

The nurse turned to Kyle. "You. Out."

"Just as soon as I'm sure that my love is okay," he said.

"I'm calling security," the nurse said and stomped away.

"Very funny, Lathey," said Corey, "but I think it's pretty clear you're not welcome here."

Kyle stepped into the cubicle and pulled the curtain closed behind him. "You guys are out of sorts now, but when the shock wears off, you'll see that this is a dream come true. You can't pay for this kind of drama. The viewers will eat it up!"

"No one is going to eat up anything—" began Corey.

"Some folks got video of these three coming in on the lobster boat and then being loaded into ambulances. Combine that with video of Ann's visits to the Spindle and of last night's fire and we're halfway to a documentary already."

Kyle pulled his phone out of his pocket.

"What are you doing?" asked Corey.

"I'm immortalizing the moment." He tapped the phone and pointed it at Ann.

Corey took a step toward him. "You're videoing her?" he asked, his voice rising.

"You'll thank me later," said Kyle. "Now, Ann, can you tell me in your own words—"

"Who else's words do you expect she would use?" said Corey. "Give me that phone."

"Corey, go stand by Ann—you're part of the story now, too."

"I am not part of the story—and neither are you." Corey reached for the phone.

Kyle waggled a finger of the hand not holding the phone. "Now, now—only one director on the set."

"Honey," said Ann to Corey, "he's annoying me."

Corey grabbed the phone with his left hand at almost the same moment that his right fist connected with Kyle's nose.

"Goddammit!" yelped Kyle, clapping his hands to his face.

"Shit!" hissed Corey, clamping his hand under his armpit.

"What the hell is going on in here?" yelled the nurse, who had appeared at the curtain followed by an elderly security guard.

"My second husband tripped and hit his nose on the—" Ann looked around the cubicle. It was admirably free of objects one could hurt oneself on. "—end of the bed."

The nurse crossed her arms.

Kyle glared at her over his hand, a trickle of blood running down his chin.

"And when my first husband tried to help him—"

Corey looked at her expectantly, gingerly cradling his hand.

"—his hand got caught between my second husband's nose and the bed."

Corey's face registered a unique combination of pain and amusement.

"Well, both of your husbands better move into separate cubicles to be examined," said the nurse, "and then they can decide whether to press charges against one another for felony clumsiness." She grabbed Corey's upper arm in one hand and Kyle's in the other and hustled them both out of the cubicle.

Their footsteps receded from Ann's cubicle, then there was a thump, a nasal *Ow!*, definitely from Kyle, and the nurse's voice.

"Oh for heaven's sake ..."

"Everything okay over there?" came Mike's voice from the other side of the curtain, sounding increasingly woozy.

"Absolutely," said Ann, leaning back with a smile.

43

Hannah sat in an uncomfortable Naugahyde chair in a motel room in Aroostook County, just a few miles from the Canadian border. A young man sat on the edge of the bed, the only other seating available in the room. The curtains were almost closed, but Hannah could see the faintest lightening of the sky through the gap.

They were waiting for word from a third associate that the plans for her crossing into New Brunswick were ready to proceed. The fact that they had outfitted her with hiking boots and heavy canvas pants made her suspect that the crossing would not be made in the comfort of a vehicle. She hoped, though, that her journey would ultimately end in a pleasant location with no extradition treaty with the United States.

"So," said the young man, in a French-Canadian accent, "the fire at the warehouse didn't work out quite as expected."

"It seemed foolproof," said Hannah. "Those ancient shingles, the light wooden trusses."

"But Kinnear and Garrido got out."

"Yes, I must admit that it was a lack of imagination on my

part not to foresee the use of the stack of lobster traps as a ladder, otherwise I could have ensured that those plexiglass windows were more securely fastened. But your organization hired me for my scientific expertise, not for my ability to anticipate escape routes." She gave him what she hoped was a conspiratorial smile. "I take it that's your area of expertise."

The young man didn't smile back. "Tell me again the steps you took."

Hannah's smile faltered. "I've already told you twice."

"Tell me again."

She reached for the plastic glass she had filled an hour ago from the bathroom tap, but she found it was empty. The young man didn't offer to refill it for her. She cleared her throat, hoping to ease the tightness that had formed, and launched into her story for the third time.

~

One Week Earlier

From her office window, Hannah watched Jonathan Garrido leave the building alone. In view of Leo Dorn's death the day before, she had given the Stata Mater staff the day off, but she was certain that there was still one person present. It would be unlike Shelby Kim to take advantage of the offer of a personal day, even under the circumstances. Perhaps especially under the circumstances.

Hannah retrieved her laptop from her desk, locked her office, and walked purposefully down the hall to Shelby's lab. Shelby was seated at the lab table, gazing listlessly past her laptop display. Hannah rapped on the doorframe. She had tried to knock lightly, but the young woman jumped, nonetheless.

"Hello, Hannah," said Shelby dully. "I didn't realize anyone else was here."

"It's just the two of us. How are you doing?"

"I'm all right."

Hannah crossed to the table and sat down on the other stool. She put the laptop on the table. "You should be at home." After a pause, she added, "Or out with Jonathan."

Shelby gave a snuffling laugh and dabbed her nose with a tissue. "That's what he said."

Hannah waited to see if Shelby would continue. When she didn't, Hannah said, "When something terrible like this happens, sometimes we want to talk about it."

Shelby kept her eyes on the tissue, which she was now shredding. "He said that, too."

"Yes, I'm sure he did. But sometimes it's easier to talk to people we don't know than people we do."

"You mean like a psychiatrist?"

"Well, yes, some people do find that helpful. And it's safe because of doctor-patient confidentiality." Hannah patted Shelby's hand. "Can't come back to bite you."

Shelby nodded. "I suppose so."

"Sometimes, though, we're tempted to talk with people we don't know who aren't bound by that kind of restriction."

Shelby blotted her nose again and stuffed the tissue into her pocket. "Like who?"

"Like the media."

Shelby looked up. "The media?"

"I just got word that a company from Los Angeles called Authentic Productions is planning on doing a documentary about Leo and his death."

"Oh." Shelby slumped again, and she twisted her fingers in her lap. "Yes, I just found out myself. And they aren't the only ones who are interested in Leo. A trespasser fell at Brookview. It sounds like he was trying to get video for his YouTube channel. They say he's going to be paralyzed."

"Yes, so I heard. I suppose one has to expect this type of event is going to grab the attention of the kind of small-time attention-seeker who will try to capitalize on someone else's tragedy. But a production company from Los Angeles?"

"Leo was an important man."

"You weren't responsible for suggesting that subject to them?"

Shelby looked up. "No. Why would I?"

"Might you have a reason to want a third party to dig into Leo's past? Into his activities?"

Shelby blanched. "Of course not. Why are you asking me this?"

"Shelby, let's not make this conversation any more difficult than it needs to be. I know you read the notebook. I know about your conversation with Leo. I know he showed you the video of Oscar Sanz."

"You were in on it, too?" asked Shelby, aghast.

"You don't really think he did all that himself, did you? Leo Dorn might have had the foresight to see what profitable purposes a slight modification of your clean agent could be put to, but you don't really think he had the scientific wherewithal to make it happen, do you?"

"That was your notebook I found in his office?"

"Yes. That's one good thing about having a largely paperless environment. No one knows what anyone's handwriting looks like."

"You blew up that man in Mexico?"

Shelby sounded as if she were forcing the words past her throat, and Hannah wondered briefly if it was possible for a young, healthy woman to pass out from stress.

"That explosion was actually Leo's work. But I can show you some more of my own handiwork. Quite recent, in fact."

Hannah opened her laptop, tapped, then turned the screen toward Shelby. A video feed, the grainy quality suggesting security camera footage, showed a woman sitting at a veneer-topped table in the dim light of what looked like a small business break room: molded plastic chairs, an ancient copier, a counter equipped with a sink and microwave.

Shelby gasped. "That's Stacy! That's my parents' bakery!" She snatched her phone off the table.

"What do you think you're doing?" asked Hannah, without much concern.

"I'm calling her!" said Shelby, frantically trying to get her phone unlocked.

"Don't be silly, Shelby. That video isn't live. It was taken several minutes ago."

Shelby gazed in horror at the screen. "Is it ... is it going to explode? Is she going to die?"

"Not tonight. At least not as far as I know. Just watch."

Stacy picked up a small pile of cash, tapped it square, and put it and what looked like a few checks in a bank envelope. She closed her laptop, put the envelope and laptop in her backpack, then carried her mug to the sink. She threw out the filter and grounds from the coffee maker, washed the mug, rinsed the carafe, and unplugged the coffee maker. When she turned from the sink and surveyed the room, her face caught the light. One cheek was mottled and puckered, the eye drawn down by the scarring beneath it. The other was unnaturally smooth, as if plastic wrap had been stretched across the skin. Stacy raised her hands to flip the collar of her jacket up around her neck, and the light revealed the discoloration and ridges on the backs of her hands.

She stepped out of camera range. A flashing red light on a

panel on the wall appeared—the security alarm being armed—and the room lights went off. A rectangle of light appeared and disappeared, suggesting a door opening onto a more brightly lit space and then closing again. The red light continued to flash for a few more seconds, then stayed steady, the alarm now activated.

"She certainly is a creature of habit," said Hannah. "The alarm goes on at the same time every night, give or take only two or three minutes."

"How can you see this?" asked Shelby, her eyes frantically scanning Hannah's laptop screen. "They don't have a security camera in the break room."

"*They* may not, but that doesn't mean we don't," said Hannah. She continued gazing at the screen with studied nonchalance. "She doesn't go anywhere other than the bakery, does she? Doesn't want to see anyone—or have anyone see her."

"Right after she got out of the hospital, when she went to the doctor for a checkup, she scared another little girl in the waiting room," whispered Shelby. "She wouldn't go out after that."

"Other people might have thought she was a monster," said Hannah, "but you've been so good to her since the fire. You gave up what should be a young woman's most carefree days to take care of her. How many parties did you miss to stay home with Stacy? How many friends did you shun because of an ill-advised comment they made about your sister—or even a poorly hidden look of disgust at her appearance? Once you left home, how much of the normal college experience did you miss out on because of your single-minded pursuit of getting to a place like Stata Mater Technology so that you could do penance for what you had done to your sister? In fact, you've devoted your whole life since the fire to finding ways to keep the same thing that happened to your sister from happening to others."

Hannah paused. "It was the least you could do, I suppose.

And your parents managed to keep the bakery going through it all. A business that starts before dawn and continues into the night, all those long days on their feet, your sister being home-schooled in the back room—the very back room where she now counts the receipts for the day. All the years with no vacations. But they finally made the bakery pay, didn't they?"

Shelby nodded, her face chalk white.

"Do they blame you for what happened to Stacy?" Hannah asked.

"No," said Shelby, her words barely audible, "but they should have."

"Yes, they should have," said Hannah briskly. "But parents can forgive their children many things. They may have forgiven you for what happened to Stacy, they may have buried their anger and grief in their work at the bakery, but what happens if you take from them the last good, unspoiled thing they have in their lives?"

"Please, no ..." whispered Shelby.

"Look closely, Shelby," said Hannah, gesturing toward the laptop display.

There was now a glow on the video, coming from near the counter area.

Shelby leaned toward the display. "What is that?" she asked, although from the dread in her voice it was clear she knew what it was.

"What does it look like, Shelby? You should have a professional opinion."

"An electrical fire? But she unplugged the coffee maker—I saw her do it!"

The glow became a flame, flickering up from the outlet.

"Did you?" asked Hannah. "It's so hard to remember these things accurately, especially when you're under stress." Hannah turned her gaze to the laptop display. "Or did Stacy leave it plugged in? Did she accidentally cause the fire? After all, there is a family history of that. In fact, that history might make it hard for your family to convince the authorities that it *was* an accident—lightning striking the same place twice and all that, if you'll forgive the metaphor."

The flame rose higher and caught a paper towel hanging from a holder next to the sink. The towel smoldered for a moment, then burst into flames.

"After all, the bakery is the only thing other than your sister in your parents' life," Hannah continued, relentless. "Maybe the investigators will decide that Stacy got jealous and wanted all the attention for herself."

"But she always unplugs the coffee maker," said Shelby, her voice tremulous. "You said so yourself—she's a creature of habit."

"Oh, really?" said Hannah. "Let's take another look. Everyone can have a little hiccup in their habit now and then."

She tapped and reversed the video, then hit *Play*.

Stacy was rinsing out the coffee carafe, her body hiding the electrical outlet. This time, when she stepped away from the sink, the coffee maker's electrical cord was clearly plugged into the outlet.

Shelby gasped. "How did you do that?"

Hannah shrugged. "It's just a matter of recruiting the needed talent. Just as we did with you when we needed someone with your special abilities."

Hannah let the video play, showing the flames blossoming to encompass the wall behind the sink, the counter.

"The police might be surprised that the fire spread so quickly—they might be suspicious that it wasn't entirely accidental—but they won't find any accelerant residue. And we have you to thank for that."

There were a few awful seconds where flames filled the camera's view, then the picture winked out.

Hannah turned to Shelby, who had sunk back onto her lab stool. Tears were streaming down the young woman's cheeks.

"Leo said it was only buildings nobody cared about," Shelby gasped through her tears. "He said no one ever got hurt."

"And you believed him? You and Leo had quite the mutual admiration society going. Leo was convinced that you would stay quiet. He convinced me to give you the benefit of the doubt. He convinced our partners to give you the benefit of the doubt. He risked everything because he trusted you. And he paid with his life, didn't he, Shelby?"

Shelby gave a miserable nod.

"But at heart, I believe you're too much of a straight arrow, too much of a law-abiding citizen, to leave well enough alone. I think that eventually—probably sooner rather than later—your regret over Leo's death and your desire to reveal what Leo was doing will overcome your fear of any reprisals I might exact. You'll warn your family to go somewhere out of reach—after all, they don't need to stay around to mind the bakery anymore—and you'll turn yourself in to the authorities and you'll tell your story."

Shelby began to shake her head slowly.

Hannah leaned toward her. "Shelby, your family couldn't go anywhere where my associates and I couldn't find them. And if you did tell anyone your story, your parents' house, with your parents and Stacy inside, will burn just like the bakery did. And I guarantee you no one will get out this time."

Shelby's headshaking became faster, a thin keening sound emanating from her trembling lips.

"Stop it!" hissed Hannah.

Shelby wrapped her arms around herself. "I won't tell," she said, her voice barely audible.

"I don't believe you."

"I won't!" Her voice was now loud with terror. "I swear!"

Hannah looked at her speculatively. "You know, there is one thing—only one thing—that would convince me that you won't tell anyone."

"What's that? I'll do it!"

"Dead men tell no tales. And neither do dead women."

Shelby straightened and turned her tear-streaked face to Hannah. "So you're going to kill me?"

"I have a better idea," said Hannah with a thin smile. "I have plenty of experience making murders look like suicides. But an actual suicide is always so much more convincing."

"So," said the young man seated on the bed, "you talked her into killing herself."

"Yes."

"There was a great deal of speculation about whether Shelby Kim's death was suicide, murder, or an accident."

"That was intentional. The more theories that were circulating, the harder it would be for the police to triangulate on any one of them. From what I saw among the members of the documentary team, it was a valid strategy."

What Hannah didn't add was that Shelby had imposed a condition of her own: that the circumstances of her death remain vague. Evidently Shelby believed that her family would prefer to hold on to the possibility that it was just a terrible accident—an ill-advised midnight stroll, a miscalculation of where the cliff edge lay, a gasp of panic, windmilling arms, a brief fall through the salt-scented air, and a quick death on the rocks. Hannah could understand how a lifetime of imagining a daughter or sister grappling with an attacker would be painful.

Perhaps imagining that she had been miserable enough to end her own life would be even worse.

Until Hannah had heard about Authentic Productions' plans for a documentary, she had had only one bad moment: at the edge of Otter Cliff when she thought Shelby Kim wouldn't go through with it and that Hannah might have to push her off the edge. But in the end Shelby Kim's guilt for disfiguring Stacy and for killing Leo had done Hannah's work for her.

The young man raised an eyebrow. "Impressive."

She couldn't tell from his tone whether he was being sincere or snide.

"It seemed it might distract attention from what Leo and I were doing," she said. "And I think circumstances proved me correct."

"But you made no effort to make the warehouse fire look like an accident. It's doubtful that a padlock would have *accidentally* attached itself to the door."

"At that point, I knew my time at SMT was up. Among other things, it was only a matter of time before someone reviewing security camera footage noticed my car following Shelby's to Otter Point."

"And even if Kinnear hadn't thrown the explosive device overboard before it detonated," continued the young man as if Hannah hadn't spoken, "no one would think the explosion on Garrido's boat was an accident."

"By that time I knew that the plan was to extract me from the situation."

The young man examined her, expressionless. She returned his gaze. She didn't want to seem to be challenging him, but she couldn't let him believe he was intimidating her. She needed to be able to negotiate her next steps in the organization from a position of power.

His phone buzzed. He pulled it out, read, slipped it back into his pocket, and stood.

"Arrangements are almost in place. Please wait here and someone will come for you shortly."

Hannah stood as well. "I did my best to take care of things."

"No doubt."

"Where will I be going?"

"The people who are coming will let you know." He picked up his coat from the bed and pulled it on. "Please don't leave the room until they come for you."

"Very well."

He stepped out the door and closed it gently behind him.

She went to the window, which overlooked the parking lot, and in a moment he appeared, got into the nondescript sedan in which he had arrived, turned left onto the nearly trafficless two-lane highway, and disappeared from sight. She gazed after the car, wondering from which direction her next escort would arrive.

She wondered what would become of *Mariposa*. Maybe once the organization got her settled, they could purchase the boat and bring it to her. She thought of all the notebooks of research findings left in her office at Stata Mater and regretted that she hadn't been more diligent about using the electronic version. At least she had had time to destroy the damning documents.

Fingers of light from the rising sun were casting the elongated shadows of pines across the highway. She wondered if she would be making the crossing to Canada in the daylight, or whether they would keep her sequestered in the motel until darkness fell again.

She was about to return to the chair when she saw vehicles approaching, silent but with blue-and-red lights strobing across the trees that lined the road. One ... two ... three ... there were at least half a dozen of them. She was not surprised when they veered into the motel parking lot.

She steadied herself on the window frame, then made her way stiffly to the chair and sank down.

She thought she had taken care of Shelby Kim—had taken care of everything—and then Ann Kinnear had arrived on Mount Desert Island, and who could have planned for that?

She had thought dead men don't tell tales.

She had been wrong.

nn and Jonathan sat on *Lisa Jane*'s engine box as the lobster boat motored toward the Spindle. The sky was a sparkling blue, and the wavelets barely registered on the sturdy boat. The Coast Guard had towed *Hotshot* to Seal Harbor and Jonathan was hopeful that it could be repaired.

Mike had opted to stay in Manset despite the calm seas. "You never know when the weather will turn, and I'd rather wait until I can get a good grip on something with both hands." He glanced down at the cast that encased his arm. "Assuming I ever decide to venture out on the water again."

As soon as Ann was warmed up and discharged from the ER, she had retrieved the rental car from Seal Harbor and driven to the L.L. Bean outlet in Ellsworth, where she had bought the puffiest down coat they had. She was wearing the coat now, her mittened hands pushed deep into its pockets, a wool watch cap keeping her hair from blowing in the breeze. Not her usual attire for May, even in Maine, but with all the news coverage the events on MDI had garnered, she suspected it was not only her eccentric clothing that was attracting people's attention these days.

The shopping bag back at the Manset house also contained a few pairs of flannel-lined jeans to send to Helen Federman in the Adirondacks and a replacement sweatshirt for Corey.

Ann peered past *Lisa Jane*'s pilothouse as it approached the Spindle. She could already see Shelby there, her gaze, as always, averted from the approaching boat. This time the tide was low, and Ann could see Shelby's feet seemingly firmly planted on the rocks, occasionally washed by the gentle waves.

"With a name like the Spindle," said Ann, "I thought it would be pointy, but it's flat."

"It doesn't need to be too pointy to do some damage to the hull of an unsuspecting boat," replied Ned, the father of the lobstering duo. He pulled back the throttle as they neared the Spindle. "How close do you need to get?"

"As close as you can," said Ann.

"As close as you *safely* can," said Jonathan. His stitches were just visible under the dark waves of his hair.

Ned goosed the throttle and the boat inched closer to the rocks.

"You can do better than that, dad," teased his son, Monty.

"As I said," muttered Ned, "they call it the Spindle for a reason."

"Don't disappoint your audience," pressed Monty, gesturing to the fringe of spectators on the cliffs. Ann suspected that some of them had been staking out the site hoping for a return engagement of what one local paper had started calling *the Maritime Medium*.

Ned finessed the boat to barely a dozen feet from the rocks. "That's it. That's the best I can do."

Ann moved from the engine box to the side of the boat. Although *Lisa Jane* barely rocked in the waves, she kept a firm grip on the edge of the pilothouse.

"Shelby, can you hear me?" she said. She was so close, she no longer felt the need to raise her voice.

Shelby kept her gaze on the rocks at her feet.

"Shelby, I came to tell you that your warning—at least I think it was a warning—worked. We decided it meant there was something you couldn't tell us—that someone was keeping a secret. Hannah Jeskie planted a bomb on Jonathan's boat, and we realized what it was and were able to throw it overboard before it exploded. Because of you. You saved our lives. Thank you."

The young woman brought her head up slightly, her eyes widening, before she dropped it again, but Ann sensed a tenuous connection that hadn't been there before.

"Hannah tried to get away," continued Ann, "but the police caught up with her. She's in jail now, accused of trying to kill me, Jonathan, and my brother, Mike. I suspect that as the police dig into what's been happening, they'll find other things to charge her with as well. I don't think she'll be getting out—at least not if Tippy Pepperidge has anything to do with it."

A look of relief relaxed Shelby's features. She closed her eyes for a moment, then opened them again, and for the first time her gaze met Ann's.

"If you can talk to me," said Ann, "it would be a great help if you could tell us what happened. I think you didn't tell us before because you were afraid that Hannah would take her revenge—maybe on Jonathan, maybe on your family—but you don't have to worry about that anymore. Obviously, the police can't use anything you tell me officially, but it might help point them in the right direction. Can you tell me what happened?"

Ann waited, hardly breathing, then saw Shelby give an almost imperceptible nod.

"Great," Ann said, her heart thumping. "That's great."

She saw Shelby's lips move, but it came across the water as a barely audible whisper.

"Shelby, I'm having trouble hearing you. Can you talk any louder?"

Shelby spoke again, but her words were no clearer to Ann.

"Hold on for one minute." Ann turned to the three men on the boat. "I can't hear her from here."

"Good thing you came prepared," said Jonathan, his eyes scanning the rocks.

With a sigh of resignation, Ann took off her life vest and pulled off the down coat, mittens, and wool watch cap, as well as a sweater, turtleneck, boots, and jeans. Underneath, she was wearing her other Ellsworth purchase: a neck-to-ankles wetsuit. She zipped on a pair of neoprene water shoes and buckled the life vest over the suit. She glanced over at the rocks, from which Shelby Kim watched her with surprised amusement.

"Okay," she said to Jonathan and Monty. "Can you guys give me a hand?"

They each took an arm and lowered her over the side of the boat and into the water.

She shuddered as the water crept into the wetsuit, although her body quickly warmed it. Accommodating the life vest's propensity to flip her onto her back, she kicked backwards until she rose on a gentle swell and felt her back bump into the rocks. She started to flip over to climb onto the rocks, but then the reverse surge of water lifted her off the rocks and back toward the boat. She repeated the maneuver two more times with the same result, to the accompaniment of what sounded like coaching advice being yelled from the observers on Otter Cliff. On the third attempt, she managed to find a handhold on the rocks. She staggered to her feet and barely avoided slipping and landing back in the water. She held out her arms like an ungainly tightrope walker until she was sure of her stance, then slowly lowered her arms to her sides and raised her head—face to face with Shelby Kim at last.

"Hello, Shelby," she said, smiling. "I'm glad we can finally talk."

Shelby smiled back. "Me, too."

45

Shelby relayed her story: her invention of the clean agent that would exponentially improve the technology available to fight fires while leaving no residue; the overheard conversation between Leo and Tippy at the celebration dinner at Blackwood's and Leo's apparent desire to profit from the invention; the spiral-bound notebook and her accidental discovery of the bastardization of her invention into an untraceable accelerant; her eventual realization of the type of clients to whom Leo was selling the technology; and her desperate plan to prevent her invention from being used to feed the flames she had spent her life fighting.

"So you found your own way of stopping his work," said Ann.

"Yes. I decided the only way to end what he was doing was—"

She stopped, and Ann was afraid she had learned all she would from Shelby Kim, but then the young woman took a deep, shuddering breath.

"I decided the only way to stop him was to kill him."

"You pushed him while you were hiking."

"He didn't fall from the path where I told the first responders he had fallen. He fell from the ledge. You know the ledge?"

Ann thought back to her nerve-racking crossing. "Yes, I know it. But how did you overpower him?"

"I used a lubricant variant of the clean agent. That morning I went to the path—by the back entrance, near Frank Judd's studio—and poured it on the ledge. It made it slippery. As slippery as ice."

"You brought it in a canteen."

"Yes," said Shelby, surprised.

"I found it—or, more accurately, Leo showed me where it was. He noticed that the rock covering his hiding place had been moved. My brother took it to a lab in Bangor to get the residue analyzed."

"I would have said they wouldn't find anything," said Shelby. "It was supposed to evaporate within an hour or so, to leave no trace. That's why I had to leave the canteen somewhere on the property—I had to get from the ledge to the house and then back to the ledge with Leo as soon as I could. But it must have still been there the next day." She looked down at her hands, her fingers twisted together. "That guy who sneaked onto the property ... he must have slipped on it. I must have formulated it wrong. "

"You didn't formulate it wrong," said Ann. "The lab said that the small amount of liquid left in the container evaporated before they had a chance to test it. It worked just as you had intended. I think it's way more likely that the guy who was trespassing at Brookview fell because it had rained and the ledge was wet. Everyone said that no reasonable person would take that path when it was wet. I think he only has himself to blame, Shelby."

"You think so?" asked Shelby tentatively.

"I do. And it looks like he's going to be okay. There was

damage to his spinal column, but the doctors think that with surgery and physical therapy, he's likely to make a complete recovery."

Shelby's expression brightened. "He will?"

"That's the prognosis. He and his YouTube partner are playing it up as a miracle, but I think it was luck and good medical care."

Ann smiled encouragingly and, after a moment, a smile flickered on Shelby's lips as well.

After a beat, Ann pressed on. "After you poured this substance on the path, then you went to the house and asked Leo out for a hike?"

"Yes."

"Wasn't he suspicious when you asked him to go on a hike with you—especially one as tricky as that?"

"He knew I didn't have a weapon—at least not a conventional one. I wore form-fitting clothes so that he could see I didn't have a gun or a knife on me, and I left my jacket in the entrance hall while I went out to my car—I told him I had forgotten to change my shoes—so that he could search it and see that I was unarmed."

"I wonder if he actually did search it ..."

"Oh, he searched it, all right. He put my hat back in a different place than I had left it." She looked down at her hands. "I guess that he figured he was so much bigger than me that as long as I wasn't armed, he didn't have much to worry about."

"And when he got to the ledge, he slipped and fell."

Shelby's fingers twisted together more tightly. "He almost fell, but then he caught himself. He asked me to hold out my hiking stick to him so he could get his balance." Her voice trailed away to an almost inaudible whisper, thick with remorse. "It just took a little push."

They were both silent for a long moment.

Finally, Shelby drew in a deep breath. "I pointed the investigators' attention to a different point in the path to give the substance a chance to evaporate."

"Was Tippy involved in all this?"

Shelby's head snapped up. "Never. She would never do such a thing. After what happened to her first husband, she devoted her whole life to making sure that other people didn't suffer that fate."

Ann's eyes drifted to Jonathan. "Was anyone else involved?"

Shelby's gaze also shifted to Jonathan, her eyes resting on his face for a long moment, then back to Ann. "No. Jonathan knew nothing. I'm certain of it."

Ann nodded. "Shelby, what happened at Otter Cliff?"

The young woman gave her a sad smile, then raised her hand and drew her fingers across her mouth. *My lips are sealed.*

"Ann," she heard Monty call from the boat. "You should come back now."

She realized that she was shivering, the breeze moving across the water starting to draw away the heat from her body.

"Okay," she called back. She turned to Shelby. "Thank you."

"Thank *you*," Shelby replied. "I hope this helped."

"It did."

"I'm glad."

"Is there any message you'd like me to give your family?"

"Can you tell them that I was just on a walk at Otter Cliff, and I slipped accidentally?" asked Shelby hopefully.

"Is that what happened?"

"That's what they should hear—that I died doing something I loved. I think—" Shelby's voice caught, and she swallowed. "I don't think they could stand anything else."

Ann nodded. "I'll tell them." She dropped her voice. "Is there any message you'd like me to give Jonathan?" She didn't want

Jonathan, a dozen feet away in the boat, to hear the question if the answer was *no*.

Shelby smiled sadly. "Tell him I wish I had gone out for drinks with him that night." She looked skyward. "Tell him it's such a pretty day, I wish we were walking the Ocean Path, one car at Sand Cliff and one at Otter Point." She looked toward Jonathan. "Tell him I know there's going to be a celebration at Stata Mater soon to celebrate a breakthrough they'll call JG-1." Her eyes returned to Ann. "Tell him I'll miss him."

Ann nodded, then waded into the water. When she reached the boat, Monty and Jonathan hoisted her aboard. Monty handed her a blanket, and she wrapped herself in it.

"What did you find out?" asked Jonathan, his eyes on the rocks.

"I can tell you on the way back," she said, her teeth chattering.

"Did she ..." His voice trailed off.

"She gave me a message for you." She told Jonathan what Shelby had said.

He smiled. "Can you give her a message from me?"

Ann looked back toward the Spindle. The rocks were empty.

"She's not there anymore."

"Maybe we can come back tomorrow."

Ann smiled sadly. "I don't think she'll be coming back."

nn folded the last article of Mike's clothing and put it into his duffle. She had interceded when she could no longer stand to watch his one-armed efforts to pack his clothes. She glanced at her watch. One hour until Walt picked them up at the Hancock County-Bar Harbor Airport to take them back to West Chester.

She had made one more trip back to Brookview, to the site of Frank Judd's studio. Ann had walked the site, had experimented with being there with Tippy and being alone, had stayed through the time when Frank had died in the fire and then on into the night. He never appeared, never gave Ann even a hint that he hadn't moved on. She had expected Tippy to be disappointed, but the older woman looked accepting—even relieved. After all, Tippy now knew that it was only tragedy that had kept Leo and Shelby behind, at least for a time.

Ann was just zipping Mike's bag when she heard a vehicle turn off the road into the driveway. She looked out the window to see Corey's Suburban roll to a stop. She slung the strap of Mike's duffel over her shoulder, grabbed her own bag from the bedroom, and headed downstairs.

Mike was noodling one-handed on the piano: *Happy Trails*.

"Corey's here," she said, dumping the bags by the front door.

Ann hurried to the back door and opened it just as Corey was climbing the steps to the porch. The pinky and ring finger of his right hand were taped together, the swelling from the boxer's fracture beginning to lessen.

"Hi, Corey. You got here just in time—we were just finishing packing up."

She stepped aside to let him in, and Mike joined them in the kitchen.

"That's good," he said, "because the house has to be ready for its new tenant. Me."

"You're staying on MDI?"

"Yup. I got the go-ahead for a new project."

"What is it?" Ann asked cautiously.

"An exposé of what Leo Dorn and Hannah Jeskie were up to."

"No kidding," said Ann, brightening. "That's great." Her expression dimmed. "What does Tippy think about that?"

"She's fully behind it. In fact, she's helping authorities go through Leo's financial records. I think Ms. Pepperidge was none too pleased when she found out what Leo and Hannah had been doing under the guise of Stata Mater research."

"Any sign that anyone else at SMT was involved?"

"Nope. In fact, Jonathan Garrido is helping out the authorities on that front. Tippy gave him Leo's old job: President and Scientific Director. He's the one who got to make the announcement about Shelby's invention."

"That's great," said Ann with a smile.

"Is Authentic Productions financing the new project?" asked Mike.

"Nope. Tippy Pepperidge is providing financial as well as investigative support."

"That's great," said Ann. "I'm glad you don't have to deal with Authentic Productions anymore."

"That's for sure," said Corey. "I'm happy to say that I have parted ways with them for good. I don't think they were thrilled that I punched their errand boy in the nose. And before you ask," he said to Mike, "I'm afraid that the new concept has been approved with the stipulation that there be no references to spirit sensing."

Ann laughed. "Just as well."

"How about Kyle?" asked Mike.

"Turns out Kyle and Authentic Productions are teaming up with the guys from *Behind the Scenes with Geary*. Brian Geary's responding well to treatment, and as soon as he's fit for travel, they're going on a nationwide tour of locations where famous people met infamous ends."

"Sounds like a match made in heaven," said Mike.

Ann heard the sound of another vehicle in the driveway and looked out the window.

"It's Garrick," she said, surprised.

"The only one who got through this unscathed," said Corey.

"Sure," said Mike, "if you just sit back and let someone else do all the—"

Ann cleared her throat.

Mike raised his uninjured hand. "Okay, okay. I'll try to curb my Pavlovian reaction to hearing his name."

Ann went to the back door and opened it just as Garrick reached it.

"Hey, Garrick. Come on in."

He stepped in and nodded to Mike and Corey. "Gentlemen."

"What brings you to Manset, Garrick?" asked Corey.

"I understood that Miss Kinnear would be leaving for Pennsylvania today."

"You came to see me off?" asked Ann, pleased.

"In a manner of speaking."

There was a long moment of silence, then Ann said, "Mike, why don't you go to Little Notch Bakery and pick up some of that raisin bread that Scott likes?"

"I'd be happy to get out of your and Masser's hair, but I'm not thrilled about driving with one arm."

"I'll take you," said Corey. "I'm quite a raisin bread connoisseur myself."

"You're okay to drive?" asked Mike, eyeing Corey's bandaged hand.

Corey held out his hand and flexed it carefully. "As long as we don't have to take any evasive maneuvers, I should be good."

Ann gave Corey a grateful smile.

Mike glanced out the window. "Masser's car is blocking Corey's."

Garrick held out his car keys to Corey. "Take mine."

"Really?" said Corey. "Sweet! I love those old Caddies. Thanks, Garrick."

Mike shooed away Ann's attempt to help him get his jacket sleeve over his cast, while Corey struggled momentarily with the zipper on his new, bloodstain-free, Acadia National Park sweatshirt and then gave up. He followed Mike out the door.

"It's not that old," muttered Garrick.

"What?"

"The Fleetwood. It's not that old."

"Ah." Ann gestured toward the kitchen's small island. "Have a seat. Hot water?"

"If it's no inconvenience."

"Anything with it? Like ground coffee beans or tea leaves?"

"No," said Garrick, lowering himself onto one of the stools.

Ann filled the kettle with water and poured the last of the coffee from the coffee maker into her mug.

"What have you been up to?" she asked Garrick.

"At Ms. Pepperidge's request," he said, "I returned to Brookview to tell Leo Dorn that his nefarious work had been discovered and thwarted."

"Where did you meet up with him? Is he moving toward the house?" She knit her brows. "Should we be worried about Tippy?"

"It doesn't appear that he is able to move much beyond the stream, where we conducted the interview. However, I encountered him at the rock steps where he fell."

Ann lowered the mug from her lips. "Really? How did you get there?"

Garrick grimaced. "Very slowly."

"How did your talk with him go?"

"Unremarkable. He seems no less present than he did shortly after his death, but less capable. I have no fears for Ms. Pepperidge's well-being, or the well-being of anyone else visiting the Brookview property, but I would not be surprised if visitors to the estate run into Leo's spirit for some time to come. Not a pleasant situation for a spirit to be in, wandering the grounds of his former home. A well-deserved consequence for the difficulties he has caused."

The kettle whistled and Ann poured the hot water into a mug and handed it to Garrick, then sat down at the island. He took a sip of water. "And you?"

"Fred Barnwell played the Pied Piper and led Jessy Barnwell out to Kebo Brook, where her grandfather died. I went out there yesterday and saw Jessy and Clarence walking along the road, the two of them chatting up a storm."

"A most satisfactory situation for them."

"I also confirmed that Shelby's gone. I went out to Otter Point—by car—and the Spindle was empty." She took a sip of coffee. "I did get to have the disconcerting experience of

standing next to a couple who were exchanging information—
most of it wrong—about everything that happened."

"Including the exploits of the Maritime Medium?"

"You know about that?"

"I could hardly avoid knowing about that," he said sourly.
"What were Dr. Garrido's feeling about Dr. Kim's departure?"

"Garrick," she said, "that's such a sensitive thing to ask."

"Nonsense. Merely professional curiosity."

Ann smiled. "Yes, heaven forbid you'd actually be worried
about Jonathan."

Garrick glared at her.

"When he found out she wasn't at the Spindle anymore," she
said, "he seemed willing to accept the situation as the best thing
for Shelby under the circumstances. I explained that it's usually
those with unfinished business who stay around, and that they
are usually hoping to move on."

"As I have no doubt Clarence and Jessica Barnwell will do
when they tire of walking the Loop Road."

"That spirit negative I saw at the top of Otter Cliff," said Ann,
"that was a new one for the books."

"Quite."

"It's a good thing you had encountered one and knew what it
was, or I probably would have wasted a lot of time looking for
Shelby at the cliff top."

Garrick was silent.

"Don't you think?" prompted Ann.

Garrick set his mug on the island. "I have not in fact encountered a spirit negative myself, although I have of course exten-
sively studied the writings of those who have. It is not ..." He
cleared his throat. "It is not a phenomenon that is usually
perceptible to a spirit senser."

After a beat, Ann said, "Really?"

"Yes." He gazed broodingly at his water, a curl of steam rising from the mug. Then he straightened. "You have come a long way, Miss Kinnear. I recall when I first met you, your ability was limited to the perception of sounds or scents—merely the ability to determine the disposition of a spirit. Then your ability expanded to include actual interaction with spirits—even, I understand, mistaking a spirit for a living person because its presence was so vivid to you. Now, the ability to sense a spirit negative ..." He stopped, at an uncharacteristic loss for words, then continued. "There are few with our ability. Fewer still with yours."

They were silent for a few moments, then Ann said, "Thank you, Garrick."

"I merely state the obvious." He paused. "Please don't tell your brother."

She smiled and drew her fingers across her lips.

THE END

ALSO BY MATTY DALRYMPLE

ABOUT THE AUTHOR

Matty Dalrymple is the author of the Ann Kinnear Suspense Novels *The Sense of Death*, *The Sense of Reckoning*, *The Falcon and the Owl* and *A Furnace for Your Foe*; the Ann Kinnear Suspense Shorts, including *Close These Eyes* and *Sea of Troubles*; and the Lizzy Ballard Thrillers *Rock Paper Scissors*, *Snakes and Ladders*, and *The Iron Ring*. Matty and her husband, Wade Walton, live in Chester County, Pennsylvania, and enjoy vacationing on Mt. Desert Island, Maine, and in Sedona, Arizona, locations that serve as settings for Matty's stories.

Matty is a member of Mystery Writers of America, Sisters in Crime, and the Brandywine Valley Writers Group.

Go to www.mattydalrymple.com for more information and to sign up for Matty's occasional email newsletter.

facebook.com/matty.dalrymple

twitter.com/mattydalrymple

instagram.com/matty.dalrymple

ACKNOWLEDGMENTS

Many thanks to the following for generously sharing their expertise and their support:

Wade Walton and Sean Cox, for information on Mount Desert Island's more precipitous and perpendicular trails—with extra thanks to Wade for creating the map of Mount Desert Island found at the beginning of this book.

John Holt and Nancy Gable, for insight into life on the waters around MDI.

Thérèse Picard and Nicole Austin for help understanding jurisdictional responsibilities among MDI law enforcement.

Wade Rogers, for information on research labs' personnel structures, processes, and procedures.

Thomas Dunne, Ken Shoemaker, and Ken Fritz, for their expertise regarding fires and firefighters.

Rodger Ollis, for helping once again with information on police procedure.

Jane Kelly and Lisa Regan, for being my (word) search and (plot) rescue first responders.

Jon McGoran, who reminded me that "reader" doesn't mean "mind-reader."

Any deviations from strict accuracy—intentional or unintentional—are solely the responsibility of the author.